TO
NO
END

By Lexy Night

Tales of Forgotten Fae
To No End
Come What May

To No End

TALES OF FORGOTTEN FAE

BOOK 1

LEXY NIGHT

Edited by Noah Sky
Proofreading by Rachel Theus Cass
Book Cover Design by Krafigs Design
Illustrations and Font Design by Jade M Design
Map Art by ©Travis Hasenour/To the Moon and Back Design
Interior Design by ©Travis Hasenour/To the Moon and Back Design

ISBN: 979-8-9908638-0-4 (Paperback Edition)
ISBN: 979-8-9908638-1-1 (eBook Edition)
ISBN: 979-8-9908638-5-9 (Audiobook Edition)
ISBN: 979-8-9908638-2-8 (Hardback Special Edition)
Library of Congress Control Number: 2024918255

First Edition January 2025
Published in Overland Park, Kansas
Printed and bound in the United States of America

Under The Covers Publishing
www.lexynight.com

For all the people who thought they knew someone…
It's not about what came before; it's about what comes next.

I hope to write about the women you admire, the friends you deserve,
and the kind of love you'd destroy kingdoms for.

THE FAE REALMS OF
DEMIR
HOUSE WICK
HOUSE TIERNAN
ELORN BASDIE
MOUNTAINS
HOUSE HUXLEY
HOUSE EVENUS
HOUSE KASPAROV
HOUSE BRYNMAWR
CAMBRIA
ENDLESS TIDES
TINSILOR CASTLE
HAVEN HOUSE
DOORLAE TAVERN & INN
ERISAS BAY
LEDOR CANYON
HOUSE BLACKTHORN
RIVERLANDS
HOUSE CORLISS
LEDOR RIVER
N
ARTUME
SADEM
NASALLUS CASTLE
THE IVORY WASTE
CAANO
DAMAS
ENDLESS TIDES

CONTENT NOTES

A pronunciation guide can be found by skipping to the back of the book.

This story contains adult themes and the mention of the following that may be concerning to some readers:

- Adult Murder (common theme)
- Attempted Sexual Assault (brief mentions)
- Branding (brief mentions)
- Consensual Nudity/Sexual Scenes (several fully described)
- Female on Male Violence (common theme in the form of training/battle)
- Infant Murder (very brief mention)
- Infertility (very brief mention)
- Language (infrequent)
- Male on Female Violence (common theme in the form of training/battle)
- Miscarriage (very brief mention)
- Self-Harm (brief theme in the form of training)
- Spousal/Child Abuse (brief mention)
- Classism (brief mentions)
- Torture (brief theme)
- Verbal Assault (brief scenes)
- Violence (common theme)
- War (reference to past, present and future)

PROLOGUE

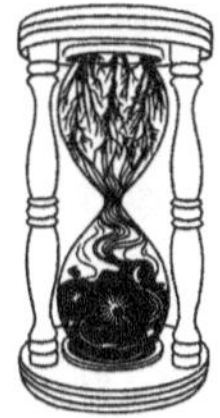

For those who see the future, speak not of it, for fear of bending its many winding branches.

Excerpt, Tome of Sight, Ch. 1. Verse 4.

After hundreds of years of turmoil and senseless bloodshed, there had finally come a time for peace between Cambria, the kingdom in the north, and Artume, the southern kingdom. A feeling of normalcy had returned to the Fae people and all other creatures who resided in these territories. Ravaged lands had been restored, trade had resumed, and people began to prosper once more. Kingsguards dwindled in numbers and assumed the lowly duties of patrolling between the borders of the Riverlands. There was hope amongst the Fae, and once again, they began to grow their families with the belief that a new generation would inherit a better place than what came before.

But peace in the land of the long-lived was a fickle thing, and fear can be more dangerous than any assassin. It behaves like a blade in many ways; with guile and precision, puncturing the confident exterior and laying bare the viscera within. A knife, when it's at your throat, presents an undeniable reality. But fear is far more dangerous because, unlike the blade, its influence is masked by other emotions: greed, lust, aggression—fear can hide behind all of these, and it is far more lethal in the hearts of those who rule.

One night, a seedling of this immense power swept gently on the tides, gliding upon the black waves as they hurried toward shore. When it crashed into the rocky coastline, it clung to the gusts of the west winds, swirling up the craggy cliffs until another torrent of air carried it through an open window, where it found a sleeping host.

King Aeon I, son of Ciaran, ruler of Cambria, awoke suddenly, chest heaving, blinking his eyes furiously to shake off the horrors his dreams had unveiled. His wife, Queen Nyla, tried desperately to console her frantic husband as he gasped the words, "A vision…! A vision! A prophecy." Sweat slicked his brow and arms, his muscles finally unclenching as he awoke fully. "I must speak to Idris at dawn," he pleaded, wide-eyed, to his beloved. At the mention of the name, her skin paled and her features hardened. Her eyes met the king's with concern, knowing what would follow.

"You know I cannot tell you what I saw, or it may not come to pass. Anything I say could alter it," the king snarled.

He stood and pounded his fists on the long oak table, gripping the edge while dropping his head in frustration. The sound echoed across the stone archways of the High Council chambers. Idris, unfazed, looked intently at the king, silently awaiting his next words. For Idris did not often stand before this table, and whenever he did, it was him and the king alone. Idris was very old, yet you wouldn't know it from the sharp angles of his appearance. He had served Aeon, and his father before him. As spymaster, he was aloof, with no friends, kin, or lovers to speak of. In truth, Idris managed to fit in wherever he went. His silent manner and calculated presence allowed him to simply exist, blending in like ivy curling around a lattice. His contributions to the realm were crucial, providing the king with information about his enemies' movements.

Idris nodded, "My king, I understand. I will not press you, as your dream sight has never failed us. But what can you tell me so that I may serve?"

The king scanned the room nervously to be sure they were alone.

"Call the Order, demand an Offering, and light the Pyres of Ennae immediately," Aeon whispered.

Idris began to rub his hands nervously. "My liege, are you certain? Once we do this, it cannot be undone. The High families of the North will not give up their sons and daughters without suspicion!"

"You know I would not ask this of anyone if it were not dire. I'd give of my own brood were they of age to serve. May we never relive the horrors of our first king's sacrifice. I would never take lightly the families I ruin and the lives I take in the Offering," Aeon said penitently, sorrow beginning to fill the otherwise regal features of his handsome face.

"I am certain our time of peace is coming to an end, and we must be prepared. We must be the ones to gather intel and strike first. I need the Order reinstated." Aeon looked flatly at Idris, the silence between them palpable.

"My lord, the sky will dance with red this eve, though it gives me no pleasure. I shall summon the others to the Elorns, where they will train the Offering until they are ready. Then we will remind our Fae brethren in the South why peace is the only option." He paused, looking away in contemplation, remembering how the winds of war always find a way of returning. And with those winds came opportunity. He locked eyes with the king and quieted his words, just above a whisper, "Remind them that they are only safe by your will, sire."

That evening, the Pyres of Ennae were lit, and one by one the red smoke from the burning Gaia Wood spread from mountain top to mountain top, sprawling across the vast territories of Cambria. The enchantments bound to the wood ensured only the lords and ladies of the High Court could see the signal. To the outsiders, there was nothing, not even the faintest scent of fire and ash. Nothing to draw concern from them that anything was awry. Idris himself stood idly on the tower, using his powerful magic to light them, one by one, without so much as lifting a finger or alerting a single Kingsguard.

The Pyres of Ennae were a symbol, a message that had lain dormant for over two hundred years. That evening, the most respected, royal, and wealthy families of Aeon's Court would know their king was calling—and they were to answer. In thirty days' time, they would each deliver one son or daughter of conscription age to the Offering, and they would never see or hear from them again.

CHAPTER 1

I wandered the halls of our home aimlessly, tired from another monotonous day. Much of which I had spent riding the small expanse of our land beneath the sunlit sky, but never going beyond the boundaries of the estate. It wasn't usually allowed without an escort— unsafe, for someone like me. So, I'd ride along its outskirts longing to go beyond the walls. As my horse trotted beside the perimeter, I'd drag my fingertips along the stone walls, feeling the rough texture of the rock broken up by soft patches of moss. When I grew bored with that, I'd race my horse from one end to the other to feel the wind in my face, avoiding the gardens so that my mother wouldn't have my head.

When my parents called me into our library at such a late hour, I knew something was off. Especially since they turned my twin sister, Versa, away when she followed me in. My mother looked absolutely distraught, and my father's brow was locked in a furrow. He looked like he had been practicing whatever he was about to say for the past hour, and yet the right words could not find him.

"Cress—my darling, you know that with being a family of the High Court, we have enjoyed the luxuries and freedoms that come with those titles."

I nodded in acknowledgment.

"But there is also a price. One we hoped we would never have to pay. All these years of peace, we have gone about our lives, prospered in all the ways your mother and I dreamt. Yet, despite the innumerable and invaluable fortunes I have beheld, I hope you and your sister know that you're our most prized treasures."

Why did this sound like a goodbye speech? Were they sick? Had they planned to travel to faraway lands? I glanced at my mother, who was doing everything in her power to not let her traitorous watering eyes stain her beautiful rose-colored cheeks.

"In times of peace, the price seems like a—"

"Father spit it out, what is troubling you?" I chimed in, impatiently. I could no longer stand the looks on their faces.

My loving father sat up straight, drew his shoulders back, and took a deep breath. "In thirty days, we journey to Tinsilor Castle to deliver you to King Aeon. From that time forward, you will serve the king and his realm in whatever way he sees fit. You will not see us or anyone else you know again."

And there it was. The truth, like a dull knife—what I had asked for. The answer to why my mother looked horrified and my father couldn't bring himself to meet my gaze.

I should have been in shock, yelling in disbelief, or possibly crying. But that's not me. In times of distress, I lean into my overly logical side and usually all I have is questions, endless questions.

But the ever-present bond between me and my twin sister was itching below the surface, and suddenly there was only one distinct question burning to be asked.

"What about Versa?"

The bobbing of my father's throat told me everything I needed to know before he even spoke.

"We are only required to deliver one of you to King Aeon, and since your sister was recently betrothed, it did not make sense to go back on our word to that family."

The words stung my father more than they did me. I already knew that if only one of us was required to go, there wasn't a chance in three moons that Versa would be the one selected. She had recently been promised a most favorable match. One that was going to seal a relationship between families leading to years of wealth and prosperity. If I was being honest with myself, it didn't make sense for Versa to go anyway. I hadn't a clue what serving the king and the realm even meant, but despite appearances, Versa and I were very different.

We were both considered stunning by Fae standards, but Versa had a unique quality where she just...glowed. When we entered a room, people's eyes settled on her, not me. She was more delicate in every way, from her dainty collarbones to her polite disposition; she's what most would want from a young lady of a High Court family. Well-bred, well-behaved, stunning, and ripe to bring even more beautiful babies into the world.

I, on the other hand, shared a face with my sister, but I was sturdier in every sense of the word. I was strong, fast, curious, and in all ways unsettled and unrestrained. My mouth and intellect often got me in trouble, and I was most certainly not amenable to betrothals.

Despite all that, I still had ideas and plans for a future of my own—one that I was in control of. But now it seemed the king would dictate my path. And while maybe I could come to terms with that, it was that last part my father mentioned that began the stabbing ache in the depths of my chest.

I would never get to see or speak to my family again. To my other half, my twin. I think this was the part I struggled most to grasp, more so than being sent away to serve the realm.

I snapped myself out of the endless well of thoughts and turned to my mother. "What does that mean? Serve the king and the realm. What will I be doing that requires I never see you again?"

My mother looked at my father almost in anger, before she spoke, as if this was something she too wanted answers for.

"The Offering is a secret. Only the High Lords and Ladies pay the price with their children's lives. Those with offspring who meet the age of conscription must answer the call with one daughter or son. No one but the families themselves will know who is offered…" My mother trailed off, trying to remain impassive.

My father attempted to fill in the gaps, still seeing the confusion washing across my face.

"The pain of your absence will not be our only suffering. We will not know where you are, what you're doing, who you're with"—his voice cracked as he struggled to choke out the remaining words—"or if you're safe. It will torture your mother and me for the rest of our days. I don't even know if Versa will be able to carry on, which is why…"

"Which is why she must not know the truth!" My mother finished sharply, sensing his inability to complete the sentence.

"Aren't they going to notice all these sons and daughters of the High Court are missing? Notice *I'm* missing?" I asked incredulously.

"Each family will create an elaborate lie to account for their sons' and daughters' absences. Versa must not know the truth. It would absolutely break her. You two have been attached at the hip since your first namesake. She'd never be able to carry on not knowing if you're okay."

I leaped up from my armchair, "And it won't break you?" I shouted at my mother.

"I've been broken since receiving word the Offering had been called, my strong-willed daughter… And the only solace I will have is the belief that whatever this is, wherever you're going, it must be honorable. Important. It has to be. King Aeon is good and would never take the sons and daughters of the North on a whim. I choose to believe that being called upon isn't a death sentence, but an opportunity, and that your life and the lives of the other High Fae will not be given in vain."

My father reached out to place his hand on top of hers. It was then I witnessed the tears streaming down her face, reflecting the light of the nearby fireplace.

"The Offering has not been called upon in over two hundred years, not since before the war ended. We're told never to question it, but I can't help but worry about what this forebodes for Cambria. And like your mother, I choose to believe if you are needed, there is a damn good reason my daughter is being taken from me."

Now my father's anger matched my mother's from earlier, and I could feel his magic beginning to ripple in the warm air of the library. He rarely ever showed his abilities; it wasn't proper, he'd say. While their concern was beginning to boil over, I was quickly becoming numb to my fate.

"So, what now?" I shrugged, disbelief and apathy deadening my tone.

"Your mother and I will determine the lie that your sister, family, and friends will be told. Then, in thirty days, we will deliver you to King Aeon as the Offering calls for," my father explained.

I rose to my feet, itching to pace, to run or scream, a roaring need to unleash building inside of me. "And what am I supposed to do during that time while you two spin elaborate lies about my upcoming disappearance?"

My mother stood and grabbed my shoulders. "Oh Cress, you do whatever your heart desires while your life and your freedom is your own. Fate be damned," she sighed.

She looked me dead in the eyes fiercely, holding a hand to my cheek with all the love a mother can offer. "No one can know what your fate holds once in the king's hands. But you have our complete blessing to live the next thirty days selfishly. Unapologetically. Drink the nectar that is freedom while it's within your grasp. I am only sorry that I cannot promise you that for the rest of your days, as you most certainly deserve. As we all deserve."

My mother dropped her hand and squeezed my shoulders, embracing me. And that's when she whispered the words that cut like daggers.

"But if you disappear, if you do not take your place in the Offering, Versa will be taken instead and there is nothing we can do."

I don't know if it was a threat or a plea, but it hurt in ways I refused to let myself feel fully. Versa had always been closer to my mother, whereas I was closer with my father. Though it was not the intent of her words, I couldn't help but feel my mother would have never let her prized daughter be the one to go. However, through this entire ordeal, I wouldn't let my parents see me fall apart. No, I'd plaster on that same stoic face I'd wear anytime hurt and disappointment came for me.

Whether it was my failure to master footwork in sparring sessions at school, facing my loneliness in the background behind all the budding relationships of my fellow classmates, or the fact that Versa was the daughter worthy of a handsome betrothal; ultimately, I'm just the "Offering" to the king and the realm.

For all they knew, I was being sent away for slavery, slaughter, or worse. So, I swallowed the hurt deep down and hugged them both tightly. Nightfall was calling me, and I knew exactly where I wanted to be when I came apart at the seams.

The three moons of Demir were bright in the night sky, each of their crescents hugging the shoulder of the other. The garden path was illuminated with their moonslight, and I followed the trail to the nearby gazebo and tree swings.

Two swings, one for my sister and the other for me. This place, which I could come to whenever I wanted, now seemed much more meaningful. Only thirty days to soak in the people and places I loved. Thirty days to do whatever my heart desired. It's a funny thing to know what you want to do the next day or even one hundred years from now, but when your freedom is limited, those priorities change.

I kicked off my shoes and felt every blade of dewy grass tickle my ankles as I approached my swing and sat down. The cool breeze comforted me as I began to swing slowly, staying low to let my toes drag across the tough dirt below.

How does one even approach planning for their last days of freedom? It could take me thirty days alone just to make a list I felt good about. A list. That's what I needed. I was going to make a list of everything I wanted to do, see, or experience with what little time I had left. After all, my mother said to be as selfish as I wanted to be. It's not like I'd be around to experience the consequences. I swung underneath that tree for what seemed like hours, watching my shadow sway back and forth across the lawn.

Occasionally, I'd glance over at the empty swing next to me, trying to ignore the growing pain in my gut. The loss of Versa might be the most painful aspect of all of this. I continued to swing higher, faster, feeling the air rush all around me. My long dark locks were flying carelessly in the wind and I kept pushing back the stinging tears building in my eyes, the tightening of my chest. The never-ending barrage of thoughts overwhelmed me, deciding what I needed to experience in the days that lay ahead.

Beginning tomorrow morning, I couldn't waste a single second of what was left of my freedom. Higher and higher the swing flew until the list building in my head began to consume me. Now motivated to action, I tucked my legs underneath me and leaned back to maximize my momentum. The rush of adrenaline took over as I timed my dismount with the highest point of the arc and leaped, landing perfectly, gracefully, almost feline.

I stood, dusted off my hands on the sides of my emerald green dress, and began to embrace the dark feeling of my life being utterly out of control. There was one thing I had to do before the Offering, one thing that was undeniably happening; I was going to lose my maidenhead.

CHAPTER 2

It was the middle of the night by the time I returned to my room. Versa was sleeping soundly across the hall, and for that, I was thankful. I was never good at lying; even worse at lying to her. The only time we ever pulled off lies was when we were in on it together and out to mislead our parents. For as innocent as she came off to others, only I knew her secrets and occasional antics.

I had no idea what story my parents would tell her in the morning about my upcoming "disappearance." I certainly didn't want to spoil things by coming up with my own falsehood. I knew I wouldn't be nearly creative enough to spin up something believable off the cuff, not with Versa's eyes on me.

I glanced around my bedroom at the wall of trinkets that I'd collected from my father's various travels. He'd always bring me back something so that we could share in his adventures. A way to learn about the people, the customs and the beautiful places beyond the sea. I noted the top few shelves consisting of a handful of unique instruments, none of which I could play, but all equally interesting to inspect and admire. My favorite was the golden flute with decorative mother-of-pearl embellishments.

To the right of the instruments were an arrangement of masks and dolls, each intricately painted in a beautiful array of colors that were beginning to fade from the sunlight glaring in through the giant windows. Each of the items made me nostalgic for my childhood, and what ordinarily wouldn't have seemed long ago, suddenly felt so far away.

My collection of books was precious to me. I couldn't fathom the thought of them covered in dust, and I hoped that after my disappearance they'd find a new home, someone to love and cherish them the way I had. I acknowledged how I had them meticulously arranged in an order that only made sense to me. Row after row I scanned, remembering how quickly they overflowed my shelves and I had to beg Versa to let me move some of them into her room. Given the questionable content, I was too embarrassed to store them in our family library.

My room was already beginning to feel lonely and foreign. I hated that this simple change of direction in my life made me feel like a stranger in my own home, my own room. A home I had made memories in for 25 years, some of which were captured in paintings displayed throughout the gallery.

On every special occasion, my mother insisted that we sit for hours while some poor artist struggled to paint our family in a way that met her extremely high standards. Mother spent weeks planning our attire for these portrait sessions, trying her best to ensure that our outfits appeared cohesive. Not surprisingly, that same rationale gave her an excuse to pore over expensive and exotic fabrics, allowing her to commission new dresses to be made for all of us.

She constantly critiqued the artist, implying that our beauty had not been captured accurately enough, but what she really meant to say was *her* beauty. For all my mother's kindness, she was also vain. Rightfully so.

I'm glad to say my sister and I did inherit her looks, but we were both much humbler. If you glanced at the portraits quickly, it was clear that we were our father's daughters. His bloodline dominated all our major features. Our heads were crowned with long, dark brown hair—so dark, it was almost black—falling like tendrils well past our shoulders. We bore the same sparkling emerald eyes as him, and nearly translucent eggshell skin. Our father's cheeks, however, were always rosy, permanently sun-kissed from years at sea under the relentless sky.

However, the foundations of what made us considerably attractive Fae were our mother's perfect nose, pouty lips, sharply arched cheekbones, and deep-set eyes.

Some might have considered her intense burgundy hair color harsh, for it appeared like blood if you stared long enough. Her olive skin was that of her mother's, and all the females who came before in their family. At least from the paintings I've seen.

She was what most would refer to as intimidatingly beautiful. Her dark eyes were like endless pools of ink. If you stared into them for too long, you'd find yourself drowning. Sometimes, I'm convinced it was her eyes that first ensnared my father.

My mother is intense. My father, on the other hand, has a light-hearted and jovial exterior, but could be brutal when it came to matters of commerce.

In my mind, they were the quintessential opposites attract love story. Since many High Fae families were focused on keeping bloodlines strong, they often denied their children the chance at finding a true mated bond or love match. Instead, they relied on favorable arranged marriages. I have never actually encountered a pair of mates myself, as my mother and father were a love match. For that, I am grateful to have grown up witnessing two people who, despite not having a mated bond, chose each other for all time.

They're lucky their families didn't intervene. I am also lucky that despite Versa's betrothal being what would be considered a financially beneficial arrangement, she was happy. The attraction was there, and I believe my father would have never forced a decision upon her. We were his pride and joy, after all, and he'd never have condemned one of his daughters to sadness… I paused, contemplating the thought that despite that, I was indeed condemned—and powerless to stop it.

Each portrait featuring two daughters now felt like it might as well be just one. Will they miss me? And for how long? Hundreds of years could pass until my family took their final breaths, and my time amongst them was a mere season. Not that they would, but there was even time for my mother and father to replace me with a newborn should they so choose. Maybe even a male heir.

It never did bother them that they only had two daughters. Even though the families of the High Court were encouraged to breed large families. It's a shock they stopped after me and my sister, but they did get two for the price of one. I couldn't help but feel some sense of impending grief, that for my mother and father these portraits which brought them joy would someday make them feel despair.

Two hundred years since the Offering had last been called… My thoughts drifted to how many other households contained paintings with generations mysteriously lost to this command.

I shook my head in frustration; I was wasting my time already with what-ifs and pointless scenarios. I had thirty days of freedom ahead, with no idea how much actual time after that. I had no way to know if I'd even make it to twenty-six, let alone two hundred. Thinking about the long lives my family had ahead of them did nothing to ease my mind. Instead, my anxiety was growing.

There were many unanswered questions; I tried my hardest to sharpen my focus on the next month and ignore whatever lay beyond. I sat in the bay window of my room staring out into the expansive courtyard and sprawling gardens all bathed in moonslight.

On the window frame, I noticed a silver spiderweb glistening and watched as a brown spider crawled from one end to the other toward a small fly it had captured. The innocent fly was so unaware of what was coming, how brief its life would now be.

I waited nervously to witness its demise, wondering if it would struggle, put up a fight, or simply succumb to its fate. The anxious feeling in the pit of my stomach grew as I grabbed some nearby parchment, ink, and a quill and rested the paper atop a hard book. My mind began to wander as I scribbled the item that would definitively sit at the top of my list.

It's not that I had been saving my maidenhead. It's more like it wasn't important enough to pursue. While some of the ladies at school spent their spare time bashfully teasing or lusting after their classmates, I was quite the opposite. I loved to learn and invested every free moment in the pursuit of knowledge.

My father's collection of maps was of special interest to me. I'd wanted so badly to learn to navigate the seas and travel with my father's fellow merchants on their voyages. He always promised me that someday, when my education was complete, he'd guide my path toward becoming a guild member.

So far our time together at sea was fleeting, I was eager to learn everything I could about his trade. I followed the deckhands around, observing their chores and adding colorful words to my vocabulary—to the amused disappointment of my father. He showed me the purpose of tying different types of knots, and we practiced them together, both laughing when I inevitably became tangled and frustrated.

"All in good time, dear. A sailor is not a master of all things on her first few voyages."

Although his travels were usually benign, some were quite dangerous. I had no fear of it, though, only a growing anticipation for the sway of the sea, and the horizon serving as my only comfort as we sailed into the unknown.

I would trace the lines on the maps for hours with my eyes, scanning in between each territory, mountain top, river and body of water. I loved the smell of them. They combined some of my favorite scents of old dusty books and sea breeze. With some of them you could even feel the sea salt on your hands when you ran your fingertips across them. Evidence of past adventures.

But it wasn't just books or curiosity about the wider world that made my wheels turn. I was fascinated with the sciences, as well, understanding how the land provided the necessities of life if one only knew where to look. Things to hurt and to heal, things to nourish us and to destroy us. I had an immense respect for all these things and the harmony in which they balanced, humbling all living creatures. One might think someone so focused on academics might be lacking in strength and agility, but in that, too, I was gifted.

It didn't matter if I was training alone, running the woods of our sprawling land, or practicing hand-to-hand combat, I couldn't get enough of that adrenaline. It soothed me. And where most felt the rumblings of fury or fear, I felt a deep sense of calm and awareness.

Although it was merely an exhibition, pure exhilaration consumed me when I was drenched in sweat and I could feel my body being molded into a weapon, like a newly-forged blade being sharpened. No matter how hard I pushed myself physically, I never felt satiated. And when there was finally no energy for sparring and training, I fed my ferocious curiosity for knowledge, consuming tomes on Fae history, politics, and commerce until that fire in me returned. Perhaps, while I was focused on the body and the mind, I may have deprived matters of the heart.

My sister, on the other hand, was doing the exact opposite. There wasn't an admirer she didn't have—both males and females. She didn't even have to try; she simply existed. My father is lucky he didn't know just how many suitors had pursued Versa in our youth. I always kept her secrets when she'd sneak out to meet them under the cover of night.

She'd return late into the evening and crawl into my bed to tell me of her adventures. We'd laugh at all their failed attempts to woo her and their weaving of poetic words trying valiantly to tug at her heartstrings. None of them were ever as suave as the romantics we'd read about in our silly little novels. And while a few may have been lucky to land a kiss here and there, it's not like she was running about giving every attractive Fae all of herself. Anything I knew or learned, I learned because Versa did it first, and for that, I was immensely grateful.

She even told me of the time she went out with a beautiful young lady named Miran. She was the only female at school whose allure surpassed Versa's, and it had made the males' blood boil that she had zero interest in them. But she had been very interested in my sister. After enough convincing, Versa finally gave in and met her one evening.

When she returned to me that night, she explained that it had been one of the most physically captivating encounters she had ever had. By far the best kisser, and when Miran traced her lips alongside Versa's neck, down her collarbone and then to her breast, she shook with a desire she had never experienced prior.

I thought this was something that would blossom, but Versa explained to me that while she was physically taken with Miran, she didn't reciprocate her feelings. She looked at me intently that night and spoke these words, which I will always remember: "You can't know what you do and don't like till you try it. You can't know your heart until your mind doesn't fight it." Versa was wise like that; an old soul wrapped in a delicate, beautiful shell.

The night Versa lost her maidenhead I was the first to know, and to say I had a hundred questions was an understatement. She didn't make a fuss of all the things I thought she would. As expected, she mentioned there was brief pain and minimal pleasure. He was proper and understood the situation, so precautions were taken. I was glad to hear he was gentle, because Versa knew I would have slit his throat otherwise. She'd have helped me get rid of the body. We were thick as thieves.

As she continued her recollection, she seemed withdrawn in a dream-like state. Changed in the smallest of ways. While she said she did not find her own climax, she treasured the memory of their bare skin against one another and was already plotting to see him again. She continued with these trysts for a while, and her stories became more passionate and detailed with experience and experimentation. Like I said, everything I learned, I learned through Versa.

I wasn't completely inexperienced. After listening to Versa's endeavors and explorations for long enough, I finally sought my own. I stopped ignoring the advances of my schoolmates and became quite obsessed with kissing. In fact, I made a game of stealing kisses between classes in the stone halls that I enjoyed more than I should have, as I was constantly putting myself at risk. Mainly of someone telling my parents what a little trollop I was being, but I didn't care. They'd judge who I was kissing rather than the act itself. No one would be good enough for a High Lord's daughter, certainly not without their approval first.

Kissing felt like everything to me. It felt like enough, and I didn't have much interest in taking things further. Partly out of fear, but also because it just didn't seem necessary. I had all the time in the world. I was more focused on excelling in my studies and thinking of a future at sea. The flirting, teasing and kissing were all part of luring them in only to catch and release. It was mostly harmless, but I knew some were quite disappointed when I didn't return any formal affections, and that's when I knew things had to end. When time is your friend, you don't have to rush a good thing.

My thoughts turned back to the present, and here I was swallowing the painful truth of how time was no longer an ally. I held the quill to the parchment and began making a list of everything that came to mind. Small and big, silly and frivolous, serious and sad.

Lose my maidenhead
Seduce a stranger
Gamble till I win
Get drunk
Alter my appearance
Help someone in need
Get a tattoo
Do something that scares me
Swim naked in the moonslight
Say my goodbyes

CHAPTER 6

I awoke to the morning sun glaring through my windows and Versa practically pouncing onto my bed. With a squeal of excitement, she exclaimed, "Father has told me all about your new adventure!"

I rolled over to face her, trying to rub the sleep from my eyes. "Huh?" I questioned groggily.

"I always knew you'd be the one to do something amazing. I'm so jealous; I wish I could come with you."

My head was pounding, not only from being woken abruptly—and this early, which I hated—but also from Versa's tone, which in no way matched that of my parents' the night prior.

Before I could even say a word, she continued to ramble on. "I mean, I am devastated you won't be here for the wedding, but who could say no to an opportunity like that? I don't blame you, not one bit!"

Versa inched closer to me as I pushed myself up on my elbows, holding my hand up to the window to shade my eyes from the sun. "I can't believe you leave in a month, but I know we'll make the most of it. You can help me finish up the planning and—"

"What are you talking about?" I snapped in confusion.

She paused and looked at me with hurt in her eyes, and I admit I hadn't noticed the sharpness of my voice until I saw her reaction.

She spoke softly and slowly this time, "You know, how you've been assigned to be a translator on a ship with one of father's guild members."

It started to make sense, as I transitioned from the delirium of sleep to a state of awake.

"You were always better at the old tongue than I was. I just couldn't see much use in studying something that was hardly spoken..." she trailed off. "But look at you now! You're going to see the world, finally."

This was it. The bold and creative lie my parents had come up with to keep my sister completely in the dark as to why I'd be leaving soon and wouldn't be at her wedding. I felt sick to my stomach that my father dared to use a real desire of mine to conveniently put a bow on this little charade. He knew I wanted to join the guild; he promised me it would happen someday, and here we were pretending he had kept his word.

I gave them credit. Saying I'd be a translator was not something I would have come up with. I'd have bet that was my mother; nice touch. Although, a good lie requires a commitment to the details.

I think I had underestimated how exhausting it was going to be keeping up with these lies around Versa, and already it made me want to flee. But, for her benefit, I swallowed the anxious feeling and replied, "Oh yes, I am so excited...but I didn't know how to tell you. I just can't believe I'm not going to be here to see your hand given in marriage."

Versa placed her hands on mine and smiled at me with all sincerity. "You're forgiven. Think nothing of it! Look at it this way, one less ball... I know how you despise them."

She wasn't wrong, balls weren't my thing, and being she was a daughter of a High Lord also marrying into a wealthy family, no expense would be spared on such a spectacle. I glanced away briefly, shielding her from the sight of the grief beginning to creep into my expression.

Yes, I hated dances—despite my skill—but I loved my sister and I wanted to be there for her on her big day. I wanted to be there for all her big days. The day she became a wife, a mother. All of it…I'd never get to see it.

Before my thoughts betrayed me, I grabbed her shoulders and pulled her toward me in an embrace. I whispered into her neck, "I'm going to miss you more than you can imagine."

As she pulled away from me, my attention was drawn to the parchment by the window, and I became nervous that she might notice it. After all, she thought I was going to be gone for a long time, but not forever. I'm sure there was going to be some grand part two to this lie that eventually explained why I never returned.

I laughed internally at the thought of the headlines and rumors. I could see it now…

Daughter of merchant, lost at sea—never returns.

Daughter of a High Lord taken to her untimely death by a creature of the sea.

Daughter of House Blackthorn taken captive and slain.

Thinking of the ways in which my parents would fake my disappearance was beyond depressing, and I immediately sought to distract myself. If I was never to return or speak to anyone I know or love again, then the only believable reason was that I had died.

If letters went with no reply, if visits went unplanned, there had to be a culmination to this lie. Because forever was what the Offering demanded.

I had to focus. I had things to do and time was already dwindling. My sister knew me too well. We were one soul split in two. Sometimes, I think she knew my motives before I did.

"What are you going to do before you leave?" she eyed me mischievously. "I hope it's absolutely debaucherous."

I let out a high-pitched cackle because she thought just like I did. Make the most of everything. I smiled at her and gave an equally deviant look back when I replied, "I have some ideas..."

My sister and I sat in the dining hall, sipping on warm tea and enjoying sweet rolls. I added two extras to my plate and chomped away obnoxiously because, if I had no future, who gave a damn about maintaining one's figure for training, attracting a spouse, or otherwise. I slapped a heap of butter onto the second roll as my mother and father entered the hall.

As they made their way toward us, my mother's deep red hair contrasted dramatically in the sunlight against the pale lilac gown she donned. It was not a flattering combination.

Normally, they sat at the complete opposite end from Versa and I, which often led to feeling like we were eating breakfast separately. They must be feeling sentimental—or wanting to listen in closely to ensure I kept up with the lie.

"Morning," my father said nonchalantly.

With my mouth stuffed full of sweet rolls, I figured I'd throw them a bone by showing them I had already been ambushed. "Father, you'll have to let me borrow some of your maps for my voyage," I quipped dryly while eying him and shoving another bite in my mouth.

My mother was already displeased with the curt manner of my speech, complemented by the completely unladylike behavior I was displaying with my food. Something absolutely out of character for a daughter of a High Fae family whose upbringing most definitely included all things etiquette.

I slurped my cup of mint tea for good measure. My prompt caught them both by surprise, but they quickly recovered and played along.

"Of course, darling," my father nodded, helping himself to the spread. "I'm sure the Seafarers will have their own, but it doesn't hurt to have extra. After all, none are as detailed as mine."

My mother nodded in agreement and spared us a fake smile before sipping from her steaming cup. I glanced at Versa, who was completely buying it, and almost disinterested, as she began glancing through the sketches of her wedding gown options. She'd only changed her mind fifty times, but who could blame her; everyone was going to be looking at her.

Before I even knew what I was saying, I spoke with conviction, "Since I have such little time to prepare before I have to leave, I just wanted you to be aware I will be very busy." I paused expecting someone to interject, but they didn't, so I continued, "I have some affairs to get in order, some friends to say goodbye to—you know, typical things…" I almost snorted at how formal I sounded, when all I was really trying to say was that I was not going to be around much since I'd be busy checking things off a ridiculous list I'd made before the king destroyed my life.

I could tell my sister was only half listening since all she did was chime in to offer, "But you'll make time for my dress fitting and provide some help planning, right?"

I rolled my eyes. She didn't take notice since hers were still plastered on the dress sketches. She had no idea the severity of my situation; how could I fault her for thinking her wedding list was more important than my end-of-freedom list?

My mother and father eyed me intently, because unlike her, they did understand. And, although they had no idea what I'd be pursuing, they had already understood that whatever these days entailed would be of my own making.

My mother, trying to keep up the act of just another casual morning, turned to my sister and quietly began to discuss the details of the nuptials.

Shoving another bite of breakfast into my mouth, I turned to my father, tilting my head with a complacent smile that read, *How am I doing?*

I was almost feeling cocky enough to throw my feet up on the table, but then Versa would have been tipped off that something was truly awry if I was going to push my father's limits unnecessarily. I kept my feet planted under the table like a lady should, but slumped my posture a little in defiance.

My father grinned, his thin dark beard framing the corners of his lips as he continued to play along. "I am sure you're going to love your time at sea, but we should make sure you pack accordingly. You'll need something more practical, as gowns won't be needed on the decks."

I tried to hide my scowl as I replied in between bites of breakfast, "Yes, I think my fighting leathers, trousers, blouses, and boots would all be better suited."

At the mention of my attire, Versa finally squeaked in alarm, "Fighting leathers! Father, what are you sending her off to do? I hope she won't have a need for that. I pray she doesn't run into those barbarians or their kind; please tell me she'll be safe with whoever her captain is!"

I knew what barbarians she was referring to. Years ago, there was an uprising led by a group of Seafarers against the merchants. They blockaded the port, took hostages, and killed indiscriminately to prove their viciousness was not a bluff.

They felt the merchants guild had become too powerful and were taking advantage of the Seafarers. Their kind weren't overly keen on negotiations, so the disagreement began with bloodshed rather than diplomacy. The horrors they inflicted were practically war crimes. There wasn't an ounce of etiquette or decorum, and my father described how the once beautiful blue bay that sparkled with seafoam was painted in blood and driftwood from destroyed ships and lives taken. To make things even more salacious, the rebels were led by a Seafarer who was, in fact, High Fae. It was treason for members of the High Court to turn on one another.

This was a very difficult time for my family as my mother, sister and I waited for what seemed like an eternity to hear any news of my father and his well-being.

Night after night we'd go to bed crying. I remember Versa and I slept together most of those nights, clinging to one another for some small sense of comfort. While his guild's fleet had lost many ships and lives, he returned to us unscathed but extremely shaken. He would not speak in detail of the atrocities he had witnessed, but one night, I had eavesdropped on him and my mother. I never shared the details of what I'd heard with Versa, and as for myself, I wish I could take back my curiosity from that evening.

My father's jaw clenched at the memory of the barbarians, "No Versa, of course not. She'll be under the protection of people I trust completely. Plus, they finally caught up with that evil scoundrel who incited that entire uprising, and he will be tortured and imprisoned for eternity."

My father paused, appearing in deep thought, probably suffering flashbacks. "Death isn't good enough for him," he added bitterly.

I grabbed my butter knife and pointed the dull end at Versa's arm, making a short jabbing motion to lighten the mood. "What, sister, you think I can't handle myself against a couple of Sea Fae?"

She cocked her head at me in annoyance that I might dare get butter on the silk sleeve of her dress. My father finally returned from his own thoughts and gave me a warm smile before adding, "Cress can handle herself, of that I have no doubt."

The frustration of this entire conversation was broiling beneath my skin. It was clear sitting around the manor all by my lonesome was just as irritating as sitting with my family and playing pretend. Versa continued to thumb through sketches. I turned to my left and saw the ornate golden clock that had been in our family for centuries, and I was reminded that each minute that passed where I sat here putting on an act, wearing a mask and stuffing my face, was one less to achieve all the things on my list.

I stood abruptly, screeching my chair across the marble floor. The unpleasant noise caused my sister to glance up at me once more and, before she could show any measure of concern, I stated flatly, "I have a lot to do today, don't wait on me for dinner."

I practically waltzed out of the room, already sweating at the thought of any of them knowing what I intended to take care of first.

As I made my way up to my room, I supposed I could have asked to speak with my father in his study, just to understand the full extent of this wild tale we'd be spinning. But it didn't matter, not when I was on a mission.

The lady's maid drew me a hot bath and I opened the windows to let in the fresh summer air and sunlight. I gave her a nod of appreciation and indicated I'd like privacy. I figured if today was the day some male was going to take me, I might as well be clean, smell delightful, and look like a lady. After a brief soak, I exited the tub smelling of lavender and I paused to stare at my naked body in the long mirror next to my armoire. I was every bit a grown female, but at this point, I felt a bit shy that I was going to have to present myself bare in the very near future.

I studied the angles, dimples, and curves of my body. Turning and posing, trying to stand in a way that I thought showed off my best assets. I opened the door to view my dresses and selected one to mark the occasion. It was not something I'd have normally worn, and in fact, it was one Versa had designed to match her own. The neckline was scantily cut to accentuate the collar, and…other things… The sleeves were long, loose, and elegant. The skirt was fitted until just past the waistline to show off the bodice, all the way down to the hips, and drew close to the leg so as not to make it unbearable to get around. Like most of my dresses, it was made of velvet and I fancied the dark teal color.

I didn't know where this passionate episode was going to take place; I certainly didn't want to be overwhelmed or distracted by my attire. I left off any jewelry as I didn't want to worry about losing it. I also changed my mind and elected to leave my hair down, knowing that if I left with it styled and came back with it looking like a bird's nest, I might not be able to hide the embarrassment on my face. I only knew this because sometimes Versa would crawl back into my room after her late-night rendezvous looking completely disheveled.

Once fully dressed, I looked myself over again in the mirror one last time. I inhaled deeply. No time like the present.

I headed to the stable and waited impatiently while the stable hand saddled my dapple-gray horse, Rain. I saw my mother staring at me from a window and gave her a polite wave.

In a flash, I mounted and took off and was immediately glad I chose to leave my hair down as the wind rushed through every strand, the breeze offering me a reprieve from the blanket of heat that had already overcome the morning.

Exhilarated at the freedom of leaving the grounds without an escort, I knew exactly where I was headed to accomplish item number one on the list; to someone who had made a bargain with me. It was time to call in that favor.

I dismounted from my horse outside of Gris's family manor and tied Rain to the stone fence near the entrance. Gris was not only a lifelong friend, but someone who I had seen almost daily for years during our education at a nearby academy.

His family was only slightly less wealthy than mine, his father being an artisan known for having access to the most rare and stunning gems. He was an artist at transforming metals and stones, making jewelry for all the High Fae families in the North—including having handmade many of Queen Nyla's diadems. It's rumored he was hired to make Versa's wedding ring. And by rumor, I mean Gris had secretly confirmed it for me. This is just one of the ways I knew she was aligned to a "favorable" match.

Nerves were already starting to settle in as I began walking toward the ornate front doors of Gris's home. I wasn't nervous about seeing Gris, more that he was going to be entirely shocked by what I would ask of him.

When I knocked three times, I was relieved that he answered the door instead of one of the staff or his parents. I needed to keep my courage up and my eyes on the prize. Which was now standing before me. All six feet of him.

Gris greeted me with a wide smile of perfectly straight white teeth that contrasted against his deliciously warm skin. I used to think of that smile as boyish and charming, but now I was doing my best to see beyond friendship and acknowledge him as a mature Fae male.

A handsome one at that, who was able to carry himself with the ease and lack of formality required of most High Fae families, since he was, in fact, not High Fae. His chocolate-brown hair was tousled and messy, and he leaned into the door frame with one arm hovering over me, accentuating his towering height. I eyed the sculpted tan muscles of his arm, his white shirt clinging to his chest in all the right spots.

"Cress, an unexpected visit. And what reason have you for gracing my doorway?"

I tried to soften my features and silken my voice before speaking. Not at all my usual with Gris.

I began coyly, "What, you don't like surprises?"

It sounded and felt unnatural. Trying to seduce anyone was going to be a challenge for me, but putting the moves on Gris was supposed to be the path of least resistance.

Before he could respond, I added, "Are your parents home?"

He looked slightly confused, "No, they're away showing my father's latest creations at an exhibition a few towns away, why?"

Perfect, I thought to myself, this is absolutely perfect. I gently grazed my hand across his abdomen and stepped under his arm still framing the doorway. "Aren't you going to invite me inside?"

I had invited myself in with a move like that, though I tried to remain sly and elusive. I didn't tear my gaze from him as he followed me from the doorway.

Gris turned to face me as I stood in the giant foyer of his home and shook his head in amusement, shutting the door behind us with a small chuckle.

"Sure, Cress, come right in. How utterly improper of me to not have offered sooner."

His remark was bathed in sarcasm, but that was our language. Our friendship had always been one of playful teasing and innuendo. Sometimes our dirty mouths would get the better of our education and standing.

I had been in Gris's home many times, but trying to figure out where I'd lead him to take my maidenhead made my memory go blank.

Gris grabbed my chin and lifted my face to meet his warm honey eyes. "Cress you're awfully dressed up today. I didn't think you knew how to ride a horse in a dress, like a lady. To what do I owe the pleasure of this rare appearance?"

Gris knew better. He knew I wasn't going to be seen in a dress unless it was some formal occasion.

Normally, I was in fitted trousers, a loose blouse, training attire—anything but gowns. Those were reserved for occasions not of my making. I took his coy words as my opening.

"Well, speaking of pleasure..." I smiled playfully as he released my chin, "I need to call in a favor. Our bargain."

Gris let out a deep, booming laugh, one that echoed throughout the massive foyer. He shook his head and ran a hand through his hair, sliding it down a cheek to rest his chin on his fist with a look of pure disbelief. I wanted to crawl under a rock, but I knew I had to keep my composure to pull this off.

"We aren't even fifty yet, and you're calling in that favor? Didn't we agree on one hundred?"

I tried to keep my annoyance at bay, "Semantics."

He chuckled again and began to usher me to the parlor. I always enjoyed the casual, relaxed feel of Gris's home over the ostentatious display of wealth that I grew up in. It was inviting. As we walked, he spoke.

He tried to give the appearance of taking me seriously, "No, Cress, it's not semantics. I'm not interested in marrying anyone just yet, and we agreed we were each other's backup plan."

I followed him closely, doing my best to sway my hips more than I should and present as gracefully as I could muster.

"I actually don't need the marriage part..." I trailed off, trying not to acknowledge the blushing cheeks that were now betraying me.

He grabbed a silver decanter from the bar and began to pour some golden-brown liquid into a glass.

"Oh, we're definitely going to need drinks for this conversation."

"But it's only the afternoon," I resisted, as he handed me the first glass and began to pour himself his own.

"Cress, you show up unexpectedly trying to call in a bargain not due for another seventy-five years and are now, what...asking me to bed you?" He lifted his glass and clinked it against mine.

That's what I loved about Gris. Like me, he never minced words. Always to the point. I looked at the tempting liquid idling in the glass and threw back a giant swig, trying not to wince at the awful taste.

"Exactly! I knew I could count on you," I exclaimed.

Gris leaned against the wall with folded arms and sipped casually from his drink. I tried not to look like I was staring, but instead mentally acknowledged all of his best features in my mind, trying to harness any attraction that I had ever felt for him buried beneath layers of friendship.

The silence between us seemed to last forever, and he just kept eyeing me. "You're not kidding, are you?" he said softly.

I shook my head in admission while taking another sip. A little liquid courage, as I knew what he was going to ask next.

"But why now? Why me? Why here?"

I took a deep breath and once more found myself putting on the mask of lies.

"I've been selected to join a merchant and Seafarers as their translator. I'm leaving very soon, and I'm going to be gone…for a very long time…" My words trailed off as I bit down on the sad truth underneath that last part.

His features gradually turned from amusement to concern. The truth settled into his rigid jawline and furrowed in his dark brow. I could tell he was realizing that meant he, too, wouldn't be seeing me anytime soon.

And at the bottom of all this, that's what we were. The greatest of friends who in the silliness of our youth made an oath, a bargain to one another that if by our one hundredth name day, neither of us were betrothed, had found our true mates or someone to love, we'd settle on each other. Maybe in one hundred years' time, we'd stop ignoring that minor attraction that treaded below the surface of our friendship and often erupted as flirtatious banter, sometimes jealousy, and quickly reconciled back to friendship.

"Surely, you'd rather wait? You have plenty of time. Find someone you actually care for…that way." His voice became unsteady as he finished the sentence, his words unsettling me, because only I knew just how long a time it would be.

"No, I do not want to wait any longer." I replied rigidly. "Please don't make me beg, Gris! Would you really have me lose my maidenhead to some grimy Seafarer aboard a ship with no privacy?"

Gris scoffed, "I absolutely can't be responsible for a daughter of a High Lord experiencing anything less than the respect and acknowledgment of her standing on my watch." He paused. "Even if they say the Seafarers are quite passionate lovers…"

I rolled my eyes into a look, like one more word and he'd be explaining to his mother why there was broken glass all over her beautiful rug.

Gris began to move slowly toward me, and I could see desire building in his study of me. Something I usually witnessed him direct at one of our many fawning classmates, but it was something entirely different to see it turned toward me.

"Are you sure about this, Cress?" He placed his smooth hand around my waist and settled it on my lower back, my breath hitching audibly from the heat.

He bent down, leaning into my ear, and said in a taunting whisper, "You're going to have to stop being so nervous at my touch if this is really what you want."

I turned my face to match his dark gaze, and I could feel his breath on my neck. I took in the citrus scent of him, and I was failing to see how this beautiful male, this friend, had never seduced me before. Here in this space, welcoming him to cross the threshold, I realized I was entirely taken by him.

He refused to speak another word, waiting for me. I did what I knew how to do and to show him I was serious, so serious that I'd make the first move.

I quickly grabbed both sides of his face, clumsily pulled him toward me and crushed my lips to his. Fiercely and passionately, I swept my tongue into his mouth, with a dominance he reciprocated. We both tasted like the golden liquid we had just consumed, and it reminded me to have courage.

For what seemed like forever, Gris and I explored each other with our mouths—and occasionally, our hands. This was unknown territory for us both, because it was crossing a line we had clearly set for ourselves.

Friends don't kiss this way, don't touch this way, but I had called in the bargain and he showed little to no reluctance acquiescing. I wondered how much of that had to do with him wanting me, or wanting someone in general. Or was he really just doing this as a favor for a friend?

Gris was far more experienced than me. From the kissing alone you would not have known how inexperienced I was. But kissing had always been my favorite. I was good at it, more than good—I was great. I felt confident that I was ensnaring his lust with each swipe of my tongue across his.

When I bit down gently on his lower lip and pulled away slowly, the surprised lust flickering in his eyes started to warm me from the inside, and my stomach felt like it was beginning to tighten in knots.

Gris was taller than me, and I had to stand on the tips of my toes to keep him close. He bent down and once again spoke quietly in my ear, "Should I make you stand on your toes the whole time, or shall I take you somewhere more comfortable?"

I pulled away and glanced up at him. Hearing that smolder in his voice was like looking at a stranger, but one that I was extremely turned on by.

"I'd like that," I practically whispered while blinking furiously to remind myself this was actually happening.

Before I could say another word, Gris picked me up and threw me over his broad shoulder, his muscular arms wrapped under my rear to hold me close while I dangled over him. This is not what I meant.

"What are you doing? Put me down." I fought while pounding my tiny fists into his back as he kept walking, heading down a hallway to a room I'd never been in.

"Cress, you're not in charge today, just let me lead."

And there it was, the dance of seduction that I was not familiar with. I was used to leading, being in control, and having a well-prepared response. I hated feeling out of control. It wasn't in my nature. I planned and prepared for everything.

I tried to lean into the moment and let Gris have his way with me, even if it meant him stupidly carrying me like a sack over his shoulder. I had to admit, this unseen side of Gris was more than just a little alluring.

He tossed me onto the bed like I weighed nothing. I looked around the room, not recognizing it and wondering where he had taken me.

He could easily read the thoughts on my face. "You're wondering why I've brought you here and not my room? Well, I don't feel like the room we've grown up in together is a setting that is going to do anything for either of us."

He wasn't wrong, not in the slightest. Gris was a quick thinker like that, but also considerate. Probably wasn't the best idea to be in a room I've seen many times throughout all the ages of our youth.

The room was filled with harsh sunlight, and I was beginning to feel shy about my body being on display in all the illumination. I hadn't accounted for the fact that my surprise visit should have been at night.

Before I could say a word, he walked over to the window and drew the lapis-blue curtains closed, leaving behind only the dim candlelight which appeared with a snap of his fingers.

It was odd to see Gris using even minor bits of magic. At school, we were discouraged from relying on our gifts and made to understand that they were a waste of focus and energy. To become reliant upon them would make us weak. It was sort of considered taboo or unbecoming to use magic for simple things.

That's when I realized that beyond lighting the candles, he was also reading my mind. It's how he knew I was fixated on the sunlight and the windows.

"Hey. Stay out of my head!"

I was quickly consumed with embarrassment. How many other times had he invaded my thoughts since I arrived? I would have to do my best to shield anything else for fear of him learning the truth. How was I ever going to focus on my mental shields while trying to be present for the task at hand? I hardly ever practiced keeping them up.

Before I could argue any further, he pounced on top of me. Both of his strong legs pinned me to the bed like a cage, and he leaned forward with a devious smile. "Make me."

He could tell I was losing all confidence and quickly becoming distracted. He grabbed my chin and straightened it to look at me. "Hey, it's ok. I won't anymore. I just really wanted to make you feel comfortable, I thought it might be an advantage." His voice softened with kindness.

If there was anything I could thank the Gods for, it was the realization that I had chosen wisely. It was treading in risky territory to pursue someone other than a stranger, but it was Gris's attentiveness to me and my needs that solidified it. Despite my anxious and eager body, being pinned underneath my gorgeous friend was exactly where I was meant to be.

Gris teased me with soft kisses and spoke once more, "Cress, you're sure?"

I nodded, and this time it wasn't with fear and uncertainty. Gris smiled, his eyes alight with a happiness that seemed rare for him. He began to kiss down my neck with a palpable hunger. His hands roamed greedily down my sides, feeling every curve of my waist and hips.

In a swift movement, he drew one hand to squeeze my breast. I gasped in unexpected pleasure, and he swallowed the sound in between our kisses. He sat up and removed his shirt, tossing it to the floor carelessly and revealing more muscles that I had refused to acknowledge any other time I had seen him shirtless.

My eyes feasted on his body, his arms, and my gaze trailed all the way down his stomach to the beautiful V that framed the top of his pants. His skin, a stark contrast to my pale flesh, even in the dim candlelight. He was unbelievably attractive; I felt very lucky. Everything in me was growing warm, hot. I badly wanted to be rid of this horrible velvet dress.

Gris crawled to the edge of the bed and began to slowly lift my dress, trailing kisses up along my leg, and while I had no idea what a climax truly meant, that alone could have been my undoing. He pulled away and I took it as my cue.

I sat up quickly, ungracefully lifting my dress over my head and tossing it to the floor beside his shirt. I realized now I was completely naked, and he wasn't. In my head, I was starting to panic. I had not worn anything special underneath. Nothing lacy like the growing collection Versa had in her armoire.

Embarrassingly, I had been so focused on rushing to the task at hand that I hadn't put on any undergarments at all. Gris had not taken his eyes off me, not once. He had a look that was bordering on feral. "You naughty thing, no layers for me to peel off?"

He just stood there, drinking me in. I did the best I could to mirror his audacity and stated plainly, "Your turn."

Gris looked shocked at my remark, then sauntered over to me as I sat in the nude at the edge of the bed. The drawstring of his trousers was now at my eye level, and it was then I could see the length of him—a hard outline straining against the confinement.

In my mind, it seemed like a powerful thing to feel like you could draw a physical response from someone this way. And in turn, he was doing the same to me; I could feel myself becoming wet like the times I had touched myself.

He began to slowly untie the top of his pants till he removed them fully, releasing himself into my view. Each line we crossed felt like the point of no return. Gris and I stared at each other's naked figures in the dim candlelight, the increasing hunger for one another edging on unbearable.

I knew there was a whole spectrum of things we could do, but I didn't know how long I was going to be able to keep up this show of confidence with him. Especially if I alluded to how little I knew or had experienced. I had come here with one thing in mind, and as long as that was accomplished, then I'd met my goal.

Gris lay down beside me, and we faced each other. He began to run his fingers idly along the side of my hip and slowly down my stomach. The light trail of his fingers sent ticklish sensations down my abdomen that I could feel reverberating, causing my muscles to throb. I inched closer to him and began kissing him again to distract myself from everything to come.

While his tongue danced along mine, I felt his hand inching down, lower and lower, before I grabbed it to stop him. Still trying to maintain our passionate kisses, I didn't want him to focus on anything but what I needed done. I was beginning to ache with anticipation and frustration, all in one.

He pulled away momentarily. "Let me help you relax."

I don't know what he meant by that, but I was trying to follow his lead.

He continued to kiss down my neck, along my shoulder, and before I could stop him, he slipped his soft hand between my legs. There was no hiding the evidence of my want, and the next thing I knew, he began to rub two long fingers up and down my slick apex.

My breathing hitched and was starting to become uneven as he continued, no matter how much I tried to clench my thighs against his hand.

He looked me square in the eyes and asked me in a hushed voice, "Do you trust me?" All the while he dragged his fingers in a slow, fluid motion.

I thought I was going to die right then and there. This was by far the sexiest thing that had ever happened to me. As I began to mouth the word "yes," he slowly slipped a finger inside of me and I arched my back, leaning into this amazing feeling.

Before I could show signs of wanting more, Gris continued to nibble, lick, and kiss my breasts, and with the next gentle thrust of his hand, I felt a second finger slide in. As the pressure built, my panting became increasingly obvious.

After Gris had stroked me gently into a mess, he pulled his fingers from me and I looked at him with intense need as I missed the feeling of his hand between my thighs.

Gris was intently focused on me; I had almost forgotten him and his magnificent body, his manhood that remained rock-hard. He lay back on the bed and ordered me to crawl on top of him. I hovered over his stomach, not knowing what to do next, and he could see the flushed nervousness canvassing my face.

"I want you to take me inside of you. Slowly."

This was finally happening. I was already hot and my body ready from everything that had come prior, but now I was perspiring out of fear.

Gris placed his hands on the tops of both my thighs and spoke with all the patience in the world, "This will hurt less if you do it this way. You're in control."

Encouragement. Consideration. Consent. My chest felt tight with an overwhelming appreciation for the way he was helping me, guiding me through all these emotions that were racing inside me. Desire, passion, confusion, fear, nervousness, tension.

I knew I was being cared for, and I let the safety of all of that wash over me as I let the tip of his length rub against me, and it made me eager for more.

He was much bigger than the two fingers he had teased me with earlier, but I pressed on. I let my body gently lower, and he didn't move a muscle. He continued to look at me like I was a powerful queen conquering him from above, and his admiration overcame me.

I accepted him into me further and could feel the tight sting my sister had warned me about. The pain was there, but I was too overcome with desire to please him, to please myself, and to fill this aching emptiness deep inside me.

As I slid slowly down on him, trying to ignore the minute pain, I realized in retrospect how grateful I was that he had helped me "relax" before all of this. I had been greedy in trying to rush when Gris was just trying to make this experience as good as it could be.

When I finally enveloped him entirely, he smiled and pulled my shoulders forward to kiss me. That was when I felt the first bit of plea-sure from this position.

Gris gently began to make small fluid thrusts upward, watching for any signs of pain, but I did not withdraw. He framed my hips over him, and for the first time he remarked on my appearance, "You look stunning from this view."

The view he was referring to was looking up at me while my soft breasts hung over his chest, occasionally grazing him, and normally I might have felt a bashful reaction, but there was nothing left to be shy about.

"Try moving until it feels good to you," he offered.

With this permission I began to rock back and forth, occasionally attempting to grind in circles until I found a sensation I wanted to keep. The whole time he patiently waited while I explored how my body felt and navigated any traces of pain.

He did his best to keep control and make this about me. He reached up and squeezed my breast and continued exploring with both hands gripping my rear to rock me back and forth. I became even wetter and more fulfilled.

After a short while, when he was confident that I was okay, he asked me if he could try something else. I nodded in agreement, and he lifted me off of him, gently laying me flat on my back.

He moved to the edge of the bed and positioned himself. I sighed in anticipation as he spread my thighs and stared down at me. A hunger glowed in his eyes and I took that as a sign that I had no reason to be embarrassed.

He moved toward me and placed himself at my entrance. I wanted to slide myself down upon him, but Gris gave me that look of *Relax, let me lead.* I tucked away my tendency to rush and let him gently enter me.

He went slowly, letting me feel each inch as he filled me. This angle felt entirely different than the one before, and I was pleased with his exploration.

Once fully inside, he began to thrust slowly, and I could feel him hitting the depths of me as I tightened around him with each stroke. He let out a groan, and I loved the thought that I was pleasing him. That somehow, in all my inexperience, this moment was not entirely a waste of time for him.

As he began to move, I urged him on. "Faster," I panted, trying to know my own body and what it was telling me. Gris began to move more vigorously, and I continued to tighten all around him.

My breaths became ragged and I arched into him, trying to feel even more. He began to move with more speed, still focusing patiently on me and my needs. As he moved in and out, he pressed his thumb down against the sensitive area above my entrance, making tiny soft circles into me that made all the nerves in my body stand on edge.

I began to moan loudly, uncontrollably, and just as I was starting to feel the rhythm of my own true pleasure, I think the sounds of me enjoying myself had thrown Gris overboard as I felt him strain into his climax.

Within seconds, he crashed into my chest and I felt his release. Our overheated bodies crumpled against one another and we lay there for a time, panting until our breaths returned to a normal rhythm. I didn't know what to do at this point. I just began running my hand through Gris's messy hair and idly dragging my fingertips along his wide back with the other.

Gris didn't look up but spoke the words sweetly against my stomach, "Are you okay?"

I cleared my thoughts and tried to focus on evaluating how I felt. I felt sore for sure, but nothing horrible. Logically, I was appreciative of the gentleness, awareness, and enthusiasm with which he handled this entire request.

But emotionally, I was an absolute wreck. I knew how fleeting all of this was. And even though I was happy to check it off the list, that it was finally something I could acknowledge and move past, I couldn't ignore this closeness I had felt with Gris.

I tried to imagine what it would be like with someone I actually cared for in that way, someone I loved or, even scarier, a true bonded mate.

It was a whole new world I had just opened the door to, and yet my time to explore it seemed limited and pointless. I concealed my internal struggle so as to not give Gris the slightest hint of concern. I would in no way have him thinking that I experienced displeasure in the slightest.

I replied, "It was perfect, Gris. You're perfect." And I meant it for so many reasons.

It made no difference that he found his pleasure before I could meet mine. That wasn't what this was about, and he had made sure to think of all the things that I did not. The only thing that would make it more perfect was if I didn't have to live with the sinking feeling that I had just lied to one of my best friends.

I felt like I used him for a reason he didn't truly understand, and that this might as well be a final goodbye because I didn't know if I could bring myself to see him again after this. Not if it meant farewell for good.

Gris rolled off of me onto his stomach, and for some reason, we both seemed entirely comfortable just lying around in the nude together. I guess Versa wasn't lying when she said things like this would only bring you closer. I certainly didn't expect to ever become this close to Gris—but he was perfect.

He grinned at me and remarked, "I should have made more bargains with you, Cress."

I gave him a snarky look and shot out my foot to push him off the side of the bed, but he caught it and pulled himself closer to me. The silence between us started to make me nervous, and I focused on keeping up my mental shields now that we both weren't distracted with each other's writhing bodies.

"You're still a great kisser," he remarked, and I remembered back to that time we had both agreed to "practice" with one another just so that we wouldn't make fools of ourselves when those that "mattered" came along.

I winked at him, "You're alright yourself."

He knew I was just holding back on inflating his ego, and just like that, we were transitioning back to friends, who we were before I brazenly showed up at his front door requesting a far-fetched bargain be redeemed.

Gris climbed from the bed and handed me my dress. He pointed me to the washroom nearby and asked if I needed anything to tidy up. He remarked that I better not go back home looking like I fell off a horse. He didn't need my father finding out where I had returned from and demanding Gris's head on a pike.

When I returned to the bedroom, it was clear that Gris had used magic to straighten the place to appear as if no one had stepped foot in there. I gave him an eye roll.

"Out here just throwing magic around?"

He sighed, "Oh, you're lucky I didn't use any magic while you were riding me."

His remark stopped me dead in my tracks, and I'm sure the shock was written all over my face. I had never considered the use of magic in the bedroom or with partners. Was that a thing? Versa had never mentioned that. Now I was exploding with curiosity.

He added, "Can't use my whole bag of tricks on the first go around."

What did he mean by that? Was he trying to imply there was going to be another time?

I let him guide me back to the foyer, asking if I wanted anything to drink. I was desperately parched, so I asked him to fill me a canteen of water to take with me.

"Leaving so soon?" he questioned with dismay.

This interaction was odd. This was not like Gris—implying a second rendezvous and unsettled by my quick exit. Was he suddenly pining for me? I didn't want to disappear on Gris, not after the kindness he showed me today. I knew he'd take it the wrong way. He'd internalize everything if I didn't at least come back to say goodbye.

"I just thought, you know, with you having to leave for your new adventure you might want to stay longer. My family won't be back for a while, we'll have the whole manor and grounds to ourselves." That last remark came with a nefarious look, and I could see the lust still lingering in his stare.

There was no possibility of me staying. I had a lot to process, and I wanted badly to speak with my sister. I also didn't want to have to spend any more time discussing that awful lie about my new role with the Seafarers, all while struggling to keep my guard up so I wouldn't run the risk of him finding out where I was truly headed.

"I have to go. My sister is going to be livid that I didn't help with the wedding planning at all today."

I could see the disappointment sprawled across his face as he went to hand me the water…to go. I also knew deep down I had no other intention than checking item number one off my list, and I couldn't get distracted. No, not now that I had other things to accomplish.

Letting myself stay longer or visit more would just send me into a spiral that I wouldn't be able to climb out of. And even though this new weird spark between us was something that I'd possibly delight in exploring, it was wrong. I didn't want to hurt him any more than I already would once he found out I was never returning. I took the water from him and began to make my way to the front door.

I could feel the traitorous tears beginning to form at the bottom of my lashes. The impending permanent goodbye loomed over me. While I could come to see Gris again, it was the reminder that these were the goodbyes I'd need to perform for anyone I cared about. The sting of that truth was becoming all too real. During this time with Gris, I had managed to mostly ignore my fate, but now it was torment. My emotions grappled with the inevitability of one of my lifelong nearest and dearest friends slipping through my fingertips.

I turned and plunged myself into him, throwing my arms around his giant torso, hugging and squeezing him tightly. His body was still radiating heat from our time together.

I was saying goodbye, even if he didn't realize it. "Thank you, Gris, for letting me call in a bargain…seventy-five years early."

He laughed, hugging me back, and gently kissed the top of my head where his chin rested.

He released me, and as I began to head down the steps toward my horse, he called out, "Maybe I was the fool for needing one hundred years."

And then it hit me like a sharp stab in the chest. Words like daggers indicating he had felt something and I had done exactly what I had hoped to avoid. I didn't want him to feel anything for me. I didn't want him to question if there could be more, because there couldn't.

I couldn't have trusted a stranger with this, to ensure I was treated properly as I knew Gris would. That's all this could be. I bit back the tears and mounted Rain.

Before I rode away, I yelled back to Gris, "You wouldn't be the first fool."

It was cocky, sarcastic, and something he and I would have said to each other before I selfishly asked to cross the boundaries of our friendship.

Just as I rounded the corner, I heard him yell out his response coated in longing, "And I won't be the last!"

CHAPTER 5

On the return home, with each stride Rain took, I felt a mixture of yearning and soreness between my thighs as my center rocked back and forth against the leather saddle. I longed for the feel of Gris between me and struggled to concentrate as I was overcome with flashbacks of what had just occurred.

I fixated on the thoughts of us riding each other as I urged my horse into a faster pace. I thought if I could get a serious distance between myself and his home, I might finally be able to calm myself. I felt as if I hadn't taken a breath since I parted from him.

All of this was overwhelming. I knew that I had the biggest grin stitched across my face. I was undeniably blushing as I replayed the moment his fingertips pressed into me. I needed to concentrate or I was going to fall off my horse.

By now, the bright sun of day was beating down on me and my body was dripping in sweat under the heavy velvet gown. I wanted to tear the clothes from my skin and drown myself in the relief of a cool bath. I felt so accomplished, despite the tinge of guilt. I had checked the first item off my list.

Once I could see my home in the distance, my mind turned toward all the things I wanted to tell Versa, but also how I needed to contain myself once I arrived. I hoped that I did not have the same glow that Versa did when she returned home from the time she had lost her maidenhead.

As Rain trotted onward, I kept making up little lies and excuses I could say about where I had been or what I'd been up to. But lying was not my talent, and I'd rather just decompress in a nice cold bath before having to face anyone at all, even Versa.

When I arrived inside our gates, I dismounted from Rain and again felt the small twinge of pain, a reminder of Gris and what he had done to me.

The stable hand walked up to me and I tried my best to conceal my embarrassment. I handed over the reins and quickly turned to head inside without a word.

I took the long way around to the back, through one of the gardens, and figured I'd sneak in through the kitchen entry. Peeking my head in the door, I saw no one of consequence and sauntered through the kitchen. Before exiting, I grabbed a piece of fruit off the counter since my appetite had become ferocious on the ride home.

I scurried as quickly as possible up the winding stone staircase, trying not to trip over the length of my dress. I would be thrilled once my body was rid of this frock.

I entered my room and closed the door quietly to not alert anyone nearby who might hear my arrival. I practically ripped the dress off at the seams to free my overheated body from this cloth cage.

Once naked, I went to the tub with the canteen Gris had filled for me. I did not want to call any of my lady's maids to fill it. I wanted to be utterly alone. I poured a small amount of water from the canteen into the large oval bath. I bent down on my knees and held my hand just above the tiny pool of water.

I knew I wasn't supposed to do this, the voices of my professors lecturing me echoed in the back of my mind, but I didn't care. It was one of the few things I was capable of. I closed my eyes and focused all my energy and thoughts. I imagined the water growing higher and higher, filling the walls of the copper tub.

I concentrated on how it would feel once it reached my fingertips and surrounded my entire hand. Within an instant, the magic manifested into reality and I could feel the chill of the water rising, expanding, enveloping my wrist, then farther up my arm till I opened my eyes, and before me the crisp bathwater brimmed to the edges. It was considered wasteful to use magic on frivolities such as filling one's bath, but it's not like I squandered my limited abilities regularly.

Unlike this morning's lavender oil, this time I reached for orange as I wanted to drown myself in the scent of Gris. I set my piece of fruit on the small table next to the bath and dipped my feet in one by one.

A shiver ran up my spine and I rolled my shoulders, trying to let the tension slide away. I sat down, submerging myself, and felt brief arousal as the temperature of the water made my nipples peak. Gods, would it be like this from now on, where even the smallest things set me off?

I rested my head against the back of the tub and watched as the citrus oils swirled in the pool of water around me. I reached for the ripe plum, and when I took a bite, the sweet flavor made my mouth water and I felt like I might never taste something this delicious again. Everything felt heightened now, and I needed to come down.

While nibbling leisurely on the plum, I closed my eyes and once again found myself replaying the scene in my head. I'm certain that everything Gris found insignificant about the encounter were the things I could not stop obsessing over.

Like the way he tilted his head back and groaned as he lost himself in his pleasure. The veins straining along his neck and how his strong hands gripped the bedsheets beside me. Finally free of the lust-filled intoxication, I was able to recollect even more detail.

I blushed at the memory of his voice having the slightest tremble when he gazed up at me and said I looked stunning above him. All of these little memories would serve as inspiration for those private moments with just me.

When I was able to pull myself from the dreamlike state, I was left with the sore feeling. Part of me wanted to leave it as a reminder to myself, but for that same reason I knew I shouldn't ignore it in case it became an unwanted distraction when I had much more to accomplish.

I dipped my hand below the chilled water and hovered it just between my thighs. I closed my eyes again and concentrated on eliminating the tiny, dull sting that lingered there. I felt a warmth right below the place my hand hovered and nowhere else, and quickly, the pain receded. The exertion made me tired and a bit dizzy. Expelling energy for small magic was proof that I did not have the endurance to pull off anything of consequence.

When I stepped out of the bath, I stood for a while naked in front of the mirror, glancing at myself from all angles. This morning where I might have felt insecure, I now felt fully rooted in my feminine body. I admired myself instead of passing judgment on every little flaw I could find. I looked at myself knowingly, that I had brought a male to his arousal. A handsome one that many desired.

I smirked at myself with a pride that I hoped would last. It was much more pleasant to finally look in the mirror with kindness. I could see out my window that the heat of the day was finally starting to let up as signs of early evening were upon us. My body was still taut, and for that reason, I did not wear my usual trousers and blouse but instead an extremely lightweight flowy dress that wouldn't cling to a single part of my body. Something much more comfortable and relaxing.

When I exited my room, I found my way to Versa's across the hall because I wanted to see her before supper. When I gently knocked on the door, I heard her sweet voice welcome me, "Come in!"

When I found her, she was sprawled out on the floor below a bay window, one that matched mine only facing the east instead of the west. It had been hours since I left her, yet she was still obsessing over sketches of gowns.

I plopped down beside her. "You still haven't made a decision?" I asked, trying not to sound disinterested.

I grabbed some of the drawings and thumbed through them. They were all beautiful, and there wasn't a single one that she wouldn't look amazing in.

She turned to me with a frustrated sigh, "I just want to look perfect for him. But I'm pretty sure the dress he'd love is not my first choice."

She reluctantly handed me two sheets of very different-looking dresses. The first had a large, round skirt with layer upon layer of fabric. It seemed heavy, with ornate beading and crystals covering almost every inch of it. I shuddered to think how difficult it would be to dance in, and that's all there is to do at a wedding ball. Stuff your face, drink yourself silly on Fae wine, and dance.

The other dress was form-fitting and the skirt, while long, was simple, elegant, and flowy. It was off-the-shoulder and had only a sprinkling of crystals in all the right places. I didn't want to tell my sister which one I preferred in case that wasn't the one she favored, so I questioned, "They're both lovely, but which one is your favorite?"

I prayed she wouldn't ask me to guess.

She scoffed. "Of course this one," she exclaimed, pointing at the simpler of the two.

I sighed in relief. "I completely agree, go with that one."

She threw both pieces of paper up in the air exasperated. "It's not… loud enough," she proclaimed. "This is the joining of two prominent families, one of which will make the other's son High Fae. Two families of new money. You know how we will be judged if we do not appear to honor tradition and if we don't make a spectacle of ourselves. He, and likely his parents, are expecting it of me."

I understood what she meant, and it finally dawned upon me why she was obsessed over every little detail. She was doing her best to bring honor to our house's name.

As part of the merchants guild, my father did not inherit his wealth nor was he born of Royal blood. He built a fortune of his own making, as did the family my sister was betrothed into. Even though the Royal bloodlines would be invited, it would be a shock if they actually attended. But that didn't mean the gossip wouldn't spread and they'd hear if the wedding had respected the old ways or not.

I'm sure our dear mother had opinions on all of this, but she was likely doing her best to give Versa the illusion of choice while she made decisions behind the scenes that would be in keeping with trying to impress all the High Houses. One such example would be making sure that only the best dressmaker was hired. One who had several commissions from the Royals and would be loose-lipped during their many encounters with the High Ladies.

I put my hand on hers. "Why not choose both?" She looked at me with confusion. "What says wealth and regalness more than wearing not one, but two wedding dresses?"

She was starting to understand what I was alluding to and a sly smile began to form across her face, stretching ear to pointed ear as her eyes widened with excitement.

I continued, "Wear the heavy gown during the ceremony at the beginning of the evening, until your first dance. Slip away in secrecy and change into the other dress that you love. Wear that for your first dance."

By now my suggestion had her glowing with delight. "Don't tell your betrothed; only Mother and Father must know. It should be a complete surprise, and I assure you there won't be a gossiper within a hundred miles that won't have your name spouting from their tongue for weeks to come."

She clutched the two sketches in her hand, now staring at them with admiration and wonder.

She whispered to herself, "I will be the most talked about bride in ages, and the little Fae girls will remember the bride who refused to choose, who was both traditional and modern."

In her excitement, she turned to me with a giddy squeal. "Oh, Cress, do you think it will start a trend? Do you think someday they will all start wearing two dresses?"

What had started as a mere suggestion to help my sister get out of an indecisive slump had now become her mission to make her mark on the wedding scene of the High Fae. I rolled my eyes at her and she nudged my shoulder playfully.

Finally, she looked at me. Really looked at me, for the first time since I had entered the room. It did not surprise me since her wedding distractions were constant.

"Something about you is different," she posed. She began squinting her eyes at me and tilting her head with assessment. "Why do you look so happy? You never smile this much. And you're helping me with wedding stuff."

Her accusations about my appearance made me want to hide and cover my face immediately. Before I could pull away, she clutched my arm tightly and gave me that accusatory use of my full name, "Cressida Blackthorn..."

"I've been with Gris." I stated plainly.

A perplexed expression spread across her face, because she knew Gris was practically like a brother to us, a lifelong friend and nothing more.

"What do you mean you've 'been with Gris,' is that where you went earlier? Oh, did you go to say goodbye to him?"

Ugh, sometimes my sister could be so dense.

"No, Versa, I've *been* with Gris…" I elongated my words, trying to make a point.

My sister's eyes widened like saucers as she realized what I meant. "You can't be serious? You slept with Gris. Gris was your first?"

I didn't know if she was saying it like it was a bad thing, or if she truly couldn't believe that Gris was the one to secure my maidenhead after all this time.

"Yes, it's true. I called in our bargain. You know, that silly one we made about being with one another after our one hundredth name day."

I had told Versa about this in passing, and she always thought it humorous and pointless as she said neither of us would end up alone after that many years.

Puzzled, Versa pried further, "Don't get me wrong, he is gorgeous and you certainly could have done worse. But why Gris, why now?"

The answer to that seemed obvious to me, and yet my sister was still oblivious to the reality of what was happening to me since she was engulfed with wedding planning. This distraction worked in my favor, and it was probably the only thing keeping her from noticing anything was off about me and our parents.

"Well, I'm going to be at sea for a long time and amongst strangers. I just wanted to get it over with," I lied as best I could, weaving small truths into the narrative.

She remained silent and attentive. "Gris was the best option. I trusted him and he'll keep it a secret."

Versa folded her arms and gave me a smirk.

"What?" I threw my hands up in exasperation.

"Details, sister, I need details!"

Finally, I exhaled, worried that Versa was displeased with me. All I wanted to do was pore over each detail with her, like she had with me after all those nights she'd crawled in through my bedroom window.

Now we convened, laying on the floor of her room surrounded by crumpled wedding dress sketches. We stared at the pastel floral fresco paintings adorning the ceiling while I recalled to her, in explicit detail, each amazing memory of my first time with Gris.

She questioned me and we giggled for what seemed like hours until twilight filled her windows and I could hear Father yelling for her to come to dinner.

They hadn't realized I was home and would be joining them after all. I gave a knowing look to Versa and said, "If anyone asks, I went riding all day."

She winked at me and pulled me up from the floor to head downstairs for dinner.

My parents were pleasantly surprised to see me at dinner. Versa did a fantastic job of leading the conversation in her direction with talks of her soon-to-be infamous wedding dress swap. I was grateful that I didn't have to spend too much time lying about being out riding all day. Well, I *was* out riding something… I snickered to myself. As the meal concluded, I witnessed my mother arguing with our chef in the corner of the dining room as staff cleared our plates. It was unlike her to have such a brash attitude, especially toward our cook. She bragged over his elaborate delicacies any chance she could; it was peculiar to see her terse dismissal of him.

Before retiring to my room for the evening, I found my father pacing the expansive hallways connecting mine and Versa's rooms to the other wings of the household. His clothes looked crumpled and his hair a bit messy, which was far from his normal appearance. He began to approach me, but then quickly turned back around, heading in the direction opposite my room like he had changed his mind.

Before shutting my door, Versa poked her head into the hallway and gave me a questioning look that said, *Will you be sneaking out a window this evening?* I rolled my eyes at her and shut my door without addressing her taunt. I was too tired from the weight of this day to do anything but retire to my bed and seek comfort in the softness of my silk sheets.

My body was sore, tired, but also ached to fill the absence. The incredible absence of Gris. I kept telling myself he was a means to an end. Stop fixating on him. I rolled to my side and reached for the tiny book on my bedside table where I had hidden the small piece of paper with my list.

I was more than pleased with myself when I crossed off the very top item. My tired eyes began scanning over what remained. There was only one thing on the list that wasn't entirely selfish of me; I figured it made sense to at least prioritize that. I lay in bed that night as the moonslight blanketed the pale marble floor, thinking about all the wealth contained in my room alone.

Wealth, after all, is what made our family Honored Fae, members of the High Court. At a certain point in history, the king of our land couldn't ignore the benefits of having allies not just of royal blood, but also those who held fortunes of their own. There would always be a divide, though. Us and them, the Honored Fae and the Royal Fae. It was extremely political because in terms of land, treatment, and respect, all High Court families were equal. But beyond the eyes of the king, these two sides would always remain divided.

The Royals found it distasteful to allow their children to marry outside of Royal bloodlines. They scoffed at invitations to attend major parties or weddings hosted by the Honored Fae and, oftentimes, these invitations were only extended to maintain a facade of pleasantries.

This is why I didn't know many of the Royal families of the High Court, because they didn't mingle with our kind. Additionally, when our family was called to court, it was standard practice that only one generation at a time travel to Aeon's castle or palaces in order to protect the lines of succession. My mother and father always traveled with heavy security in tow.

Sadly, a lot of the High Fae families had been intentionally killed off during the war, so the Royal and Honored families were especially keen to protect those that remained. Many High Fae families had to relocate when peacetime resumed to spread farther out and maintain governance over all the territories.

Despite the Royals being invited to attend Versa's nuptials, it would be unlikely that they'd make any appearances. But boy did they love to gossip and one-up each other. The Honored Fae lived on the cusp, always trying to be acknowledged or buy their way into acceptance.

The Royals were secretive and conniving, often avoiding sending their children to the same academies, instead opting to provide private education. Years and years of deeply-held beliefs passed down from one generation to another, creating endless cycles of unwarranted division.

Regardless, at the end of the day, we were all the king's pawns. This had never been more evident to me, now knowing I would be called to the Offering. It didn't matter your bloodline or your fortune, all would be required to make a sacrifice.

I folded my list and placed it back inside my book. My eyelids were heavy, and as I rolled onto my side to pull my pillow into my chest, I thought of Gris and his formidable muscular frame and how nice it would be to feel his warmth cradled against me under the soft sheets. I drifted off to sleep, hoping if I kept his handsome features in my mind's eye, I'd be lucky enough to dream of him.

CHAPTER

6

hen the sunlight began to peek through the soft sheers at my window, I reluctantly stirred. I hated mornings, but my new circumstances called for a make-every-minute-count approach. I completed my normal routine, but instead of dressing to impress, I once again donned my brown riding pants, a loose-fitted cream-colored blouse, a dark blue vest, and black riding boots.

As I walked past the mirror, I felt more like myself than the day prior. But today I was once again met with the look of a new person staring back from my reflection. A confident female; one who still blushed at the notion that she had commanded a male's desire. I smirked back at the girl in the mirror and made my way to my armoire. I pulled back the drawer to uncover jewels of immeasurable value, all laid out in a display atop a blanket of black velvet.

The display looked like a museum exhibit, as if it had never been touched and these items were arranged just for viewing. Although I wasn't big on wearing jewelry, our merchant father was insistent on spoiling his daughters every chance he got with shiny, sparkling baubles from all over the world.

I lightly ran my fingers across each piece, touching the brilliant stones ranging from small to large, intricate and ornate to simple and minimalist; there were too many to count.

Necklaces, earrings, bracelets, brooches, rings, diadems. My sister's drawer overflowed even more than mine, as she enjoyed collecting such finery. And my mother, well, let's just say a drawer wasn't enough to contain the luxurious accessories that she had accumulated.

The worth of these pieces was exorbitant. And for me, these were now just pointless material things that would no longer carry space in my life. Where I was going, whatever I would be doing, wouldn't be a place to bring such things. It made it very easy to reconcile that just a few of these wouldn't be missed by me or anyone else, and I had an idea and a better purpose in mind.

I gathered the pieces into a small drawstring bag and tethered them under my riding cloak to avoid questioning on my way out the door. I'm not sure my father or mother would have stopped me if they knew my intentions, but many were gifts from special occasions and I couldn't bear to look them in the eye and see the hurt. They no longer held meaning to me if I was going to be erased.

That was how I felt. My emotions passed over me in waves. Some were low and steady, easy to control and accept. Occasionally, I was unexpectedly drawn under treacherous tides of anger, frustration, and sadness. I knew I had to keep a lid on all of it or I'd end up saying hurtful things I didn't know if I meant. Just because they felt true now didn't mean they were.

I didn't bother to stop for food in the dining room or say farewell to anyone. I was eager to get out of the manor and be on my way. It was still early by the time I reached the stable, but I was lucky to find the groom already engaged in the day's chores. He walked Rain up to me and prepared to hoist my usual saddle, embossed with the emblem of House Blackthorn—but I did not want to stand out in any recognizable way.

I halted him with my hand and asked for an unmarked saddle instead. He looked at me with confusion, but did as I asked.

I pushed past him hurriedly as he was brushing away the dirt and mounted. He questioned, "When shall I expect your return?" but I was already galloping away in the direction of a nearby town.

The surrounding towns were lively and filled with busy markets, shops, and pubs full of unique sights and sounds. I had been to the occasional atelier with my mother and sister for dress fittings, but never this part of town.

Our staff normally shopped for us, so it was very unfamiliar. I did not want anyone to know who I was; I kept my chin down and tried to act like I belonged, like I knew where I was going.

My plan seemed simple but, in execution, it was more complex. I wanted to find people in need and disperse the jewels currently weighing down the right side of my cloak. I could hear the jangling with each step that Rain took.

But I knew if I just handed out jewels, the people would end up suffering interrogation, possibly even be accused of thievery. Honestly, I wasn't convinced that I wouldn't be accused myself.

I found a horse stall and was able to rope Rain, this way I could move about the town and explore more freely.

This place was buzzing with all kinds of Fae doing their errands and bartering; the sun overhead casting shadows all along the roads. The smell in the air was ever-evolving with each shift in the breeze. Sometimes it smelled sour, like rotten fruit or stale beer. In other wafts it smelled earthy, like dirt and farm animals. Sometimes scents of sweet sugar from a nearby bakery would mask the less pleasant odors and create an intoxicating swirl in my nose.

I moved swiftly from building to building and stall to stall, looking for a place where I could convert the jewels to coins, when I finally found what I was looking for at the end of a long dirt road.

The sign in the window read *Wendell's Exchange.* The glass panes appeared dirty and curtains were drawn from the inside so you couldn't see beyond. The exterior looked unwelcoming and the wooden steps creaked as I made my way to the door.

I only knew about this place because Gris had once admitted to me that he pawned some jewelry his father made to get some fast coin, but he never told me what he needed it for. I twisted the brass knob and quietly stepped into the establishment.

The inside was dark, and I could see dust flying about in the few sunbeams peeking in slits through the windows. A very old heavy-set male with ebony skin and white frizzy hair sat behind a giant wooden desk. He beckoned me forward with his hand while he rattled around his desk, finally finding a tiny pair of spectacles and placing them on the bridge of his freckled nose.

"How can I help you?" he said. His voice was deeper and warmer than I expected. He felt oddly safe and friendly, despite the rather drab appearance of his business.

I sat down reluctantly in the chair on the other side of his desk and said, "Is this a place where I can find a fair value of coin in exchange for jewels?"

I had no idea if what I was asking was correct but I tried to sound like I knew what I was doing. I wasn't sure what the jewels were worth, but I knew it was a lot and I feared being cheated.

He let out a hearty deep laugh. "Ha! Has someone accused me of not being fair?"

My fingers twitched anxiously against my thighs. I was worried I had offended him with my wording, which was not my intent.

"I'm sorry, sir, I didn't mean—" He cut me off, "Oh dear, I'm just yanking your chain—or should I say, your jewels," he smiled.

I let out an audible sigh of relief.

"Why don't you show me what you've got, and we can discuss from there." He waved his hand across the table, pointing to a candlelit soft pad on his desk where I assumed he wanted me to display the items for exchange.

I lifted the bag from under my cloak and, one by one, laid out each piece almost like it had been displayed in my drawer. His eyes widened further with each item I pulled from the bag.

"These are very beautiful, very valuable," he looked up at me between his spectacles, eyes squinting with some accusation. I figured there was no point in mincing words.

"They are mine, and I have no use for them anymore, but I do have use for the coin they'd fetch." I stared him down with all the confidence I could muster.

From the pocket of my cloak, I pulled out a silver medallion. On it was the embossed crest of my family. It was the unquestionable proof of my High Fae status, and what he needed to know to ensure that I was indeed the owner of the jewels and not a thief.

There wasn't usually a need to show a family medallion, but they did serve a purpose. Once I was old enough to understand, my father and mother emphasized the importance that my sister and I always had these medallions with us whenever we left our home, even with escorts.

They were made by the king's blacksmith, and if lost, you would not receive another. I can't remember the last time I had even shown anyone mine. It had seemed unnecessary. But today, it finally served a purpose.

I had heard that lost ones were invaluable, but to sell them rather than return them was a high crime. Having a medallion that wasn't yours meant you could pretend to be someone of high standing.

I'd been told they were imbued with blood magic, but I didn't recall ever knowingly granting my blood for my medallion. But the blood magic rumor often kept people afraid of attempting to imposter anyone. This is why they were more commonly referred to as "blood" medallions.

The male across the table almost got up to bow, but instead dipped his head low in respect. I would never get used to that. It seemed ridiculously formal. Only the Royals expected everyone to bow.

"I'm sorry for even questioning, my lady, but you know I have to be certain. I can't have a reputation for dealing in stolen goods."

"I understand," I replied and pocketed my medallion.

The dealer began to gently pick up each piece, inspecting it from every angle in the candlelight.

After taking his time, he said emphatically, "Do you wish to sell immediately or consign and wait till I can find buyers? The latter would bring you more coin but will take time."

I appreciated his guidance, but time wasn't something I had. "I need coin, today."

A small hint of concern flashed across his face. After all, what was a young High Fae lady doing disposing of this much jewelry?

"I can give you five hundred Lorcs for all of it today, but it's worth double or more if you consign."

I was shocked at how much he was offering in exchange, and even more shocked by its worth should I choose to consign. Gods, we were spoiled, I thought to myself. Five hundred Lorcs would be more than enough to make a huge impact on the people of the town who needed it most.

It pained me to know I was letting go of it for less than half its worth, but I reasoned with myself that it was mine to do with as I wished, and I refused to let it collect dust in my absence or be added to the heaping pile of jewels already in the Blackthorn household.

I reached my hand out across the table, "It's a deal!"

He placed his soft wrinkled hand atop mine, sealing the arrangement.

He must be very old; hundreds of years, to have any signs of crinkles on his skin. The Fae aged very slowly, and it made me wonder just how many jewels, trinkets, and treasures had crossed his desk over those years.

As our hands parted, he introduced himself, "Wendell's the name. It's a pleasure exchanging with you."

I knew he was waiting for me to offer up my name, but when the long silence continued and I looked away, I think he understood I wasn't going to share. He had already seen my house emblem on the medallion, and that was risk enough. This entire endeavor was meant to remain a secret.

Wendell disappeared behind the counter to gather my payment from his safe. He graciously counted each Lorc in front of me in small piles to show that I was not being cheated. I appreciated his professionalism and scooped all of the coins into the bag that I had carried the jewels in.

"Please be careful with that coin, my lady, someone might do very bad things to take it."

He looked at me with the warmth of a father, and I couldn't help but wonder if he had children, or perhaps grandchildren. While I appreciated his sentiment, I knew that by the end of the day, there weren't going to be any Lorcs left to steal, and the thought of what was next brought a smile to my face as I quickly exited his establishment.

Before shutting the door, I gave him a tiny smile and said, "Thanks, Wendell, it was nice knowing you."

When I re-entered the bustling streets of town, the scene had shifted as shops and food carts began to prepare for the early lunch hour. Smoke from the chimneys billowed across the sky, and for a brief minute you could ignore the stench of the streets and instead be enveloped with the scent of freshly cooked meats and savory stews on the open fire. A burning campfire has always been a soothing smell that engulfed me in nostalgia.

As I slowly meandered along the road, I thought back to the times my sister and I would make a firepit in the garden and curl up with a book while we waited for the sun to set. My mother had no doubt lectured my father incessantly that we were going to accidentally burn her rose garden to ash. My father never entertained her exaggerations, in favor of letting us have these small moments. We were daughters of a High household, it's not like we were living the life of a wild huntress.

My father encouraged us to gather our own wood and taught us how to make a kindling without magic. Just like our professors at the academy, he lectured us regularly on needing to have our own skill sets based on knowledge and practice, not magic.

Now with the weight of so many Lorcs weighing down my cloak, I reminded myself to stay focused and seek out the various alleyways that would lead to the backhouses and residential establishments that encircled the town center.

Passing through one such alleyway, I encountered a young female. Her clothes were tattered and her hair was in a disheveled bun. She was wringing out wet clothes and preparing to take them to a clothesline. It was pretty obvious she was likely the servant of one of the nearby residents who could afford staff.

I didn't know exactly how to approach someone without giving them cause for alarm. Especially since I was very clean and neatly dressed, despite my attempts to blend in. My skin was clear of dirt and soot, my clothes pristine and pressed and looking freshly dyed.

I quietly greeted her with a "Hello," and she briefly glanced up at me. Then she looked side to side down both directions of the alley to make sure I was actually addressing her and not someone else.

When I paused in front of her, I noticed what terrible condition her shoes were in. I had never really done anything like this, and I couldn't help the well of sadness building within me or the tight lump in my throat at just seeing the complete and utter inequity just a few miles from my home.

My home stood like an untouched fortress in the solitude of a beautiful forest, sprawling with lush green. Such a contrast to this place, shielded from the hardship and decay of lands piecing themselves back together after years of being war-torn. A mere matter of chance was all it was. The difference between me and her. That she was born into this life, and I was born into mine.

I prodded her with more questions, trying not to be overly intrusive. "Do you work nearby?"

She nervously answered, "Yes, I work—I mean, we, my family and I, we work for a nearby household..."

I nodded with encouragement so she understood I wasn't a threat. "I see, and do you have any siblings?"

The question weighed heavily on me as thoughts of Versa idled in the back of my mind.

"I do. I have two very young siblings...and an older brother." She began to look around for signs of someone who might be displeased with our encounter.

"I'd like to give you something, but it's under one condition." Before she could ask what that condition was, I said, "Complete anonymity. If I give you this, you cannot ever tell anyone where or who it came from, or what I look like. Nothing. Do you understand?"

My tone was serious, but I simply could not have her describing me to anyone.

She looked somewhat concerned but nodded and said, "I promise."

From my pocket, I pulled out a handful of shiny Lorcs. At the first glance of them, her eyes widened dramatically. She began to shake her head, stepping back, almost bumping into the stone wall behind her, because surely a stranger was not offering her this without some sort of catch. A debt she could not pay, a deal or bargain she could not honor.

"I can't, I'm sorry," she whispered, shying away from all those Lorcs.

"Take this to your family. Your parents will know what to do with it. There's no catch. I'm not going to hurt or follow you; just take them."

She took a long, silent pause, surveying me and the coins again.

"What am I supposed to tell them? They will think I've done something terrible to get them. We don't even make that much money in a season."

"Tell them a person of sound standing gifted them to you with no strings attached. They will serve you better than they ever could serve me. Where I go, there is no need. Do not tell them if this person was a male or female, don't mention any defining features ever. Tell them these were the terms of you receiving them."

She remained stunned, but she began to pull her hands out from behind her back where she hid them away, and slowly cupped them together to take the coins.

As I quickly poured them from my hands to hers, she looked up at me. "How will you know that I will keep my promise of anonymity?"

She had a fair point, not that I didn't trust her, and although I wouldn't be around if someone came searching or questioning, I just didn't want it ever getting back to my family what I had done.

"Fine, a bargain it is." I clasped my hands around hers while she still cupped the Lorcs between us and spoke the binding words, "Do you agree to my terms of anonymity in exchange for these coins, and know that should you break these terms anything that remains of them and anything purchased with them shall disappear?"

She looked up at me between her greasy orange bangs and nodded, "Yes, I promise."

And with her acceptance, I closed my eyes, mustering the energy to bring forth the binding magic and seal the arrangement between us.

I hoped this wasn't going to be necessary with each charitable act. I did not like making bargains, let alone with strangers, and rarely sought to seal them with actual magic.

When I pulled my hands away and the weight of the Lorcs remained in hers, I could see for the first time blood rush to her cheeks and warm them with a rosy pink that sat just below the surface of her freckles and soot-splattered face. She finally offered me a smile of relief that this encounter was real. Not a trick or a dream.

She quickly pocketed them and began to gather her laundered items and basket. "Thank you! Gods bless you," she practically squealed, and I hushed her so as to not draw attention to us.

The Gods had nothing to do with it, just my family's habit of exorbitant luxuries and my doomed fate.

I spent the rest of the day wandering throughout the nooks and crannies of the town, mostly seeking out young Fae that looked in need. I preferred to make my encounters with solitary individuals, this way people could not corroborate the story or compare details of what I looked like or where I went.

I wanted to remain aloof when handing out my small fortune. I'd walk a fair distance in between each dealing to try and cover as much ground between townspeople. I did not want to cause alarm in case anyone took notice that there was a sudden influx of wealth amongst the underprivileged in the days that would follow.

I avoided making bargains with anyone else, as they became more eager to accept the terms without question. I didn't need the magic being traced back to me, either. I wanted to leave as little of a trail as possible.

Every person who skipped away with the Lorcs brought an undeniable smile to my face, and I felt guilty that I hadn't done this sooner—or simply done more for the town around us in general.

Being High Fae could be very isolating. From prestigious academies to refined social circles, and with expectations to remain on grounds as much as possible, it created an extremely narrow worldview. I felt naive and ignorant of the realities outside of my perfectly manicured little bubble. There was peace in the ignorance of not knowing where I was going in thirty days, but the other side of that coin was fear of the unknown.

All day I grappled with this guilt-ridden feeling in between the small pieces of joy it brought me to hand out each and every Lorc. By late afternoon my pouch was empty, my cloak no longer dragging from the weight of the coin.

I made my way back to the stable where I had left Rain, and made sure to keep the hood of my cloak up and my head tilted down in case any of my newly made friends saw me making my way out of the town.

Just to be sure, I sneakily took a left instead of going right when exiting the main entrance to throw off anyone who might be paying attention. I made a large loop in the forest and took the long way back home just to keep prying eyes off my trail.

It was funny to assume any of these people would notice me while going about common things during a common day. It brought me a slight rush of excitement to pretend I was on a mission to go unnoticed, almost like a spy.

⊂⊂⊂✦

At dinner, I intentionally donned a canary-yellow diamond necklace that I had received as a gift one year during the Winter Solstice. I wore it because the diamonds, albeit stunning, were small and understated. Maybe I was playing with fire to bring attention to the family jewels after spending the day selling a small fortune, but I also knew that I had an excuse in my back pocket.

Dinner was small talk, as usual. Mother and Father were on board with the dress swap idea and had now moved on to bickering with Versa about floral selections. Gods, was I happy to not be planning a wedding for myself. Not that being shipped off to the king sounded any more appealing, but I had to tell myself that I'd rather take this fate than spend my day debating flowers that would wither and die in an evening. I tried not to take it personally that Mother and I had spoken very little since the secret news of my departure. This, along with the wedding, created a distance between us—and everyone else for that matter. Even the staff, typically in her good graces, had been reprimanded for the tiniest of infractions lately.

I had spent all day up close and personal with the injustices of this cruel world, and now I grappled with the fact that what I'd done hadn't even made a dent in how we should have been helping our people all along.

I stuffed my mouth with honey-glazed roast and practically burst at the seams of my trousers. Versa eagerly pulled me aside, begging for details on if I had revisited Gris. I hated hearing his name and being reminded of everything I was trying desperately to ignore. Repeating to myself over and over that he was just a means to an end. To her disappointment, I confirmed that I had not seen Gris again and currently didn't intend to.

I cupped my hands around my bloated lower belly, regretting how I had gorged myself. I hadn't eaten all day during my very important mission, and now I was paying for overeating. I gave Versa a look and then glanced down at my stomach. If you didn't know better, you'd have guessed I'd been with child for nearly five months.

I wanted to lie down. I was exhausted from walking all day and remaining cloaked in the unbearable heat. Oh, how I longed for autumn.

I retired to my room, less than gracefully plopping down on the bed fully clothed, searching for the energy to disrobe. I rolled over on my side, once more reaching for the book where my tiny list was hidden. I reviewed the remaining items after checking off today's activity. I had helped more than one person in need. And, if I'm being honest, I could spend the rest of my time left giving away all the wealth I had access to, and it would still feel like I wasn't doing enough.

This hollow feeling was a new one to navigate, and I slowly drifted off

to sleep with the somber memory of the day and all the unfair hardship
I had witnessed.

~~Lose my maidenhead~~
Seduce a stranger
Gamble till I win
Get drunk
Alter my appearance
~~Help someone in need~~
Get a tattoo
Do something that scares me
Swim naked in the moonslight
Say my goodbyes

The next morning brought with it cooler temperatures as the forest was blanketed with dense fog, making the grass slick. Glancing out my window, I tried to see beyond our lands but couldn't make out much. I welcomed this type of weather. I awoke, still feeling a bit melancholy from the day before. I wanted to tuck away this shame and instead replace it with numbness; find some way to ignore the fact that my family and I remained untouched by the harsh realities of village life.

We oversaw the territory on behalf of the king. Beneath the veneer of that honorable duty, I was just now seeing the layers of hypocrisy and apathy. I didn't want to confront the thought of just how spoiled we were. Why should anyone go hungry at all? Why should a drawer full of jewels collect dust while small Fae children have hungry bellies?

Between my education and isolation at home, it seemed like all they wanted us to be good at was looking away and ignoring problems instead of solving them. When Father spoke of his travels, he rarely mentioned people suffering or blighted lands. He focused on the exciting things, like the riches and the beautiful sights. I understood that the generations before us had suffered hundreds of years of instability and bloodshed during wartime, and now they wanted to leave their troubles in the past. Professors liked to say the land and its people were healed, but that's not entirely true. People are still recovering; plenty are still suffering.

I dressed quickly and apathetically. Haphazardly throwing on a few layers, just comfortable clothes for riding. I tied my hair back into a loose braid to help keep my locks out of my face. I grabbed an entire coin purse filled with plenty of Lorcs and tied it to the inside of my lightweight cloak. Today, I didn't entirely have a destination in mind, but I knew I'd find a way to check something off the list and lift my spirits.

When I ran into Father in the hallway, he gave me an approving nod and informed me that Versa and my mother had already left earlier in the carriage. They were both attending a dress fitting, and I tried to ignore the stinging reminder that I didn't need one. He looked at me knowingly as I lowered my eyes in quiet sadness.

"Where are you headed?" he asked curiously, quickly changing the subject. Before I could answer, he continued, "We could always find something to do together..." he trailed off, as if pleading for more time with me.

I didn't mean to come off as dismissive to my father, it was just that I wanted to be alone. "I'm going riding."

Before he could offer to join, I added, "Alone. I'm sorry. I just feel like being alone."

He put his hand on my shoulder, pulling me into him a little and giving me a gentle peck on the top of my head. "I understand. Please be safe."

I admired that my father wanted to be protective as long as I was still his to protect. I knew as my time here dwindled, it had to be eating away at him. I could tell because dark circles were beginning to form around his steely green eyes.

Perhaps he hadn't been sleeping, or maybe he's been trying to find some way to get me out of my obligation, but I already knew that it was fruitless. I wasn't about to get my hopes up.

I stopped by the kitchen and grabbed a couple of small items to snack on along the way and a giant canteen of water. I looked around at the kitchen staff, who were utterly annoyed that I was helping myself. It was more apparent than ever how ridiculous it was to have staff on hand to do these simple things for us, especially after yesterday. I'm quite capable of making myself a lunch to go.

Upon arriving at the stable, the eager hand greeted me. He was sharper than I gave him credit for, because today he asked me which saddle I preferred. Once again, I pointed to the unmarked saddle, and he quickly began tightening all the straps around Rain. He blushed when I thanked him, and I left, making my way beyond our land into the still fog-ridden forest.

Rain sprinted for what seemed like ages, weaving through the shadowless forest. In the distance, I saw a small, dilapidated cottage and pulled the reins to slow him into a steady trot. As we got closer, I could make out the aged hand-painted wooden sign which read *Fortunes, Favors, & Fates* and had the symbol of the three crescent moons of Demir on it.

It had to be a Seer's establishment. I had never encountered a place like this, but had heard of them in an eccentric bedtime story or two when I was little. People said that some Seers can only be found when meant to be, as if they had some ability to disappear and reappear at will.

I nervously approached, clutching the leather reins uncomfortably. I glanced around in all directions, concerned. There were many reasons that I should have ridden on and ignored this place, but there was an aching curiosity that propelled me forward. Was I being opportunistic or foolish? I quietly dismounted and tied off Rain on the short, rickety picket fence surrounding the house.

The area was lush with flora, but the overgrowth in this particular yard had taken over every inch of the exterior of the house. A giant dead tree that appeared to be charred loomed over the cottage and was anything but welcoming. It was out of the ordinary, one giant dead tree surrounded by all the teeming green. I wasn't sure if anyone was even home. There were no obvious signs such as smoke coming out of the chimney or candlelight illuminating the glass windows.

I was hesitant to knock, but still curious enough to see if this supposed Seer had any legitimacy. Maybe, by chance, I'd get some insight into what my dark unknown future held.

Before I even lifted my hand to knock, the door opened, and before me—or rather, below me—stood an old tiny female who looked like she hadn't seen daylight in a very long time. She couldn't have been more than five feet tall, and her tangled hair was a mess; her skin pale, almost gray and sickly. Her fingers were bony, but none of that was the most shocking part—it was her wings.

Her wings were out on display. And not in the poised way you might think one would show them off; instead, they were just there, calmly folded behind her shoulders. They were almost bigger than she was. Each wing contained the same mesmerizing pattern you'd commonly see on a moth. A gradient of browns, black, and beige, all culminated in a circle that looked like an eye assessing me. One on each wing.

I must have been stunned, mouth agape, because she remarked in a displeased raspy voice, "Are you going to stand there and stare or come inside?"

I certainly was staring. It was extremely rare for Fae to have their wings out, especially in any sort of casual manner. But here she was, answering the door for a stranger with her wings out, as if it meant nothing at all.

Wing display was typically only used in times of defense, either to shield or fly. Some Fae wouldn't even show their wings at all, unless in the presence of their mate. Thousands of years ago, wing type provided evolutionary advantages to adapt to the region and climate where one had settled. As time passed, Fae clans expanded their boundaries across the lands and cultures blended together, making their wings more indicative of their lineage.

She turned her back to me and with one long spindly finger ushered me to follow her into the home. With her back to me, I was able to get an even better view of the majestic moth-like patterning.

"Girl, do you always gawk like this? It's very rude."

I tried to make an excuse, "I'm sorry, I didn't…I mean, no one ever shows off their wings where I'm from."

She interrupted, "Yes, yes you particular Fae and your silly customs, etiquette, and nonsense. I don't subscribe to that."

She waved her hand in all directions, and with each passing gesture, little candles began to flicker to life throughout the house, unveiling what could only be described as a hoarder's treasure trove.

Every inch of the walls and floors was covered in things. Dusty books, knick-knacks, paintings, sculptures. Nothing was adequately displayed or even cared for, just piled all around. I had likely already offended her once, so I did my best to conceal my reaction and seated myself in the chair across from her at a small cloth-covered table.

She leaned forward in her chair and put her hand out to greet me. "I'm Asterius, but you can call me Aster if you'd like."

Despite her lack of refinement, she knew the proper etiquette, holding her hand out to me flat, palm facing upward in accordance with the Fae custom. I noticed an odd black mark around her wrist, almost like a handprint. She caught my stare and quickly pulled down the sleeve of her dress. I placed my hand gently on top of hers and held it there for a moment. The icy touch of her skin sent a chill up my spine, and I did my best to spit out a flustered introduction in return.

"I'm Cress. I like your name, it's very beautiful."

There was no sign of warmth in her cheeks like a normal reaction when someone received a compliment. She nodded and pulled her hand away from mine.

Between us on the table was a large, round, golden bowl, at least a foot wide, filled almost to the brim with water. I'd never been to a Seer, but had heard that the way in which they use their gift can vary. Some needed to touch you, while others used cards, stones, or other natural materials. Some were believed to have visions in their dreams. And still, some even claimed they could convene with the dead.

Most people avoided Seers, due to the abundant rumors. Some said that the payment was steep, or that it required dark bargains to be fulfilled. She was very odd, but she did not scare me. At least, not yet.

"What brings such a beautiful young thing to my doorway? Seeking answers, are we?" She clasped her hands together, resting her fingertips against one another.

"I'd like to know what my future entails," I replied softly.

She let out a snort and rolled her eyes. "Well, child, if you wanted to know your past you wouldn't be here now, would you?"

I was feeling sillier and more uneasy as each minute passed. I pondered for a moment, and then I re-worded the question. "I want to know if I have a future."

Aster smiled at me with an odd satisfaction. "That's more like it."

I was too terrified to ask if I was headed straight for death's door. I intentionally worded it the way I did to go easy on myself, though I had a feeling Aster wasn't keen on taking it easy on anyone.

"Please grip the side of the bowl with both hands and dip only your fingertips into the water." She pointed encouragingly at the object between us. "Do not remove them until I tell you to. You may look at the water, but do not try and interpret what you see, that is my job."

I did exactly as she requested and submerged my fingertips slowly into the warm water. Aster reached into the pocket of her tattered apron and withdrew a vial of black liquid. Opening it, she then poured the entire thing into the bowl. I watched as the liquid swirled like oil, remaining separate from the water but still within it. Then she performed the same placement of her fingertips in the bowl across from mine and waited.

When I finally stopped staring at the black liquid dancing around our fingers, I looked up to see that her eyes had both gone milky white and I could no longer see her pupils. I gasped audibly, but quickly remembered not to pull my hands from the water, even though her appearance was frightening.

She was such a tiny, frail thing, but it was clear she possessed strong magic and I wasn't going to underestimate her. I kept my fingertips firmly planted on the side of the bowl and turned my attention back to the water, trying to make out whatever image or message it might show me.

I squinted my eyes and strained to understand what I was seeing. In some ways, it seemed like the black liquid showed both calm tides and then rough seas.

The fuzzy images constantly changed and shifted. She told me not to try and interpret them, but it was beautiful and I was transfixed.

Then Aster spoke, her voice no longer deep and raspy but this time melodic, almost like someone else was speaking through her. My breath hung on every poetic word that left her crinkled lips.

> *The ink is dry on pages past*
> *but shines anew on skin.*
> *Behold! When cursed die are cast*
> *A conflict builds within.*
>
> *Which path is safe?*
> *Which door is locked?*
> *How strong is faith*
> *When arrows nocked?*

Let loose, they'll pierce the golden mask
that hides beneath the surface.
The sands of fate within your grasp
Reveal a darker purpose.

When Aster's voice went silent, I watched as her eyes returned to normal. She looked at me like prey, cocking her head with a sly smile spreading across her face.

"You may remove your fingers from the water."

I pulled myself away from the trancelike state, and when I looked down, the black liquid was no more, the water crystal clear again. I didn't know how much time had passed, but I felt like I had been staring into that bowl for an eternity.

Her puzzling words echoed in my mind over and over. It was one giant riddle. Anger swelled in my chest. Is this what I was paying for, nonsensical rhymes? I wanted answers!

She could tell I was on the verge of unleashing my displeasure.

"Your fate is entangled with Gaia Wood enchantments."

My eyes narrowed with annoyance.

She continued, "This vision is unclear. It ensnares my tongue to speak to you in riddles and rhymes because it doesn't want to be revealed and can only be understood when it comes to pass. Your fate doesn't want to be known."

My hands clenched in tight fists. "But I want to know! I *demand* to know." This outburst had been building in me for days. After all the hours of placating my family and pretending to be fine, I wanted to know what my future held.

"Your foolish outrage doesn't change a thing," she chided. "Gaia Wood enchantments are extremely rare and powerful. Whoever bound it did so intentionally to ensure its secrecy. I'm not about to go meddling—nor should you. Whatever you're fighting, accept it."

I pushed back from the table, rising to my feet defiantly. "I hope the price for this babble isn't absurd."

Aster clenched her teeth and began to look irritated—very, very irritated, and somehow her tiny size meant nothing as fear began to pulse through me.

"You insolent brat. You wanted to know if you have a future, and not only did I show you that you did, but I conveyed it's one of importance, of secrecy, and yet you continue this ungrateful tantrum."

I folded my arms across my chest, trying to ignore the bitter truth. I'm almost certain all of this secrecy and importance had everything to do with the king's Offering, which I already knew, and didn't get me any closer to the details I needed.

I did my best to keep replaying the words she said in my head, memorizing them so that I could mull through them later in peace and quiet.

"My apologies, Asterius. You're right," I replied curtly. "How much do I owe you?"

She began to walk me toward the door, and just as I stepped outside the threshold of the cottage, she stood there smiling at me slyly. "You owe me nothing. You're about to lose everything, anyway."

Before I could even respond, she closed the door in my face. I practically stomped my way back to Rain, who was still waiting at the fence nibbling on clover. I mounted and took one last glance at the dilapidated shack. I could see Asterius in the window, staring back at me with an ominous grin, and my stomach roiled.

This whole morning was a complete waste. I wasn't any closer to answers and, in fact, now I was stuck with a senseless riddle that only concerned me more. I wanted a drink; Gods, I *needed* a drink.

Rain and I continued north in search of a pub where I could drown my sorrows and ignore the fact that I had been accused of being a brat!

CHAPTER

8

We traveled deeper into the forest until I'd lost track of how far we'd come or how long we'd been gone. The daylight shifted across the sky, indicating many hours had passed. I satiated the growling in my stomach by stopping occasionally to snack on the items I'd brought with me, feeding what remained of an apple to Rain.

Finally, we found a clearing, and in it I could see a tavern inn marked by small stone walls surrounding it. As we made our way closer, I noticed they had a stable where Rain could rest safely. I didn't remember the last time I had ridden him this hard and for this long of a distance, but I think he was grateful for the freedom and adventure.

After getting him settled, I made my way to the threshold of the door noting the sign labeled *Doorlae Tavern & Inn*. The ceiling was lower than I'd expected and everything felt tightly cramped together. The main room smelled like stale beer, and my boots clung to the sticky floor with each step I took.

All around me were every manner of gruff-looking Fae minding their own business. I tried to blend in, but it was impossible. I had to have been the softest, most delicate thing the place had seen in some time. I held my chin up confidently and made my way to the bar.

A very tall and broad-shouldered bartender approached from behind the counter. He had a bald head, an extremely uncommon look given how most Fae fancied their locks. He also donned a dark brown mustache, with the ends curled up on each side.

"What's the lady having? That is, if you're sure you're in the right place."

His wide smile showed off all his teeth along with one silver-capped tooth, and I didn't know if his tone was meant to be friendly or judgmental.

I tried to sound like I had ordered a drink from a bar before, but in truth, I hadn't. I'd drunk before, but never in a setting like this one. Usually wine at parties, and never to the point of being drunk or out of control.

"What do the locals recommend?" I parried, feigning confidence.

He gave me an amused look, eying the options over his shoulder. "The locals drink mead, but if you've got deeper pockets, I propose the braggot."

Maybe this was a trick to see if I had money. It's possible I was walking into the trap of being robbed, but I figured why not splurge, especially since I had every intention of drinking my share of this place.

"A braggot will do. Please bring it to me over there." I pointed at a nearby booth in the corner.

He let out a deep-chested laugh. "This isn't that kind of place, m'lady. Give me a second and I'll have your drink."

I smiled nervously back at him, knowing I had made some sort of mistake implying that someone should bring me anything. Within a minute he showed back up with a giant foaming mug of ale, the spillage drenching his already sticky hand. I tried not to scrunch my nose at the powerful scent as I grabbed the drink, threw him a few coins, and made my way to the corner booth I intended to claim.

I sipped the ale slowly and thanked the Gods I'd spent the extra money; I could only imagine how terrible the cheaper ale must be if this was the expensive stuff.

For the first hour or so, I made my way through two mugs while I people-watched and assessed my surroundings. The sun was slowly setting outside and the place grew dimmer, orange hues from the sunset peeking in from the various windows. I knew that with darkness the tavern would only get rowdier, but with each sip of ale, the numbing warmth I had been seeking replaced the swirl of emotions I'd battled for days. Guilt, longing, sadness, confusion, and anger. With every swig, I felt those tiny agonies lessen.

When the bar was at its busiest, I finally got brave enough to ask some fellow to join me in a game of cards, to which he snarkily replied that he only played for stakes. And since, along with getting drunk, gambling till I won was also on my to-do list, I welcomed it, even though I knew I was terrible at cards, and that being intoxicated certainly wasn't going to help my cause.

But I had Lorcs burning through my pocket and nothing to lose; I gestured for him to join me in the booth.

Because I was feeling loose and gutsy, I yelled to the barkeeper like I owned the place, "Bring my friend a drink! The good kind." My words slurred a little, but the rosy-cheeked male sat down across from me, looking more than eager to take all of my money.

 For what seemed like hours, we played hand after hand. Every time I lost, I'd fish out another Lorc from my pocket and giggle while sipping at my ale. I'd lost count of the drinks and the rounds of cards, but I was having the best time and I was too stubborn to quit. I was going to beat him eventually, I had to. It was only a matter of odds.

Occasionally, other people would stop by to watch us or join in on a hand. I wasn't quite sure if people actually enjoyed my company or enjoyed the fact that I kept paying for the beverages and made for a lousy gambler. From a more sober point of view, I'm sure it looked like I was being taken advantage of, but I knew what I was getting into and I enjoyed every minute of being a sloppy mess with my new "friends."

Despite my appearance, I was trying to focus. With each hand that he played, I learned more about his strategy, and this time I felt like I had him in my trap. I was confident I finally had a strong hand to play, so I decided to up the ante and go all in with a large handful of coins. He eyed me suspiciously, but had also underestimated me since hours of losing had his confidence sky-high.

He matched my bet and we proceeded. When he laid out his hand fully prepared to mark another victory, I slurred, "Not so fast!"

I laid out my own, trying to hide just how proud I felt.

"Victory is mine…for once!"

I looked up at him, smiling, expecting to meet composed disappointment; instead, all I saw was rage and disbelief pooling in every angle of his face.

Before I could react, he yelled, "Cheat! You lousy cheater!"

I leaned back to put space between us and replied brashly, "Me? A cheat? Are you kidding me? I've lost every round. You lost fair and square."

I cupped my hand on the heaping pile of coins between us, preparing to slide them to my side of the table when, all of the sudden, the enraged player across from me reached out abruptly and grabbed my wrist, holding me firmly in a painful grip.

"You're a cheat and a filthy little wh…"

Before he could finish his verbal attack on me, there was a shiny silver blade held firmly against his throat.

My eyes scanned up the gloved hand holding the dagger, which was attached to the arm of a very tall, hooded male in all black—who had made this act of aggression so discreetly that no one else around us noticed anything was awry.

The stranger in black bent down to the card player's ear and quietly said, "Tsk, tsk, very poor form. The lady beat you fair and square. You'd dare deprive her of the spoils of her victory? And that tongue of yours… well, had I let you call her what I think you were going to, you might just find yourself without one."

I was equal parts terrified and exhilarated. But I couldn't decide if I was more frightened of the guy still clutching my wrist or the one with the blade to his neck.

He sloppily writhed against the weapon. "She cheated, I know it."

"Release her. Right. Now." Each word was like a sharp staccato from his lips.

He pulled the knife even tighter against his skin, and below it I could see a tiny dribble of blood appear. He did not back down or loosen his grip. With one swipe of his hand, he could easily take this male's life. The drunk finally released his grip on me and I pulled my sore hand to my chest, rubbing it for relief.

"When I remove this blade and let you keep your tongue, you're going to get up, quietly leave this establishment, and never return." He paused, as if expecting him to fight the instructions.

From the look in the male's eyes, it felt like he hoped he did fight him just so he could enjoy the feeling of pressing the sharp edge even deeper into the offender's throat. And just like that, I witnessed the anger slowly fade from the gambler's face, his shoulders relax, and the dagger lift away from his neck, allowing him to stand.

He did exactly as he was told. Not a single word or gesture to draw any attention to us or what had just happened. I watched nervously until he exited the tavern. The next thing I knew, I was sitting face to face with the rogue who just forcibly removed the drunken gambler.

I fumbled over my words trying to make sense of what just happened and shake a modicum of sobriety into myself.

"How did you know I didn't cheat?" As if that mattered—I had been attacked!

"I've been watching you lose hand after hand to him all night. You didn't suddenly get good at cards. You got lucky," he replied, unimpressed.

He was absolutely right, of course. I didn't cheat, I had just bided my time and waited for my strategy to kick in—wait, did he just say he had been watching me all night? How did I not notice someone spying on me this whole time? Especially him?

I say this because the male now sitting across from me in this booth was hardly someone you could ignore. He was scary and sexy all wrapped in one, and I had to check myself to make sure I wasn't drooling. I took another sip of my drink while further assessing him, just to give my hands something to do. Was he really this attractive, or was the alcohol clouding my judgment?

He slid his hood back revealing his inky black hair, messy and tousled. It contrasted greatly with his pale skin and hazel eyes. The look he was giving me bordered between disapproval and disgust. It's not like I had asked for his help, though I was grateful.

That look made me feel years younger than I was, like I was some sort of child to be scolded. While I was seemingly a complete and utter annoyance to him, I, on the other hand, found him stunning me into silence with his brutally attractive masculinity. An alluring viciousness radiated from him.

I set my drink down and offered him my thanks. "I…uh, appreciate what you did. Can I buy a round of drinks in gratitude?"

He stared out the window, not meeting my gaze, then turned back to me, answering irritably, "I think you've had enough to drink."

His posture was tense and guarded. I finally relaxed a little, but he remained alert and kept scanning the rest of the room with his eyes. It's like he was trying to look everywhere possible except directly at me.

While I did appreciate him intervening, I wasn't about to let him continue to talk to me like a child.

"I think I can make my own decisions, so do you want a damn drink or not?" I asked through gritted teeth, trying to match his intensity.

He immediately stood up and turned his back to me, and I almost instinctively reached out to grab him, but he had already walked away. Disappointment began to sink in as I was now left alone in the booth with nothing but empty mugs, a mess of cards, and a pile of Lorcs.

Within a minute he returned, two beverages in hand. He placed a glass of water in front of me and an ale in front of him. "Drink," was all he said.

His voice was demanding, and a part of me wanted to obey him, even if another wanted to push back against his commands. We both sat sipping in silence for what seemed like an awkward amount of time. If he didn't want to interact with me, why was he still sitting here?

With the liquid courage still coursing through my system, I figured why not boldly ask, "Why were you watching me this entire time?"

He rolled his eyes in aggravation, taking another sip of his drink before responding.

"A young, pretty girl in a tavern gambling away a small fortune while drunk out of her wits…you had the attention of every male in here, whether you noticed it or not."

I tried to conceal just how pleased I felt that he had referred to me as pretty.

He continued, "And when you decided to leave here in the sloppy state that you are in now, how did you think that was going to fare?"

I hadn't thought that far ahead. I was having too much fun not caring and overthinking. He was probably right. I was being more than reckless, and I knew my safety was questionable given the situation and environment.

Instead of addressing the point that mattered, I ignored him and spat back, "I'm not young, I'm twenty-five."

I watched as he clenched his teeth, holding back what might have been a laugh at my expense. While shaking his head he retorted, "My mistake, you're clearly very mature."

I ignored his icy words because this was the first time he actually looked at me directly. I adjusted my posture a little, trying not to appear like a slob.

"You know, my previous guest didn't sit here and insult me the entire time. You haven't even bothered to tell me your name."

He took another giant swig of ale and I stared as his tongue grazed his lips, licking away the foam.

"Trace. My name is Trace."

He leaned in closer across the table and I did the same to hear whatever quip came next, "And your previous guest insulted you the entire evening by robbing you of all your money without so much as a second thought. Let's not pretend you are a good judge of character."

Our faces were much closer to one another now and my eyes tightened as I glared back at him. The audacity. I might have punched him if I wasn't so tempted to kiss him, unable to avert my gaze from that beautiful mouth of his. It was infuriating.

I had never been spoken to like this. My whole life, everyone had calculated their words to ensure they never offended or misspoke to a member of the High Court. But Trace didn't have a clue who I was, and I liked it that way. Maybe too much. It was in that singular moment where we just stared at one another, sparring with our gazes, that I decided this was the stranger I was going to seduce.

I softened my features and gently pulled my braid over my shoulder. I dipped my chin and looked up at him through my thick lashes. "I'm Cress." I held my hand out palm up, licked my lips for good measure, and waited for him to meet my introduction.

He looked back and forth between me and my hand and let out a wicked smile. The first and only one I'd seen during our entire interaction. He slowly pulled the black leather glove from one hand and set it on top of mine.

He held his hand there for an uncomfortable amount of time. Long enough for me to notice the black ink vining across the top of his hand and leading up his sleeve. A tattoo. My mouth began to water a little with the intrigue of wanting to see all of it.

Our hands still touching, we were interrupted from our awkward haze by the mustached barkeep towering over our booth.

"Folks, it's near closing time."

We abruptly pulled our hands back from one another and Trace replaced his glove. I frantically looked out the window and saw nothing but pitch black and moonslight. A sobering thought washed over me as I realized I had no idea how I was going to get home in the darkness. It was at least a few hours' ride. I had gotten caught up in my antics and hadn't even made a plan for the return.

In unison, we both turned to the barkeep and said, "I'll take a room."

The barkeep laughed back at us and said amusingly, "Lucky for you two lovebirds, we only have one room left."

I couldn't believe he had called us lovebirds, and the same thought was written across Trace's face as he looked up, clenching his jaw.

Before I could interject, Trace responded, "Fine. We'll take it."

He handed him a few coins and the barkeep smiled at us both, unable to hide the pleasure of having unintentionally orchestrated this conundrum. He laid down the key in front of Trace as if it were already his room, and I reached across the table, snatching it so fast it probably gave them both whiplash.

I stood up from the booth, thanked the bartender, and made my way to the staircase leading to the inn portion of the tavern. With each step, I swayed my hips and walked as gracefully as possible in front of Trace.

He followed behind from a farther distance than I'd like. It was probably a good thing, since my conscience was fighting with what was left of the alcohol still in my system about sharing a room with a stranger. One that I desired, badly. I was playing a very dangerous game and the excitement made me tingle.

The key slipped into the lock snugly, but wouldn't budge. Hearing Trace's measured strides reach the top of the stairs behind me, I began to turn the key back and forth frantically, desperate to have this situation under control. I gave it one last emphatic turn and tried the handle. Nothing.

"I think the barkeep gave us the wrong key."

"Hmm. Possible, but unlikely, since it is the last room and all the other patrons are clearly in theirs—not locked out," Trace said, with what I determined to be way too much sarcasm.

"Excuse me…" I started, indignant but then relieved when he clutched my shoulder and moved me aside and, with one swift motion, unlocked and opened the stubborn door.

The room was pitch black, and for a moment we both stood there in the dark, close enough to be touching. Close enough that I could feel the heat between us, despite the chill of the room.

Before I could break the awkward silence, he turned his back on me and bent down in front of the fireplace, working quickly to establish some light and heat other than our own.

"I admire that you took the time to make a kindling rather than just relying on simple magic."

He glanced back, eyeing me sharply, the flickering light of the fire creating shadows across his handsome angled features.

"Everyone should know how to make a fire. People should be prepared to help themselves."

I could hear my father's voice echoing in his sentiment, and something about that made me feel more at ease.

Once lit, the fireplace allowed me to assess the tiny room. The space was tight and, by all accounts, plain. There was a medium-sized bed against the back wall that could fit two people if they managed to lay very close. By the fire, there was a tattered-looking armchair, still plush, nonetheless. And lastly, a small writing desk to the right.

"Well, it's not the royal palace by any means, but it will do for the night," I proclaimed, setting myself down on the edge of the bed, trying to sound friendly and amusing.

Trace had such a hard exterior shell about him, I had to find a way to soften it. I wanted to show him that I wasn't a threat and that he could relax a little. All he offered me was a small grunt in agreement.

He continued to stand uncomfortably in the center of the room, as if remaining there was going to make the reality of only one bed disappear.

I began to unlace my boots and placed them by the bottom of the bed, leaving my stockings on. He started to carefully disrobe, removing his cloak, gloves and weapons. A sword, two daggers, and another small blade. He had been concealing all of that under his cloak. I quickly recognized the small blade as being the one he had held against the gambler's neck earlier.

My throat bobbed with a small tinge of fear that this beautiful stranger was indeed very dangerous. This combination of fear and lust was a new sensation for me. His long sleeves hid that tattoo I was still curious about. I hung my cloak on the wall next to his, made my way back to the bed and laid down in the middle, propping myself up on my elbows.

I eyed him up and down. Trying to make it obvious just how much I wanted him; how much I liked what I saw. He had chosen his words carefully thus far; but I wasn't here for his words, just that mouth of his.

"Which side do you prefer, the left or the right?" I asked playfully.

Without hesitation, he retorted, "I'm not sleeping in that bed with you."

There was no way to hide the rejection from my expression.

I snapped back harshly, "What, you're afraid I bite? You don't give an inch, do you?"

He looked down at me and surveyed the length of my body sprawled out across the bed. Once again, I got to witness that wicked smile of his when he responded in a deep, eerily calm manner, "Oh trust me, I give…"

He stared at me intensely, and I could feel the space between my legs begin to pulsate with heat from that look. Against my better judgment, I mustered every ounce of courage I had and gave him an equally wicked reply, "Prove it." I slowly began to spread my legs apart in a seductive welcome.

In a split second, I felt him grab my ankle and abruptly pull my whole body down, sliding me across the top of the bed closer to him; now I was lying flat beneath him. He hovered above me, still holding my ankle firmly, not in a painful way but possessively.

He lifted my leg, cupping the heel of my foot and began slowly, painstakingly removing my stocking. Oh my Gods, it was happening. It was working. He was mine. All the while, his eyes were fixated on the curve of my foot, admiring it like it was something delectable.

He gently set down my bare leg and proceeded to lift the other one, performing the same act of undressing me one piece at a time. I practically shivered at the feel of his fingertips along my skin. The silence between us, punctuated by nothing but the crackling fire, was palpable.

Once he had my second leg bare, he continued to hold it up tenderly and said, "If…" he paused. "*If* I were to fuck you, you're going to be sober when I do. There will be nothing to dull your senses and no chance of you forgetting a single minute of you begging me not to stop. You will call out my name till you no longer can."

He paused and placed my foot back on the bed. My eyes were wide with shock. No one—and I mean, absolutely no one—had spoken that way to me in my entire existence. His words were filthy and unrefined, yet I craved him desperately.

"Go to bed and sober up, sweetheart."

With that final remark, he stalked back over to the armchair and made himself comfortable. He had no intention of taking the bed—or me. But by Gods, I clung to his words like a promise of what was to come.

Every ounce of me regretted every single drink I'd had earlier that evening, unaware it was destroying my chances of having Trace's wicked mouth crushed against my lips and every inch of my body. I crawled beneath the covers as if they would conceal the aching want unfulfilled deep within me.

I replayed his words over and over in my head, trying to sleep. Lying on my side facing away from Trace, I wanted to glance back and see if he was struggling to get any rest like I was. Was he as tempted and as tortured as I was? Of course not. He was the one doing the torturing. Refusing to give in. Holding out on me with demands of my sober attention. Well, he had my attention, alright.

I felt the burning sensation in my eyes as I fought to stay awake, hoping that the vision of me laying there for the taking would change his mind; but alas, I could fight sleep no longer. I drifted off, afraid I had lost my shot and that tomorrow this growing tension between us that he wished to ignore would have faded like stars into the light of dawn.

When I awoke in the morning, I rolled over, half forgetting where I was, with a small dull headache reminding me that I wasn't a drinker. At least, not of ale. But then the echo of his voice and the memory of Trace came rushing to the forefront of my mind.

I sat up abruptly, glancing toward the armchair to find it empty, along with his belongings nowhere in sight. I was alone. Alone and unfulfilled, disappointed that I'd never see that mysterious stranger again. I began to collect myself and my things when I noticed a small piece of parchment on the writing desk in the corner of the room.

Meet here this afternoon. Stay out of trouble.

— Trace

My breath hitched as I reread the words, trying to determine if I was still dreaming. I finally came to terms with the fact that he wanted to see me again. I was treading in dangerous waters. I tried to simplify the situation to the meaningless task of seducing a stranger. After all, that was the item on my list. Yet, for some reason I couldn't identify, a deeper emotion bubbled to the surface. The thought of his hands, strong and purposeful, tearing at my blouse. I flushed at the idea. A successful seduction surely did not include such a lack of control. I felt infatuated with him. His cryptic words were an intoxicating rope pulling me closer. The promise of his words from the night before carried me every mile of the ride home.

CHAPTER

9

When I arrived home, I discovered Versa had already covered for me, providing a decent excuse as to my whereabouts last night. I was now indebted to her and owed her, at the least, an explanation as to why I had planned to be gone another night. At least one. I tried not to get ahead of myself or take too much pleasure in the thought of being gone multiple nights.

I told her I had met someone, but they were farther away and I was going back later that day to meet them again. As expected, she was concerned about my safety and just how far away I had wandered off without an escort. I reassured her that I was going to be fine. I argued with her that I was about to be entirely on my own, no escorts, with the Seafarers, so she might as well get used to the thought.

I returned to my room, bathed quickly, and did all the necessary primping in anticipation of the evening ahead. I had not given up on my endeavor to seduce Trace. This time I packed a small bag of my things. Just in case I was going to stay the night—or two—again. I selected each item intentionally, trying to avoid anything that would indicate I came from wealth. He had already seen me gamble a good handful of Lorcs, but he didn't have to know where they came from.

I liked being just as much a stranger to him as he was to me. The excitement of playing out this other identity coursed through me. That's when I decided to take the biggest risk of them all. I plucked my blood medallion from my cloak pocket and hid it under some clothes in my drawer. Leaving it behind was dangerous enough, but I didn't want to risk him ever accidentally seeing it and what that might mean for the both of us.

I was certain a commoner knew better than trying to bed a daughter of a High Lord. And worse, I still wasn't entirely sure Trace could be trusted; I didn't need to end up being held for ransom or something just as terrible.

Before I made my exit, I remembered two things: the list and Aster's rhyme! I scurried to my bedside, pulling out the book where I had hidden the parchment containing my list. I grabbed a quill and repeated the rhyme to myself over and over till I was certain I had recorded it accurately. I hadn't put any thought into it since meeting Trace, but I knew at some point the frustration of that entire encounter would get the best of me and I'd need to pore over those words more intently. But that day was not today. I turned over the paper to the side containing the list and began to strike through another two items before hiding it away again.

~~Lose my maidenhead~~
Seduce a stranger
~~Gamble till I win~~
~~Get drunk~~
Alter my appearance
~~Help someone in need~~

Get a tattoo
Do something that scares me
Swim naked in the moonslight
Say my goodbyes

Trace's note requested that I meet him this afternoon, meaning there wasn't any time to hang about the manor since I'd be making the hours-long ride north again. Though Rain galloped confidently, as if he knew the way to the Doorlae Tavern & Inn, I still focused intently on trying to successfully memorize the way back.

I couldn't imagine anything worse than getting lost, him thinking I had spurned him and disappearing before my arrival. I had to admit, I was a bit nervous that he wanted to meet in daylight; after all, the activities I was seeking out were more suited for after hours.

As Rain traveled on through the forest, crystal clear thoughts of Gris came to mind; like him shutting the curtains to shield us from the harsh light of day. My cheeks were warmed by those memories. I allowed myself to revisit them in detail—for educational purposes.

Replaying my body intertwined with his, the intentional breath whispered in his ear, my yearning, stifled at first, but turning to reckless abandon beneath our writhing bodies. I concentrated on what to do differently, do better, once I finally ensnared Trace. If his words were any indication of experience, then I was certain I was no match for him; I was going to have to pull off another impeccable acting job.

If I had to guess, we had been on our journey back to the tavern about an hour, and this should have been around where we encountered Aster's house. But it was nowhere in sight as I glanced around in all directions, trying to establish if I had gotten us lost somehow. Come to think of it,

I didn't recall seeing that house on the return ride either. Had I set us on an entirely different path?

I was keeping Rain at a slow pace while I continued to search for familiar signs when I saw the startling sight of the charred dead tree sitting in complete isolation. No picket fence, no dilapidated house or signage. Was my memory untrustworthy? I could have sworn that it was the very same tree that loomed over Aster's house, but it was surrounded by nothing but more forest. It had to have been the very same one I witnessed just yesterday.

Rain and I passed the tree with trepidation. I urged Rain onward quickly, working to put distance between us and that eerily familiar place. Was it possible that the rumors were true?

For the remainder of the ride, I tried to distract myself with thoughts of Trace and the exciting game of what was to come. Our limited words and short time together could be described as nothing more than sparring. Each reply a jab, every unenthusiastic retort an effort to conceal. I was going to break him down bit by bit; he just didn't know it yet.

When I could finally see the tavern, I approached nervously on horseback, scanning the area for any sign of Trace—as if he'd be waiting for me. Trace did not seem like the type to fawn over anyone. I walked Rain into the stable looking for the largest stall to give him plenty of room for the evening when I suddenly felt a hand wrap around my waist. I jumped in surprise, turning quickly with my hand already curled into a tight fist.

To my chagrin, I found Trace towering over me, a smirk plastered across his face. He took his hand and cupped my raised fist, pushing it down to my side.

"You don't want to try that."

I stepped back from the overwhelming presence of his stature. "Do you always go around grabbing people by surprise like that?"

He nonchalantly began tying up his horse next to Rain.

"Only the ones that try to bed me on the first night."

He turned and winked at me.

Before I could point out that I had claimed this stall, he eyed me and said, "You don't mind if Alcar shares? You do share, don't you?"

He was even more attractive than I remembered from the night before, and I was no match for this kind of banter, so I replied sweetly, "Of course, be my guest."

The dappled gray of Rain was a stunning compliment next to Alcar's crisp white body and solidly black mane. After situating the horses, we stood there like two strangers, silence filling the void between us...

"You should eat." He sounded bossy, but I had to admit that skipping breakfast along with the long ride had built up my appetite.

We made our way back to the tavern, the place feeling both familiar and unknown.

This time I had arrived with someone, I knew my surroundings, the bartender, and I had no intention of sparing even one drop of sobriety as Trace's words echoed through my memory. *Sober...and nothing to dull your senses.*

Trace led us to the very same booth from the night prior, where he had intervened on my behalf. A barmaid quickly appeared, and from the looks she was giving Trace, it was clear she would love to sink her claws into him too. I did not like her eyeing my target and I made a sour face at her when she greeted him but not me.

She was short, big-busted, and showing off her assets with a low-cut blouse. Trace didn't seem to pay any attention when she leaned further into him asking, "What can I get you, handsome?"

"We'll take one braggot, one water, and two bowls of the stew with bread." His dry reply gave her no indication that he returned the same affections. She flitted away in disappointment to fulfill his request.

"Ale?" I questioned. "What happened to not dulling the senses?"

"I never said a damn thing about myself, Cress. You're the one who hasn't proven you can drink responsibly."

I clenched my teeth in annoyance that he continued to treat me like a child by ordering my meal.

"And don't think I can't read that look on your face. The stew is the only edible thing on the menu; consider that before you decide to hold a grudge."

I relaxed my shoulders and managed a gracious, "Thank you."

Trace leaned back into the booth, relaxing, still adorned in his cloak and those concealing gloves. Once again, he donned all black.

My chest tightened at the thought of us having to make small talk for an entire meal and, perhaps, an entire afternoon. It's not that I wasn't deeply curious about him, it's just that I knew the more we talked, the more I was going to have to conceal the truth.

There were parts of me I just couldn't share or I'd be putting myself at risk. I wasn't a good liar, and bound to be even worse at it when his perfect lips were distracting me from damn near everything. I went with the simplest start that I could muster.

"Why'd you name your horse Alcar?" His gaze shifted into something softer, almost sad, like I caught him off guard.

"He's named after a story from my childhood." He paused, looking away, then finished, "One my mother used to read to me when I was very young."

I have no idea why that minor admission appeared to pain him, but I felt like it wasn't the right moment to pry any further. I replied, "So where are you from, and what brings you to these parts?"

I had no idea why I had stupidly asked that question, but we were likely to get around to that subject matter anyway. I just needed time to prepare my lie.

The eager barmaid arrived, setting down our drinks and meals in front of us, giving Trace time to formulate a response.

"I'm on leave from the Kingsguard."

Ahh…military. Made sense given his rigid demeanor and all those weapons he kept under his cloak.

He took a swig of ale and I continued with the interrogation. "But where are you from?"

He shook his head, replying, "When you're Kingsguard you're never really from anywhere. You're always on the move; you learn to call home wherever you are that day."

I took two giant bites of stew, grateful that Trace had some insight about the menu.

"Well, everyone is from somewhere," I prodded, spooning away at my meal.

"North of North. That's where I'm from. You wouldn't know of it."

The way he evaded the question was condescending, but I was intrigued. Little did he know, my sister and I had studied maps of the kingdom from a young age, especially when my father was away. It comforted us to see the destinations he was traveling to up close. It helped bridge the seemingly unfathomable distance between the span of a thumb and forefinger. I let him move on for now but stowed further questions in my mind for later.

"And you…? Where are you and that beautiful horse hailing from?"

I fidgeted anxiously. Maybe he had noticed too much about Rain. To the average eye, he was simply beautiful—but to someone who knew horses, he was expensive and rare. Not an animal you'd see tied up in a run-down stable. I decided to downplay it, assuming that a common Kingsguard likely didn't have awareness of rare horse breeds.

"Oh yeah, Rain, he's a looker," I took a gulp of the water. "As for me, I'm from south of South. You probably wouldn't know of it."

I knew my reply was snarky and he was unlikely to buy it, but it was the best I had at the moment. I could have lied and mentioned the town where I had visited Wendell's Exchange, but then I might be expected to know all about it on the off chance he'd been there…then I'd really be in trouble.

He let out a small unimpressed laugh and took another gulp. "Well played, Cress, well played."

I breathed an inaudible sigh of relief that he took my response as just more evasive banter.

"South of South you say? What brings you this far north?"

Of course, he had follow-up questions. "I'm just killing time, exploring. I leave in a couple of weeks to serve the Seafarers on a ship."

I had to admit the half lie rolled off my tongue naturally, and I knew sticking with my parents' story was going to serve me well. But instead of him thinking that I was educated, versed in languages, and familiar with the merchants guild, I needed him to think I was nothing more than a commoner in need of labor and a wage.

As I mulled over the different aspects of the lie in my mind, I realized there was an extended, thoughtful silence. He moved his empty bowl to the side. "I think I can help you kill some time. Would you like that?"

The question slid off his tongue like silk, laced with the intoxicating promise of what was to come. My thighs pressed together tightly. I wanted to kill all of time with the stranger before me.

My throat bobbed, and I think I could hear my heartbeat pounding as I nodded in agreement. "I'd like that, Trace."

I said his name melodically, thinking of how he promised me I'd be saying it until I no longer could. A wicked smile spread across his face, exposing his teeth and accentuating his predatory gaze. "What do you have in mind?"

I glanced out the window, the daylight still burning strong. It would be too forward to drag him up to the room and strip him. Which was what I had in mind.

"Actually, I have a list," I said boldly.

"Oh, do you now?" His interest was piqued. He continued, "And what's something we can check off today?"

He hadn't a single clue that he was the next thing on the list, but I had to dredge up something else or I'd blow my cover.

"Do something that scares me," I replied, trying to sound intriguing and adventurous rather than innocent and meek. He cocked his head to the side.

"I think I've got an idea that suits this request," he offered slyly.

He threw some coins on the table to pay for our meal and began to usher me up and to the exit.

"Hey, I can pay for my…" Before I could finish, he interrupted.

"I know you can, but I'm not allowing you to." He continued his stride to the exit and I quickly followed, making up the distance between us.

We headed back to the stable, and he told me it wouldn't be too long of a ride.

"We'll take both horses," he nudged me toward Rain and Alcar.

"What, you think I can't keep my hands to myself?" I quipped flirtatiously.

He continued to prepare our horses and replied coolly, "I know you can. But I cannot."

I was shamefully blushing at his response and almost blurted out an excuse that Rain was too tired, but that was too desperate. Trace had this way of being salacious but then acting as if he were commenting on the weather. It was infuriating, but also the exact reason he was so damn alluring. He exuded experience and casual confidence. I shuddered to imagine the number of lovers he'd taken with this charade of interested indifference. It was certainly working a number on me.

We both mounted, and he uttered, "Follow me."

Before I could even question the destination, he took off at full speed, but I met his challenge with enthusiasm.

Rain and I kept pace with Trace and Alcar for the majority of the distance. I was probably being quite stupid, putting this much trust in him as he led me farther and farther away from anywhere I had been or could find my way back from. For all I knew, he could have been leading me to my demise. A place so isolated no one would hear my screams. But at this point in time, I would have followed this cloaked rogue into oblivion.

I tried not to let him notice my stolen glances of his wind-blown hair being swept off his face, revealing more of his sharp, handsome features in the sunlight. When he slowed Alcar, we followed suit, and arrived upon a small body of water surrounded by trees and a rocky backdrop. The center of the water was terrifyingly dark, the bottom impossible to see, implying it was very, very deep.

He dismounted and casually tied Alcar and Rain to some trees off to the side. I dismounted and began to pace around the edge of the water, "What are we doing here?" I questioned anxiously, since Trace hadn't indicated what his idea was before we arrived.

"You want to do something that scares you. This will do the trick." He pointed at the body of water.

"I'm not scared of swimming," I remarked.

"Of course not. Someone who's going to spend so much time with the Seafarers surely isn't afraid of the water..."

His intent was lost on me. Was this some sad attempt to get me naked in the water, because I had saved that item on the list for another time.

"However, the Sav eels can be quite intimidating. What with those rows and rows of razor-sharp teeth, they could skin a tiny thing like you in mere seconds."

My eyes widened with fear, and I felt myself holding my breath as I took a step back from the water I had been peering into. He continued to look at me knowingly, like he expected me to just welcome the insanity of his proposal.

"You're crazy if you think I'm getting in there with those eels."

He laughed. "You said you wanted to do something that scares you."

"Yeah, Trace, but I'm not trying to die today!" I exclaimed, as if that needed any further explanation.

He walked up to me and placed his gloved hand on my lower back, as if that would bring me comfort. He nudged me closer back to the edge as we both peered into the pool of water.

"The good news for you is the eels are nocturnal; they'll remain in the dark depths of this pool until sunlight no longer blankets the surface." He paused, as if explaining that made the situation any more enticing. "That is, if you trust their natural instincts."

He certainly had found something I was scared of, but this went beyond that. Frankly, I was terrified that some brave eel was going to make a meal out of my leg. But what would Trace think if I backed down now? After all, I was the one who had prompted this absurdity. This was a reminder that I needed to be more specific about my list in the future; that is, if I made it past this challenge.

I mustered every ounce of courage I had and turned to Trace defiantly. "Fine, I'll do it, but you have to join me."

"That's not possible, dear. On the off chance anything does happen to you, we'll want to make sure I'm there to be able to pull you out quickly."

His point was fair—and infuriating, as I was faced with the reality that I'd be going in alone. Before my building adrenaline wavered, I marched over to the tree, walked around the horses, and began to quickly strip down. I was too focused on the task at hand to care if I was giving Trace a show, or if he was even interested. If I didn't take care of this quickly, I was going to talk myself out of it.

I walked out from behind Rain, into the bright sunlight with my undergarments hanging loosely over my now goose-bumped flesh as I watched Trace attempt to ignore my lack of clothing.

Trace held out his hand to help me step down carefully into the still water. I shivered as the cool liquid enveloped me one limb at a time. I told myself if I was really careful and quiet about entering, then I'd be lucky enough to avoid disturbing any of the hostile eels resting in its depths.

Before letting go of Trace's hand, he looked down at me with a taunting smile. "Any last words?"

"Yeah, don't miss me too much."

I yanked my hand away from him and carefully immersed the rest of my body up to my neck, as I slowly waded out farther toward the middle. Trace stood idly at the edge, waiting and watching for anything alarming. I was terrified, and I felt myself curling my toes in an attempt to keep them from accidentally drifting any deeper into the water where sunlight didn't touch. My bones rattled with fear, but I grit my teeth and continued to stare back at Trace on the shoreline, who smiled back at me proudly and made a slow clapping motion.

All of a sudden, I heard a splash behind me, and then another. In complete panic, I began to flail and scream, hurriedly swimming with all my energy back to the shore. I was certain that there had to have been a swarm of eels coming straight for me.

When I reached the shoreline, I grabbed for Trace's wrist, pulling myself, soaking wet, out of the water and into his arms. I stood there for a minute or two, panting and trembling, barely able to stand. Trace was holding my drenched body close to his chest when I heard him let out a laugh.

As he held me, one laugh became many. Infuriated, practically unable to see straight, I shoved myself back from his embrace.

"Was that you?" I screeched in anger.

He shook his head back and forth, raising his hands in surrender. "I'm sorry, I couldn't help myself."

The fury that coursed through my veins removed any embarrassment I might have felt as my soaked undergarments clung transparently to my skin. Trace kept laughing, clearly amused, but there was something else behind that look as I confronted him.

"You could have gotten me killed! What if you disturbed the eels?"

He had gambled with my life. He tried to approach me slowly, but I took another step back from him.

"Cress, I wouldn't have done that to you." He pointed at the pool of water to our side. "Sav eels are saltwater creatures. You're not going to find them in a freshwater pond."

If it was possible to catch fire in that very moment, I think I would have exploded as pure rage pulsed in my temples; he had not only lied to me, but also played a prank at my expense. I felt stupid and angry, unable to reconcile that I hadn't been in any real danger since he'd used magic to scare me.

I charged at him, shoving him with both my hands and yelling, "You ass! You lying, ass!"

He stumbled back a little upon my impact. "Hey, you said you wanted to do something that scared you, not that you had to be in actual danger. I think this was actually the more responsible choice."

His logic was irrefutable, but did not make me any less pissed off. I marched over to Rain, stepped behind the tree to strip off my wet undergarments and replaced them with my dry clothes.

I yelled out from behind the tree, "That was a real cheap shot, Trace, and trust me, you're going to pay for it."

When I came out from behind the tree, he had moved closer and fiendishly replied, "I'm counting on it."

He eyed me up and down as if disappointed that I was no longer on display. I strode past him, bumping his side with my shoulder.

"Ass," I muttered under my breath while wringing out my clothes and loading them into my pack.

❈❈❈✦

I was grateful for the silence and distance between us on the ride back to the inn. I was still fuming, and doing my best to remain steadfast in my desires.

Upon arriving, Trace stowed the horses together in the stall, and I was secretly hoping that Rain might give him a good kick in the balls; wishful thinking.

Trace tossed me the key. "Same room as last night, go wash up. You smell like pond water."

I could have spat at him, but he wasn't wrong. My damp hair reeked, and I could use a hot bath to relax all this tension I was carrying. Not to mention I wasn't interested in bedding anyone while like this. I took the key and marched off without a word, afraid that I might say something so harsh that there'd be no wooing my way back into his good graces.

The room was exactly as I remembered, but this time, it held a lot more potential. I spent an inordinate amount of time lounging in the bath. It wasn't remotely as nice as my own back home, but it did the trick.

Steam circled above the water and I tilted my head back to relax, but all I could think about were those Gods damned eels. What a fool I had been! I couldn't believe I ever fell for that. I wondered what Trace was up to, down in the bar. Maybe the barmaid had returned with her antics, or perhaps he was playing an even worse prank and ditching me with the bill and a lonely room.

No. That was unlikely, not after seeing the sinister way he had looked at me when my soaked undergarments clung to every inch of my nude body, displaying me like a statue carved of pale stone.

Whether he wanted to admit it or not, he wanted me. Was this his thing? Did he like playing hard to get? My undergarments were still damp and saturated with the unpleasant aroma of wet earth and stagnant water.

After exiting, I submerged them in the bathwater, wrung them out and hung them on a line in the washroom. I didn't have many options in the way of clothing, since I had only packed a few things—which didn't include extra undergarments.

What was I thinking? I buttoned some fitted trousers and threw on a loose blouse and another corseted vest to accentuate my curves. Snickering to myself, I recalled how I had shown up at Gris's place with nothing underneath, and here I was again.

If Trace was going to be disappointed that he had nothing to peel off me, that was of his own making, and maybe he'd think twice next time. I braided my damp hair and looked back at that tiny bed, taking a deep breath and reminding myself to be confident. You've got this.

Upon returning downstairs, I scanned the expanse of the room and discovered Trace occupying our booth. The thought of anything being ours delighted me more than I wanted to admit. I could see the sun in the early stages of setting outside the tiny windows.

The tavern had once again filled up with a lively crowd, all of them buzzing with conversation and sipping their beverages. This evening, a fiddler had taken up a spot on the other side of the bar and began playing a medley of merry tunes, hoping for anyone to spare a coin or two for his talents.

When I took my seat across from Trace, he had a glass of water waiting for me, and I rolled my eyes as I watched him enjoy his drink—which most certainly wasn't water.

"Ahh, there's my little nymph," he coaxed playfully.

I tilted my head, giving him an unenthusiastic smile, unable to hide my annoyance.

"In the flesh," I retorted.

"I ordered some cheese, bread, and cured meats. It's the second most edible thing they have, and I figured you wouldn't be interested in eating stew twice in one day."

Despite his jokes and indifference, he was attentive. Telling me to stay out of trouble, as if hazards and mishaps followed me wherever I went. All his words were filled with heavy innuendo and a lustful tone. I had to admit, I liked being cared for despite how he bossed me around. His words held power over me. Gods, I wished I had that kind of power over him.

I began to silently eat my food. The adrenaline rush of the pond debacle had left me famished. I continued to go about my meal, giving him a coy silence. I wanted him to feel as awkward as I was annoyed. I knew hoping for an apology was expecting too much.

"Let's play a game," he said, breaking the silence between us.

"You know I'm terrible at cards," I replied indignantly.

"No, one where we each win by getting something from the other."

"And what's that?" I replied, munching on my bread with disinterest. At this point, my seduction efforts had gone by the wayside.

"Information. We haven't been extremely forthcoming with one another. And…if I'm to share a room with you this eve, then I'd like to get to know you better."

I almost choked on my piece of bread. Was that genuine interest I just heard coming from his mouth?

I was still chewing, and he added before I could reply, "Unless bedding strangers is your thing…? Is that your thing, Cress?"

The insolence. Before I even registered what I was saying, I snapped, "No, I don't go around bedding strangers. I'm not some sort of strumpet. Or did you forget you almost slit someone's throat last night for implying that about me? I've only slept with—" I caught myself before I could finish my anger-fueled diatribe and was shocked at just how close I had been to revealing my severe lack of experience.

I bit my tongue before I said anything else. Trace just smiled back at me. It wasn't the kind of wicked smile he usually gave me. One that implied I was going to regret something. This one was softer, kinder, maybe even understanding. He probably felt bad for me because it was clear from my outburst that I wasn't exactly sporting a list a mile long.

"I was simply asking if that was your thing. I didn't say I minded it," he replied.

"Well, aren't you open-minded," I retorted. "What's the game?" I was attempting to get this conversation on a different track.

I had no idea what my thing was, but I was pretty certain he'd have no problem figuring it out.

"Five questions. We each get to ask five questions of the other, and you have to answer honestly."

I was interested, but it was risky. He was asking for honesty, but I knew there was only so much I could offer in the way of truth. I told myself if I could lie to my sister and Gris, then lying to Trace shouldn't matter. After all, I'd never get to see him again once this was all over; how bad could the consequences be?

"Deal. I'll go first," I demanded eagerly.

Trace leaned back in his seat, looking just as intrigued as I was and where this little game would lead us.

"What does your tattoo mean?" Trace's expression perked up at my first question.

"You don't even know what it looks like; don't you want to know that first?"

Coyly I said, "I'll be seeing it later tonight. I'm not wasting a question on what it is, I want to know what it means," I restated firmly.

Trace never blushed, but if he did, I'm certain he would have in that moment.

"You're pretty clever sometimes. It's a military tattoo; my brethren and I have them. It's a reminder that we bleed for our king and his people. That we don't take life without cause. You cannot wash away the lives you take, even when you've cleaned their blood from your hands."

My breath hitched with the nervousness that he might as well have confirmed he'd killed someone—or maybe even multiple people. I had suspected the very first night I saw him, based on how comfortably he'd held a knife to that poor gambler's neck.

No remorse or concern, just a singular focus. I knew better than to waste a question and ask something as crude as how many had died by his hand, but curiosity hung on the tip of my tongue.

"Do you have any family?"

What an odd question for him to ask. Did he guess that I was an orphan?

"My parents are alive, if that's what you're asking. And I have a sister. She's a little older than me."

It wasn't entirely untrue. I just avoided mentioning that I was a twin and that she was only older than me by a couple of minutes. I don't know that I entirely cared if Trace had family, but something about the look he gave me almost invited the question in return.

"Do you?"

His features softened into that same disheartened look he'd had when he told me about where Alcar's name came from. I was beginning to worry I had hit an unpleasant nerve. He took another gulp of ale.

"I come from a large family. All sons. I have a handful of brothers, four to be exact. I'm the youngest."

How odd, he didn't mention his mother or father and it seemed intentional. The thought of four strapping young lads all with the same gorgeous features as Trace was practically unimaginable. Thank the Gods I only had to suffer the solitary brutality of his undeniable beauty, and not all of them at once.

I hadn't noticed just how long I'd been lost in the thought of his brothers when I heard his voice, "Spare me a minute longer of you daydreaming about all my brothers, you wound me."

I smiled back at him and held both my hands up, palms facing him in surrender. "Guilty as charged."

"So, you're heading out to sea? Is that something you want to pursue, and if so, why?" Trace asked with a tone more concerned than curious.

I was sure he had heard of their brutish reputation, and of course you had to have been living under a rock to not know about the rebellion. I thought for a moment about the answer, because the truth was that the lie was entangled with real desires. Ones I'd had since I was a little girl.

Hours of studying maps, days looking at paintings, sketches, and drawings of the sea—it had all captivated me. I had always felt the sea calling. My father's influence aside, I had always known in the depths of my soul that the place I had called home for many years was not where I was truly meant to be. I longed for that future, but that was under different circumstances than the lie we'd spun. I would never get to experience that life. Not when the king had other plans for me.

"Yes, very much so."

I spoke from my heart. From a place I had not let myself acknowledge since things were taken from my control. *My* truth.

"I've been landlocked my entire life, but it doesn't mean my heart doesn't long for the sea. I have an adventurer's soul, and I am meant for the horizon."

I caught myself in the embarrassment of how silly I sounded with my confession—but I didn't care. It was the truest thing I had said in days, and if he didn't like me for it, that was fine. Trace remained silent, like he was hanging on to my every word.

"You probably think that sounds stupid."

He chimed in before I could chide myself further.

"Not at all. I know what it's like to feel like you're meant for something else."

I think this was the most genuine interaction we'd had yet. This rawness was something new and different from our usual banter.

My hands fidgeted with the new energy pulsing between us. I grabbed another piece of cheese to distract myself and continued, "Do you have any hobbies? You know, when you're not doing whatever the Kingsguard requires of you?"

I shoved the food in my mouth to give him space to answer me—and because the rapid-fire questions weren't giving me any time to plan. I only had a few questions left and hadn't put any good thought into what else I wanted to know. Besides what he tasted like. What his rough hands felt like running across my bare skin. I was getting carried away with my imagination.

"The military is a lot of hurry up and wait. When we're sitting around for days at camp, you have to find ways to fill your time or you'll lose your mind. That, or form other bad habits… I've been prone to sketching every now and then."

He paused, looking at me for any sign of judgment.

"I draw mostly landscapes. To remember the places I've been and the lands I've seen."

I couldn't for the life of me imagine Trace doing anything artistic. It was pretty bewildering, but I needed to see these sketches with my own eyes.

"Are you any good? Shit, wait. Don't answer that. I'm not using a question for that."

Trace let out a small laugh, an amused smile framing his lips.

"I'll give you one free of charge. Just because I like you."

My eyes widened, but I dared not speak.

"Sketching isn't exactly considered a very masculine activity, Cress. I don't go around showing off my art or making it apparent that I do it at all. You think having brothers give you crap is tough, try a military-minded father who might teach you a lesson for catching you in such a frivolous act."

Trace's expression changed and a wave of melancholy swept across his face. "I don't know if I'm good, to answer your question."

I imagined Trace wanting to do something that brought him happiness, but being forced to hide it. While my dream of being at sea had not yet been realized, I knew that my mother and father would embrace that path, even celebrate it.

In Trace, I sensed the uncertainty and disapproval of the people he held most dear, and it saddened me. He still hadn't made any other mention of his mother, not since telling me about Alcar's name.

Momentarily, I realized how loud the bar had gotten. All this time I had been tuning it out, dialing into Trace's every word like we were the only two people in the room.

Time had passed unnoticeably and with each question, the mystery of Trace was unfolding with more twists and turns. He was becoming more than a target of my desires, and I didn't know what to do with that or the feelings that were bubbling up along with it. I wouldn't allow myself to feel for this person or anyone.

I was struck by the sobering thought of time dwindling and, how soon, my decisions would no longer be my own, including the company I sought. Not Trace. Not Gris. No one. But the longer we sat here conversing, the more I was seeing the person that was Trace, rather than the meaningless, wicked stranger I was tempting.

I was lost in thought when Trace interrupted, "Why aren't you scared of blades?"

The question was an odd choice with so few questions left, but it was clear that Trace was very observant.

"Don't pretend to be surprised, Cress. You didn't flinch, not once, when I pulled out that blade and held it to the gambler's neck. You also didn't show any signs of concern when I removed all my daggers last night."

He was right, the blades didn't concern me at all. I had spent years training in sparring at school. Blade, bow, sword—you name it, I've wielded it. Never in a situation of need, but I was no stranger to them. So, I lied.

"It's dangerous out there. Especially for females. I'm not going to be caught helpless. My friend back home taught me. I made him practice with me and demonstrate everything he knew. I'm comfortable, but not an expert or anything." I added, "Plus, it doesn't hurt to know how to hunt, just in case."

I hadn't a clue if I sounded believable, and from the unconvinced look on Trace's face it didn't seem like he was buying it, but he elected not to pry.

I went to change the subject immediately and blurted out an entirely selfish question, "If you've been with the Kingsguard all this time, do you have someone waiting for you somewhere, or back home?"

He displayed a small disbelieving smile and shook his head. "No, there isn't anyone waiting for me. If there were, I wouldn't be entertaining this evening with you."

Well, that was a relief.

"I don't let myself get attached to anyone, anywhere, or anything. When you're always on the move and your life belongs to the whims of the king and commander, you learn to settle for dalliances and stealing brief moments of joy."

I should have bitten my tongue, but I couldn't help myself. "Is that what I am to you…a dalliance?"

I can't believe I asked that aloud. I also did not intend for that to be my next question. I wanted to take it back as soon as the words left my mouth.

"I don't know what you are yet."

His carefully worded response had me on edge. Was I being toyed with, or was this just the same smooth talk he used on every female he took to bed?

"That doesn't count as a question, by the way," I said casually, when what I really wanted to say was, *Well I don't have time for you to figure it out anyway.*

"Of course." He nodded, taking another sip of his drink. "That brings me to my fifth and final question. I suppose I better make it a good one, right?"

I didn't know how much time had passed, but I could have sat there for hours going back and forth with this game of questions.

"I suppose you should."

He paused briefly, waiting for me to acknowledge his gaze. "Cress, share the night with me?"

Was he really asking me a simple yes or no question? Something that I thought was obvious. Did it even need to be asked? Was he asking at all? The sound of it came out more like a command than a request. I channeled every ounce of desire and audacity I possessed to answer his question with one of my own.

"That depends on you telling me how you're going to make sure there's no chance of me forgetting a single minute of tonight. How will you make me beg?"

I matched his gaze with even more intensity, and it felt like I had struck the match to light a flame that could not be tamed.

Trace held out his hand to ask for mine. "I'd rather show you."

And with that, I took his hand and let him lead me back to our room.

CHAPTER 10

The door closed behind us, the air thick with lust. I was grateful for the ruckus coming from the bar downstairs, because there was nothing but charged silence between us as Trace bent down to light a fire. I stood there in the dark, recalling how we had performed these same motions the night before. But this time was different. This time there wasn't an ounce of liquid courage to carry me forward, and I was certain something was going to happen.

My mouth was dry, but elsewhere I was slick with eager anticipation. Despite the excitement, I was still so unsure of myself, unable to bring myself to make the first move. This was very different from my time with Gris. He and I were friends, we knew each other well, and there was an air of lightness between us that made things easy.

With Trace, things were not going to be as easy. Who would speak first, who would yield? We knew each other a little better, but there hadn't been years of trust built up like I had with Gris.

I was starting to wonder if I was going to be able to follow through.

It wasn't because I didn't want to—I *really* wanted to. I watched as Trace began the familiar routine of removing his cloak and daggers, placing them one by one on the small writing desk. The dim, flickering light created a display of shadows all along the walls of the tiny room. Trace towered over every piece of furniture around us. He finally turned to me, single silver blade in hand, and began stalking over slowly.

I gulped, looking up at him and licking my lips in preparation to take that beautiful mouth of his. I stood there frozen, unable to move my feet. Internally, I was itching to touch him, but I couldn't bring myself to lift a finger.

Trace moved the blade to hover just between my aching breasts where the laces started on my vest corseted in front. The tip of his blade pulled the strings taut, and I couldn't refrain from gasping when each one gave way to the sharp edge in one swift motion downward to the top of my belly.

The blade did not scare me. I was confident that he knew exactly what he was doing—and I was equally sure that I was coming as undone as this corset. He had barely laid a hand on me, and yet I was transfixed with the way he worked slowly and meticulously to drag out the act of removing it.

When he was done, he took his hand and gently slid the vest from my shoulders until it fell to the floor behind me. From the corner of my eye, I could see the tattoo on his hand, distracting me. I wanted to see it all. He then lifted the blade to my braided hair and did the same to the tie, unleashing long waves down my back.

"Much better," was all he said.

He circled me like a predator stalking prey, and I could feel his muscular chest now pressing against my back as he stopped behind me. I leaned into it, wanting to feel his warmth, but all I could focus on was how aroused I'd become; my nipples poking against the thin white blouse, betraying me.

Trace ran his rough fingertips along the side of my neck, pushing my long hair to the side as I tilted my head, baring myself to him, willing him onward. That's when I felt the warmth of his mouth nestled between my shoulder and the curve of my neck.

The first time those magnificent lips graced my skin, they melted into me. He began to slowly place soft kisses all along my neck. His breath was a low hum at my earlobes, the tickling sensation nearly unbearable. I felt his lips run up along the tip of my pointed ear, followed by his face pressing into the back of my hair. He was breathing me in, the scent of me. I just stood there letting him explore me at a painstakingly slow pace.

When he returned to face me, it was like a different person. The once slow, patient, calm Trace was gone as he grabbed both sides of my face in his hands and crushed his lips to mine, sweeping his tongue into my mouth with the desperation of someone who has longed for this. I, too, had longed for this very encounter.

I stumbled backward slightly, but he stepped forward, keeping himself close and pinning me against the door as he continued to ravage my mouth. I worked to keep pace as our tongues clashed. I returned his frantic passion and bit gently on his lower lip; he groaned in response. I angled my body into him, willing him to continue.

With one arm bracing himself against the doorframe, he used the other to run his hand up my side and under my blouse where he cupped my breast, rubbing his thumb in a circle across my nipple. Between our kisses, I gasped in pleasure with each tender squeeze he made.

Everything was moving at such a fast pace; I wasn't having any time to overthink. I was not remotely in control of the situation, and for some reason, I liked it. I couldn't anticipate my next move or his; I was entirely lost in the moment.

Gathering my hair with one hand, he pulled it tightly, forcing my head back to give him better access to my throat. He continued with endless kissing and the occasional graze of his teeth, until his lips returned to mine and I felt him run his hands between my legs and squeeze.

I let out a gasp, which he swallowed with another kiss and sweep of his tongue. He continued to rub and tease me over the soft fabric of my pants, and I worked hard to hold back a moan, but the sensations he created exposed my want. He pulled back for the first time, giving me a second to catch my breath.

His hazel eyes were dark and heavy with desire. He grabbed at my waistline, his fingers dipping just below the fabric, pulling me toward him. He leaned closer and growled, "You're so fucking beautiful, I can't wait to taste you."

My breath hitched, and I barely had time to comprehend his words before he began slowly pulling me away from the door, toward the bed, unbuttoning my pants as we went. By the time I felt the back of my legs hit the edge, he had already made his way to the last button and bent down to his knees. He quickly unlaced my boots, and I had enough sense to be grateful that he didn't use that knife to destroy another piece of my clothing; I'd have nothing to wear home.

He remained on his knees as he began to slowly remove my trousers, one leg, then the other, baring me. It was at that moment that I wished we were back against the wall; the embarrassment of standing there half-naked was more than I could handle.

"Sit," he ordered, as he had done before, but this time, he did not sound like someone to ignore.

I did not dare disobey or return some smart-mouthed quip. I did as he commanded. As soon as I did, he sat up on his knees and spread my legs wide in front of him. My Gods, I wanted to die. Cover me now. He just sat there, taking me in.

"I've wanted to do this all day."

Before I could react, he leaned in and began passionately kissing up the insides of my legs with as much speed and force as he had taken my mouth with just minutes ago. My legs were quivering and all of my nerves went into overdrive as he continued, occasionally biting at my thighs and then sending me over the edge as one hand began to lazily run a finger along my dripping apex.

I laid flat on the bed, unable to do anything but arch further into his hand. There were no kisses to catch the sounds he drove from me. As Trace slid a finger into me, I let out an audible gasp, and from this confession of pleasure, he showed me no mercy.

The next sensation I felt was entirely new. Trace's tongue swept back and forth across my clit while his finger plunged in and out of me. I began to moan and writhe against his motions. Gods, this was the most incredible feeling. I propped myself up on my elbows to gaze down upon him and was met with the intensity of his stare. His eyes darkened and he continued to work me over, languishing me with the strokes of his tongue. The desperation for more built when I let out a traitorous cry and called out for him, "Trace!"

As soon as he heard his name leave my lips, he shoved another finger in and increased the unrelenting pace and motion. My breathing was uneven and I found myself unable to catch my breath. My body responded to this in ways I had never experienced.

The passion continued to grow as he worked, and I found myself in a cadence of whimpered cries and calling his name over and over, trying to gain control over this unruly and maddening feeling. Suddenly, he stopped.

I was left feeling empty. I was worried I had done something wrong, but I sat up to find Trace now standing at the edge of the bed.

He had removed his boots and began lifting his dark shirt over his head. Had I not been entirely distracted by the sight of him, I might have been more disappointed that he had teased me to the brink and then left me there. But I couldn't be mad because I was already enamored with what stood before me.

His body was perfectly proportioned for his tall stature. He was muscular, but not bulky, and chiseled everywhere you'd hope. I was now distracted by the distinct tattoo starting at his left hand, running up his arm, and stopping just above his collarbone at the base of his neck.

It was difficult to make out clearly in the light of the fire, but it looked almost like black ink had been spilled down his arm. And that's when I remembered what he had said about it being a military tattoo and never being able to wash away the blood of the lives you took. That's exactly what it looked like, spilled blood running the entire length of his arm, almost covering him entirely. Very little of his pale skin remained visible. He stalked toward me, noticing my distracted gaze, and grabbed my chin, tilting it upward, forcing our eyes to meet as he towered over me.

"I like hearing you say my name."

He ran a finger across my lower lip, looking me over as if he were inspecting me. Like he was considering if I pleased him or not.

"Let's see how loud you say it this time around, and perhaps, I'll give you what you want."

Trace was going to be the literal death of me. He was a mystery, a male of few words, but he sure did choose them wisely. I was wrapped around his finger in a fog of lust, and my mouth watered at the sight of him straining against his pants. It's a good thing he didn't encourage me to unbutton him because I was pretty sure my hands would have fumbled clumsily.

"Remove your shirt," he demanded.

There was no room to be shy, after all his face had been between my thighs only moments ago. I did as he instructed and tossed the shirt to the floor, moving my now fully naked body farther back onto the bed to welcome him. He did not take the invitation. He continued to stand at the edge of the bed, just looking down at me.

"Spread your legs."

Again, I did as he commanded, still feeling a bit embarrassed to be doing so.

"I want you to look at me and begin touching yourself. Touch yourself the way you do when you're alone."

My eyes widened at the filthy request he was making of me. But Trace wasn't making a request. He was instructing my every move this entire evening, and with a slight hesitation, I lowered my hand.

Trace stood there watching me intently, and I could see him take a sharp inhale as he watched me push a finger inside myself. As I began to circle my finger over and over in a rapid motion, my breathing became difficult to control. I tried to keep my eyes focused on him like he had ordered, but it was more difficult than one might think.

Trace freed himself from the constraint of his tight pants and I practically gasped, witnessing him take the hard full length of himself in his hand and begin to stroke. He did not waver. He continued to stare me down as I watched desire build in his gold-flecked eyes.

His jaw clenched tighter when a small moan escaped my mouth. The tension felt like the physical embodiment of all our verbal sparring. It was killing me. I wanted him and I wanted him now. I knew exactly how to bait him to me.

I shoved a second finger in and when I did, I threw my head back in a passionate release and gasped his name loudly, "Trace!"

Within seconds he was over me, between me, arriving like an answer to a prayer. He ran his hands along every bare inch of me. I stopped pleasing myself, unaware if I was going to regret that, and grabbed his face pulling him toward me, tasting myself on his lips. Now I was the one crashing into him. I frantically ran my hands over his arms, feeling every sculpted muscle, wrapping my legs around him and sliding my hands across his bare chest.

I felt him adjust himself at my entrance and eagerly spread my legs wider. He brushed a lock of my hair out of my face and just held himself there, looking down at me. Tenderly. I didn't know how I knew what he wanted; I just did.

I pulled his face close to mine and left gentle kisses along his neck, slowly working my way up to his ear where I exhaled a pleading whisper. "Trace."

It was his undoing.

I felt him thrust into me all at once, and the intensity was indescribable. The length of him was brutal, but welcomed. He began to thrust in and out, holding our bodies so closely together I could feel my breasts skimming his chest with each powerful movement. His bare skin felt magnificent against mine, and I curled my legs around him tighter, unable to get close enough to him. Urging him deeper when there was nowhere else to go.

His pace became unyielding, and his ragged breaths began to match mine in between our all-consuming kisses. Occasionally, he would bite down on my shoulder, and the painful sensation of his teeth contrasting the pleasurable ones elsewhere was a sinful combination.

Before I had time to react, Trace swiftly rotated, pulling me on top of him as he now lay beneath me. I adjusted and quickly remembered the pleasure I had found in this position before. I began to roll my body against him and quicken the pace, when suddenly I felt his thumb in the same place it had been when he almost took me over the edge earlier. He continued to caress me, and I felt the pressure increasing with each movement I made against him.

My back bowed as I lost myself in the pleasure that he brought me. The sensation was quickly becoming uncontrollable, but I could not stop my writhing. I prayed he stayed with me just like this. I didn't have words or thoughts for what was happening, but the sensitivity of it all was beginning to feel almost unbearable, but I pushed onward, teetering between pleasure and release, and when I could no longer control myself, I moaned, "Trace. Trace." He increased his pace. "Trace," I rasped.

All of a sudden, I felt a dull familiar pain coming from my back, and within seconds, my wings burst forth splaying out fully on both sides of me as I crashed against the pinnacle of my desire, with Trace finding his mere seconds later.

Oh no. Absolutely not. What had just happened, and why were my wings on display? Shit. *Shit.* I quickly crawled off of Trace and moved abruptly to the other side of the room, working to calm my breathing as quickly as possible and regain some semblance of control.

I had not called forth my wings, it just…happened. It was beyond my control, and I felt myself growing redder by the minute with embarrassment. I must have been turning in circles trying to find a way to sheathe them when I felt Trace grab my hand. "Cress, are you okay?"

"Ugh, I'm sorry. I don't know why that happened. Just give me a minute. I can take care of it."

But no matter what I did, they would not return. Trace and I stood there, both naked in the firelight, and I felt awful that I had entirely ruined our bliss with whatever this was.

Trace turned my body, forcing me to face him. After everything he had witnessed me do tonight, something about this was worse than all of that. Fae do not go around showing off their wings, and they certainly didn't do it by accident. Gods, why was this happening to me?

"You don't need to be embarrassed. You can learn to control it," he offered softly.

"…What?" I questioned.

"It's not uncommon that when we lose control from things like…like climax, that you have to exert control in other ways."

I stared at him blankly, realizing that this had never happened before. Not alone. Not with Gris. Had that meant this was my first true climax? Why did this have to happen now? In front of him, of all people. I would kill Versa for not warning me this could happen.

"Stop shaming yourself."

As he offered the kind words, his eyes began to scan the ridge of my iridescent wings and I couldn't stop staring at the shadows they cast on the wall, reminding me of the horrible error I had made because I lacked experience and control. One minute, I was riding high on my pleasure, and now, I felt unbelievably naive.

"I think they're stunning…like you." He lifted my chin to seal his words with a gentle kiss.

Nothing like the way he kissed me earlier. After a few more minutes passed, I was finally able to feel my breath even out and the calm spread over me as my wings lowered, slowly sheathed, and disappeared.

Now that I was finally free of the embarrassment my wings had caused, I found myself bashfully standing naked in front of a still-nude Trace, looking for any piece of fabric to cover myself. Trace swiped the blanket from the bed and wrapped it over my shoulders, but unwilling to let go, he instead pulled me in close to his chest.

He leaned in and whispered against my ear, "I'm really glad the eels didn't get you."

"You fucking piece of work," I shoved him away, taking the blanket with me.

I couldn't believe such foul language had left my mouth, but there wasn't anything ladylike about what I had just done—so why pretend?

Trace laughed and began to put his pants back on, while I sat back on the bed, covering myself to warm up. Trace moved to sit in the armchair by the fire; the same place he had slept last night, and I was worried he was about to make some sort of unexplained exit. Was he done with me?

I moved to one side of the bed and patted at the empty space beside me.

"I'm willing to share, you don't have to sleep in that uncomfortable chair."

Trace let out a frustrated breath. "It's not you. I'm just used to keeping watch at all hours, and I find it difficult to sleep."

He must have read the disappointment on my face because he stood and made his way toward me. He crawled into the spot I had made, and now that we were both in this bed without any distraction, the tiny space felt noticeably smaller. He pulled me to him, coaxing me under his arm as I rolled on my side and relaxed into the comfortable crook of his body.

"You don't seem like the cuddling type," I remarked teasingly.

He began to trace lazy circles on my arm with his hand. "The pleasures of the flesh are fleeting, we must enjoy them while they last."

His words were truer than he realized, but I refused to dwell on them.

"Did you read that in some clever book of poems?" I playfully mocked.

He scoffed, disregarding my remark. "I'll stay with you till you fall asleep, but please take no offense when I make my way back to the chair; old habits die hard."

I'd take what I could get. I nuzzled myself further into his side, taking in the scent of him. Now that I was paying attention, I realized he smelled like sandalwood and pine. It was a comforting scent that reminded me of riding Rain through the forest in the early morning when the ground was moist with dew.

I began to run my fingers gently across the line of his waist, feeling each ridge of muscle. He grabbed my hand. "That tickles, and if you don't stop, I'm going to be forced to do terrible things to you."

While the challenge was more than enticing, I knew better. I was exhausted and sore—and rightfully so, given Trace's size. I pulled my hand away and lifted it instead to his chest. He leaned in and left a gentle kiss on top of my head, lingering seconds longer to smell my hair like he had done earlier.

By now the tavern had closed and the only sound was the crackling of the fire. I tried to fight sleep, afraid of losing this moment with the dawn. The last thing I remembered was the sight of Trace's tattooed hand intertwined with mine.

I was foolish to think there was a chance that in the morning I'd awake in his arms. After all, he had warned me. But I did not expect to find myself entirely alone. I glanced around the room from the bed and saw that all of his things were gone. This was what I got for bedding a stranger. Should I have expected anything more than this? I was heading toward the washroom to retrieve my now-dry undergarments when I saw the note on the table.

> *Meet me in a week. You showed me yours. It's only fair I show you mine.*
>
> *— Trace*

Laying across the top of the parchment was a solid black feather, as dark as night. Trace was a Nightwing. Not only that, but he had left me a literal piece of himself.

I carried the feather over to the window sill, letting the morning sun shine brightly over it, illuminating the green hues that only appeared at just the right angle. Nightwing Fae hailed from about as far north as the maps go. They were mountain people. He wasn't exaggerating when he said he was from north of North.

I held the feather closely to my chest, letting out a sigh of relief that he wanted to see me again. Another part of me knew that missing him already was a horrible sign, and that I needed to cut off whatever this was. That returning to see him in a week was only going to make things harder.

Maybe I shouldn't return at all. I'd just never show up, he'd realize I had no interest and move on. What good was it going to do, my having any feelings for him? I had accomplished my goal. I seduced him, I bedded him, and I should check it off the list and forget all of this.

The entire ride home I gently thumbed the feather tucked away in the pocket of my cloak, unsure if I was ever going to be able to shake the memories of Trace. Unsure if I wanted to.

When I arrived back at the manor, I intentionally sped past my mother and father who were lounging in the parlor and headed straight for Versa's room. I barged my way through her doorway and found her fiddling with jewelry and diadems; another frivolity of being a bride-to-be.

She turned to me in excitement, but I slammed the door behind my back and screeched, "I have a bone to pick with you, sister."

"What?" she exclaimed, bewildered.

"In all your wild stories you shared with me, in all the recounting of your escapades, do you think you could have mentioned the fact that our wings can just uncontrollably unfurl with climax?"

I was still fuming from the preventable embarrassment I had experienced with Trace. I blamed my naivety on Versa. Of course, she had to have encountered this before. My sister's cheeks turned red as she tried to hold in an audible laugh.

"How was I supposed to know you didn't know?" she pleaded, her eyes seeking forgiveness. She wasn't going to get off that easily. I could still see that twinge of amusement in her features.

"How many of your trysts have we discussed, and not once did you ever mention it," I complained, waving my hands in disapproval.

Versa nervously twisted the necklace in her hands and looked up at me through her angelic lashes.

"Well, sister, if you must know, it's never happened during one of my so-called trysts."

I had already planned my retort but paused.

"What do you mean? It's never happened to you, like ever?"

Versa smiled back at me sweetly. "It's only ever happened when I'm with myself, alone. I taught myself how to control it so that it wouldn't happen unless I wanted it to. I didn't think I ever needed to mention it; you may be inexperienced with others, but it's not like you've never been alone with yourself."

She had an extremely valid point. But all those times I'd never even felt the slightest stir of my wings. My sister's eyes widened with the same realization.

"Not even on your own? Never?" she said, aghast.

I shook my head. Before I could spend another second wallowing, she was in front of me, squeezing both my shoulders in enthusiasm.

"My Gods, who was this stranger you were with and what did he do to you?"

My sly smile betrayed me.

"Tell me everything," Versa beseeched me.

My parents were more than happy to see me at dinner that evening. I had to admit, spending all afternoon recounting the details of my and Trace's time together had done a fair job of distracting me from the uneasiness I had felt on the return home.

For those few hours in Versa's room, I embraced the feeling that I could ignore my impending reality and just gossip with my sister like it was any other day. I had felt weightless, but now that the distraction had passed, I couldn't deny the heavy feeling in my chest that had returned.

The heaviness was more than just these feelings toward Trace. It was the unbearable sadness of being separated from my sister for the rest of my days. It made me hope that my days with the king would be short. Fleeting waves of incapacitating grief continued to flood over me. I didn't want to live without her—or my parents.

They comprised my entire world. My family, my friends from the academy, and even the staff at the manor. I loved them all. This small piece of the world was mine, and I could feel it slowly cracking all around me. And I knew that in just a few short weeks it was going to completely shatter.

My heart was breaking at the thought of leaving them.

Leaving on a lie.

I was glad Trace had said he didn't want me to return for a week. It was a built-in excuse to stay close to home. The moment I stopped to pause, breathe, and look around the dinner table at the smiling, jovial faces of my loved ones, I knew that this was where I wanted to be. Everything seemed natural. They ate, laughed, and discussed normal things as if nothing awful was about to tear through this family.

It made me realize that since the horrible news had been delivered to me, I had been moving so fast. Focusing on the list, I hadn't slowed down to take it all in because I didn't think I would be able to bear the weight of the truth. But today I was feeling a little bit stronger. I needed to sink myself into this chaotic storm of feelings or I wasn't going to make it out alive.

I wanted to stop feeling like I was suffocating in this house at every chance of seeing their faces. If I didn't spend this time committing all the details to memory, then how could I ever expect those memories to carry me forward? Through whatever lay ahead.

After all, by serving as the Offering for the realm, I was serving my family too. That's what I told myself. I would muster up the courage to leave them so that they would be safe, and, most of all, so that my sister would never feel this indescribable loss that I was now grappling with.

That night I crawled into my bed, noting the incomparable difference to the one from the inn. The cool chill of the bedsheets and the noticeable absence of Trace's warmth brought back a flood of memories. I felt the heat of the blush coloring my cheeks. I rolled over to pull out the infamous list from my nightstand and crossed through another two items with a smirk.

~~Lose my maidenhead~~
~~Seduce a stranger~~
~~Gamble till I win~~
~~Get drunk~~
Alter my appearance
~~Help someone in need~~
Get a tattoo
~~Do something that scares me~~
Swim naked in the moonslight
Say my goodbyes

(Twenty-five Days Remain)

In the early morning, I awoke with an idea burning in my mind. Another item to check off the list. I rushed to make myself presentable, hoping that Versa would be willing to go along with my bold proposal. I knocked on her door and was shocked to find her still in her bed, hardly stirring. A few beams of light seeped through the window, drawing lines across her bed and the floor. She had always been much fonder of mornings than I.

I cozied up beside her and whispered playfully in her ear, "I have an idea, if you think you're brave enough."

She rolled over to face me. How is it possible she looked this pretty in the morning? Did I look even half this lovely in the early light of dawn? She nudged me and replied sleepily, "I've always been braver than you."

"Prove it," I said, pushing aside the memory of taunting Trace with the very same line.

"Get up," I continued, standing to rip the covers off her body.

I walked over to the window sill, yanking the drapes open wider to let more light canvas the room. I recollected the number of times she had done this to me, and I had to admit, it was amusing to be on the other end of it.

"We're getting marked today," I stated plainly. Versa sat up abruptly in surprise.

"What! A tattoo? You're kidding, right?" she exclaimed.

"Why not? I'm going away. You're starting a new life with your fancy husband-to-be. We should mark the occasion. Permanently." I turned to her with a mischievous look.

Tattoos weren't considered very becoming, especially for High Ladies like ourselves. My mother always showed distaste for my father's: a small symbol showing his allegiance to the merchants guild. I thought he liked to pretend it was more serious than it was.

I was solidly convinced they all got them while drunk and abroad, then had to find some cover story to tell their spouses. I didn't mind it at all—in fact, as a child I found myself envying my father for it and wanting my own to match.

It was on the inside of his wrist; a small anchor with a Seafarer's knot tangled around it, and at the top of the anchor was the letter N for North. It irritated him when someone pointed out that the N was not directionally aligned with a real compass. He'd explain that the N was figurative, meaning true north. It was a reminder that no matter how far away from home his travels carried him, *we* were his true north, his final destination.

I adored the meaning and was shocked he'd even come up with something so thoughtful. He wasn't the overly sentimental type.

Versa didn't take much convincing. At breakfast, we were extremely nonchalant about our intention to head into town that afternoon. My mother tried to insist on sending an escort with us, but when I gave her a look, she did not put up any further disagreement.

When we entered the stable to gather our horses, the hand didn't miss a beat. It was the first time I had seen my crested saddle atop Rain in days. I gave him a small wink of gratitude and headed toward the town with my sister at my side. By the time we arrived at the artist's shop, I had still been waffling about exactly what I wanted.

She and I sat nervously in the front of the shop, trying not to giggle at the absurdity of what we were doing. My mother and father likely cared little for anything I'd do with my body. But, Versa, on the other hand, was about to be on display at her wedding in front of many well-to-do nobles.

An extremely tall and very slender female approached us. Her black hair was short and choppy, not a style you'd commonly see on females. Her appearance was a bit androgynous; attractive, in any case. Tall cheekbones and all sharp angles. She had a bare midriff, seemingly uninterested in the current styles.

Perhaps the oddest aspect was that we were supposed to believe she was the artist who would be tattooing us when every inch of her greatly exposed skin was devoid of any marks. Not a single tattoo in sight. I was becoming more anxious with each passing minute.

"Are you…are you the artist here?" I muttered.

"Don't look so disappointed."

Before I could even get the words out, Versa chimed in with the same thing I had been thinking.

"But you don't have any tattoos," she said with a concerned look.

With an indifferent tone, the female said, "I'm covered in tattoos, maybe you're just not looking hard enough."

My eyes widened with her admission. Was she glamouring us? That was the only way to explain her claim.

She waved us toward the back of the shop with a look of annoyance, like she'd had this discussion many times before.

"My tattoos are for myself, and those I choose to let see them." She pointed at the chair.

I eyed Versa, trying to give her a look that said stop staring.

"I'm Taran. Now that the pleasantries are over, what are we doing today?"

I could hear Versa snort at the curt introduction. I supposed she had the personality I'd expect from someone who had to deal with all kinds of unique patrons.

I tried to sound confident in my decision. It had only come to me a short moment ago, and already, I was beginning to doubt myself. I really should have spent more time thinking it through.

"I think I'd like the three moons of Demir."

She showed no reaction to my request.

"Where?"

"Uh...behind my ear, if that's alright?"

I figured it would be easy to conceal with my hair in most styles, and that way I wouldn't have to deal with any sort of scolding from my parents or outside judgment in the future. I thought back to Trace's massive tattoo covering his arm, and it made me wonder if he was ever treated differently for it. He wasn't a member of the king's court like we were, so it was unlikely. A different life, with different expectations.

Taran nudged me to lie down on the table with the side of my head angled toward her and the sunlight beaming through the window. I lay there facing my sister, preparing for what, I didn't know. I wasn't sure how painful this was going to be, but she held my hand for courage regardless.

I could feel Taran move my hair aside and gently run her fingers behind my ear. A shiver ran down my spine with a flashback of Trace and his breath.

"Why'd you choose the three moons of Demir?" Versa asked.

"You'll probably think this is silly, but one moon for each member of my family: Father, Mother, and you. And because when I'm away at sea, they will be my constant. Depending on where they are in the sky, I'll always know which direction leads home."

Before I could finish my words, Versa added, "Like true north, guiding you back to us."

I could feel the stinging in my eyes as I fought back the tears; she had no idea how much I wanted that to be true.

Taran asked, "You ready?" I nodded and Versa squeezed my hand tighter.

From the mirror on the wall, I could see Taran begin to work. She closed her eyes and raised both her hands, palms facing inward. She began to move her hands slowly in what looked like an intricate and delicate dance, and as they swayed in unique patterns in front of her, I felt it. A burning, heavy sensation behind my ear.

Though I couldn't see it, I could feel every single piece of the design come into reality. My palm was sweaty in Versa's hand and I squeezed hard, attempting to ignore the pain while also relishing the unique sensation. A cross between tiny blades slicing and a hot burning, like a brand. I couldn't have been more thrilled to have picked such a tiny design, because despite the beautiful movement of Taran's hands in the mirror, I knew without a doubt I could not handle this feeling much longer.

I tried to imagine someone doing this to her; covering her entire body, and the pain she would have endured to achieve that. If I had gone through that I would probably be showing off every inch of my art to the entire world, so they knew just how strong I was.

When Taran dropped her hands and opened her eyes, I could feel the burning subside. She grabbed a small can of salve and dabbed a bit across the new tattoo behind my ear. The sting that lingered was minor, and the cooling salve was already doing its work. Versa grabbed a small mirror and held it up above so I could see. There it was, just like I had imagined, three tiny crescent moons hugging each other nestled behind my ear. It was perfect.

"Your turn," Taran directed Versa, who laid down where I had just been. "What'll it be for you?"

"I hadn't come up with anything half as good as what you did, Cress, but I love it. Would you mind if I get the same?"

Honestly, I hadn't thought there was a chance she'd even go through with this, and I certainly didn't mind the idea of hers matching mine.

"Of course not," I replied gladly.

Suddenly, Versa sat up and rotated, "But I want mine on the opposite ear. She is my other half, after all."

I was grateful Versa was now facing away from me because there was a swelling tightness building in my chest, and I was doing everything possible not to cry at her words.

I held Versa's hand as she did mine, and as Taran began her beautiful movements once more, I heard Versa's cracked whisper, "I hope it does lead you back to me."

I swallowed the lump in my throat and squeezed her hand tighter, unable to utter a single word.

CHAPTER
12

Matching tattoos with Versa accomplished checking another item off my list, making the time I spent at home with family still feel like progress. I did my very best to make those days feel as normal as possible. For them and for myself. I had realized that if someday Versa learned of my implied death, these were the days she'd think back on. I wanted them to be happy ones for her. Not ones where I hid away because I couldn't get my grief or anger in check.

Even though my mother and father knew where I was truly headed, they had no idea the outcome and never would. For them, too, these would be our last days together, and I wanted to show my gratitude for the amazing life they had given me.

I ate all my meals with at least one of them. Most dinners involved all of us together, just like when I was young. Midway through the week a letter was delivered to me, and I carried it back to my room to open in private. When I saw the crest on the wax seal, I knew exactly who it was from. Gris did not waste an inch of parchment with hollow greetings or misguided flattery.

Cress—

Maybe we don't have to wait another seventy-five years… I know this isn't what you were expecting, and it's not what you asked of me. I haven't stopped thinking of you since you left. Everything feels different for me (now). I know you're leaving, and I couldn't bring myself to say all this in person in case you could not return the feelings. I needed to tell you before you left. I'm not asking you to stay, but I need you to know I'd wait for you; just say the word. If by chance you felt something too, send a reply by letter and I'll come to see you off. But if I do not hear from you, then I will assume you do not return my affections and I wish you safe travels as my true friend, until I see you again.

Yours, Gris

I had been unconsciously holding my breath while reading every word, again and again. I couldn't have felt any worse. This was exactly what I did not want to happen, and it was all my fault. Perhaps if I wasn't leaving, I'd have entertained this. If…if I hadn't met Trace. I was still in shock that Gris had put himself out there like this. This was very uncharacteristic of him. He was too prideful for something like this.

Anytime Gris was seeing someone, I was always the one pushing him to make his feelings known, teasing him that not everyone was going to read his mind just to get to the bottom of his true intentions.

No, this was very unlike him. I wanted to write him back, but only to apologize, tell him the truth, and let him change his sentiment from affection to disappointment; even disgust would be fitting and what I deserved. If he had known how I had used him, how I'd lied, he wouldn't feel this way. I had already moved on to all-consuming thoughts of another. What I had done was not honorable. He didn't deserve that.

I spent most of the afternoon deeply saddened in my room trying to decide what to do. There was no making this right without telling him the truth, which I could not do… By early evening, I had decided the best answer was no answer.

Like he said, if he didn't hear back then he'd assume my feelings weren't the same. I went to the fireplace in my bedroom, eyes watering, my hand shaking with nervous regret as I dropped the letter into the flames, watching it quickly shrivel and turn to ash.

If I had kept that letter, I might have looked at it every day until I left. I might have changed my resolve and wavered on what needed to be done. The idea of bringing pain to Gris had me spinning out with thoughts of Trace. Was I doing the same thing to him? Would my attractions lead me to an inescapable web? Had the silks already begun weaving?

I had the luxury of walking away from whatever destruction I left behind, they did not. There were times I had myself convinced that I wouldn't return to Trace, but there was an undeniable pull. It wasn't just physical. The intrigue ate away at me almost every night.

I wanted to know more about him. He had shared so little, and I could tell there was much more to him. He was always holding back, carefully crafting his responses while trying to come off nonchalant. But it was in the between moments where I saw glimpses of it. A small cracked grin, a tamed laugh, a tightened jaw, a quiet sadness. I was immensely curious to understand the enigma that was Trace.

To get through the days leading up to my return, I reminded myself that it was a choice. I had decided I would meet him as he requested, but I knew I had the freedom to alter my plans. It was these small reminders of freedom that brought me a reprieve from the fact that it dwindled with each passing day.

I spent the next two days helping my mother and sister with wedding activities. Cake tasting was one thing I was not disappointed to partake in. My mother kept giving me disapproving looks as I finished off every full piece of cake, which they had only sampled. It's funny how pleasurable things could be when you didn't care.

One evening, I joined my father privately in his study. I found it hard to spend time with him, and I think he knew why. The unspoken guilt of what he was about to put me through. The helplessness spanned his every feature, making him appear gaunt. When he saw me enter the room, closing the door behind me, my heart fluttered at the small bit of warmth that returned to his expression.

He spoke cautiously, unsure of himself. I was pained by the uncomfortable energy wafting between us.

"I'm, uh, glad you've decided to join me."

I nodded. "I've been very busy, but I've missed you."

I offered him what I could in the way of verbal affection, so that he knew this was not easy on me either. The awkward silence stood between us, making the air seem stale. I struggled to reconcile this foreign sentiment between he and I, all our other encounters having been so warm and effortless.

Remembering how I had been meaning to bring up Mother's recent treatment of the staff, I mentioned, "Have you noticed how rude Mother has been toward the servants? It's really unacceptable."

He sighed before answering. "Your mother has been… Well, she is struggling. She should not be taking it out on the others as she has been, but you must know how hard this is for her. Even if she isn't open enough to discuss it with you directly. Your mother is not accustomed to being denied what she wants—keeping her daughter."

I hadn't realized that maybe her behavior had more to do with losing me than the stresses of the wedding. Since we hadn't really spoken of the Offering, I had begun to feel like she'd accepted my fate more than either me or my father.

My father could see the contemplation in my expression.

"I don't think she has felt this powerless since I was kept away during the catastrophe at Erisas Bay. Let her process it all in her own way. Her distance is not directed at you, just as her outbursts toward the staff are not about them."

"I see your point," I answered.

"You know, Cress, I had hoped to give you what you wanted. You deserved to see the world. To sail the ocean by my side. I'm so sorry we waited…" He paused. "…We waited too long."

I rested my head on my hand, sharing that regret. "I know. It's not your fault, Father."

He looked over at his desk and shelf, full of books and maps.

"I would have loved for it all to be yours," he said with a choked smile.

My eyes widened as he continued, "I have always known you weren't going to choose the life of a High Lady, like your sister. You are wild and untamable. It would have been silly of me to try. You were meant for more, for adventure, just like me."

My father wasn't usually long-winded; I did my best to let him speak what was on his mind.

"I don't have much that brings me peace these days. I suppose I've spun a story in my head that you're headed off into a great adventure, an unknown that not even I have explored. That whatever you're doing for King Aeon will bring continued peace to all. That my daughter isn't offered, but chosen."

His eyes welled with tears, and he wiped them away on his shirt. My tears had betrayed me as well. I wanted to believe my father's words, desperately. This romanticized version of what was happening to me, to them. Instead of fighting it, I let us both believe, in that moment, that it was true. He would never know if it was or wasn't. I would let him have this.

"I think so, too, Father. I will make you proud. I promise."

He smiled back at me through wet lashes, making his eyes sparkle like emeralds in the firelight. The same eyes I bore.

The raw emotion between us fashioned an opening, and before I knew it, I had begun an onslaught of questions that had been locked away in my mind for days.

"How many other sons and daughters do you think will arrive with me?" I asked quietly, just in case prying ears were listening.

My father looked pained, like he wanted to offer me answers he didn't have.

"I'm not entirely sure. There aren't many High Court families left to begin with. Not since the war. That goes for Royal and Honored members. The age of conscription is twenty. Our honored allies in House Huxley and House Kasparov have children too young to conscript."

I clung to his every word for any bit of information that I could deem valuable.

"I have no idea if it's true, but rumor amongst the High Court is that they do not accept those who are with child or raising children under the age of conscription. One can also assume they only accept those in good health," he said.

I rolled my eyes; obviously, to protect and continue the bloodlines. Legacy and heirs above all else, right? Thinking through what he had said about how few families made up the court, I wondered to myself how many of those included ones with children younger than twenty.

Is that what I had to do to be excluded, just get myself pregnant? The pieces swirled in my mind like a puzzle as I tried to make sense of what was happening. Young, but not too young. Free of obligations like giving birth or raising children. Healthy. Independent. High Fae. Well, so far, they had me pegged.

"Is there anything else you've heard?" I questioned, hopeful for more information.

"It is said that the Offering came about because the first king of our lands was faced with a dire decision. One that required him to offer up all of his sons and daughters. They were referred to as the Forgotten Fae."

My eyes widened at the horrible thought of a father giving away all of his children. But I remained silent and let my father continue.

"Henceforth, the king decreed that all families of the High Court would be required to make tribute as well, if called upon. Every family complied to show their gratitude for the great sacrifice, and it's been upheld ever since."

I took a deep breath, trying to fathom how many years back this had gone, wondering how many times the Offering had been called, how many faces and names were lost to time.

"Father, is there anything else you can tell me? Perhaps you have some books or texts on our histories?"

I prayed he had something that I could scour for more information, anything at all that might give me more insight regarding what was in store for me or that I could use to further decipher Aster's words.

"Sadly, no. On this matter, little more is known, for the knowledge is protected and dangerous to seek." He leaned forward and lowered his voice.

"I need to tell you something, Cress. You must protect yourself. At all costs. I don't care what you've been taught about etiquette, using your abilities, being a lady. None of that means anything now. Just please be careful, and survive. Now is not the time to hold back. Guard everything, including your heart."

I had never heard my father use such a direct tone with me. There was no longer sadness or worry, just intensity burning with a protectiveness that I knew had always existed in him but rarely needed to be shown. Before me was one of the guild leaders who had survived the Seafarer rebellion, who had encountered all sorts of vicious creatures and peoples along his travels and returned without a scratch. His words became brands in my mind. I spent the rest of the evening in his study, silently thumbing through random books and maps by his side.

We no longer offered each other words, only the comfort of one another's company. A scene we had played out many times before, when he was preparing for travels or returning from them. Together in the study, we could pore over the things that excited us. Things that were a bore to Versa and my mother. This was ours.

Outside these walls, there was expectation and tradition. But alongside my father is where the dream of a life at sea was born. I kissed my father on the cheek before heading to bed.

That night, I tossed and turned in bed with the complicated decision of whether or not I'd spend the next morning packing things to make the return trip to Trace, or continue to play out my remaining days at home.

With the normalcy of daily life, the house felt more like home again. My leaving and all the lies we'd told no longer had to be the center of attention. With that, my anxiety and tension subsided.

When I awoke the next morning, I felt free and clear-minded. For the past few days, I'd wrestled with the decision of whether or not I'd return to Trace. Gris's letter did not help ease my resolve. Once again, I couldn't help but ask myself if I was I putting Trace in the same position, where I'd leave him wanting more than I could give? What mental state was I putting myself in, knowing I had developed deeper feelings? I knew this now, because each day apart, the longing and doubt ate away at my every thought.

Even though I had made my mind up to return to Trace and fill the void of his absence, I was able to be present at breakfast. I enjoyed witnessing the playful flirting between my mother and father. No matter the years that passed, their love for one another was obvious. I silently hoped the same for Versa and her betrothed. That her love would be a great one. But I would not have this luxury.

The gift of time and some long-drawn-out love story wouldn't be mine. But I did have this—whatever this thing was—with Trace. I would relish that.

I gathered a much larger pack this time, filling it with more than a handful of undergarments, which made me smile to myself when folding. I wouldn't be caught without them or smelling like pond water again. I was preparing to be gone for at least a week. I didn't have a clue what he had in mind or how long he'd want to spend together, but I was going to make sure I was prepared. I included a handful of toiletries, but nothing fancy to keep up the charade that I did not come from wealth.

Versa came into my room as I was preparing my things. I had already warned her that I was going to go back to him and that I might stay longer than last time. She did not try to dissuade me, and only teased me to exercise some self-control this time. Each time she joked, I rolled my eyes.

I wished her luck with the nuptial planning and encouraged her to pay a visit to her betrothed. She was all in a tizzy about adhering to the customs of not seeing him in the couple of months leading up to the event, but I said, *What would a bride that wears two dresses do?* She couldn't argue with that.

In her world, all of these things like tradition, customs, and expectations still carried weight. To me, they now seemed silly and meaningless. I knew she wasn't able to relate, but that didn't mean I couldn't encourage a little recklessness. Before leaving my room, I took one last glance at what remained on the list.

~~Lose my maidenhead~~
~~Seduce a stranger~~
~~Gamble till I win~~
~~Get drunk~~
Alter my appearance
~~Help someone in need~~
~~Get a tattoo~~
~~Do something that scares me~~
Swim naked in the moonslight
Say my goodbyes

I was too embarrassed to explain to our parents why they might not see me for a little while. Though they likely wouldn't pry, I told Versa to cover for me and I'd go along with whatever lie she made up.

Once more, the stable hand prepared Rain with the unmarked saddle that had become standard for these solo trips. Together we took off into a sprint through the forest, and I was overcome with the anticipation of finally returning to Trace after what felt like the shortest and longest week of my life.

(Nineteen Days Remain)

There he was, leaning against the large oak tree beside the tavern as I approached, and the sight of him took my breath away. I assessed him fondly from a distance. Admiring the utterly casual state of him. It was a pleasant vision to see him so relaxed. Trace always seemed uptight and tense. Probably comes with the territory of serving in the Kingsguard. This time, he seemed at ease. I was half tempted to not even approach, but that feeling that had called me back to him all along was now burning stronger than ever.

He looked up as I approached on Rain, and I blushed at the small, almost unnoticeable smile in my direction. Relief washed over me with the confirmation that he was happy I had returned. When I stopped by his side, he stepped up to help me off my horse—not that I needed it. Another protective gesture that I allowed with no complaint.

Our faces were positioned closely as I looked up into those intense eyes I had missed, noting the strong cleft in his handsome chin.

"Miss me?" I questioned.

"Like the eels miss darkness," he replied teasingly.

It did him no favors to remind me of the line he had crossed, and I recollected the promise of payback I had made him.

"What's the plan?" I tried not to sound overly eager. I was desperate to be alone with him again, but I exercised what little self-control remained and waited for his answer.

"I was thinking, a quick bite to eat and then we ride to our destination. It's a surprise, so don't even try to interrogate me."

My interest was more than piqued by the proposition.

After lunch, Rain and I followed Alcar and Trace. He had warned the ride would take a bit and to yell if I needed a break. I took note that he did not have a large pack attached to his horse like I did mine, and was quickly becoming self-conscious that I had assumed too boldly how much time we'd spend together.

An hour or so passed, and the verdant foliage and russet underbrush of the surrounding forest blurred together like watercolors. As we increased our speed, the once gentle breeze now whipped into a frenzy, and I narrowed my eyes to keep focused on Trace.

When we finally slowed, confusion set in. I did not see any visible shelter. Not an inn, a house, or even a tent. I would have settled for a tent over nothing. I dismounted and began to meander about, seeking any signs of why we were there. Trace stood impatiently underneath a massive tree and ushered me to his side with a gesture.

"Look up," he said with a twinge of excitement I hadn't yet heard.

To my utter surprise, above me was a small tree house. Hidden by thick leaves and branches, you had to be standing right underneath to take notice of it.

"How did you find this? *What* is this?" I questioned in amazed curiosity.

"This is a haven. Left behind from the war."

My eyes widened. "Like a safe house?"

"Basically," Trace confirmed. "These are scattered throughout the land and served as a place of refuge for the military when they needed it."

He reached up, untying a rope that unfolded into a ladder and created an entrance.

He pointed at it. "Ladies first."

I gave him an uneasy smile but withheld any judgment. I had climbed trees in my youth, but had never been inside any kind of treehouse or otherwise. When I got to the bottom of the structure, I pushed up on a flat door that opened into the main—and only—room. I was grateful I hadn't worn a dress, even though I toyed with the idea, thinking it might have been flattering for my figure; something I had rarely considered before Trace.

I glanced around the space, taking it in before watching Trace make his way up through the same door on the floor. It was a bit amusing trying to see someone of his size fit through that tiny opening, but he made it work, nonetheless.

On one side was a small stovepipe, a shelf for storage, a small table with two chairs. I took special note of the only bed, no bigger than the one at the inn. The space was plain in every sense of the word. No frills, decoration, or non-necessities. Which made sense given he had said it was a military haven, not some kind of retreat.

Trace waved his hand to encompass the space.

"It's not much, but it's why I needed a week. I couldn't bring you here in its prior condition. Pretty sure you would have killed me."

I tried to imagine a condition any plainer than this.

"Me? I'm still unsure you're not the one who's going to do the killing. Given the fact that you've brought me to the middle of nowhere, as far as I can tell. No one would even hear me scream."

I realized the unintentional innuendo as soon as the words left my mouth, and Trace's devious smile was a confirmation of that.

"I was tired of the males in the bar gawking at you. Figured we could enjoy some privacy. Plus, I have some other surprises up my sleeve. That is, if you play your cards right."

"They were not gawk—" he cut off my protest with a kiss.

Grabbing my chin and pulling me into him, suddenly I didn't care where we were because this was what I had longed for. This was worth the wait of every agonizing day apart. He pulled away first, leaving me breathless and hazy.

"Privacy is good," I admitted, defeated.

Trace helped me bring up my pack and find places for my things alongside his, like we both lived here. He didn't have a lot, a few changes of clothing, more weapons than I cared to take note of, and a leather-bound book that caught my attention. I was almost certain it was a sketchbook, and I was going to make it my mission to see what was hidden inside of it.

He had already stocked the place with food and water. The only thing eating away at me was the absence of a washroom. I didn't want to upset him by making mention of it; so, I kept the concern to myself for now.

It was only a short time before the twilight hour arrived and Trace encouraged us to eat again before he unveiled the next surprise. He was always insistent about eating, drinking water, and taking care of oneself. I don't know that I'd ever get used to this rigid and regimented behavior that was ingrained in him. On one hand, I felt cared for, and maybe a little controlled, but in a way that I found oddly satisfying.

When darkness veiled the area, he led us by lantern light a small distance from the haven. When we approached the destination, my breath hitched.

Before me was a small body of water, blanketed in moonslight. But it wasn't the light that stole my breath. It sparkled, actually shimmered, as if lit from within. I had only ever read about springs like this. They were rare, so much so that I had just accepted that I'd likely never see one in person.

From my studies, I knew they were unique hot springs, and that the minerals in the pool created the luminescence that I was now enamored with.

"Surprise," Trace said nonchalantly, with a smirk I could faintly detect in the dim glow radiating off the water.

Next thing I knew, he began stripping down. I watched as he removed his shirt, as if in slow motion, revealing that body that I craved. My eyes trailed down the length of his tattoo. Without a second of hesitation or doubt, he removed his pants, unveiling a fully naked Trace in all his glory.

There wasn't a hint of embarrassment on his face, and I envied the confidence. My mouth watered with desire as he strode casually to the edge of the pool and lowered himself into the steamy abyss of the water.

"Just in case you wanted me to prove it, there are no eels."

He pushed himself back from the edge, casually wading deeper. Waiting for me to join him.

A bath sounded truly amazing, and I was grateful to have fewer concerns about a washroom knowing we had this nearby. Relief set in, and I made my way to the edge of the water where I was certain Trace could see me. If he was going to give me a show, then I was going to do the same.

I slowly began undressing in front of him, removing each item piece by piece until there was nothing remaining, all the while, holding him with my gaze. I could see him lick his lips in anticipation. I stood there for a moment longer, naked, moonslight reflecting off my pale skin, letting him appreciate the sight of me. Letting the want build between us.

I stepped gently into the pool, lowering myself into the warmth, trying to stay focused on him. I had to admit it was hard, being distracted by the magic of the water as I was. Magic was the only word to describe the intoxicating beauty of the shimmer, swirls, and glow. The comfort of the hot spring only made it that much more enjoyable. The pool of water wasn't very deep, making it easy to wade in some areas and stand in others.

Trace made his way closer to me and, despite the heat of the spring, I could feel goosebumps all along my skin that hovered above the waterline. I tried to think of something cheeky to say, to taunt him with, but before I could, Trace said huskily, "Don't speak. I missed this."

His lips crashed into mine with more intensity than the last time we were together. Our bare bodies intertwined naturally as I wrapped both my legs around his waist, feeling his excitement pressing at my entrance. I was frantic and greedy, intoxicated by every sweep of his tongue against mine.

The warmth of the water cradled our bodies, making me tilt my head back toward the night sky, and he ran his lips across my throat with fervor. He gathered my hair at the nape, fisting it in his hands, pulling my face every which way to kiss all parts of me. My lips, throat, ears, neck, shoulders. I could wait no longer to feel him and as he palmed my breasts greedily, I let out a pleasurable gasp of his name, "Trace!"

He answered when I called for him. With one fierce thrust, he was now inside me, consuming me. He pushed me against the edge of the pool as our bodies writhed. His mouth grazed my nipples, gently, teasingly, and then forcefully with small bites. The back and forth of soft pleasure and pain was indescribable.

This time would be different; I knew how to find my pleasure. To exert self-control and release at the same time. All this time apart had built up to this, and it did not take long for us to find our climax, together. We stayed there in the water, still entwined, chests rising and falling together. As we caught our breath, I could not possibly imagine myself anywhere else than in his arms.

When we returned to the haven house some time later, I was tired. The weight of the day and reuniting with Trace in every way had brought me to a state of exhaustion. We dried off, changed into comfortable loose garments to sleep in, dimmed the lanterns, and crawled into the bed.

Cradled in the nook of Trace's warm chest, I let myself relax and listen to the soft rustling of the wind and trees like a lullaby. Trace leaned in and whispered, "I have another surprise."

My eyes were heavy, and I didn't think I could handle anything more today. Trace sat up, and behind him, near the headboard, he tugged a tiny rope that led to the roof above us. A small skylight opened, creating a view straight to the doorway of the Gods, to the stars. I couldn't believe what I was looking at.

It was magnificent; the view of bright twinkling lights, but none were as bright as the three moons of Demir. Trace ran his finger gently along the back of my ear; I had forgotten about my tattoo!

"I was going to save this for tomorrow night, but then I saw this new addition." He smirked.

"Oh, yeah," I replied bashfully. I did not want to talk about Versa, otherwise I might not be able to keep the emotions at bay. Instead, I coyly asked, "Do you like it?"

"There's not much I don't like when it comes to you," he said, nibbling on the tip of my earlobe. I could feel the throbbing ache of desire beginning, but I could not let this go there again. Once was enough this evening; I was still recovering.

"It's amazing. The view, thank you."

Luckily, Trace took the hint that I was not going to survive a second round and relaxed back into the bed. We lay there in silence for a long while. My eyelids were heavy as Trace twirled the ends of my hair in his fingers. Such an odd thing to witness, knowing how far I'd come in breaking through that hard exterior from when we first met.

Trace reminded me that if I awoke and he wasn't beside me, not to worry, he was likely just sitting in the chair or had made his way outside to relax beneath the tree. Yes, old habits die hard, I remembered.

Before he'd let me succumb to sleep, he nudged me playfully. "Cress, five questions?"

Before I could protest he said, "Nothing too difficult, I know I may lose you here any minute."

I couldn't fathom how he was still wide awake and I was on the verge of letting sleep take me. I nodded in agreement, unable to deny him almost anything he asked. He proceeded to make his way through a handful of light questions, and to make it easy on my tired mind, he provided them all and we both just answered.

Small insignificant things like our favorite season, favorite meal, and I recollected drifting off into slumber as I told him my new favorite scent was him.

❮❮❮✦

When I woke in the morning, Trace was not there. But this time I wasn't alarmed. I dressed myself, unaware of what the day would entail, and found my attention drawn once more to the leather sketchbook sitting on the table. I seized the opportunity and began to thumb through it. The whole front half were drawings of landscapes. Trace may not have ever shown anyone, but he was quite gifted.

They were made of charcoal, devoid of color, but I could still imagine the sunsets he had seen, the mountaintops and riverbends; many wondrous places. Signs he was well-traveled, and I was struck with a jealousy I had not expected.

Just as I had planned to set the book down, I turned the page and there it was: a sketch, not of a landscape, but of a female. She was peacefully sleeping, and it was like staring in a mirror. Trace had drawn *me*. I didn't know when. Maybe last night, possibly before at the inn? Just like the landscape, it was well done.

I closed the book quickly and set it back on the table, feeling partly ashamed for snooping, but also satisfied at having found myself in the position of being his muse. There were no other sketches of people, just me.

In the days that passed, we enjoyed each other's company in all ways. Often the silence between us said more than words. This was our language. Everything we could not or would not say, we showed in the way we knew how. Without restraint.

By now, I had memorized every inch of Trace's body. We'd continued our escapades in the tree house and on our visits to the hot spring. Anywhere, as we often found ourselves unable to exert any semblance of control.

At dinner, we'd play a game of five questions and, for the most part, I could be honest. Now and then I'd have to change an answer ever so slightly to avoid giving myself away as someone more affluent or educated than I was pretending to be. We'd hunt, and I'd act like I was a worse shot than I was. Granted, I had never needed to hunt, but I knew how to hit a target, even a moving one.

If I were being honest with myself, these days of playing house with Trace were perhaps the most normal I'd felt since the news of the Offering. The importance of the list was unusually far from my mind.

(THIRTEEN DAYS REMAIN)

I sought out my revenge on Trace's prank about a week into my visit. When I was young, I learned a trick with Rain that sent my parents into a near panic. It consisted of pretending I had fallen off my horse and hurt myself, when in actuality, it was an acrobatic feat that I'd practiced many times with Versa as my audience.

We were riding together, with me trailing a short distance behind Trace and Alcar. Close enough, though, that they'd hear a commotion and stop. As planned, Rain slowed a little, stood on his hind legs, let out a deafening squeal and I "fell" and rolled to the ground. Like clockwork, Trace turned just in time to see enough of the act that looked real from a distance.

I lay there, not moving, pretending to be completely knocked out when Trace galloped to me, lunging to my side. I could feel the horror emanating from him. I reveled in his fear, remembering the exact moment I had tried to escape the flesh-eating eels.

He held me in his arms, cradling my face, asking over and over again, "Cress, Cress, are you okay? Wake up!"

When I finally decided he'd had enough torture, I opened my eyes wide and smiled directly up at him. Now that my eyes were open, I could see the concern and fear settled deep in his brow. He was scared. Had I truly rattled him that badly? The look on his face when he saw me smile and knew what I had done in jest was a mixture of relief and an inexplicable anger that I'd never encountered.

Before I could respond, Trace had lifted me like I weighed nothing, hoisted me over his shoulder, and began carrying me toward a nearby tree.

"You want to play damsel in distress?" he said with an eerily calm ferocity.

"You deserved it!" I tried to sound playful to offset the intensity radiating from him.

Trace set me down and turned me toward the tree, facing away from him. My body was limp and pliable as I let him have his way, unsure of exactly where this was headed. I began to look over my shoulder to peer in his direction. "Don't look at me. Don't move a muscle," he ordered.

I heard him rip the fabric from the sleeve of his shirt, tear it in two, and suddenly, a strip of cloth was being wrapped tightly across my eyes, blindfolding me. Another piece quickly found its way across my mouth. I had been so distracted by the urgency of his actions, I didn't have time to process if I was scared or turned on.

I trusted him completely, but this was all truly surprising. After some brief rustling noises, I felt the feeling of worn leather binding my hands tightly behind my back. Now the nerves were setting in as bit-by-bit Trace rendered me helpless.

The forest seemed still and silent. I could feel the hot, heavy breath of Trace's lips near the back of my ear, hovering close to my neck. He used his knee to nudge my feet into a wider stance.

"That was a very big mistake, Cress," was all he said in a low, almost predatory manner.

My body was becoming hot with desire; the suspense of not being able to see, speak, or use my hands was alluring. Trace reached his arm around my waist, taking no time at all to plunge his hand down the front of my trousers and run his long, rigid fingers along my slippery heat.

I arched my body into him, seeking more. He began to draw pleasure from me in rapid circles, my ragged breaths inaudible through the gag. I could feel myself reaching a climax, as he did not relent, and just as I was meeting my end he stopped and removed his hand, leaving me practically aching for him. Why would he do this to me?

"Are you distressed?" he asked, toying with me.

I whimpered with a nod. He turned me around so I was now facing him, but alas, I could still see nothing beyond this blindfold. My fingertips itched to touch him. He yanked my boots from my feet, removed my pants swiftly, and if it weren't for the absolute certainty that we were utterly alone in the middle of nowhere, I'd have feared for my propriety.

Trace was now clearly on his knees before me as he swung one of my legs over his shoulder, forcing me to balance on the other. A near-impossible task as I was still trembling from minutes before. And then his mouth was consuming me.

Firm brushes of his tongue, light flicks across my center, his fingers working me into a frenzy. I had nothing to steady myself. My hands were rendered useless. I leaned into the amazing feeling of his mouth against me, and in minutes, I was chasing that climax again. I could feel the intensity of it building and once more, as I thought I would topple over the edge—he stopped.

Once more he deprived me of his touch, of the sensation. All of my muscles tightened, building with the anxiety of being taken close to release and then denied.

"Are you distressed?" he asked again.

If only I could see, I was more than certain there would have been an absolutely sinister look on his handsome face. I was unbelievably distressed—so much so that the aching was borderline painful, and I could feel the beginning of stinging tears hovering below my lashes beneath the blindfold.

Once more, Trace turned my half-naked body to face the tree, away from him, and wedged his knee between my legs to spread them. I heard the unbuckling of his belt and the sound was that of salvation. I yearned to feel every inch of him inside of me, to set me free from this torturous build-up.

Trace forcefully bent me over, taking me abruptly and without warning. His thrusts, short and rapid, had me taking deep breaths through my nose, as I could not get enough air with the cloth gag in my mouth. The lightheadedness caused by this created an unnatural, almost euphoric sensation.

He punished me with a vigor I had never felt from Trace. If he did not bring me to an end soon, I was going to fully collapse. I had already been bracing most of my weight into the tree in front of me, the rough bark irritating my skin, a sensation that could only be ignored by the countering force of Trace. His pace edged me toward eruption and as I tightened all around him, the bastard did it again.

He stopped. Standing completely still, unmoving, but inside of me and he began to slowly pull out.

"Are you distressed?" he panted the words in my ear.

I nodded yes, anything to get him to stop this cruel madness. I felt him untie the fabric gagging my mouth and when it fell to the ground, I took in deep heaping breaths for the first time since this all had begun. He spun me around, facing forward now, but still blinded.

"Say my name," he commanded.

My dry lips rasped, "Trace."

When I did as he asked, he gripped my leg, wrapping it around him. Trace placed himself at my entrance, holding himself there. He teased me with a fraction of his length, refusing to push past the threshold.

"Again."

I licked my lips. "Trace."

He pushed himself into me just a little farther. I wanted more, all of him. I craved the true fullness that I had seconds ago.

"Are you sorry?"

Yes. Yes, is all I wanted to scream, because never had I imagined pretending to fall off a horse would have led me to this game of unrelenting, sensuous torture. But I knew what he wanted.

"I'm sorry…" I paused, letting the silence fill the air between us, "Trace."

The sound of his name once more drew him to me, fully filling me, and he pounded into my core with a rapid pace, carrying me with him to a climax that he finally allowed both of us. It culminated with his lips pressed against mine for the first time since he had rendered me helpless. I collapsed into him fully, unable to hold myself up any longer.

In contrast to his earlier intensity, Trace gently removed my remaining bonds and dressed me carefully and slowly. He took note of my exhausted state and brought me water. He pulled my disheveled hair back and tied it with the ripped fabric that had previously veiled my eyes.

Once we were somewhat presentable, I looked at Rain, and the mere thought of having enough strength to ride seemed unfathomable. Trace let out a small laugh and shook his head in disbelief.

"You'll saddle with me and I'll tether Rain. I'm not letting you fall off your horse for real this time."

I didn't have the will or energy to argue with him. Not after what he'd just put me through. He hoisted me up onto Alcar and saddled behind me, holding my body tight and close to him the entire way back to the haven house.

"You need a good warm soak this evening, you're going to be very sore."

That night we lay in bed together staring out the skylight at the stars. This was our usual activity after dinner and a game of five questions.

"I've always loved the stars, they're one of my few constants and bring me solace." There was an air of sadness in Trace's admission.

"The stars are like seeing something that's already gone, it's terribly sad," I said before realizing it was highly unlikely someone who was less educated would know anything about the astronomical sciences. They believe the light we see is actually from stars long dead, only just now reaching us. I changed the subject immediately.

The days with Trace blurred together, and if I could, I would have bottled up that brief time of happiness for eternity. As my freedom dwindled, I tried to ignore the overwhelming feeling that I awoke to each morning. More pictures of me appeared in the sketchbook, but he never showed me directly. I only ever saw them when I had a chance to sneak a glance.

I had planned to spend at least a week with Trace, but now, one week didn't feel like nearly enough. I wrestled with the desire to stay as close to him for as long as possible and the need to see my family. Before I left, things at home were manageable, but that didn't mean there weren't hard days. My father withered more each time I saw him, his appearance falling further into disarray. My mother remained distant, unless it involved wedding plans, allowing her to placate herself with a semblance of normalcy. Keeping up the lie in front of Versa was the worst of it all, though.

As my feelings for Trace intensified, I found myself daydreaming in bouts of jealousy of what my sister would get to have with her betrothed. Sure, there were moments where we all successfully pretended like it wasn't eating us alive…but there were others where any one of us appeared as if we were about to crack. I was keeping it together for them, they were keeping it together for Versa, but *I* was the one who was keeping it all together for me. Here, with Trace, it was much easier to ignore. I loved them dearly, and maybe I'd spend the rest of my life missing them, but I relished in this escape where I was the center of attention for all the right reasons, instead of for what awaited me at home.

I had made it known to Trace when I needed to part ways, noting that I had a fair distance to travel to meet up with my new crew. He reluctantly acknowledged that he, too, would need to return to his post soon. Together, we set a date, knowing that in a week this would all come to an end, and I could tell leading up to that we were both eager to ignore it as much as possible.

There were days where we spent more time locked in one another's embrace than doing anything else, hidden away under the canopy of the treehouse, fugitives from sunlight. We teased each other to the brink of madness in the pools of the hot spring, creating swirls of luminescence with each passionate exchange. We were determined to defy time; too certain our nights were endless; too foolish to know it wasn't true.

The night before we departed, there was no way to hide from reality, to delay the coming of the dawn.

"I think I've been falling for you since the moment I saw you, how could I not?" Trace said.

It was unexpected. He was just offering up his truth from seemingly nowhere. The candor of it caught me off guard. I remembered when Trace said he had been watching me all night at the tavern when we first met. Though our first interactions were not the smoothest, I replayed them often in my head to remind myself of how far we'd come in such little time. How oddly connected I felt to him. Unable to accept the weight of his words, I remained silent.

He half joked, half pleaded, "We could both just run away from our obligations, but there would be consequences."

"Yes, consequences…" I said, dismayed, thinking of Versa and what would happen to her if I made such a selfish decision.

"Wherever you're going…I want you to be happy. Don't wait for me, Cress. Kingsguards' wives make for lonely widows. Just promise me you'll go and be happy."

He had no idea how much I reciprocated that sentiment. I was leaving to Gods-knew-where or what, and I wanted to be mature enough to believe that if I couldn't have Trace, then I wanted him to be happy as well. I think we knew now was the time for words, because in the morning there would likely be none.

Tomorrow we'd say what we needed to, without words. That night we didn't sleep. Beneath the stars, surrounded by the sounds of tiny woodland creatures, we made passionate love to one another over and over. It felt different than all the other times before. It felt like goodbye.

I dreaded the orange and yellow hues of sunrise peeking through what little light the tree branches allowed into the haven house. I looked around the tiny room, at all its simplicity, grateful for the memories he and I had made. He made me breakfast and packed my things for me, giving Rain a few gentle encouraging pats along his mane. I was lost in thought for much of the morning. Staring at Trace, trying to commit every possible detail to memory.

He kissed me deeply, neither of us wanting to be the first to pull away. He hoisted me up to the saddle, though by now he knew I did not need the help. But he liked doing it, so I didn't protest.

I sat there, gazing down at him, trying to keep the tears from falling. He grabbed my hand and placed a gentle kiss on my knuckles.

"I put something in your bag for you, for when you get wherever you're going, Cress."

He said my name as if he just wanted to hear himself say it one last time in my presence.

I gulped in the air to give myself time to say anything without my voice cracking, but it was impossible.

"Wherever you're going, think of me. When you're lonely or alone. I won't be forgetting you any time soon."

It was obvious the last remark broke me, and I kicked Rain into an urgent sprint as tears streamed down my face, unable to glance back even once.

CHAPTER 14

(Six Days Remain)

Painful. It was the only way to describe the entire trip home. My emotions ranged from numbness and rage to despair. It was a terrible mistake, to let myself feel like this. I didn't have anything else to compare to, and I was glad for it. My chest felt incredibly tight, like I was struggling for breath. I was so Gods-damned angry at what was happening to me. Why did I have to find Trace, why now? The silly list I'd made had delivered me into chaos of my own making. I had spent too much time by his side. Given too much of my heart. I would pay for this trespass for far too long.

When I arrived home, I absentmindedly handed Rain over to the stable boy then made my way through the manor in a fog, hoping to not see anyone. Back in my room, I was reluctant to unpack. I didn't want to know what he'd given me, and yet I ached to feel any sort of connection to him. When I opened the satchel, I saw a folded piece of parchment.

I knew what it was before I even unfolded it. A sketch of me, sleeping soundly with the stars above and my tattoo peeking out from behind a few strands of my hair. Below the drawing of me were a few words of handwritten text.

Like seeing something that's already gone.

The uncontrollable sob that wrenched forth from my heart was loud and desperate. Tears streamed down my cheeks, and before I knew it, Versa had rushed into the room. I quickly folded the piece of paper and shoved it back into the bag before she could take notice.

Without hesitation, she pulled me into her chest and let me hang limply in her arms and just cry for what was not meant to be. "What's wrong?" she asked, her voice laced heavily with concern.

I looked up at her, more tears welling in my eyes, and choked out, "I should not have gone back to him."

"It's okay, it's okay," Versa tried to console me. "Maybe you'll see him again when you return. You're not going to be gone forever!"

She had no idea how devastating those words were. I remained silent and continued to cry it out in her arms. When she finally thought she'd calmed me, she urged me to wash my face and try to join us at dinner, reminding me how much our parents had missed me these past couple weeks.

⟪⟪⟪✦

Dinner wasn't any easier. I could see the worn look on both my mother's and father's face. An expression that said they had spent the last two weeks imagining what it would be like without me. Neither looked like they'd slept in days, and I felt selfish for doing that to them. An air of awkward silence hung heavy in the room, only punctuated by the metallic scraping of cutlery on my mother's favorite dishes.

"We hope you enjoyed your time visiting friends," Mother finally said, following with a gulp of wine.

It was no coincidence that she had a decanter entirely her own, indicating this was one of those evenings she was going to drown her sorrows. Versa gave me an encouraging nod, implying that I should go along with it.

"I did, very much so," I replied, eying Father to discern if he was buying anything I was saying. "They're mostly excited for me, when they weren't complaining about how much fun I was going to miss by not being at the wedding." My sister smiled at me softly, as if to say *It's ok.*

"Yes, well, your sister and I made lots of progress while you were away, I'm sure she'll bring you up to speed on it before we have to leave."

I smiled at my mother, feigning interest in the update.

I could hear the hint of a crack in my father's voice. "Speaking of, we will be leaving in a day so your mother and I can properly escort you. It will take us awhile to reach our destination; we'll need to make haste."

"I thought we had more time?" Versa questioned. "I shall come with you."

"No!" my mother interjected without hesitation. "You must stay and oversee the household while we're away. I've made wedding appointments for you to tend to."

Versa gazed at me dejectedly.

The remainder of dinner was unpleasant; the uncomfortable silence settling back in until my mother inquired, "Cress, honey…what would you like for your farewell dinner? Chef D'eliar is eager to prepare you any of your favorites."

I turned to glance over my shoulder, eying a few of the wait staff, knowing my departure wasn't lost on them either. Just more people to miss me, more for me to miss.

"Tell him I appreciate it and to surprise me."

He'd never cooked a bad meal in this household, so I trusted him. And I wasn't about to treat this like my last meal.

"If you don't mind, I must excuse myself. I need to begin packing."

I pushed away from the table and noted each staff member performing a small bow as I passed. Two weeks away and I'd forgotten all about the pomp and circumstance of being a member of the court.

That evening, I attempted to get as much packing done as possible. This way, I could spend the next day with Versa and my parents. Plus, keeping myself busy made it easier to ignore how I was feeling. With no actual explanation of what I was headed into, I found it difficult to pack accordingly. Blouses, trousers, multiple sets of fighting and training leathers, undergarments—no frills—a few pairs of comfortable shoes, a modest dress—Gods knows for what—some basic toiletries—brush, hair ties, soap, hand mirror—perfume—perhaps for a formal event in one of the palaces—and a handful of other items that wouldn't take up too much space.

I figured what good were fighting leathers without weapons? I took a leather pouch and placed in it a couple of small blades and daggers that had been made specifically for me. I hadn't planned to take any jewelry, but in combing through my drawers, there was one piece that caught my eye. A tiny silver bracelet.

It was simple in every way. The braided chain featured no stones, only a small charm of a rose, Versa's favorite flower. This one little piece carried so much meaning. She and I both had matching ones adorned with the other's favorite flower. These were bracelets representing our sisterhood that we had given to each other on our tenth namesake. I had no idea if I'd be permitted to wear it, but I packed it anyway in an attempt to take a piece of Versa with me. Hopefully, I'd get by with my parents thinking I'd taken more than that when they noticed the other pieces that had gone mysteriously missing.

I looked at my collection of books, and it was crushing to accept that I likely couldn't bring more than one or two. I wanted to pretend that wherever I was going, I'd still be permitted such frivolities as time to read.

I made sure to pack my family medallion as my father had instructed, the weight of it heavier in my hand than I ever recalled it feeling before.

I tossed and turned most of the night, unable to get any rest until I'd finally become so exhausted that slumber took me without warning.

My final day at home began with a routine like any other normal morning. A long soak in the tub, styled my hair, dressed in something lovely—since this would probably be the last chance—and headed to breakfast.

Breakfast was my favorite meal of the day; which usually meant brunch, given I wasn't an early riser. Chef knew me too well. I indulged in every type of pastry. There was enough food on display for an entire party.

I spent the morning listening as Versa and my mother provided me updates on all the wedding decisions they had finalized while I was away. I smiled and nodded, giving no hint of disinterest; just one last day to soak in every boring detail of a simple life.

Lunchtime was another exercise in excess. Chef had prepared delightful tea sandwiches. They were scrumptious, but not as much as the petite cakes which I gorged myself on in a truly unladylike fashion. Fruit fillings and frostings, peach, apricot, pear—all fresh from our very own orchards.

That afternoon, I relaxed in the library reading a book; nearby, my father was captivated by the trade reports. Time passed quickly, and each chime of the clock echoed noticeably louder.

Before joining my mother and Versa for dinner, my father pulled me aside by my elbow.

"Did you pack your medallion as I requested?"

Our gazes remained close and locked; there was no discussion needed. The implication of the request was enough. I nodded and proceeded to dinner, pulling away from his grasp.

When I arrived in the dining hall, I was shocked to find a majority of the kitchen staff lining the walls dressed in their finest attire. Chef D'eliar stood at the head of the table and gave me a welcoming smile. As soon as we took our seats, a few of the staff stepped forward and placed soft white linen napkins across our laps. The formality of this all was absurd. I glanced at my mother and her wide-eyed stare said *Do not resist.*

Chef cleared his throat and pronounced loudly across the room, "My lady Cressida, it has been our honor to serve you all this time, from your youth and all through your days. You've blossomed before our eyes. We are sending you our best wishes as you head out on what will be an amazing journey, and we hope you return safely."

D'eliar gestured and the staff stepped forward between each of us, and in unison, they placed covered meals in front of us and removed the silver lids to unveil our dinners. The delectable smell wafted into my face; tenderloin, fingerling garlic potatoes, and butter rolls. If I hadn't been practicing sufficient self-control the entire day, the scent alone and overwhelming gratitude would have had me in tears.

"Thank you, Chef. All of you, you've outdone yourselves. Truly."

Before lifting my fork and knife, I looked all around the room at the smiling faces glancing back at me. The faces of the kind and helpful people who I had come to know as an extension of my family. This was their goodbye. They exited the room, heading back toward the kitchen.

Our bellies were already full from dinner; we were not prepared for the chocolate fondue dessert placed before us. I would not offend Chef after all he'd done for me, and I found myself making room for two helpings.

We all sat there silently, each of us trying to ignore the empty table before us.

"We'll be leaving at first light; we should all get some rest. Versa, say your goodbyes this evening. We won't want to wake you."

And just like that, the crescendo of the moment we had all been avoiding crashed down. I followed my sister upstairs to her room, making an excuse that I still had a bit more packing to do, so I wouldn't be able to stay very long.

We sat closely on her bed, but I still felt distant, trying to reconcile the fact that we'd never been apart this long before. I was overcome with the urge to unravel secrets and lies that had become tangled in my mind. I wanted to warn her to never have children, so as to ensure no one else from our bloodline would ever succumb to the same fate as me. I wanted to tell her the truth of what was happening and set fire to these past weeks, to the charade we'd been made to keep up with.

But looking at her, the innocence and naivety, it seemed wrong to hurt her unnecessarily. I started to believe that the lies were the best way. It was better for her to believe I was away, happy, doing what I longed to do, and then something tragic happened. That would be easier to overcome. I wondered if she did have children someday, would she learn of the debt all families owed the king? Would she surmise that is what had happened to me?

If she knew the truth, she'd never let me leave—or worse, she'd attempt to join me, and I couldn't allow that to happen. If she knew the truth, she'd never forgive our parents. She'd likely even fear having her own children one day. The dream of being a mother, was I willing to ruin that for her? Never.

I leaned over and embraced her, holding her longer than usual, as I wasn't normally one to hug. I squeezed her tightly, taking in her floral fragrance, and savored the feeling of my other half for the last time.

When we pulled away, she looked at me and said, "Promise you'll write to me, when you get a chance?"

I nodded, unable to lie again. She moved a strand of hair behind my ear, giving her a glimpse of our matching tattoo. Holding my hands in hers, she said, "May the light of the moons guide you back to me."

She pulled me into another tight embrace, and I rested my head there on her shoulder for as long as she let me, doing my best to fight the sting of my tears.

Before returning to my room, I snuck down to the stable to say goodbye to Rain. I found him relaxed in his stall and began to brush long lines across his side, in between planting kisses along his snout and cheek. The stable hand appeared from the darkness, patting Rain gently.

"Fear not, my lady. I will take good care of him until you return."

I nodded, unwilling to let him see me cry, and made my way back to my room. Upon arriving, I pulled out the list. It seemed like forever since I had last looked upon it. I crossed off two more items, trying to ignore the memories flooding through me of Trace and I swimming night after night in the spring.

Only one item remained. I argued with myself that I had already accomplished it. Doesn't getting a tattoo count as altering my appearance? I thought back to the night I'd made the list, unsure of what I had even imagined for that item, when an idea came to mind.

Carrying my bedside lantern, I walked over to my writing desk and sat before my mirror. I opened the drawer and pulled out a small sewing kit. I grabbed the black feather from Trace's wing that he had given me, that I'd hidden away. From my jewelry drawer, I took out a small plain earring and untangled the wire from it, re-wrapping the loose end around the shaft and fastening the feather in place to the earring.

I pushed back a strand of hair, allowing the lantern light to reveal a reflection in the mirror of the one small earring already there. Then I took out a sharp silver needle from the kit and eyed it intently, twisting it between my thumb and forefinger. Hovering the needle above my ear lobe next to the first earring, I didn't question if it would hurt.

I pushed the needle through. Rejoicing in the pain, glad to feel anything at all since numbness had been battling to consume me since leaving Versa's side. I wiped away a tiny dribble of blood and pushed the feather earring through the new hole.

I tilted my head, admiring the look of the shiny feather peeking out in between locks of my dark brown hair. Wherever I went, his memory would be with me. I crossed the last item off the list. I turned it over one more time to reread Aster's words. I had told myself I'd remember them but, honestly, didn't know if I would. What did it matter anymore? I was about to find out what was in store for me, regardless. The need to unravel the riddled words felt like a hollow and empty endeavor. I lifted the parchment over the flame of a candle and let it all burn to ash.

I hadn't managed to get much sleep before the sun rose. I located the two notes and the sketch Trace had drawn. I tore off the bottom part of the drawing—his message to me—and added it to the pile of letters. I then folded and shoved them into my pack, unwilling to part ways with these pieces of him. I snuck quietly into Versa's room and left the sketch of me on her bedside table for her to find when she awoke.

One might consider it bizarre to have a sketch of your sister sleeping, but I had reasoned that someday when I tragically didn't return, she would be glad to have it. I took one more glance at her soft, sleeping face, my face, and turned away from her for the final time, my heart aching.

Downstairs, I stood alone in the dim, quiet foyer. Not even the staff were awake this early. The eerie silence was a somber backdrop to my departure. The pristine shine of the marble floors, the smell of floral arrangements wafting through the halls, the arched ceilings featuring detailed frescos, and the winding staircases leading towards the east and west wings. I closed my eyes to picture the expansiveness of my home, to take it all in one last time.

The elegance of the set table in the dining room. The family portrait hung proudly over the stone fireplace in the library, its ornate frame reflecting the pale blue shafts of light that streamed in through the windows high above.

My father's office desk, laden with endless scrolls of maps and paper-work. My mother's closet of fineries; fabrics of every color, shade, and texture. The two swings near the gazebo in the garden, where my sister and I competed to see who could go the highest. The sound of Rain's hooves beating in an even tempo across the expansive grounds. This had been my home, and I wanted to preserve every detail in my mind.

Finally, with no more tears to shed, I opened the front door and crossed the gravel path to where my mother and father stood, a large carriage looming beside them. They seemed lost, out of place. A wave of sadness began to wash over me, blurring my vision.

But then I saw it. I wiped my eyes to be sure. This carriage was not our family's coach. Its dark chestnut frame was not lacquered to a pris-tine shine, but dusty and ordinary. There was certainly no family crest to be seen on the door. I shifted my gaze to the driver and then to the guards on horses that flanked the carriage. Their clothes were pedestrian, but they were visibly armed.

"Come now. Time and tide wait for no one." My father extended a hand to help me into my seat.

I tried to smile at this tired old saying of his, but I was too focused on the seriousness of this journey.

As the carriage rattled along the road leaving the grounds of our home, I watched the manor blanketed in sunrise, once and for all, thinking of a future that might have been.

CHAPTER 16

Four excruciatingly long days, that is how long I'd be stuck in a tiny, uncomfortable carriage alongside my mother and father. I was informed we'd only be making brief stops along the way to relieve ourselves. Chef had already prepared meals for us to eat on the way. We were instructed to keep moving and told that we wouldn't be allowed to stay overnight at any private residences or inns to avoid bringing attention to our caravan. Hence, the unmarked carriage and lack of regalia on our company's attire.

We each mostly kept to ourselves, napping, reading, occasionally forcing small talk and then staring out the window at the passing scenery. My mother gave me a silent but questioning nod at the feather earring peeking out from between strands of my hair, but with a single eyebrow raise from me, she did not pry any further.

I had not been to Tinsilor Castle since I was very young and had forgotten how monotonous the trip was. Occasionally, I'd find myself daydreaming about Trace and where he might be with the Kingsguard.

My father informed us we'd be arriving around nightfall and that they had a strict timeline and very clear instructions for the Offering. My mother and father donned their normal attire, but I was provided a plain white, long-sleeved dress to change into.

The material was cheap and thin, the texture slightly itchy. There wasn't a single marking or design to be found anywhere on the fabric. Lastly, and most uniquely, the top of the dress included a hood, and attached to that was a thinner, sheer-white fabric meant to be pulled over my entire face as a veil. When I pulled the veil over my face and sat across from my father in the carriage, he began to panic.

"Seraphine, we can't do this. I won't!"

He began to move about the carriage in a flustered manner. My mother's eyes widened with concern.

"They must accept something else. Surely money, jewels, a fleet of ships. Anything but her!"

My mother was on the verge of tears, witnessing my father's breakdown. He fidgeted with his hands, unable to sit still or calm himself. I lifted the veil to reveal my face to him, hoping the gesture would bring him some sense of relief.

"Father, I've accepted my fate. Don't waste the last moments I have with you."

My words broke him and he began to cry too, reaching for my hands to clasp in his. He apologized profusely over and over in a whisper. My mother shook her head in despair, unable to tear her gaze from the window and face me. She placed a hand on my knee but kept her eyes averted. I removed one hand from my father's grasp and placed it on top of hers.

There was nothing I could do to console them, but I was steadfast in my courage. I was done crying and feeling sad for myself. I wanted no pity, not even my own. The silent tears carried us like a river the remainder of the journey to the castle's doorway, where outside our window, pitch black consumed the starless night sky.

They each placed a kiss on my cheek, and I took one last look into their eyes without the constricted view of the veil. Mother's dark eyes contrasted Father's green, but the whites of their eyes were both moist and red with the same agony.

"I love you, and I always will." I imparted my final words to them before pulling the sheer veil across my face and turning to the carriage door. To become an Offering.

My mother and father escorted me up the steps of the castle and into the expansive great hall. The room was concerningly empty, except for a few individuals at the dais. The king and queen, another male who looked unassumingly dangerous, and a female who most certainly had to have been a priestess given her ethereal beauty and attire.

The hall was absent of any tapestries or banners of the great Houses. Not a single family crest in sight, no tables filled with gold plate settings, no silk draperies. None of the usual symbolic decorations were displayed to welcome an audience. This, combined with the secrecy of our caravan, only further assured me that we were not an audience they wanted the kingdom to be aware of.

With each step we took forward, I felt like heavy stones were weighing down my feet. The barely-there gown did little to shield me from the breezy halls of the castle.

When we arrived at the foot of the dais, the male standing at the king's right spoke, his voice smooth and confident.

"Who presents this Offering to his majesty, King Aeon I, Son of Ciaran, ruler of Cambria?"

My father answered, his voice still trembling with emotion, "We do, Your Majesty. Niall, High Lord of House Blackthorn, and my wife, High Lady Seraphine. We present to you an Offering. Our daughter, Cressida Blackthorn. May she serve you and the realm for all her days."

At the closing of his remarks, he and my mother bowed, and I quickly followed their lead, dipping my veiled head.

Aeon's mouthpiece continued ceremoniously, "The king accepts your most precious Offering with humble gratitude. He shall now gaze upon her unveiled face in recognition of who she is now, who she has been, and who she will always be to you."

Aeon stepped forward, and my hands began to tremor nervously at the prospect of the king approaching me. He lifted the veil with both hands, holding it above the brim of my eyebrows and stared down at me like he was peering into my soul. I could not bring myself to blink. I just stared back, a well of emotions pooling in my chest at what he was doing to me, to my family, and with zero explanation for his actions.

A king was accountable to no one except the Gods. His face remained solemn as he nodded and lowered the veil back down to cover my face. He returned to the throne and seated himself.

The mysterious male carried on, "As generations have before, so too are you now required to sacrifice an Offering. Know your king takes no pride or pleasure in breaking the sacred bonds of blood. This loss will not be in vain. The Gods smile favorably on the protectors of the realm."

He paused briefly. The air was still and silent but for the faint crackling of the torches that lit the room.

"Lord and Lady Blackthorn, we thank you for the sacrifice you've made today, and for your unwavering fealty to the king's cause. You may kiss the Offering's hands in parting."

And just like that, they were expected to leave. I turned toward them, fighting back tears with all the strength I could muster. I was not sad for myself. No, I was angry for the sadness my parents had been forced to endure, and will likely endure for the remainder of their days. My mother grabbed my hand and raised my knuckles to her lips, kissing gently, holding her lips there for a few seconds. She released me and I turned to my father, who gathered both my hands in his.

He bent down to kiss them both. I could feel his wet tears fall on my fingers, and he then pressed them hard against his forehead and stood. Leaning in closely, he whispered the words, "You are chosen, not offered." I do not believe he was permitted to speak, but no one intervened.

They both turned from me and began to walk the long distance of the great hall back to the entrance. I stood there watching, willing them to turn and look at me once more, but they did not. I was starkly reminded of my inability to turn back and glance at Trace as we parted ways, and it was then I understood.

When I turned back around, the priestess who had been silent the entire time was standing before me. She beckoned me to follow her and the strange male behind the throne, where I discovered a large, elevated, round fire pit glowing bright and hot. I noticed the king followed behind us quietly, the steps of his stride echoing.

When she spoke, her voice was melodic, almost entrancing. I think she could have requested anything and I'd have complied without hesitation.

"Please present your family medallion."

My breath hitched with worry that I had forgotten where I'd placed it, but then I remembered the side pocket of the dress. Fetching it quickly, I felt the heaviness of textured metal in my hands and was reminded of how little I had cared for this thing, how unimportant it had seemed before now.

I handed it to the priestess, who placed it in the center of the flames before us. Behind the veil, I watched as our house crest melted away into nothing, and soon after, the medallion lost all shape and meaning.

"Cressida, you will soon be born anew in the Bath of the Four Mothers. With you, you'll take a name, but not a house. Your new brothers and sisters await you, and together you will take an oath. But first, a tribute. As the bonds of familial blood have been severed, so must you make a new one. Please hold out your wrist."

Before I could even react, the priestess lifted a tiny metal rod from the fire, its tip glowing orange with heat, and pressed it against my wrist. I did not recognize the symbol she branded me with.

I quickly clutched my hand to my chest, the pain pulsating from my red and pink flesh. The king, now uncomfortably close to my side, held out his wrist to display the very same brand long healed over. His skin was shiny, almost silver where the mark resided.

"My blood is my bond; you shall be reborn in the name of the nameless. May the Gods favor the protectors of the realm, and may you be protected all your days, until your last breath."

His voice was even more hypnotic than the priestess's. I clung to every word, distracted from the pain. The king clasped his hand around my wrist, and when he pulled it away, the wound had healed just like his. Like it had been there for years, not just mere seconds. He then waved his hand over the top of the healed symbol and it disappeared completely. It was gone. Not even a scar remained visible. My skin was restored, only the memory of pain remained.

I had just lost my medallion, my family name, been branded, and yet I still had very little understanding surrounding what I was here for or who I was to these people. Was this just a bunch of ceremonious nonsense before I was sacrificed to the Gods in the name of the king and the realm? The priestess directed me to follow her out of the great hall, and I did so despite the mounting list of questions confounding my head.

As I walked behind her, still veiled, I ran my thumb over my wrist trying to see if I could feel any sense of the symbol, but I felt nothing. She led me down a narrow, winding stone staircase. Lower and lower, to the unknown depths beneath the castle.

This is where I was going to be murdered. Somewhere the staff couldn't hear our screams. Trying to ignore the endless steps, I found myself wondering about the other Offerings. Were they down here as well? When I saw a faint blue light ahead, I surmised the steps were coming to an end and we were nearing the bottom. If not, would I be led farther into some sort of catacombs? I could feel the muggy steam and moisture hanging in the air.

I turned the corner, and through the veil, I could barely make out a glowing pool in the center of the room. My surroundings felt constricting. The ceilings were low, the stone walls wrapped around the circular body of water, and the only exit appeared to be another dark hallway.

Tall figures dressed similarly in all-white and veils were encircling the pool of water. After indicating to me that I should remove my slippers like the others, she pointed me to an open spot near the pool. By now I had confirmed it was a hot spring, given the steam hovering around my toes.

"Everyone, please kneel."

As each of the strangers lowered themselves, I couldn't help but feel the utter subservience of the action. A bow was respectful and honorable, but this felt different, almost wrong. When we were all clearly kneeling on the slick hard ground, she spoke again, weaving her words like poetry.

"Each of you has been offered willingly, and each of you has performed a tribute in blood. Before you is the Bath of the Four Mothers. Tonight, you will be cleansed of your former life and blanketed in the waters of eternity. Your body is a vessel for the will of the Order. Within these waters, there is no past, there is no shame, there is no regret. You are forgiven before forgiveness is asked."

I stared down at the pool below the edge of my veil and noted the milky consistency of the water; how it glowed like moonslight regardless of being in this deep dark place shielded from the sky.

"You may stand, and I ask that you each carefully enter the pool as you are for the cleansing."

I took that to mean fully clothed and veiled; I focused on my footing, ignoring the others' entry, trying to make sure that I didn't fall face-first into this water. The liquid was warm and inviting. Beneath my feet, I could feel a stone ledge running along the perimeter of the pool, making a space for me to sit and submerge myself up to my neck.

I had only been submerged briefly when I began to feel a hum deep in my bones. It was faint, but occasionally felt stronger in tiny, almost unnoticeable waves. The bath, itself, felt strange in all ways. If I had to give a description, it was like feeling younger, cleaner, stronger, more powerful all in one but light not heavy.

We all sat there in silence. Our clothing was fully soaked through as we awaited guidance from the priestess.

"May you be born of the waters and receive the blessings of the Four Mothers at first breath. Please submerge yourself fully, and upon rising, you may remove your veil and witness your new family."

I took in a shallow breath of air and ducked under the water, drenching the final inches of my body. When I arose, I inhaled sharply, the fabric of the soaked veil pressed firmly against the outline of my face. I lifted the veil over my head and looked up, only to see familiar eyes staring back at me in horror.

I gasped in shock, trying to calm myself at the sight of Trace standing before me. The thin fabric outlined every dip and curve of his body; my eyes were unable to stop scanning the shape of him. I became instantly bashful, realizing that I, too, might as well have been naked given the fabric, and went to shield my chest with folded arms, angling the front of my body away.

I was once comfortable in the complete nude with Trace, and now I shied away from the male looking back at me. As the others exited the pool, I struggled to follow suit without tripping.

Trace and I stared at each other; our gazes filled with unimaginable confusion. My mind was unable to reconcile seeing Trace in anything other than the color black. I noticed his eyes dip to where my new earring rested; his jaw tightened. This time not in lust, but in anger, pure and raw. I had completely forgotten about the feather earring until I felt its damp barbs tickling my cheek.

I might have been embarrassed at his realization, except my attention was drawn to the thin scar splitting the fine dark hair of his eyebrow. An old wound, not new but healed. Below the soaking-wet sleeves of his garment, I saw the dark lines of his tattoo on not one but both arms. Was I hallucinating? Who in Gods' names was this person standing next to me?

We were directed to a set of rooms where our belongings awaited us and instructed to dry off and change into comfortable attire as we'd be traveling. If I hadn't been entirely consumed with disbelief over Trace, I might have been more irritated at the thought of more travel after having spent four full days in a carriage.

Digging through my articles of clothing, I tried to grasp what this meant. Was Trace High Fae like me? That was the only logical possibility. Only members of the High Court were called to the Offering, according to my father.

More importantly, why did he look so different from the last time we parted? I dressed as quickly as possible, eager to find a way to be alone with him. I was too angry and confused to find any relief that someone I knew and trusted was here with me. My trust in him was now entirely in question.

With my belongings in hand, we made our way through another door and up a staircase. I walked a few persons behind Trace, angling my head behind their tall stature, trying to catch glimpses of him. Upon reaching the ground level of the castle, we were escorted to a group of large carriages by the male who had been at the king's side earlier.

The priestess was nowhere to be seen. He handed us each a vial of liquid and instructed us to drink it without question. I eyed Trace nervously, and we watched each other raise the vials to our lips.

"You will each enter a carriage. In a few minutes, you will be asleep thanks to the liquid you just ingested. Do not worry, it is safe. You will be transported to our next destination and likely awaken upon arrival.

Where you're going is not something you're privy to at this time."

Trace intentionally waited to see what carriage I boarded and did not join me. I leaned back against the seat, utterly exhausted by everything that had just transpired.

My eyes became heavy, my vision blurry. The last thing I saw were the long blonde curls of the beautiful female sitting across from me.

CHAPTER

16

I awoke to the sound of knocks on the carriage door and the rustling noises of the other individual across from me. My eyes stung from the glare of sunlight casting through the windows. My neck and back had horrible cricks, telling me I had likely been seated in a poor position long enough to leave me feeling sore for a few days. I rubbed my forehead, trying to shake the disorientation and slight throbbing headache. Likely from the strange drink that had knocked us out.

I followed behind the blonde female exiting our carriage, only to be greeted with a gust of cool fresh air that sent stray locks of my hair into a tangle. A crisp chill caused my skin to ripple with goosebumps. When I rubbed the sleep from my eyes, I took in the otherworldly sights surrounding me.

We were somewhere nestled in between stunning gray mountains, hidden away from everything. I had never seen mountains this close; I'd never actually been there at all. I had traced many mountain ranges with my fingers along my father's maps, but I had no way to approximate where

I was or what mountain range these belonged to. I was so distracted by the cresting sun over the cliffs, I forgot Trace and my other companions were standing nearby also taking in our surroundings.

Glancing over my shoulder, I silently counted how many of us comprised the Offering. Six…there were only six of us. I don't know how many I'd expected. With so few Houses and the criteria for being conscripted, it had been impossible to guess. I tried to ignore Trace's presence from the corner of my eye but noted that he was back in his all-black attire that suited him better than anything else.

"Ahem, may I please have your attention? I am Idris, and I am your good King Aeon's spymaster. You have been delivered safely to the Elorn Mountains, and this place is called Basdie." He paused, folding his hands casually in front of himself, before continuing.

"You may have heard of the Elorn Mountains, but you will not have heard of the Basdie stronghold. This place does not exist. Not to anyone who is not meant to know about it. The only reason you are alive, standing within its boundaries, is because my enchantments permit your presence."

I glanced around anxiously, trying to see if any of the others showed any indication of the same concerns I was feeling. Again, I could feel that faint hum similar to the one I'd first felt in the Bath of the Four Mothers, but I ignored the sensation and tried to focus on Idris' words.

A spymaster? No wonder he acted aloof; I knew there was something questionable about him the minute I heard his voice. No one spoke, just listened intently.

"The brand you received at the ceremony is the key that allows you to pass into this sacred place—but that very same key is also a lock. Should you choose to leave the perimeter of the grounds without explicit permission, you will find that it will be your first and last attempt. Please do not make me explain this further. There are so few of you, and you are precious to the realm. I would hate to lose even one."

I caught myself grinding my teeth at the harshness of his warning and the realization of being trapped here against our will. What exactly would happen if we crossed the boundary without permission? Were they even clearly marked?

"Grab your belongings and follow me inside. I know you all are very interested in answers to more of your questions. All will be explained in due time."

I walked over to the carriage and found my pack among the others sitting on the ground. Before I could bend over to retrieve mine, my carriage mate politely handed it to me. "Thank you," I said, finally taking in the full view of her.

She was nothing, if not beautiful. A stark contrast to myself. She dripped with femininity. Her long blonde curls framed both sides of her voluptuous breasts. I tried not to appear like I was gaping at her curvaceous body; a tight-fitting dress accentuated her feminine shape. Her eyes were warm, like honey glistening in the sunlight. She looked untouched by the disaster of our recent sleeping quarters. Okay, I was officially staring. I pried away my gaze, trying to reset my expression appropriately.

She held out her palm facing up, waiting for me to return the greeting. I had never been so grateful for that small gesture of normalcy. Customs, etiquette—call it what you like; it was the first moment since arriving I felt okay.

I put my hand palm facing down and placed it atop hers, holding it there briefly.

"I'm Cressida, but please call me Cress."

The ease with which I omitted my House name saddened me, remembering how that had been taken from me only a short time ago.

As if her beauty wasn't intriguing enough, her voice was velvety smooth. The slow, raspy cadence was like a lullaby.

"I'm Gianna, but I prefer Gia; and if I decide I like you, then you can call me G," she said teasingly with a smile. A smile that I was certain could destroy the resolve of even the strongest.

She pulled her palm away from mine and, without any concern for personal space, she ran her fingertips down the long black feather hanging from my ear and gave me a smirk. Wordlessly, she turned to carry her bags and follow the others.

What was that look for? Did she know it was a Nightwing feather? It could have been anything. A raven or a crow—but no, she looked at me like she knew exactly what it was, and I blushed, following closely behind her.

The giant wooden doors to Basdie were built into the side of the mountain. This was not a structure built on top of or adhered to the mountain, no; it was part of it.

Idris waved his hand and the doors opened. I gaped at the casual use of magic. He had already mentioned enchantments; it was clear he had no qualms about wielding magic, but I had a feeling he was just getting started.

With another flick of his wrist, the torches lit up the stone walls of the expansive atrium. The ceiling was jagged and raw, with sharp points jutting out from every angle.

"Don't worry, the rest of it is only slightly more welcoming," Idris attempted to joke as we continued to follow him through another smaller set of doors.

When we passed the threshold, there were two sides of a stone staircase wrapping downward, each in a half circle arriving at the same lower level. A handful of us went down the right side. I followed Gia down the left, still lugging my pack over my shoulder while doing everything in my power to avoid looking at Trace where he walked across from me on the opposite staircase.

When we all arrived at the bottom, those lanterns and torches flickered to life as well. It was easy to ignore the coziness of the room, a mix between a library and a lounge. Just beyond the burning fireplace, bookshelves and plush couches scattered throughout the common area, and the ceiling sloped steeply to accommodate the crystal-clear glass window.

A silver decoration outlined the panes, but behind it…Gods what was that? Was that…was that a waterfall…? Inside of a mountain? I walked toward it, my mouth gaping at its impossible beauty. Was this real?

I put my hand up to the glass, feeling the deep vibration of the water pounding down from unimaginable heights. Sunlight from the opening above illuminated the narrow crater containing the falls. Mesmerized by the sight, I jumped in surprise when suddenly Idris appeared by my side.

"Beautiful, isn't it?"

I turned to him, nodding in silence, unable to come up with the words.

"This glass is very thick, intentionally so; otherwise, it would be very loud in here. But if you put your ear to the glass and listen carefully, you'll hear a sound that only a few have ever heard."

I glanced at him as if asking for permission, and he gave me an encouraging dip of his chin.

I leaned in, bracing myself with both hands against the pane, and held my ear directly against the glass. I closed my eyes and began to listen closely, as Idris instructed. The sound was deep and strong, unlike anything I'd ever heard or imagined; like wind, rainstorms, and the earth quaking all in one. The sound was enticing, and I imagined if there were a walkway to the Gods, this is what it would sound like.

All that power; barely contained. Idris smiled at me and, despite his friendly behavior, I did not trust him.

"These falls are sacred, tucked away and hidden by the mountains because the power of their waters contains rare healing properties. You'll be shown the healing pools later on."

He had piqued my interest, but before I could indulge my curiosities, he stepped away from me and back toward the group.

I turned around to see the others milling about the room, taking long glances at the waterfall in between inspecting the titles of books on the shelves and trying to discreetly size each other up.

"You may leave your bags here," Idris instructed. "I have much to tell you, and perhaps I will suffer fewer interruptions if you're busy with full mouths and raised forks. Follow me, let's eat."

To the left of the glass window was a long hallway, which we followed him down. Once more I stuck close to Gia, trailing her like a shadow. On the left side of the wall, we passed a series of closed doors. On the right side, the stunning view of the waterfall continued, though it grew narrower. The glass pane lined the entire wall. The bright blue glow of the crashing water helped light the winding hallway, along with various torches placed outside of every other door.

He finally turned into a small dining hall with a long wooden table at one end and a giant fireplace at the other. I looked at it, trying to understand where the smoke was going, but there simply was none. Just a fire burning, giving off heat but no ash or smoke. Each of us took a seat around the rectangular table. There were more chairs than there were people.

The group spread out awkwardly, clearly uncomfortable with one another. I, however, took a spot directly next to Gia. Trace located himself to the farthest possible seat from me. Idris stood at the head of the table and let out a small, amused laugh. It was odd to see him demonstrate any sort of amusement. Up until that point, he had been mostly buttoned up, almost detached. I gathered that the small smile he had given me earlier was not going to be a frequent occurrence.

"I remember the first time I sat at this table. Like you, scared and untrusting of everyone in the room. But I can assure you, you will come to trust these people with your life."

A few of us glanced around at one another, absorbing his grave words.

"I'd like each of you to clear your mind, cut out all the noise, and think only of the most delicious breakfast you've ever had. Nothing is off-limits. Your favorite food and drink."

After giving Gia a confused look, I turned away, doing as Idris requested. I thought of Chef's giant cinnamon rolls and fresh squeezed orange juice from our orchard. I thought of the delicious eggs from the farm nearby and a medley of fresh-cut fruit. The memories alone made my mouth water, and I knew if I continued this any longer, I might have become teary-eyed over food.

A short time later, the table went from barren and empty to completely covered and full. Platter after platter, servings of every imaginable type. Hot steam rose from plates, the overwhelming scents wafting all about the room. Directly in front of me was a place setting with every item I had just imagined. Just how unburdened was Idris' magic?

Absolutely parched, I reached for the glass of juice and gulped down half of it. How had he done it? The drink tasted just like the very oranges from my home. But that was impossible. Some of us dug right into the food, desperate to satiate the hunger from traveling to the Elorns. Others hesitated, scrutinizing the food. I didn't blame them; after all, they had drugged us. Idris sat down at the head of the table, absent a place setting.

"Each of you is now a member of the Order. The Order is a faction of his majesty's kingdom that has existed in secrecy for millennia. We have served the king, and all kings before him. We do not have the same constraints as the king's military, because we do not exist. As a member of the Order, you are bound to complete anonymity and total secrecy for the remainder of your life in service to the realm."

Idris paused, looking around the room, acknowledging the weight of his words. I took another large gulp of juice to hide my fearful expression.

"Your familial bonds were severed in the Offering ceremony. The Order is your new family. You do not exist, except to each other. You've made a tribute in blood, binding you to your king and this cause. You will remain here in Basdie and be trained in the ways of the Order by those who came before you. When it's determined that you are ready, you will take the final oath and pledge your commitment to the cause.

Only then will you learn how you will serve King Aeon."

By now, the seriousness of Idris' diatribe had waned as many of us began shoveling large heaps of food into our mouths and chewing without a care in the world. Like a bunch of people who had just been told they'd lost all freedom and autonomy over their entire lives. No friends, no family, no name.

A nervous giggle almost escaped my mouth at the absurdity of it all. The food was a fantastic distraction from this madness. By now it was pretty clear how important we were and that I needn't fear them killing all of us. At least we weren't here to be sacrificed to the Gods. Just to sacrifice something as small and insignificant as our entire identities.

"As I mentioned outside upon your arrival, this place does not exist— but its boundaries are very real. Should you choose to explore beyond them without permission, or should you choose to abandon the Order completely, your life is forfeit. You will come when called upon. No matter where you are, who you are with, or where life may take you, you will come when called upon. Later, you will meet your teachers who know all too well the lifelong commitment of serving the Order."

So, there were other people here. The place had been silent and absent of anyone but the six of us and Idris. Who were these people? If they were members of the Order, did that mean they were once High Fae like all of us?

"It goes without saying that you may never see or contact your family or anyone you knew ever again. To do so is considered treason, punishable by death. Again, you are rare, few, and important. Please do not make selfish decisions."

I had managed to rationalize most of what he had said until he reassured us that trying to contact family was explicitly forbidden. Until then, I had convinced myself that someday, no matter how long it took, I would send word to my family. It was the least I could hope for. But at the cost of my own life?

"Your mentors will explain more to you about your training after introductions have been made. Now that we've discussed all the heavy unpleasantries of your new life, shall we get to the good stuff?"

I almost choked on a bite of my food. I'd be shocked to discover any upside to this arrangement. Overwhelmed with the thought of never seeing anyone that knew me again, I thought to myself how serendipitous it was that Trace was here. But who was he, really? He'd lied about a lot. Was it a good or bad thing that I knew someone here?

"The king's demands are severe; he has taken a lot from you, but he has also given. You have each bathed in the waters of Mirtith. The Bath of the Four Mothers is the bath of the Gods, the anointed ones. Each of you, being of Royal or Honored bloodlines, possess a strong potential within yourselves. Many of you have lived under the guise of being less powerful than you are. Call it restraint, etiquette, culture, what-have-you, but you are now free of those constraints that chained you to a life of mediocrity."

He continued, "Magic, like all things, is finite. Wielding it frivolously means running the risk that it would not come when called upon in true need. Each of you has received a gift from the Gods; a blessing given for what your king has taken."

I had to give it to Idris, he had my attention. But in between all the fancy words and promises of Gods and gifts, what did it actually mean for us?

As if he had read my mind, Idris spoke once more. "It means your magic has the potential to become more powerful than you ever imagined, and you must learn to control it, master it, shape it into a finely tuned weapon and use it to protect our people. The very same people you left behind. Now is the time to remove the bonds of your previous life and be free. Release yourself from the expectations, rules, and limitations. We answer to no one except the cause."

Gia and I glanced at one another for the first time since Idris had started speaking. His words were undeniably motivating, and it was now abundantly clear why Idris used magic freely and without consequence. Flicking his wrists and fingers all about the place, lighting torches and fireplaces, presenting us with homemade meals like he had breathed life into the whims of our imaginations.

He was very powerful, and I couldn't deny the intrigue he had sparked in me. I hungered for that kind of power. I craved to know what it felt like to completely free-fall into the depths of my magic like never before. We were never permitted those dreams before now.

After breakfast, Idris led us all back to the place where we had left our bags and took us down the other hallway to our dormitories. The rooms outnumbered us, which meant he allowed us to choose whether we roomed alone or with others. I considered rooming with Gia, but I didn't want to impose.

Some rooms were bigger than others. Following an investigation of my options, I settled on a room with two full-sized beds, throwing my bag on the floor. We each entered separate rooms, still unsure of one another and the entire situation. Idris did not look surprised. The room was plain and windowless. Frankly, I didn't care much about the room. I was far too interested in everything else Idris had told us to put too much thought into the lodging situation. I did take a mental note of which room Trace entered, a few paces away from mine.

Idris instructed us to unpack later and continued his tour into another room that was deemed to be a classroom. Unlike most classrooms where all the seats faced forward toward a teacher presumably standing at the front of a room, this one had a very large round table at its center. Surrounding the table were large high-backed wooden chairs. This meant that for the first time since arriving, we'd all be forced to face one another and get a real good look.

My eyes scanned from left to right. First was Gia, followed by an extremely petite female with short, choppy, bright-red hair. Her tiny nose was upturned and her slim lips made her appear extremely youthful. Her eyes, almost black, were her most intense feature. If it weren't for those dark eyes, she'd seem entirely harmless, but there was something about those eyes that scared me.

One empty seat down from her was Trace, who continued to do everything in his power to avoid making eye contact with me. The two chairs to his left were also vacant, and the third was taken by another male. Were the ladies the only ones brave enough to sit next to one another? I continued to assess the next person at the table.

Even seated, he was slightly taller than Trace. His hair was pure white and messy curls sat like laurels in a crown around his head. His skin was somehow golden, like the sun was always shining on it even though this place possessed none.

Suddenly, he turned and stared directly at me, his gaze unmoving and fixated on mine. His eyes were the iciest color blue I'd ever seen. When I finally blinked, his sharp jaw flexed and two prominent dimples appeared alongside his cheeks as he tried to conceal the minutest of smiles.

We continued to stare at each other, unsure which of us would turn away first. Before I showed signs of blushing from the intensity of this game he was playing with me, I shifted my gaze to the seat next to him. He turned his head ever so slightly, revealing his profile.

That's when I saw it. I inhaled sharply at the sight of them. Three tiny lines behind his ear—gills! This male had gills behind his pointed ears. My thoughts grappled to catch up with what my eyes were seeing.

He was a Sea Fae!

But wait, if he was here, that meant he was a member of the High Court. And *that* meant… He was related to that heathen that had led the rebellion at Erisas Bay!

My momentary infatuation with his looks quickly turned to fury. I wanted to lunge across that table and cause him serious harm for what his line had put my family through, and for all the senseless loss and bloodshed they'd caused. I was seething. He did not turn his attention back to me.

There was only one person left at the table; his hulking frame dwarfed the chair he sat upon. Muscular didn't even begin to describe his rock-solid body. His tan face and dark eyes were accentuated by his long brown hair, a portion of which was tied back. The rest hung in unkempt strands along his cheekbones, barely grazing the top of his shoulders. From what I could tell, his massive hands were bruised and scarred. For all the strength and beauty surrounding this table, he's the one I would not have messed with.

"Well, I'll leave you to get acquainted with one another," Idris said, exiting the room.

We all sat in silence, staring at the walls and avoiding eye contact, when a tall, slender female came strolling through the door. Her long blue dress had a slit running up the side, exposing one leg. The dress was corseted tight, accentuating a thin waist, and her pillowy breasts practically fell out of her top. Her brown hair was tied up ornately in an updo, showing off her beautifully pointed ears and the hollows of her cheekbones.

The males at the table straightened in their seats, especially the hulk at the end, clearly unable to control themselves from gawking. I couldn't blame them; she was the only one in the room that closely rivaled Gia.

She walked over to the muscular one, swishing and swaying her hips with every step. She leaned into him, angling herself seductively, and grabbed his chin, running her thumb across his lower lip. The sight of their interaction felt inappropriate for us to witness. He angled his head up as if to welcome her in closer. He was powerless to her charms. She released her teasing grip on him and walked away.

Back toward the far side of the round table, she turned her back to us, and when she fully faced us again, what appeared was no longer a seductress. She had transformed into a handsome male with a tightly shaved beard and an eye patch over his left eye. Her once voluptuous figure was now masculine and donning a completely different attire. All black, with a long silver talisman hanging around his neck. It appeared to be the same symbol as our brands. The hulk at the end of the table jerked his chair back in disbelief, seeing the truth of what he had just pined for.

"Your eyes deceive you. All of you. Abandon your misguided senses. Leave such foolishness behind and accept that desire and attraction is a spectrum for which you can learn to control if you're willing to manipulate it."

His voice was deep, gravelly, and wise. He leaned inward, resting his body weight against the table, inquiring, "Do any of you know what kind of magic you just bore witness to?"

The little redhead chirped, "You glamoured us, didn't you!"

The male gave her a disappointed look that broke her confidence.

"You're a shapeshifter," Gia stated plainly, and the male snapped his gaze to her and a sly smile crept across his face.

"Yes, exactly! Glamour is easy, boring. A mere shade of what can be accomplished with shapeshifting for those who can master it."

He eyed all of us slowly.

"Glamour takes creativity and accuracy, but shapeshifting takes all of that plus endurance."

He sat and folded his hands with a glance toward Gia. "Not all of you will have the talent required for it," he added nonchalantly.

Suddenly, he clapped his hands together, drawing our attention back to him. "Well let's get some introductions out of the way. My name is Saryn and I am a member of the Order, of which you all are now inductees, trainees—call yourselves whatever you want, I don't care. You're stuck here just like me." His terse words were far less inspiring than Idris'.

"After years of not having to return to Basdie, I've received the fortune of being called back to help reinstate the Order by training you lucky individuals. Congrats, life as you knew it is gone, as is your freedom, and I won't sit here and romanticize it the way Idris does."

Maybe I had it wrong and Idris was the warm one after all.

"Idris has spent far too long at the castle, dawdling alongside politicians and sycophants. He's forgotten what it's like to be in the trenches. But that's why I'm here; to make sure you're prepared for exactly what is ahead of you."

"Why don't you just shapeshift or glamour away that patch on your eye?" The audacity of Gia's interruption had us all gaping.

Saryn smirked back at her. "Because mature ladies find it attractive; it's not for little girls like you."

I was nervous that the bitter exchange of words between them would continue. Gia was most certainly not a little girl. She bit her tongue, however, and did not grant him a retort. I didn't get the feeling she would have won that match anyhow.

"Since you seem keen to speak, why don't you introduce yourself next?" he prodded her.

"I'm Gianna of House Brynmawr—"

Saryn cut her off, "Tsk, tsk, Gianna, we care not for your House name. Remember, *we're* your kin, now."

Gia gritted her teeth and cocked her head. "I'm Gia, former daughter of High Lord and Lady Brynmawr. I hail from the western territories. Pleased to make your acquaintance." Each word was sharper than the last.

Saryn eyed me next, implying I was to go. I cleared my throat. "I'm Cressida, but I go by Cress," I paused, then followed Gia's lead. "Former daughter of High Lord and Lady Blackthorn, I hail from the southern-most territories." I eyed Trace while stating my introduction, but he did not look in my direction.

"Nori Evenus," the small redhead added. Despite her unthreatening size, she was quite brave to state her full name, in spite of Saryn's harsh warning to Gia. I had to give her credit; it was a bold move. Saryn rolled his eyes at her and turned to Trace. I braced myself to hear his voice for the first time since reuniting under these unexpected circumstances.

His jaw tightened and he finally looked directly at me, hints of apologetic sadness swimming in his eyes. "I'm Trace, and I'm from north of North." The familiar words taunted me, making my chest stiffen.

The golden figure sitting nearby scoffed in disbelief. "Oh, come on… you're not going to tell them who you really are? *What* you really are?"

Trace shot a glare to his left and his features began to roil. I knew Trace well enough to know he was exerting an extreme amount of self-control. I watched as his hands resting on the table before us now curled into tight fists. He remained obstinate and silent.

"Why so shy? Not proud to be Commander Wick's son?"

Commander… Did that mean his father led Aeon's military?

Finally, Trace could no longer refrain from engaging. "You really want to get started on the topic of fathers? As if you know anything about me," he spat back.

Trace had made the same correlation I had.

"I know that for someone who doesn't want to own up to who they are and what they've done, you sure are flaunting those tattoos like a badge of honor, black cloak."

His words were venomous, and they had hit their intended mark because Trace stood abruptly. His antagonist sat there unmoving and unbothered.

Saryn began to laugh again. "This is fun, truly, watching you all continue to act like anything from your pasts even matters. Perhaps it's been too long since I was in your shoes. Takes time to adjust to being nobody; each of your histories washed away like silt in a river."

Trace resolved to take his seat again, unsure of what would result if he acted out against one of us. I made a mental note to find out later what a black cloak was and why it vexed him to be called that. I already knew the meaning of the tattoo, or at least, I thought I did.

"Just when I thought we weren't going to be graced with anyone mouthier than darling Gia over there, we have you to thank. And who might you be?" he questioned, pointing his finger at the white-haired antagonist.

"Varro." He paused. "And yes, if it weren't already obvious, House Corliss. I find the mountain air displeasing, but I suppose I wasn't asked if seaside accommodations were an option."

He was about as smug as they came. Exactly what I'd expect from the son of the barbarian who slaughtered an entire bay of innocent people.

Saryn smiled. "I think I'm going to like you. You've got humor, and you're going to need it." He then turned away from Varro saying, "And last, but certainly not least, who are you?"

"Cairis Tiernan, bastard son of his most ardent Lord Magnus Tiernan and the lucky winner of this 'lottery of heirs' we all happen to be a part of."

Cairis' words dripped with sarcasm and a hint of an accent I wasn't familiar with. Who refers to themselves as a bastard when introducing themself? Maybe he just wanted to get it out of the way before anyone else made a point of it, since that was becoming a theme. I guess I could admire the transparency.

"Well, aren't we just an enthusiastic bunch? I can already tell we're going to have a lot of fun training together. You all need some time to cool off, let's call it a day. Tonight, another one of your instructors will arrive at dinner. Until then, explore, relax, and get to know one another. I need to speak with Idris before he departs."

With that, Saryn made his exit, and we were all left seated and aimless. Never in my life had introductions felt this combative. The air was thick with tension. This wasn't going to be anything like what I'd experienced at the academy.

We filed out of the room in silence, all of us heading back toward the common area and dormitories. I followed at an inconspicuous distance behind Trace as he made his way back to his room. I wasn't about to let another minute go by without getting to the bottom of a very long list of questions.

215

CHAPTER 17

I glanced over my shoulder to make sure no one was watching. He shut the door behind him, but I caught it with my hand, slipping into the room quietly. When he didn't hear the click of the door, he turned. He inhaled sharply, and I stood there staring in silence, unsure of who should speak first or what to say.

"What are you doing here?" His words were harsh and cold. Not what I had expected.

"I could ask you the same thing."

"I knew you were lying about something, but I never imagined this," he said, shaking his head in disbelief.

"What made you think I was lying to you?" I tried to think back on our time together. I thought I'd done a pretty decent job of avoiding anything misleading.

"Your hands. They've never seen a day of work, they're too soft. Not to mention that purebred horse of yours costs more than a house."

He sat down on the edge of the bed, resting his head against his hand in frustration. "Gods, I thought maybe a rebellious daughter of a wealthy noble, but not this. The daughter of a High Lord. I'm a fool."

Why was that such a bad thing? My chest felt flustered with sad disappointment. He did not seem happy or relieved to see me in the slightest.

"I know we both lied, but is it possible we're somehow lucky to be here together? I mean, I thought I'd never see you again," I said shyly, trying to conceal my feelings as best I could.

Momentarily, I set aside my anger about his lies and the ever-expanding list of questions I had for him. I stepped toward him, and he flinched—physically recoiled from me.

"Cress, we aren't lucky. This place might as well be a death sentence. There's a reason they want us to cut ties with our former life."

His assumptions were bleak. I don't know that I could argue with them, but I couldn't ignore feeling relief that a familiar face was here; his face. Everything about this place still felt unknown, but I felt safer just knowing he was here too.

"We have no idea what they might do if they knew we had known each other in that way…" his words trailed off, almost too ashamed to acknowledge the truth.

He sank his face into both hands, rubbing his palms against his temples. I crouched down to eye level with him and slowly reached my hand out, longing to console him, but again, he pulled away.

"How am I supposed to ignore the fact that you're only a few doors down from me? I despise that you're here. You were the last good thing from the life I left behind, and now I can't even take solace in that."

"I'm sorry," I whispered, trying to hide the cracking in my voice.

My presence here had upset him. I couldn't deny that the thought of him being mere steps away at night was going to be nearly impossible to ignore.

Trace finally looked up from his hands and I felt myself drowning in the green and brown flecks of his eyes, remembering all the times I had looked into them with deep, unwavering affection.

"Promise me you'll do this my way. Just let me figure out exactly what's going on here and if it's safe or not. I want to protect you, protect us both. For now, we can act friendly, like acquaintances, but they cannot know our history."

I didn't know what else to do other than nod. I didn't have the same concerns as Trace, but maybe I was being naive. It wouldn't have been the first time.

"I'll follow your lead, for now, but I have more questions and you *will* answer them," I acquiesced.

"Later, I promise. When I can find somewhere safe for us to talk."

He suddenly lifted his hand and ran his palm across my cheek, pushing aside a long piece of my hair to expose my ear. And the feather earring.

I tilted into the warmth of his hand against my skin, beginning to crave him in all the ways I could not act on. He ran his finger down the length of the black Nightwing feather and leaned in, resting his forehead against mine. "You're going to be the death of me," he rasped.

Everything in my body wanted to press my lips to his, but I knew if either of us crossed that line, there would be no coming back. Not after all the loss we'd faced, only to be gifted each other back in the strangest of circumstances. He pulled away from me to stand, and I did the same, feeling empty and unfulfilled.

"Please don't wear that. It will only make this harder for me. And whatever you do, please work on your mental shields. I don't trust these people; they'll crawl inside your head and use anything they can against you."

I wasn't sure if it was all the years of Trace being a black cloak—whatever that was—or just paranoia, but he didn't give much weight to Idris or Saryn saying these people were our new family. He was operating like they were quite the opposite. Trace peered out into the hallway, ensuring no one was watching, and urged me to make my exit.

I stopped briefly by my room and laid the earring down on a table next to my bed. I looked at it with far too much longing and hurt from being told to take it off. Shortly thereafter, I made my way back to the common room to find the others scattered about, lounging on couches—except for Nori, who was nowhere to be seen.

Varro was sitting in a far corner by himself, perusing a book, and I couldn't stop myself from glaring anytime I looked in his direction. I sat down next to Gia, who appeared to be overcome with boredom, and Cairis, who was cleaning the underside of his nails with the tip of a dagger. It became apparent they hadn't gone through our bags and removed any weapons, which was promising. A detail to later point out to Trace about why we should trust them. If they had wanted us unarmed, that might have been cause for concern.

"It's a shame you'll be missing your sister's wedding," Gia said with disinterest.

I turned my head in surprise. If I was being honest, I didn't know anything about these people, well except for Trace and Varro's father.

"How do you know about that?" I inquired.

"All the members of the High Court received invitations, did they not? My mother, being the absolute snob that she is, was gossiping to my father about it, despite their unwillingness to attend."

"Does that mean you're of Royal blood?" It was highly likely given the statement that they wouldn't attend.

"Yes, not that it's ever made a difference to me."

I was relieved to hear her say it. It would have been a shame if the only person I had attempted to befriend so far had ended up being pointlessly judgmental.

"I think you're the only Honored Fae here, anyway," she added.

Suddenly Cairis chimed in, "I'm only a half-blood, so feel free to bucket me in with Cress."

He shot me a smile of camaraderie. I grinned back at him, trying not to laugh at the obvious fact that he was entirely too large for the chair he was relaxing in.

"That must mean that Saryn and Idris are from Houses long disappeared since the war, if they were conscripted just like we were and yet none of us know them," I hypothesized.

"Well, aren't you the ever astute one," Gia complimented dryly.

"I don't care about any of that, I'm still curious about Saryn. You think he fucks as a female?" Cairis inquired crassly.

I could not believe the audacity of his foul-mouthed question. Gia rolled her eyes and I sat there, mouth agape.

"Wouldn't you like to know!" Gia teased back playfully.

Cairis cocked his head, raising a curious eyebrow at us, indicating he was considering it.

I guess it was good to see that at least the three of us got along. Even if we were talking about our teacher like he was some piece of meat.

"I don't think fucking the teacher is going to earn you any points, Cairis."

My eyes widened at Gia's equally inappropriate remark. What happened to propriety and etiquette? Was I the only one who hadn't completely abandoned our upbringings in a matter of a day?

"You two have quite the mouths on you for being a Royal and a half-blood," I pointed out jokingly.

"As far as I'm concerned, my lot has improved greatly since coming here. Guess I'm lucky that Lord Tiernan's rugrats were too young for this spy stuff. Better than being stuck working long hours in the mines and being treated like a lowborn. I suppose it was finally convenient to acknowledge I was his son and seize the opportunity to be rid of me."

The scars and bruises on Cairis finally made sense. He had certainly not grown up with a silver spoon in his mouth like the other sons and daughters of the court. I found his honesty refreshing. That, and I liked listening to him talk; his accent was like music to my ears.

"Where's Nori?" I pried, seeing if anyone else had taken notice of her whereabouts.

"Quiet, that one is," Cairis answered.

"She's in her room," Gia noted. "I get the feeling she's in denial of being here."

You can never be certain, with the graceful way Fae aged, but I had a hunch that Nori was the youngest of all of us. For a brief second, I felt almost protective of her, like an older sister. I considered seeking her out but settled on giving her some time and space to wrap her mind around this place. Who was I kidding? I still was, too; it wasn't like I was going to have any sage advice to offer.

I continued to take awkward side glances in the direction of Varro, who seemed to take pleasure in acting like none of us were here. I felt guilty for holding his father against him, especially when I had no idea what role he had played, but one could imagine the apple doesn't fall far from the tree. I also disliked how he sought to incite Trace.

Then I heard his voice echo across the room in our direction. "Cress? That's your name, right?" he asked, somehow sounding bored while still flipping the pages of his book with indifference.

"It's very unbecoming to hold the crimes of my father against me when you don't even know me." I almost gasped at the intrusion. "And yes, it's very easy to read your mind, even from a distance. You should work on that, or be brave enough to say those thoughts to my face."

My cheeks flushed pink with embarrassment and Cairis let out a boisterous laugh. Before I could even pause to consider if my reaction would give away my loyalties, I marched angrily toward him.

"I'll go ahead and give you a piece of my mind since you seem intent on prying. For someone who doesn't want to be judged by their father's actions, you're quite the hypocrite given your remarks towards Trace."

I had no idea what I was even really defending since I lacked the full context of their exchange from earlier, but Varro had had me fired up since I first laid eyes on him, and he'd done nothing but irk me with his arrogance since.

I'd made my way to his seat and hovered over him. He set the book down nonchalantly, giving me a modicum of his attention. Both Cairis and Gia had perked up in their seats, staring at the impending altercation.

"Do you even know who the Orni are?" he questioned me, and when I held my silence for too long, he proceeded, "Ahh, thought not. Well, let me educate you, Cress." I hated the way he over-enunciated my name. I swallowed the lump in my throat.

"The Orni, or, as many call them, the black cloaks, are the things of nightmares. Those who encounter them don't live to tell or see the light of day. They follow no laws, they have no decorum, and they will torture or kill whoever, as long as the price is right. Probably why the entire Wick family has always been Orni. They are all sick and twisted."

The room fell into silent tension. No one spoke a word. Neither Cairis nor Gia's expressions hinted at any sort of surprise, given the graveness of Varro's words. I thanked the Gods that Trace hadn't been in the room to hear these accusations, or Varro may have been without one of his well-defined limbs.

My mind wrestled with his words, trying to make sense of what he was implying. Trace was military…or at least, that's what I had thought. I'd seen his vicious side firsthand with that gambler, but torture and senseless killing? I refused to accept that as being true. I'd never heard of the Orni or the black cloaks, and I was going to give Trace the benefit of the doubt until I could speak with him privately.

"And how would you happen to know so much about them if most don't live to tell," I spat back.

"Because they're the ones who came for my father."

I thought back to my own father's words when he'd said they'd finally captured the barbarian and that he'd be tortured and imprisoned forever.

Rightfully so, but still I shuddered at the thought of Trace, his father, brothers, or really anyone for that matter being the one to execute those orders.

That annoying humming feeling was back again. Low and steady, but I shoved it aside when Varro stood up in front of me angling his body into my personal space. He lifted his hand and gently moved a strand of my hair to the side, revealing my bare neck. He let out a *humph* and stepped away before I could reprimand him for touching me. He strode past Cairis and Gia, making his way to the dormitories, completely disengaging from any further conversation.

Utterly irritated by him, and now filled with even more questions for Trace, I'd had my fill of socializing.

"I'll see you both at dinner," I offered while passing them on the way back to my room. I needed to get my thoughts together in peace.

CHAPTER 10

Unpacking what little I was allowed to bring did nothing to distract me or pass the time. I laid in my bed, staring at the ceiling and empty walls. I imagined this was what the cell of a prison felt like. But it wasn't a prison, and the food we'd had earlier was a sign of some semblance of hospitality. Despite the fact that we weren't allowed to leave, they hadn't treated us poorly. Yet.

When I heard the rustling of footsteps in the hallway, I took that to mean dinnertime had finally come. I was anxious for a number of reasons. Seeing the others—seeing Trace—but also intrigued to meet the new instructor. Would they be like Saryn? He was unbearably prickly in his demeanor. The others may find his dark humor amusing, but to me, it was disarming.

We made our way to the dining hall where food was displayed buffet style on a table toward the back of the room. We formed a line, making our way through and filling up our plates. A late breakfast plus no lunch had clearly built up an appetite in most of us. I watched as each person piled heaps of food onto their plates and took a remarkably similar seating arrangement to this morning. Saryn sat idly at the head of the table, and beside him was another empty place setting, presumably for whomever would be arriving shortly.

Before I could enjoy a bite of my meal, the door to the hall burst open and a cloaked female carrying two large bags made an entrance. Like Saryn, she was wearing all black and had the same long silver talisman around her neck. The amber glow of the fireplace flickered across her deep umber skin, and when she removed her hood, dark thick locks hung across her shoulders.

Her bright silver eyes glanced toward Saryn and he practically barreled toward her from across the room, embracing her tightly and ushering her to sit next to him. It was interesting to see the warmth Saryn showed her, almost like welcoming a sibling after a long time apart.

"Everyone, I'd like to introduce you to my friend, your instructor, the merciless and magnificent, Theory."

Theory nudged his shoulder with her fist, clearly annoyed with his grandiose introduction. "Thank you, Saryn, for the warm welcome, but that charm of yours does not work on me."

She smiled, looking out across the table at each of us eyeing her with curiosity. She seated herself and sipped from a cup Saryn had poured for her. While the others returned to their meals, I kept alert, trying to listen in on their conversation.

"There's so few of them," she said sadly, turning to Saryn with concerned eyes.

"It's true, but it will have to do," he replied while shoving another bite in his mouth. She continued to take brief glances, sizing up the lot of us.

"The place is just as I remembered it. It's been too long." She set her hand atop Saryn's briefly, giving him a knowing look.

"Not long enough," he snarked.

I peered over at Trace, noticing he was doing the same thing as me.

Trying to appear inconspicuous while eavesdropping in between bites. He may have his suspicions about this place, but I was going to make my own conclusions. Theory cleared her throat in an attempt to gather the attention of the room and silence befell us once more, all eyes transfixed on her.

"I imagine the past two days have felt much like a whirlwind, and I'm sure you are tired and will sleep soundly tonight. I am certain that Idris has given you some romantic notion of your role here, and that Saryn has countered that with something grimmer, but I am practical, so consider me the voice of reason."

Nori began to fidget, nervously biting at her nails and waiting with bated breath as Theory continued.

"You are here to learn and train. Plain and simple. What you are good at, we will make you great. What you cannot do, we will make you do well enough. Your strengths will be someone else's weaknesses and vice versa. But you are a team, a family, so you will be accountable to each other. You are going to be pushed farther and harder than you ever thought possible. We are going to try and break you, that way when you face the enemy, you have no fear of the consequences."

Theory took a deep breath.

"So, what are you training us to be? Spies or assassins?" Gia chimed in with an impatient expression.

Theory took no offense, answering her quickly. "Both. You must be all things. The Order is proof that the deadliest things are not your weapons but when *you* become the weapon."

I gulped down my drink; the intensity of this dinner discussion had rattled me. Being a spy was one thing, an assassin, another thing entirely...but all things? What could possibly be worse? Up until this point, I had been confident that I could handle whatever might be asked of me. I knew it would involve secrecy, and likely some deviant acts of violence, but now the worst possibility had been confirmed.

They were going to turn us into hollow shells of our former selves no matter the cost. Theory's eyes radiated a still, vibrant beauty; yet, the longer I looked, they stirred and swirled, conjuring images of dangerous, murky depths lying beneath. Everything else was just a facade meant to draw us in, make us trust her, but now I could read her. I could finally see her and there was no mistaking that she was not someone to cross.

Suddenly, my appetite disappeared. I had finally hit a wall, the pressure of the day eating away at me. I felt my chest tightening with anxiety and wanted nothing more than to escape to the deafening silence of my room.

I would have crawled into Trace's arms, granted myself a moment of vulnerability and let myself cry—if that were an option. I wasn't cut out for this, and yet, it was this or nothing at all. They were monsters, and they were intent on turning us into monsters as well. I blinked my eyes, fighting the stinging feeling, fighting back angry, scared tears.

Just when I thought I couldn't take anymore and was going to flee from the room, I caught Varro's gaze and it held my attention. Relief slowly washed over my body, my heart rate slowed, and I felt as if I had been pulled into a dreamlike state. My tightened muscles unclenched and my shoulders relaxed into the chair. Before turning away from me, he gave me a small nod paired with the hint of a smile at the corners of his mouth.

At my side, it was clear Nori was having similar sentiments. I could see the terror written all over her face. I wish I could bring her some sense of calm, but I wasn't entirely sure where my own sense of control had just come from. Theory was practical, alright; she didn't mince words and had made it abundantly clear we were going to be trained in a manner unlike anything I'd ever experienced. I didn't know about the rest of them, but Nori and I were far from prepared.

Dinner carried on with small talk here and there. Theory spent the rest of the meal catching up with Saryn. Cairis and Gia joked, and Nori and Trace sat in silence. I tried to seem engaged in Gia's conversation, but I kept getting distracted every time I saw Varro taking brief looks in my direction. He had been so harsh earlier, taking much pleasure in educating me about the black cloaks. I was quickly reminded of my distaste for him.

"We will see you all bright and early. Training will begin promptly after breakfast. If you know what's good for you, you'll get some much-needed rest. I do not intend to go easy on you."

Theory's words were a promise, not a threat. She exited the dining room and Saryn politely carried her bags. She didn't seem like the type to need any assistance from anyone, but she let him anyway. Once more, we all sat in uncomfortable silence, this time with full stomachs.

That night, I laid in my bed, grappling with thoughts of Trace being nearby yet so distant in every other way. It was unfathomable to me that since we had parted, all I had done was long to see him again, to touch him, and here we were, mere steps apart and having to show the highest level of restraint. It was an absurd form of torture, only to be superseded by the fear of what Saryn and Theory had in store for us.

I ran my fingertips along the soft edge of the Nightwing feather and closed my eyes, remembering Trace's scent and his rough hands running along the dips and valleys of my body. I needed him to find a way for us to be alone together; the separation and proximity were already destroying me. I thought of the times I had lain awake in bed beside Trace, fighting sleep with all my might. Despite my best efforts, I quickly fell into a heavy, dreamless sleep.

CHAPTER 19

With no windows or sunlight, I'm uncertain how my body knew it was morning, but I somehow pulled myself from slumber still feeling exhausted and already anxious. Given that we were beginning our training today, I chose a set of my fighting leathers, clothing that would allow me to be protected and as agile as required. I braided my long hair and tucked the loose strands behind my ears. In the washroom, I tried splashing cold water on my face, but it did nothing for the dark circles forming around my eyes. I looked like I had been through it, and I'd only been here a day.

At breakfast, I made sure to eat a well-rounded meal, knowing I'd need the energy since Theory was likely to work us into submission. Once more I seated myself next to Nori, doing my best to make small talk and complimenting her attire. It wasn't exactly ideal for fighting, but it was loose and flowy; hopefully, she'd still be able to accomplish whatever was expected of us.

She gave me a sweet smile and thanked me for the kind words. Her dainty frame appeared lean and light as a feather, not to mention she was the shortest one. I did feel some trepidation for her and what combat training might do to a body like hers.

We ate and I casually remarked on how nothing had been as good as when Idris had served us a meal. Nori agreed and pointed out that what Idris had done was very powerful magic. It wasn't a shallow trick; he had used mind-reading and transfiguration to provide us each with individually tailored meals, and then with mesmerization convinced us through our memories and desires that what we were eating tasted just as we had remembered or hoped.

On top of that, he did it nearly instantaneously and somehow managed to be inside all our heads at once. I hadn't put much thought into what he'd done until she remarked on it, but it all made sense when she explained it. I didn't get the feeling that Saryn or Theory were going to be doing anything out of the goodness of their hearts to make us feel welcome. Thinking further on it, the act was not one of kindness but rather a display of power and manipulation on Idris' part.

Theory came to fetch us from breakfast and we followed her to a new section of Basdie with Saryn trailing close behind. The stronghold was like a volcano, hollowed out over years by the powerful waterfall. The remaining rock created a funnel shape for the water to empty into. Hallways twisted and spiraled downward.

We circled our way lower; to our right was clear glass letting sunlight from the top of the waterfall leak in, illuminating the crashing waters. On the left-hand side, doors led to rooms carved out of the stone mountain. So many unexplored doors.

A couple of levels farther down, Theory welcomed us into a giant open room in the shape of a square. It was not much different from the training room at the academy. Once again, firelight was the only thing illuminating the windowless space, and if anything, that made it more intimidating than necessary.

That was unquestionably the worst part of Basdie; it was nothing but room after room cloaked in darkness. It made being in the hallway with light from the waterfall feel like a refuge.

The group entered, spreading out while some of us explored the items hanging along the walls. There were sections lined with every weapon imaginable. This place had it all. Swords, daggers, and blades of all sizes and shapes—curved, straight, and serrated. Spears with sharp tips glinting in the candlelight, ropes of all thicknesses, short and long bows. I'd be lying if I didn't admit to myself that the sight of it all both excited and terrified me.

Folding her arms closely around herself, Nori distanced herself from the weaponry. She exuded fear; it was written across every inch of her face. I made my way over to her in hopes that she'd feel a little less tense with me at her side. Cairis touched a wall of spears and clumsily knocked one from its stand. He gave us a sheepish smile of embarrassment, and I found amusement in the fact that even the spears looked like twigs next to him.

I tried to imagine sparring with him and shuddered at the thought of him throwing his full weight against me. The only way to beat him as an opponent would be with agility and speed, evading until he tired out.

There were still a lot of unknowns about Basdie and the Order, but the training room brought me a sense of familiar comfort. I was good at this sort of stuff. I enjoyed it and, in fact, I thrived in it. But these were skills I'd used for sport, for entertainment not survival. Everyone I ever trained with was for fun or competition. I struggled to conceive an emotion that would lead me to drive a real sword into my opponent, to intentionally bring them harm or worse...

In the center of the room, Theory ran her thumb in circular motions around the talisman hanging from her neck.

"Here is where you will train the body and teach your mind to overcome pain and exhaustion. Your senses must be sharp enough to anticipate your enemy's move before they make it. It is inexcusable to have brute strength but yield due to poor endurance. It is inadvisable to wield a blade but have no use of your fists."

Saryn leaned against one of the four stone columns framing the square training floor. He had a mischievous look about him. Like he was just waiting for Theory to unleash her madness upon us.

Theory continued, "You will bleed in this room. If you're not bruised, battered, and bleeding then you're not working hard enough and I will know. You do not want me to be the one to push you, so push yourself. And, I will state this plainly for anyone who is feeling chivalrous or shy: If you hesitate to treat any person in this room as anything other than equal, as anything other than a threat, regardless of their size, shape, or gender, you will not like the punishment that I will inflict."

I looked across the room and Varro's eyes were once again upon me. His jaw was set in a tight line and I could see a flicker of disagreement in his expression, but he did not dare speak out against Theory.

"For those of you who are not able to truly master the art of healing, you will find respite in the healing waters of Basdie. Surely, you didn't think that waterfall was just for looks?" Saryn chimed in.

I had never used my magic to heal anything major. Minor aches and pains here and there, but nothing of consequence. The idea that after each of these sessions we were going to require experienced healing abilities was nauseating. I might be able to fake my way through the combat training, but I knew I'd always been reliant on salves, tonics, and the like for any sort of severe recovery.

Given the lifeless rock I was trapped inside of, I highly doubted I'd be able to lean on that knowledge. I could only hope that there was either some untapped magic I could eventually hone, or that these so-called healing waters lived up to their name. But there would be no healing waters wherever they were sending us after here; I resolved to make sure I mastered it somehow.

It wasn't long before Theory had us all standing spread out and practicing various movements in repetition to warm up our bodies, leading us through stretches. Saryn circled the room, surveying us in quiet contemplation. The cave-like rooms of Basdie were normally cool, but the exercise had most of us already breaking out in a sweat.

I tried to avert my eyes from Trace. Images of his slick body brought back inappropriate memories, and I tried to focus on my mental shields while continuing the movements Theory commanded of us.

Next, she instructed us to pair up for some hand-to-hand combat. I anxiously watched Trace approach Cairis. I feared the inevitability that Varro and Trace would have to face one another eventually. But it would not be today, and the relief of that spread through me. Gia stepped up to Varro, taking spiteful pleasure in pairing with a male. It was so like Gia to want to test the waters of Theory's equal-means-equal training methods.

I went to pair with the only person left in the room, but when I turned to face Nori, I found her sitting against the wall in the corner, her legs tucked tightly into her chest. What was she doing?

I went over to inquire if something was wrong or if she wasn't feeling well. Given the options, I was the best partner for her. I wasn't going to go easy on her, at least not in a noticeable way, but she seemed entirely too breakable to spar with anyone else.

I crouched beside her. "Hey, come on, what are you doing?"

She wouldn't even look up at me, remaining firm and unmoving.

"Nori, we have to practice. You heard Theory. If we don't push ourselves, she's going to be the one doing the pushing, and I don't want to find out what that means on day one."

Before my pleading could get me anywhere, I felt the presence of Saryn hovering over us both. "Ladies, do we have a problem here?"

"I'm not sure." I tried to make an excuse for her. "I don't think she feels well enough to practice today."

Before we even had a second to see if Saryn had believed a single word of my lie, Nori gritted out, "I'm not doing this."

Saryn let out an amused laugh. Nori was small and meek, no match to be squaring off with Saryn in any sort of altercation, but the intensity in her dark eyes seemed to be boiling over. Saryn crouched down and menacingly whispered to her, "Your Goddess isn't here. Get up, now!"

I took a step back, feeling the energy shifting between them. Nori looked infuriated with Saryn, and it was clear he had struck a serious chord.

Theory yelled from across the room, "What's going on? Why are those two wasting time?"

Saryn stood and barked across the room, "We have a follower of Ilithyia amongst us."

He said it with such distaste, I could feel his annoyance permeate the air. The Goddess Ilithyia. I tried to remember the histories of our religious texts. If I recalled correctly, she was one of the old Gods, a herald of fertility, and lived her life as a pacifist. It was all starting to make sense. Nori was refusing to fight because she abhorred violence. Oh Gods, how in the three moons of Demir did she end up here?

Suddenly, my protectiveness of her heightened, but Saryn was intent on breaking her. They had told us this is exactly what they'd do. They didn't care about our beliefs or reservations, and especially not who we were before the Offering.

Theory yelled across the room coldly, "We have no need for that nonsense here; I suggest you make yourself useful to us."

Nori didn't waver; she was resolved to ignore their insults. I understood her beliefs, I really did, but now wasn't the time to be idealistic. They can refer to us all as family, they can trap us here if they like and force us to train, but that doesn't mean they have to keep us if we aren't useful to them.

I gave Nori a pleading look, one begging for her trust. She ignored me, leaving me without a sparring partner. I looked nervously at Saryn who had already come to the same conclusion I had.

"Pity when grapes wither on the vine," he chided, walking away and leaving Nori curled up on the cold floor. He beckoned me to follow him.

My nerves had shot through the roof and I couldn't help but fixate on Saryn's patch, wondering how he had lost his eye, when suddenly he open-hand smacked me across the face. The room went silent and the others turned to face us in disbelief.

"Be careful, Cress, or you'll lose an eye, too."

I cupped my hand to my throbbing cheek, trying to come to terms with how hard he had hit me with no warning. "Keep me out of your head or suffer the consequences of your distraction."

I clenched my fists in anger, everyone around us disappearing from my vision as I attacked Saryn. I swung angrily, but he ducked and dodged all of my attempts, avoiding every blow. I moved with speed, dancing around him, thinking it might be possible to catch him in a literal blind spot, but he anticipated my every move. I continued my assault, letting every bit of rage flow through me. Rage for how they treated Nori, for being stuck here, rage for how Trace was avoiding me, and for what they wanted me to become.

Despite Saryn's size, he was nimble and managed to keep up with me. I was already tired, and he was not showing any signs of slowing down. In an act of desperation I yelled, "Gia, blade… Now!"

Without hesitation, Gia lunged for a short sword on the wall and threw it to me. The second I caught the hilt, I could see pride flicker across Saryn's face—but I didn't care.

I swung the blade wildly in his direction, left then right, again and again, forcing him to back up farther and farther with each step until his back hit the stone corner post. In one fluid twist, a motion I had practiced many times, I lunged to one knee now holding the blade right against his lower belly, and yelled, "Yield!"

In a real fight, with one slice of that blade, his innards would be on the floor.

Saryn did not respond and instinctively, my training taught me to yell again, "Yield!"

Saryn looked down at me with his one good eye, unyielding. I pushed the sharp edge of the blade into his shirt, applying pressure, trying to show him it was over.

But he was daring me. He wanted me to cut him. Everything about this uncomfortable silence told me to do it, but something in me wouldn't allow it. I had never purposefully cut anyone in my life. Worried that Saryn would do something to force me into action, I stood abruptly, still firmly holding my blade against him, and before he could say another word, I slapped him right across the face in the same way he had done to me earlier.

I stepped back and watched a broad smile curl across Saryn's face as he went to wipe away the blood I had drawn from his lower lip. Suddenly, I felt a firm grip on my shoulder and Theory was standing beside me.

"It's always the ones you least expect. Well done. At least you made up for that disappointment of a girl in the corner."

I felt my hand clench the hilt tightly and tried to calm myself. I was exhausted, and there wasn't a doubt in my mind that now was not the time to try my hand against her. Fighting one teacher was enough for today.

When I finally slackened the blade at my side, the rest of the room and its occupants came slowly back into focus. Gia looked splendidly tickled. Cairis and Varro smiled in my direction with pride and amusement. But Trace, he looked…disturbed. His skin was bone white and both his fists were clenched tightly at his sides. While everyone else in the room had been impressed with my improvisation, Trace looked pained.

Perhaps he could not bear witness to Saryn laying his hands on me in such an offensive manner. I could not offer him anything in the way of empathy. That was what we were here to do. What they wanted from us; I felt strong for the first time since arriving here.

Theory circled back to the rest of the room. "You should all take note of what happened here today. A male will hit a beautiful lady. A female should be able to defend herself from someone twice her size. And when there are no rules, then there are none to break. Resourcefulness and quick thinking may save your life, but most importantly, rely on your team. That's why there is no room for useless people at Basdie."

She gave a scornful look in Nori's direction, and whatever brief pleasure I had taken in my victory was now overshadowed by the reminder of what had led to this altercation.

Saryn walked past me and waved his hand in a fluid motion over his cut lip. When he pulled his hand away the wound was gone, completely healed. He winked at me with his one good eye and retreated towards the entrance of the training room.

"Theory will focus on the physical aspects of your training, and I will focus on helping you hone your magic. If your body doesn't tire of her, I assure you that your minds will tire of me," he said while making his exit. "Meet me in the common room in an hour, I will show you another place we will be training."

Theory followed Saryn, and we all looked around at one another, questioning whether we were meant to keep training on our own or if this meant we were allowed to take a break as well. I was parched; when neither of them returned to provide any instruction, I was the first to head to the door in search of water.

Having found my way to the kitchen, after a few minutes alone, I was suddenly alerted to another's presence. I turned and looked down to see Nori. She reached up and held her hand to my face, cupping my aching cheek. I could already feel the bruise forming from where Saryn had struck me. Nori closed her eyes and I felt warmth radiate outward from her palm, and when she removed her touch, she took the pain with it. There was no longer a dull ache and I could feel that the swelling was gone. "Thank you!"

She nodded. "They would seek to have you harmed, when we should only ever seek to heal."

I hadn't heard Nori speak much, but suddenly she sounded wise beyond her years. Maybe outside of this place, in our former lives, what she said would be true. But it's clear that was not our destiny, and I feared for her safety if she fought the inevitable much longer. I sought to understand her in hopes that I might be able to appeal to her sensibilities.

"You're a disciple of Ilithyia?" I pried.

"Yes, I took my vows on my eighteenth namesake," she replied, exuding pride.

"Candidly, I don't know much about what that means. I just know she is a Goddess whose blessing bears fertility. She has often been referred to as the Eternal Mother."

Nori smiled, looking eager to educate me. "Yes, that is true. As a follower of Ilithyia, we take a vow of chastity. It's seen as a way to continue to imbue her with the powers of fertility. To give our own so that she may bestow it upon others."

"And the pacifism?"

"While the vows do not include pacifism, explicitly, most of us try to honor her by living in the image of her likeness, which includes never bringing harm unto another," Nori elaborated.

While I admired Nori's commitment and that she had made such a huge decision at such a young age with so much life ahead, I was certain there was no worse place for her and those beliefs than the Order. I don't know what they had in store for us, but some of Saryn's indications made me fear even more for Nori.

"Was there no one else to take your place here?" The question left my mouth before I had even taken a second to consider whether it was rude or if it would strike more fear and concern in her.

"No, I am an only child—and a miracle, at that. My mother was unable to carry. For years, she prayed to the Goddess Ilithyia to bring her a healthy child. She and my father suffered many losses in their attempts to bring a child into this world. But she believed her prayers would be answered, even prayers to the old Gods who do not often listen."

Nori seemed lost in her storytelling. "Finally, after much heartache, they brought me into this world. I arrived early, without warning, and I was small and frail, but I was everything they had hoped for."

I began to feel a well of happy tears.

"You can imagine how awful it was to receive the news that your only child and heir was to be taken from you."

I thought back to Versa and how leaving her behind at least meant the bloodline and legacy of our family would be carried on. Given the trouble Nori's parents went through just to bring her into the world, it was unlikely they'd be that lucky again. By the look she gave, she could obviously read the expression on my face.

"How old are you, if you don't mind me asking?"

She let out a cynical laugh. "I had just turned twenty before my parents received my calling to the Offering."

As I'd suspected, she was the youngest of us, and because of that she had nearly escaped this fate.

"The whole reason I swore my vows to Ilithyia was in hopes that she would bless my parents again. Not that I wasn't enough, not that they could have known what would happen to me, but because my mother was born to be a mother. And like all High Fae, a large family full of heirs was the one thing they desired."

Her honesty reminded me of the truth I had told myself during the thirty days before being delivered to the king. If my parents truly wanted to, they had plenty of time to bear more heirs.

Now that Nori had shared this piece of herself with me, I felt our connection growing. I couldn't really explain my feelings. Perhaps it was the absence of Versa that made me long for another sisterly bond, but with each encounter with Nori, I found myself feeling more protective of her in the same way I was of my own sister. Still, not even I was naive enough to believe I could shield her from this place.

"Please be careful," were the only words I could offer her. She didn't say it, but I heard it quietly in her thoughts, *They can only make you a monster if you let them.*

The hour-long break passed quickly, and we soon joined the others in the common room just as Saryn had requested. "Follow me and keep up," he demanded.

Once more, we paced behind Saryn and Theory through the winding halls of Basdie. My eagerness to explore and uncover where they were taking us was hampered by heavy thoughts of Nori and what they might do to her if she continued to resist.

We arrived at a large door, and when it opened, I raised my arm to my face to shield my eyes from the blinding brightness. It was unfiltered daylight and the crisp air blew through the corridor. We walked toward the light, eventually making our way outside.

The fresh mountain air overtook me and I inhaled deeply, letting the sunlight blanket me and warm my skin. A stone landing had been carved into the side of the mountain. I deduced this was the opposite side of the mountain that we had entered from. The ledge overlooked a valley of dense forest with tall gray mountains jutting up on all sides. Once my eyes adjusted to the natural light, I squinted, noticing a tiny river carving its way through the trees in the lower valley; runoff from the mighty waterfall within.

Saryn stood at Theory's side, a remarkable mountainscape as their backdrop. "Some of you might be shy or embarrassed about this, depending on how you were raised. Some of you won't care. In either case, it's time to get over any of those sensitivities immediately. This valley will also be your training ground—and sky. Show me your wings, now."

The impropriety of her instruction was outrageous. The last time someone had seen my wings, I was with Trace, and that was an accident. Before that, I don't recall the last time anyone but family had seen them. Aster's words echoed in the back of my mind. All of us stood there with similar reactions, unwilling to acquiesce.

Unexpectedly, I heard footsteps scraping against the rocky ground as Trace stepped forward.

"Ahh, at least one of you is going to make this easy," Theory remarked with a pleased look in his direction.

Trace waited for a moment, looking out upon the valley, his gaze turning upward toward the steep mountains. He turned his head slightly and locked eyes with me, narrowing his attention so it was as if we were the only two people here on this landing. Suddenly, his shoulders flexed and his wings spanned out. Wide, strong, giant wings covered in black feathers of all sizes, just like the one he had gifted me.

The sunlight highlighted the green iridescence that shimmered across each feather as they blew lightly in the breeze. He continued to hold my gaze and I felt like I was the only one witnessing his beauty.

We were interrupted when Saryn impatiently called out, "Alright, who's next?"

I couldn't tear my eyes away from Trace. I was bothered that everyone else was being allowed to look upon him like this, but I knew we had no choice. This was just one more step in breaking us down and forcing us to leave behind the ways of our pasts.

Cairis stepped forward and, without hesitation, he unfurled his wings. They were slightly larger than Trace's and different in every way. His were heavy looking, whereas Trace's were light like a bird's. Cairis' wings were also black, but thick, almost like leather, and only when the sun hit them at a certain angle could you see a hint of light trying to shine through in the thinner spots. At the top of each wing sat a sharp curved talon, and on the bottom ends were pointed tips. He did not appear shy at all; in fact, that smirk of his indicated he was putting on quite a show like a preening youth.

Varro then stepped forward, giving himself space away from the splayed wingspans of Trace and Cairis. In typical male behavior, neither of them tucked their wings, continuing to keep them spread wide on display as if this were some sort of pageant.

Varro looked to Theory, then called forth his wings. When they appeared, I think my jaw might have dropped. They were light and wispy, a transparent blue-green. Equal parts aggressive and delicate. The tips appeared like a serrated fin that you might see on a more exotic species of sea creature. The longer I looked, the more I got lost in the swirling shades of aqua and teal. Every time the light hit them; it was like seeing the sparkle that appears on the horizon line where the ocean meets the sun.

I was suddenly taken back to the few times I had witnessed such a horizon, and I was lost in the memory of a place I longed to be.

And I was finally seeing Varro in direct sunlight, and just like I had imagined, his golden skin glowed with even more vibrancy. He looked like he could melt a frozen pond with just the touch of his palm. I tried to imagine all of the Sea Fae and how wondrous they must look with their wings out like this.

I stood a fair distance from him, but time seemed unmoving; I could feel the urge in my fingertips to reach out and touch them. As if he could hear me thinking it, Varro turned to meet my stare, and in those crystal blue eyes of his was the look of pleading. But pleading for what?

Distracted by the sound of Trace rustling his wings, I turned to see who might be next. Should I go? I was still trying to build up the courage, though the others had taken to the assignment without much hesitation.

I stepped forward in line next to Varro, keeping a fair distance and trying to ignore all the wonderful colors I could see reflecting off the panels of his wings. He gave me an encouraging nod, and my brow furrowed in confusion. What was with this guy? One minute he's jumping down my throat, the next he's showing me some semblance of kindness.

I inhaled another breath of cool mountain air, focusing and trying to clear my mind of all distractions. It took me longer than the others, but I could finally feel them stirring below the surface as I did my best to will them forth. Finally, they answered my call, and the iridescent green with hints of yellow and gold was bright in the sunlight; the same type of wings many in the southern Riverlands bore. Never in my life had I seen such a display of how different the Fae could be. It all depended on where they were born and what the generations of Fae before them needed to survive, blend in, or coexist with their surroundings.

The Nightwings of the North, the Sea Fae of the Endless Tides, and the Leatherwings hailing from the rocky cave territories in the Northeast. It was fascinating to see in person rather than just illustrated on the pages of a textbook. My excitement overwhelmed me, and we hadn't even seen everyone's yet.

I had no idea what Ilithyia would think of Fae showing their wings, but I was relieved to see Nori step forward in compliance. She looked at me and permitted herself a small smile before a set of perfectly petite wings burst forth from her tiny shoulders. Hers were the smallest amongst us, but if they had been any larger, then she might have toppled over from the weight.

They were stunning in their own right; milky white and sparkling, giving the appearance of tiny clear crystals speckled across every panel. If anyone should be proud of their wings, it was her—they were truly something special to behold, as if they were made by the hands of the Eternal Mother herself.

We all stood there baring ourselves to each other and the mountain-tops. Nowhere to hide and nothing to be ashamed of. In one sense, it was freeing, and I started to wonder why there had ever been any etiquette around wings at all. This was our natural state, why should we hide from it or each other?

There was only one of us left to complete the exercise, and I turned to Gia, surprised that given her boisterous attitude, she hadn't been the first to show off the goods. But to my confusion, she looked truly distraught. She stepped forward slowly, and I felt a lump in my throat building. I couldn't help what happened next, it just…happened. I found myself slipping into Gia's mind during her moment of weakness while her mental shields were down.

I gasped at the flashes of her pain. Pain that felt like a hundred daggers were splicing through my own heart. She had a broken bond. A mate. Gia stared straight ahead, refusing to look at any of us. I could see the droplets of tears now streaming down her face as they crested the ridge of her cheek. Her hands were shaking despite her clasping them tightly together.

When Gia's beautiful wings finally appeared, it felt like a crime to look upon them. Knowing she had once had a mate and now concealed the heartbreak of a broken bond, it felt like seeing something that should have been just for them. But if etiquette wasn't a valid reason to keep our wings private, I knew there was no arguing with the sacred act of only revealing them to a true mate. I couldn't imagine the pain she was enduring by putting them on display for all of us, as if it meant nothing.

The bright ruby red color, regal like Gia, suited her in every way. Similar in size to mine, but far more alluring and far less transparent. Delicate, yet bold. They absorbed the light, creating an ombre of red like a blood rose, each shade waterfalling into a deeper crimson.

I am certain Cairis, and perhaps the others, were amazed at the sight of them. She just stood there, silent, stoic, letting the tears fall.

Suddenly, Theory clapped her hands together, the sound echoing in the mountain valley and drawing our attention back to her.

"Your wings are first and foremost part of what makes you a weapon.

Secondly, they are transportation. And lastly, to be used as a means for seduction, but we'll save that for later."

The word seduction caught me off guard, and I could practically feel Nori recoil at the statement alone. I brushed it off and tried to focus my attention back on our instructor.

"When you're not working on your combat skills in the training room, you'll be doing so out here. You must be as equally agile in the skies as you are on the ground. For those of you whose family taught them of the long war, then you know many lives were lost due to Fae civilities causing a shortage of those who could defend themselves by air. Forget those nonsensical customs and learn to use your wings. This is what they're made for."

Anytime Theory spoke, she was challenging us in more ways than one. It was easy to rely on our old customs, but what she was saying made sense. She was merely asking us to live authentically and use what had been given to us; such a different perspective from the one I was raised with.

While many of the Fae people shared that view, a feeling of dread crept from the corners of my mind, suggesting the long-held peace was more fragile than ever. Why else would they be training us like this? And why just us? Shouldn't everyone in Cambria be prepared? So many questions to keep track of. I wanted to learn, and I had no problem with training, but the *why* behind everything remained a mystery, and that was the most frustrating part of it all.

"Now that you've had a thorough introduction into how you'll spend your time training under the watchful eye of Theory, it's time you learn about my syllabus." Saryn directed us back to the classroom with a roguish expression as each of us passed by.

I found it difficult to leave the warmth of the daylight as we made our way back into the cool, dreary halls of Basdie.

CHAPTER

20

I promise you that your bodies will be nowhere near as exhausted as your minds when I'm done with you." It was about the least motivating way to begin a class, but at this point, I'd come to expect nothing less from Saryn.

Before he divulged his own plans, Theory made a point to explain how general studies would work. These instructions felt more akin to my time at the academy than anything else we had covered thus far.

Saryn went on to explain that between our physical training schedule and our curriculum with him, we wouldn't be setting aside formal time to spend on typical academics—we'd need to use our free time for that. Despite there being no official classes on the subject matter, we'd still be required to master this knowledge; he noted the library in the common area.

Any of us who didn't already know the histories, politics, and religious texts of the last few hundred years would be expected to learn them. Those of us who already did were encouraged to dive deeper.

They emphasized that we must be able to blend in with the nobility and common folk alike. This meant knowing the histories from all angles to avoid the risk of bias revealing our true identities.

I had never really thought of viewing text in this way. Usually, I just read books and took them at face value, black and white, facts and figures. But now they encouraged us to read between the lines, question everything, seek out all truths and use our peers to garner a more worldly view.

Cairis was the least academically inclined since his father had sent him to work in the mines rather than affording him the education of his legitimate siblings. I made a mental note to set up an arrangement whereby I'd tutor him in general studies if he showed me some sparring tips and tricks. If Varro had grown up sailing the Endless Tides, then he was likely the most worldly of us all, but I wasn't about to go rub shoulders with him. Not until I figured out what involvement he'd had with his traitorous father.

I was curious to know if he spoke the old tongue like me, but secretly I hoped I was the only one that could. I didn't think there was much that made me special or unique in this group. If I could have just one thing that only I could do, I'd consider it an accomplishment.

There was also no doubt that Nori likely knew the religious texts better than any of us. Honestly, I hadn't been a believer in much of anything; those tomes seemed more like fables to keep the questionable morality of the Fae in line. I supposed I'd always thought of myself as someone with an intrinsic moral compass, but I was unsure what good that would do me now that I was expected to go against everything I'd been raised to do. Be a lady, be polite, be smart but not smart-mouthed, know how to fight but never raise a hand, represent my family well, maintain a good reputation for the Honored Fae, serve as a member of the High Court, marry, carry on the family name and brings heirs into the world. None of that seemed to be the case anymore, and that sent my moral compass spinning.

In summary, the message was straightforward: read in your own time, tutor each other, and don't waste Theory and Saryn's precious attention with general studies unless you have an important question. I was curious to see if there were any recorded histories of the Offering and the Order. It was unlikely, but if they were anywhere to be found, wouldn't Basdie be the safest place to house them? Unless the Order and everyone in it truly was lost to time.

"Now that we're past the boring stuff"—Theory rolled her eyes at Saryn as he continued—"let's discuss my area of expertise...magical abilities. Power."

"Over the next few days, I will be doing private evaluations with each of you. This is for me to determine where your current strengths and weaknesses lie, and where you're lacking entirely." He eyed Nori.

He continued, "I don't need you distracted by the judgment of your peers during these evaluations, as it may impact your performance. Once we find a baseline, we can improve, and that includes confidently channeling your capabilities in the presence of others."

I was secretly grateful that these so-called evaluations would be behind closed doors. After spending most of my life suppressing the use of magic, I wasn't entirely sure what I was capable of. Now that we had all been imbued with more power, I was eager to discover what that meant—but not at the risk of becoming a source of amusement for the others.

It was clear some of us had grown up using less magic. Never did I think I would be grateful for getting the chance to be alone with Saryn, even after the altercation in the training room. This was the only exception.

Over the next few hours, Saryn explained each type of ability we could potentially have in our arsenal with enough training. He emphasized that not everyone could or would be expected to master them all. He'd snarkily mentioned which ones would require more skill, focus, strength, and energy, implying that some of us weren't cut out for it. But that didn't mean we'd be considered total failures, so long as we showed promise in other areas. The lesson began simply enough, but every transition revealed new complexities and difficulties.

The first and most basic would be healing. Being able to heal our small wounds was where the bar started. Healing ourselves from more critical injury was the next level of difficulty, and thus would require more energy. Lastly, the gift of being able to heal others. I thought back to when Nori had held her hand to my cheek, nonchalantly removing all pain and swelling with a brief touch. It made me want to lash out at Theory and yell that Nori wasn't useless like they all assumed, and that she showed more promise than I did in this area.

The next item discussed was glamour. The mere mention of it made me start to fume in Trace's direction as my eyes scanned the scar across his eyebrow and both his fully tattooed arms. All the energy he must have expended to keep his true appearance from me, and for what?

I had to admit I still found him just as attractive, if not more, but it felt like a betrayal, nonetheless. Saryn spent a lot of time discussing how this skill must be honed so that one could uphold a glamour toward individuals, small groups, even large audiences for short and long durations. It made me wonder if the entire time Trace and I were at the tavern he only bothered to glamour me, or if that included all the other patrons too.

Discussing glamour naturally led to the conversation about shapeshifting. A much more difficult power to master. I had practically given up any chance of being able to do it at the first mention. To my knowledge, the first time I'd ever seen anyone shapeshift was when we first arrived and Saryn transformed from a sensuous female into the handsome and cunning male before us now.

Unlike the trickery of glamour, shapeshifting was much more than some vivid illusion. You could touch it, feel it, and everything about it would seem real. By the end of his explanation, I pretty much resolved to master glamour long before I'd attempt shapeshifting.

The discussion of mind reading went hand in hand with mental shields. Many Fae had the ability to read minds; it was just terribly impolite. Most people were out of practice, eventually tuning it out completely. This is why many didn't bother expending the energy to keep up their mental shields. With everyone minding their own business, there wasn't a need.

Now and then people would slip up and follow it with an apology. I thought back to Gris and how he'd known I was self-conscious in the sunlight, then had proceeded to draw the curtains and dim the lights without me asking.

We were growing tired of hearing Saryn stress the importance of learning to live with our mental shields up at all times. While I understood the importance of it, the idea of it sounded utterly exhausting. He then proceeded to point out that all mind-reading is one-way, and only true bonded mates possessed the two-way communication known as mind-melding. In the old tongue, this was usually referred to as *fideli cœur*.

I glanced over at Gia, not surprised to see an expression of melancholy. I couldn't imagine being cut off from someone the way she had been by coming here. To have had that kind of intense connection with another and have it severed seemed like an unimaginable level of heartbreak I did not want to ever experience.

Saryn snidely remarked that while that two-way skillset might come in handy, it wasn't worth it to have to deal with a bonded pair, and he thanked the Gods as this was no place for mates.

Next, he covered the act of mesmerization, more commonly referred to as "pushing" someone. In a way, this felt like the most intrusive of the powers he'd listed thus far. It was one thing to listen in on someone's thoughts, or manipulate what you looked like, but this is when we started to ignore boundaries entirely. Using eye contact, or sometimes a simple phrase, even a change in tone of voice could cause another person to do your bidding.

It was stripping someone of their freedom and control over their actions and decisions. I'd never experienced anything like that; an act like that toward someone of a High household is considered treachery. If you truly mastered shields, then you could not only block someone from reading your thoughts, but your mind would also be impenetrable to mesmerization.

It felt like Saryn had been rambling on forever, as if he enjoyed the sound of his voice. Admittedly, the discussion probed further than I'd ever allowed my thoughts to explore, and that alone was enough to intrigue me. Yet, rapt as I was, a certain weight of expectation pressed down heavily, causing me to slump further into the chair.

He saved the most rare and difficult abilities till the end of his diatribe. Elemental manipulation and transfiguration were two additional, similar powers, but had distinct differences. Wielding elements meant that you could shape the natural material that made up our world. Earth, air, fire, and water. It was practically unheard of to channel the creation of the materials and then wield them. Most who did master this required some form of the element to be present or nearby already, no matter how small, then they could manipulate it; that could mean turning it into a weapon or some form of defense like a shield.

Filling my own bath to the brim with a small amount of water from a canteen is a mere shade of what water wielders could do, but perhaps that meant there was promise for me.

Much of the magic discussed today I had barely read about and certainly never saw in person, so I wasn't feeling very worldly or useful. Sometimes I found myself daydreaming in self-doubt while Saryn droned on; thinking about all the years of my life that had gone by without attempting to master any of this. I wasn't certain I could, and that scared me. I wanted to be useful, but more than that was the desire to be powerful. To do rare and difficult things, and perhaps, even impress my peers beyond some reckless sparring.

I already knew what transfiguration was and had seen Idris wielding it on full display. Still, Saryn went over it in detail to ensure everyone understood that the ability to physically change any handmade object, no matter what it was made of, was a rare and useful ability. A useful example included the ability to alter one's clothing when shapeshifting.

Theory made a morbid joke about being able to transfigure wine into poison with a mere wink. A few of us let out a small laugh, but I just looked at her with trepidation because I was certain she was not joking regardless of her playful tone.

The thought of people out there who would do such evil things freely and think of it as creativity or problem-solving was one of the many reasons I struggled to fathom myself being a valued member of the Order. But I had no other choice than to try until I resembled what they wanted me to become.

The second to last power he covered was dreamwalking. Until now, I hadn't believed this power was real. It was mentioned often in bedtime stories from my childhood. While tucking us in, Mother would tell Versa and me tales of strange figures that danced while you slept, bringing sweet dreams to good children—and nightmares to those who misbehaved. Although it seemed silly now, the story made me think twice about disobeying my mother and father when I was little.

This was the ability to gain access to someone's mind while they slept, and in doing so, you could plant ideas and visions to influence them, or you could simply watch their dreamscape to learn more about their innermost desires and plans. People were always at their most vulnerable when sleeping, as their shields would be down.

Theory implied that this power was extremely rare and we would not be expected to master an ability that was considered more of an innate gift. She also mentioned that the only Dreamwalker she had ever encountered was now dead, their head on a pike in a town square for all to see when their master learned of the trespasses that had been made.

I shuddered at the thought of it, because Theory had intentionally let her shields down and her thoughts were practically screaming the visuals of it at me, to the point where I could detect the faint copper taste of blood on my tongue. I clenched my fists, trying to break myself away from her barrage of thoughts replaying the savage act.

The final power was the gift of vision, and those with it were commonly referred to as Seers. Much like Dreamwalkers, people didn't believe in them. Most people treated them like crackpots or individuals who had lost their minds. I thought back to Aster in the woods. Her riddles and rhymes were cryptic, and yet something about her had made me feel like she could see a picture of which I could only see a fraction.

Saryn assured us that while some people pretended to have the gift of vision to swindle a passerby, Seers were real, rare, and born that way.

"A Seer is only as valuable as their ability to interpret their visions," he added.

"And most refuse to speak of their visions for they believe that increases the chances of them being altered," Theory noted.

That lined up pretty accurately with the fact that for as much as Aster had told me, it made little sense, and she offered no clarity other than my future was being intentionally hidden. Now that I was here in Basdie and part of a secret order, it all added up, and I had a funny suspicion that Idris was behind the enchantments blocking my future from being seen.

Nonetheless, pieces and parts of the riddle began to consume my mind, slipping in from the corners of my memory. My attention returned to the classroom when a long pause of silence occurred. More silence than I had heard in a long while.

Saryn must have finally grown tired of talking because he dismissed us for dinner, and I had to admit I was relieved. If he had put any more thoughts in my head, I might have exploded. By now, I was questioning which part of my training was going to be the death of me. Saryn wasn't kidding, my mind was exhausted and all we'd done was discuss magical abilities; we hadn't even begun attempting them yet.

All the action of the day had built up quite an appetite in me. In the dining room, I decided I was tired of the routine we had all settled into. Sitting in the same order room after room was beginning to irk me; I made a point to wait till Trace sat down, and then I intentionally took the seat next to him before Nori could. She had a confused look when she arrived at the table, but she didn't make a fuss about it and happily took the seat on the other side of me.

He began to eat with a begrudging look that probably only I noticed, and that's because Trace had worn a scowl on his face ever since arriving at Basdie. There was no hiding that he was displeased, so the slightest increase in that displeasure was imperceptible to the others.

I looked down at his arm to my side, noting the black tattoos peeking out the end of his sleeve by his hand. I had been too brave, too bold with my decision to swap seats, because now I had the burning desire to reach out and touch him. Even if I could just place my hand on his, and feel the warmth of his skin against mine, I might be able to relieve the heavy lump that sat in my throat every time I looked at him.

Trace wasn't exactly soft or sweet to begin with, but with me, he had been vulnerable—I knew that to be true. It was almost painful to feel the repulsion he emanated toward me. Did this place erase everything for him? Did I mean nothing to him now? He certainly still meant something to me. I had to find a way to talk to him.

After dinner, the others hung around in the common area, perusing the books. Now that we knew it was expected of us to be studying whenever we had free time, it seemed like people wanted to ensure they weren't stuck with the undesirable texts. Most of us were quiet, likely fatigued with the same exhaustion of the day.

I noticed Nori at a table fiddling with a small sack of items, and I sat down to join her.

"What's that?" I asked.

She looked up with fond excitement that I had shown any interest at all.

"It's a game; I brought it from home. You probably think I'm silly for bringing something like this, but I packed it before I knew what this place was really about..." She trailed off, looking disappointed.

Trying to make her feel better and play along, I continued to feign curiosity, "What's it called?"

"Bones and Stones. Do people play it where you're from?"

I witnessed Nori pour the contents of the sack onto the table: a number of smoothly polished stones and small bone fragments. My sister and I played many games growing up, but I had never heard of this one—and given the name, I don't think my mother would have let us play. I wondered to myself if they were animal bones... Certainly a pacifist wouldn't be carrying around a bag of Fae bones, right?

"No, I can't say I've ever encountered it. How do you play?"

She placed a long stick in between us on the table.

"You're bones and I'll be stones. The stick represents our sides of the board. You take your 5 pieces into your hand and hold them in a fist with your arm straight out in front of you over the center of the stick. You close your eyes and then call your hand, evens or odds."

I listened to the rules intently, hoping that it did not get any more complex than this. I was not one for games with a never-ending list of rules to follow.

She continued, "Once you've made your call, release the pieces from your hand without looking. When you open your eyes, we count the number of pieces that fell on your side of the stick and if it's a sum matching your call, you get a point. However, if the amount on your side of the board is the opposite, then I claim the point. Then we switch turns and repeat till the first person reaches 12 points and is deemed the winner."

Upon her explanation of the rules, I considered how juvenile the game was. There wasn't really any strategy to be had, but I was trying to forge friendships and didn't have much strength to do anything else. After a few rounds of persistently losing to Nori, I began to wonder if she had been cheating or perhaps was able to see through her eyelids. Maybe next time I'd propose blindfolds. It was eerie how accurate she was at guessing on her turn, but I resolved to believe it was because she had played this many more times than I had, or perhaps, next time I'd play stones instead of bones.

Trace may have thought he was being inconspicuous, but I noticed him watching us from the corner of the common room while he pretended to show interest in a book. He retired to his room as soon as Nori let out a small cheer as she claimed her victory point.

Training with Theory, exposing ourselves on the terrace, and then listening to what might as well have been a monologue on magic from Saryn had made for a very, very long day. I found a piece of parchment and scribbled a note on it. Before the others returned to their rooms, I made my way back first and slid the note under Trace's door asking him to meet in four hours after we were certain everyone else would be asleep.

I lay on my bed, waiting for the time to pass and for the hallways to go still and silent. When I was certain everyone else was asleep, I made my exit and was pleased to see he had decided to follow through. Honestly, I had thought there was a very good chance he would ignore my request entirely. His hair was a tousled mess and his eyes looked worn and tired like mine. He was in a loose-fitting black shirt with the sleeves rolled up to his elbows, exposing both marked arms.

I had no idea where I was going to take us to find privacy, but I led the way down the spiraling hallway. That tingling sensation had returned briefly but then quickly waned. Trace kept his distance from me but followed in silence. We walked for what seemed like forever till we reached what presumably was the bottom, as the hallway came to an end and the sound of the waterfall through the glass was even more deafening than it was higher up. We hadn't been shown this part of Basdie yet; we'd both need to act surprised whenever we were brought here later by our instructors.

To my recollection, they hadn't called out any specific rules about staying up late, being out after hours, or wandering Basdie. As Theory had said: *If the rules aren't stated, then there are none to break.* I reflected on the memory of yelling for Gia to throw me a blade before I attacked Saryn.

There was an arched doorway and we wandered through it, unsure of what to expect on the other side. What we discovered was a small circular room with a steaming pool in its center, not unlike the pool at the castle where we had bathed in the waters of Mirtith.

Using his magic, Trace lit more torches lining the walls—a stark contrast from when he insisted on building his own fires. The water glowed and steam hung heavy in the air, making our skin hot. A sheen of sweat formed along my arms, and I removed one of my layers to relieve myself from the heat. I figured why not dip my toes in while we talked?

I removed my boots, placed them to my side, and sat on the damp ground, dipping my feet into the pool. It felt like warm bath water. Trace took a spot on the ground too, but kept a small distance that made the tension obvious.

The silence between us had begun to feel like a unique form of torture. I wasn't normally one to apologize, but I figured the only way to get him to be vulnerable was to do so first.

"I'm sorry that I lied to you. I hope you can see why, since we were both in a similar predicament," I offered, somewhat timidly. "Would it have made a difference?" I anxiously asked for an answer I wasn't entirely prepared to hear.

"I don't think anything could have stopped me from wanting you," he replied, taking a long pause before adding, "My whole life has always been intertwined with every whim of my father or the king, and you were the first thing that made me want another life. One of my choosing."

He turned to look at me directly—one of the few times since we'd arrived. "I knew where I was headed, but I wanted to believe you were somewhere living your life, freely, and that someday you'd find the happiness you deserve."

I tried to interject, but he stopped me before I could get a word in.

"I have this rage inside of me now, a rage I've been unable to quell since seeing your face unveiled in that pool in the depths beneath the castle. You don't deserve this, to have your life taken from you. I cannot bear to see you become the monster they want you to be, and for you to see the monster that I already am."

I reached for his hand, finally feeling the touch of his skin against mine, and I held it tightly, trying to reassure him that I did not see him the way he saw himself. "You're not a monster, Trace, don't say that!"

"Cress, you know nothing about me or my past." His eyes were wide and his words pained. It hurt to hear him say I knew nothing about him, but it also felt true.

"You heard Varro, I'm a black cloak. We're lethal and savage, we do things I won't allow myself to say out loud. I don't even deserve to be in your presence."

I tried to console him. "You're military, you were only doing what was commanded of you."

Trace scoffed and began to shake his head. "We are not military, Cress. The Orni exists in the shadows. We don't belong to the king, we belong to no one. You know what we black cloaks say? *'For coin or Cambria.'* Yes, sometimes our king has employed our services when his own couldn't get the job done, but we serve whoever can pay the price for our services."

I was trying to reconcile what Trace was implying. So, he wasn't Kingsguard, or military at all? He was nothing more than a paid assassin? Someone who just killed for money? My chest tightened with concern, not for my safety, because I was certain he'd never hurt me, but for the looming fact that perhaps the lies Trace had told during our time together concealed much more than I ever had.

My thoughts were a tangled mess trying to make sense of it all. "But how did you become a member of the High Court if you committed these terrible misdeeds?"

"Many years ago, the daughter of a High Lord needed a favor, something unspeakable and unforgivable. She enlisted the help of the Orni, but the price was enormous. Coin alone would never be enough; he demanded a bargain. Her hand in marriage. Thus, he made his way into the High Court via marriage to a Royal Fae. This solidified his power and rank, but he did not settle for the life of a lord. He had far too much bloodlust for a simple life."

Trace's voice was shaky; he struggled to get the words out, and that's when I knew exactly who the daughter of the High Lord was. The female he'd spoken fondly but briefly of—his mother.

I reached for his face to cup his cheek in my hand, and he leaned into the feeling of my caress. His eyes closed briefly, and it was like a world of sadness pooling heavily in my palm. I ran my thumb across his eyebrow with the thin silver scar. He opened his eyes and the hazel bored into me with a beseeching look.

"How did this happen?"

He pulled away from my hand and replied, "Varro isn't the only one with a terrible father."

My eyes widened at the thought of Trace's own father laying a hand on him.

"It's a brand. All the Wick brothers have this. When we were barely adolescents, he tore us away from our mother to begin our 'training.' It began with him holding a scalding hot knife against our brow. I wish I could tell you that the act taught us some insightful lesson, but it was just a sick way to signify to the others that we were his sons and to set us apart like livestock. We weren't allowed to heal ourselves, and nobody else was allowed to help. That's why we have the scars. Pride can lead one to do terrible things, Cress."

I longed to hear my name from his mouth, and each time he said it, I had to restrain myself from pressing mine against his. But everything he said was terribly tragic, and I felt overwhelmed with despair for what he had been put through. His father sounded truly evil, and it was hard to fathom that his father might be the same if not worse than Varro's.

I hadn't realized just how much normalcy and love I had been raised around. Everyone here had some sort of tragedy befall them at one time or another. Cairis, the bastard half-breed. Nori, the miraculous only child. Gia, the broken bonded. Trace, the tormented. As for Varro, I did not know him well, but House Corliss would forever be stained due to his father's treachery. Then there was me. Not special, or unique, just a twin, born into a good family who gave me a good life. It felt unfair, and in some weird way, I felt uneasy about my peaceful life.

My peers had been hurt before they came here. They had motivation to be angry and vengeful, but I had no such thing to drive me.

I knew there was a part of me that was speaking with the real Trace for the first time, but there was also a part of me that wasn't listening, wasn't accepting it. I had spent so much time with him that there was an idea I'd built up of who he was—and who he was to me.

I did not fear him, yet I should have. I should've cared about the lives he'd taken, but I didn't. My feelings and thoughts were mired in contradiction, and my instincts danced between longing and wanting to run.

I leaned in closer to him, his scent further intoxicating my will. This time, Trace did not back away. I could feel my feet lightly touching his below the water. Eventually, our foreheads rested together, our breathing heavy. I could feel the rise and fall of his chest with my palm resting above his heart. I wanted him to know that if he was a monster, I wanted him to be *my* monster. Nothing so reckless had ever felt this right.

Our mouths hovered close, the warmth of our breath swirling together in a whirlpool of lustful anticipation. "We can't do this," he rasped.

"I know," I replied.

"Cress…" he said my name like a quiet prayer.

"Yes?"

"This place is going to make us do terrible things. Things far worse to witness than violence."

"I don't care," I said breathlessly.

"Don't promise me anything beyond this moment," he panted.

His request sounded like he was begging for a reprieve only I could offer him. Promises didn't seem like something either of us could make from here on out, so I acquiesced.

"I won't."

Before I could say another word, Trace's lips were pressed firmly to mine and his hands roamed over every curve of my body with the ferocity of someone starved for touch. It was messy and rough; the steam of the room made it more difficult to breathe as we gasped from one intense kiss to the next.

Beyond the first time with Trace, I had never felt nervous—but something about this act rattled me. It felt wrong and desperate, like we were both clinging to something unattainable. It was frantic with unspoken fear and sadness. I fought back the feeling of tears in my eyes and continued to sweep my tongue across his, running my fingers through his hair, tugging and tilting him to my will.

He pulled me on top of him, encircling my legs around him while his were still submerged at the edge of the pool. He ripped my top open and began to place rough kisses all along my moist body. I could feel his excitement between the thin layer of my pants, and the familiarity of his body against mine felt like home, like the most comforting thing I'd felt since arriving here. I rejoiced in it.

He palmed my breast furiously, and each time he pinched my nipples I let out a small noise of pain mixed with building pleasure. I dragged my nails along his back until I couldn't stand it any longer. I needed the feel of his bare skin against mine. I lifted his shirt over his head and tossed it to the floor.

Trace began to rub his hand between my thighs, causing me to grind my hips. He wasted no time in giving me what I wanted and plunged his hand into my pants, meeting my slick core. My small whimpers echoed in the tiny room, and the sound of them only caused Trace to work me harder.

There were no gentle movements. I began to untie his pants to free him of his constraints. I wanted to see him again; wanted to take him in my hands and mouth. I couldn't take any more of this foreplay, the desire to have him inside me was too great.

Trace picked me up and laid me flat on the hard stone floor beside the pool. He pulled down his trousers far enough to free himself. Impatiently, he pulled my pants off as well, tossing them aside. He spread my legs apart and wasted no time in tearing the thin undergarment from my eager body. It reminded me of all the other times he'd found himself carelessly destroying my clothing.

I gasped when he entered me, reminded of how good this had felt all those times leading up to the day I was delivered to this place. A feeling I thought I'd never have again, from someone I thought I'd never see again. It felt like a fever dream, having him here and now.

Trace pumped in and out of me with fast, shallow movements, and my body arched against the floor, wanting all that he could give me. I felt the stone scraping my back, but I wouldn't waste time trying to re-position. Not when everything else felt so good. Trace shifted into slow, long strokes and leaned over me, running small kisses along the side of my jaw till he hovered just above my mouth. I could feel his words flutter against the soft edges of my lips.

"Say my name, for I may never hear you say it like this again."

The truth of it hurt, and I felt the full weight of what he was requesting. All we had was this moment. There were no guarantees beyond this. We wouldn't survive if we avoided the reality of our circumstances.

I whispered back to him, "Trace."

He rewarded me with another hard thrust, but stalled again till I repeated his name.

"Trace, please…don't stop," I said loudly, the words now echoing.

He began to pace himself, continuously building my pleasure just like he had all the times before. He knew my body and how to work me so well.

"Trace!" I let out a moan while saying his name again.

I looked up at his face, seeing the scar across his eyebrow and then the dark ink running along both his arms, feeling like I had finally seen him for the first time. His eyes darkened, and I saw a glimmer of the viciousness that lay beneath the surface. Perhaps a cruelty I had never imagined. I tried to ignore the parading thoughts of bloodshed and torture that threatened to consume my attention and distract me from this pleasure.

I wrapped my legs around him tighter, forcing him closer and deeper. With each unrelenting thrust, I screamed his name until I was hoarse and, together, we met our climax. Catching my screams in his mouth as he kissed me. We lay there pressed together, his chest heaving against mine as we attempted to calm ourselves.

I wanted to stay with him in that room forever, or make our way to the terrace and escape together into the night sky, but the very real consequences of doing so loomed silently over us both.

What followed felt like a ritual. Together we bathed in the waters.

Trace held my nude body and tilted my head back into the pool, letting the water soak through all of my hair as he gently moved wet strands along the sides of my face. He ran his hands across the scrapes and bruises on my back that had already formed, healing them instantly. I did not know if it was the result of him or the healing waters.

If I'd had a choice, I would have kept them. The pain was a reminder of this tryst that would fade with each passing day. He looked at me with tender sorrow.

I ran my hands along his strong arms, tracing the tattoos with my fingertips now with a different understanding of what they represented. A life he did not choose; one he escaped only by having another chosen for him. I wished for him a world where he did not have to use his hands for violence and revenge. His were already stained, and I feared that for me this was just the beginning. Goosebumps rippled across my skin despite the warm waters.

When I could no longer stand the silence between us, I made my way from the pool and began to put on my clothes. He followed suit behind me until we were both fully dressed again. For a long while, I stood there in his arms while he caressed me gently.

We made our way back toward the dormitories. Our steps were intentionally sluggish, trying to keep a slow pace and relish these last minutes together where we could pretend that we weren't about to be torn apart by duty, yet again. When he stopped at my door, he whispered, "Be careful. I can't protect you from everything."

I placed a gentle peck on his lips. Anything more than that and I wouldn't be able to tear myself away. I'd make the mistake of pulling him into my room and risk exposing us both.

"I didn't ask you to." I squeezed the hand I was holding, let go, and turned to enter my room, closing the door behind me without another glance.

I leaned against the door, exasperated from all of it. I wanted him to believe I was confident that I could take care of myself. I wanted to believe it, too. I *needed* to believe it. But for now, I slid down to the ground, pulled my legs tightly against my chest, and began to let out quiet muffled sobs.

I mourned many things that night. I had to let many parts of myself disappear and die. There was too much to learn, to master, and I did not want to be distracted by my past. Despite Trace being here, I needed to treat him the same as everyone else if I wanted any chance of becoming a different version of myself.

A stronger, more powerful, more devious version. I would not leave here the same person I had arrived as. I drifted off to sleep, feeling heavy and broken.

CHAPTER 21

The next morning, I woke up feeling alert and determined. When I looked in the mirror, the dark circles and exhaustion had mostly disappeared. Perhaps the healing waters of Basdie along with my resolve allowed me to wear a new face this day. Dare I say I looked somewhat attractive for the first time since arriving?

Breakfast provided an interesting turn of events. All of us were instructed to begin a daily regimen of Doorberry tea, both the males and females. Anyone with common sense knew what the tea was used for; I just couldn't fathom why we were required to take it. Doorberry tea was a naturally occurring contraceptive, and taking it regularly over a few weeks would eventually lead to infertility over longer periods.

My cheeks warmed with guilt and embarrassment. Did Saryn or Theory somehow know about mine and Trace's encounter? It was awfully suspect that this had begun just after. I drank the tea without question, but remained worried that we had been ousted. Was this to ensure none of us became inconveniently pregnant by our peers?

Not surprisingly, Nori refused to drink the tea. Doorberry consumption was against her beliefs, since the act of impeding fertility would be taken as an offense by followers of Ilithyia.

Over the next few days, we rotated between physical training with Theory and being pulled away, one by one, to Saryn for individual evaluations.

As expected, Nori did not participate in any of the combat training. Occasionally, she'd perform endurance exercises, stretching and flexibility, but as soon as sparring began, she resolved to sit on the floor against the wall. Theory's patience with her was growing thin. Her approach of ignoring Nori in an attempt to alienate her would eventually unfold into something far worse.

Nori did participate in flight agility out in the valley, but I was certain as soon as we were asked to practice aerial combat, she would sit again. It was hard to watch Nori continually isolate herself from the group. I was the only one who attempted to connect with her in spite of her lack of participation.

The others seemed content to act like she wasn't there, as she continued to remain "useless." I wanted to tell Gia and Cairis why Nori felt the way she did, but it didn't feel like my place to tell them. They'd probably just see my defense of her as a weakness anyway.

One day, it reached a particularly heated moment when Saryn marched across the room, unable to control his anger at her refusals. "You're nothing but a spoiled little noble. You're worthless to this team, which makes you worthless to your people and your king. You'd best learn to fight, to fly, and to fuck if it means saving lives."

The words seared through us all, though Nori remained stone-faced. She let no cracks appear. If Saryn had been in my face yelling like that, I would have immediately broken down into tears. I'm also certain Trace would have become enraged.

He and I had done a decent job of creating a platonic facade in front of the others. He no longer avoided me. We had been successful thus far in appearing cordial rather than awkward around one another. Trace's protectiveness over me hadn't yet been put to the test—at least, not to a degree where he'd struggled to contain himself.

I thought back to his parting words about how he could not protect me; perhaps I was mistaken in thinking he would intervene. But I was also reminded of the time I pretended to fall from my horse and how distraught he was—and how he had punished me after…

Despite seeing me get knocked around a bit in training, there had been nothing to trigger him. Truthfully, I'd hoped that it would happen sooner rather than later. I felt the impending dread of waiting for something to happen that he or I could not withstand, tempting us to come to the other's aid. We needed to move past it, for there would be many others just like it to overcome.

The day Saryn called my name to leave the training room for evaluation, I could feel my hands begin to tremble with nerves. I shoved them into the pockets of my fighting leathers, trying to hide any signs of fear. When I entered the room, I made certain to reinforce my mental shields, as I had already been warned by Gia that he would be monitoring for that at the start.

He began a methodical set of tests; I wondered if the others had received the same ones or if they were created uniquely for each individual. Before me there was a stone, a bowl of water, and an unlit candle. I had reservations about where this was headed.

"Overflow the bowl," he instructed dryly.

I focused, clearing my mind of distractions, and stared intently at the surface of the water as it began to move with small ripples. Excited at the prospect that I could actually do it, I thought of the time I had poured Gris's canteen in my bath and filled it to the brim. I let the clarity of that memory guide the magic and watched as the water began to spill over the sides of the small bowl onto the wooden table. My attention broke when I smiled in contentment. Saryn simply moved on to the next item.

"Light the flame."

Concentrating on the small candle, I hoped for some new power to stir, but nothing came.

Saryn slapped his hand on the table abruptly. "Stop trying to call forth fire, you're not gifted like that. Pull from your surroundings."

Embarrassed by the correction, I turned, looking at the walls and noting the torches lighting the room. He had simply wanted me to draw fire from another source like I'd done many times before. I was so nervous, unsure of how these tests would unfold and if his instructions were a test in and of themselves. I used the fire from the nearby lantern to ignite a spark on the candle, which quickly formed a solid flame.

"Extinguish the candle," he ordered.

I closed my eyes, trying to feel even the slightest rustle of wind or breeze in the room, but the air was stale and still. I had never wielded wind magic and no matter how long I tried, nothing stirred.

Saryn rubbed at his temples in disappointment.

"Move the rock."

I bent down low, putting myself eye level with the stone on the tabletop, thinking maybe proximity had something to do with it. I gritted my teeth, feeling nothing but frustration as I could not get the stone to so much as wiggle.

He made a couple of notes in his journal; they couldn't have been any more critical of my performance than I was already.

It took no time at all for him to determine through various questioning and other tests that I had probably wielded magic the least. Shots at mesmerization were fruitless, and my attempts at shifting were laughable, at best.

He assured me that it did not mean I didn't have potential or that

I couldn't improve, but that it would be hard for anyone who had it ingrained in them not to practice it or rely on it, while for others it might feel more like second nature.

He was right, I was inclined to avoid magic. I had tried to take on a different mindset over the last few days. Doing little things like warming a bath or healing scrapes and bruises from training were just a few examples. The non-existent staff at Basdie made it easier, since there was no one to rely on for these menial things. But that was the crux of it; everything I had been toying with was simple magic. Nothing that would be considered useful in the field.

While I did not impress Saryn much, he was pleased to discover that I spoke the old tongue quite well. He noted that Varro could speak it a bit, but not nearly as convincingly as mine, stating that he lacked the proper inflection which only came with practice. I felt like he was implying I should tutor Varro, and the mere thought displeased me greatly.

I did make sure he knew that despite none of the proper materials being in Basdie, I was quite comfortable in chemistry. With that information, he requested that I read some of the books available to us and begin redirecting that skillset toward the art of poison-making and antidotes. I'd like to say I was shocked, but I wasn't.

This was not something they taught at the academy; it was forbidden. But the skills were largely the same; it was just the knowledge of ingredients and outcomes that I lacked.

We hardly ever heard Saryn or Theory compliment any of us. Their praise was often veiled in layers of critique. He did mention that he was very impressed with my ability to improvise and lean on my team, and that he did not hold it against me that I threatened to expose his entrails with a blade. He made no mention of the slapping.

His summary of my evaluation was that while I was academically inclined and showed promise in physical combat, I was severely lacking in magic-wielding and all things flight-related. He encouraged me to master the basics quickly: mental shields, basic healing, followed by glamour. If I began to show progress, he'd find other ways to challenge me.

I felt relieved that he hadn't deemed me entirely worthless just because I wasn't an experienced wielder and had no obvious unique gifts to exploit.

"Cress, the fact that you're well-read means you possess the gift of knowledge. You may not feel that this is valuable during your training at Basdie, but we're not training you to stay here. What lies ahead will require you to navigate many complex decisions. Stay sharp and you will be valuable to your team. But that doesn't mean you won't get yourself or them killed in the process. Focus or perish."

That was Saryn's way; build you up only to break you down. His words would stay with me in the days that followed my evaluation. Frustrated with my performance, I glanced back at the objects on the table and focused my magic, causing the water to displace unevenly so that the bowl tipped over, extinguishing the tiny candle. I looked up at Saryn, worried he would be angry with me, and instead I was met with a knowing smirk.

Following the week of evaluations, our instructors directed us to have an early dinner and to meet them in the common room after our meal. We all gathered and lounged about, awaiting Saryn and Theory's arrival.

"Most of you have done well enough this week," Theory said, giving Nori the side-eye.

"In the coming weeks, your physical training with me will escalate and your practice of magical abilities with Saryn will become more focused." Theory's expression went rigid. "You will need opportunities to practice these skills in private, after hours, and during your free time.

"There are some skills that are best practiced in private until you become bold enough to demonstrate them in the presence of others, or because they won't be useful until you're behind enemy lines. The intensity and shame of such practices must be overcome."

Saryn instructed us to follow him as he began to lead us downward toward a section of Basdie we had not yet been shown. As we followed, my cheeks heated at the thought of Trace and me in the depths of the waterfall.

He pointed to a series of doors all in a row along the hallway. He opened the door to one of them and ushered us all into the very small space, causing us to squeeze tightly together. The room was cold and empty. There was a small cot and not much else.

My eyes scanned all about, trying to take notice of any other details, but there were none. Suddenly, from the dark corner of the room beside Saryn, a glowing orb appeared, floating in place. Its light illuminated the room in a warm amber hue. I had never seen anything like it.

Turning to the group Saryn asked, "Does anyone know what this is?" The room remained silent; our gazes fixated on the glow like moths to a flame.

"Thought not," he said with disappointment. "This is a Vesper. They are an extremely rare creature with even rarer magic." He continued, "Vespers have sometimes been referred to as 'Small Gods' or 'the Infinite Ones,' and that is because of their unique abilities."

I could not look away from the floating orb. It was as if it had attached itself to me, drawing me in and locking me in place. My limbs felt heavier the longer I stared at it. There was no sound, yet it called to me in a silent song. That faint humming sensation returned, and I struggled to distinguish between it and the feelings caused by the glowing entity.

"Each of these rooms contains a Vesper, and these will be at your disposal whenever you need to use them, as frequently as you need to use them. It is best not to think of a Vesper as a creature or thing, but rather as pure energy. To the best of our knowledge, Vespers do not have feelings or consciousness. Their identity only exists in your mind, and they feed off of your imagination to acquire shape, form, and function."

The silence was so thick you could cut it with a knife. Everyone appeared to be just as transfixed by what was presented before us.

"When you are ready, you simply need to welcome the Vesper into your mind, set your intention clearly, use your imagination, and allow it to serve you." Saryn paused, making a bit more space between him and the glowing orb. "Let me demonstrate."

We all looked on as Saryn closed his eyes briefly, and when he opened them, the glowing orb began to shake and shift before our eyes. Expanding and changing, it morphed into a beautiful Fae female. I and a few others let out a small gasp in surprise. Theory did not move, indicating there was no threat. Seeing a new face in Basdie was jarring in and of itself. She looked real in every possible way. She *was* real.

Saryn began to move closer to her, and before we knew it, we were watching him full-on lean in and kiss her. It was unbelievably awkward standing practically shoulder to shoulder with everyone watching this unfold.

Their kiss deepened passionately. Had it not been for the dim light of the room, my blushing would have been obvious. He snaked one arm around her waist to pull her flush against him, and she bent to his will, letting out a small whimper of pleasure.

One second, we were witnessing an almost erotic private encounter and the next, Saryn had removed a small blade from his back pocket with his free hand and plunged it into the stunning female's side.

Pulling his lips from hers, he held her as her body went limp and blood began to seep from the wound, spreading across the pale blue dress she wore. Shock and horror spread across her face as the expression of trust shifted to vulnerability and fear.

Nori screeched, trying to push forward to help the girl but Theory flung out her arm. We all watched as the light left her innocent eyes and her limp body lay on the floor at Saryn's feet.

He wasn't showing the slightest hint of remorse, and I was still grappling to understand what in the three moons of Demir I had just witnessed. Had he killed the Vesper? Was that girl real? What in Gods' names was he expecting us to do with what he'd just shown us? Suddenly, the body on the floor disappeared, transforming back into a floating, glowing orb.

"In this room, you will discover your demons and darkness. Face them head-on and learn to control rather than be controlled by restraint and reluctance. Here is where real fear is overcome. Here you can practice anything you can imagine. In these rooms with the Vespers, you will harden yourself and find the necessary callousness that it takes to survive. The disciplines of violence and seduction seem estranged, but their mastery is born of similar principles. Learn to manipulate all things in your favor. One cannot defeat what one refuses to face. Nothing that we teach you or train you to do outside of these walls will ever be viable if you don't put in the real work here."

Saryn paused, allowing us to take in everything we'd just seen, everything he'd just impressed upon us. Could the Vespers truly take on any form we imagined? Did they truly not feel pain? Could they hurt us back?

In a moment of shock, I'd failed to keep my mental shields up, and my barrage of thoughts became fodder for Saryn.

"Cress, what have I told you about shields?" he scolded me. "Yes, a Vesper can take on any form, so long as it comes from your imagination or memory. You give it the details to provide its form, and your will gives it action. No, we don't believe they feel pain, as they are a form of unending energy. And they will only hurt you back if you want them to."

"What do you mean if we 'want them to'?" Cairis asked casually.

Theory nodded at Saryn, implying she'd take this one.

"Violence is a very unique thing to master. There is inflicting pain to defend oneself, there is also inflicting it as a means of extracting information. With two sides of this coin, one hopes you'd be the one inflicting this pain, however that may not always be the case."

My eyes widened in fear and my breath hitched.

"If you happened to be captured, how much pain could each of you endure? What kind of pain could you withstand? How long could you witness someone else undergo such horrific treatment? And even worse, what if you cared for that person?"

Torture. She was describing torture, and instinctively I glanced over at Trace, who had a hard line set across his jaw and his arms folded tightly over his chest. He stared ahead, never meeting my gaze. Is this what he meant he couldn't protect me from? Are these the horrible things they wanted us to do?

Realistically I could fight someone, I could defend myself and others by magic or other means, but this was something else, entirely. This required cruelty. But then the words echoed through me—what if I was on the receiving end? What, if anything, would I be able to withstand? If someone tried to hurt Trace or even Nori, I don't think I'd be able to contain myself, but moreover, I'd probably be as good as dead if someone wanted to torture me for information.

"In time, when you find the courage—and I hope each of you does— then you should explore your limitations with the Vesper. It is the safest way to do so, because as soon as you wish for your pain and suffering to cease then your commands will be followed," Saryn explained, as if that did anything to calm my nerves or resolve my concerns.

The underarms of my shirt were now damp with sweat and my hands were moist and sticky; my anxiety seeped out of my skin. I began to feel nauseous in the tight space surrounded by my peers.

Theory snapped her fingers at us, trying to draw our attention back to her. "I will warn you all explicitly. I cannot stop you from doing what you want within these walls with the Vespers, but I recommend you do not spend your time with them dwelling in the drowning pools of the people from your past. It's an undertow from which you may not escape."

I found myself drawn to new ideas I had only just now realized. If the Vesper could take on any form, then that must mean I could see Versa again, or anyone else of my choosing. Did that include the people who were here?

Saryn led us out of the tiny room, where the glowing orb remained, unbothered and in darkness. He pointed to the row of rooms in the hallway, one for each of us.

"They each contain a Vesper. It does not matter which one you occupy, and you don't have to choose the same room each time. Remember, the Vesper is merely a vessel to bend to your will. It cannot manifest anything on its own. You provide it with thoughts, feelings, and form. It's only as good as what's in your head. What you give it is what it has. Before, it has nothing, and after, it takes nothing with it."

Thoughts of those powerful orbs and what was possible with them overwhelmed me as we paced back to the common room.

That night I was too distracted by thoughts of the Vespers to do any reading; never mind the growing collection of books I had stacked up in my room. I lay in bed thinking about what I'd witnessed and how we'd been encouraged to use them. I had no idea if any of the others had made their way back down to the Vespers that night, but I lacked the courage to return.

Instead, the possibilities formed a mental list of all the things I feared most. My mind raced in circles until I fell into a sleep that danced with more dreams than I'd had in a very long time.

CHAPTER 22

The following day I didn't see Nori at breakfast, training with Theory, or lunch. When no one else knew her whereabouts, I began to worry that Saryn might have done something to get rid of her. When I sought her out, I was relieved to find her in her room. She sat on her bed, seemingly unaffected by my barging in without invitation.

"Why aren't you training?" I exclaimed.

"Train for what? To run a knife across a stranger's neck? To degrade myself in front of others? To witness someone I care for be intimate with another?" Nori yelled back, showing more angst than I'd ever seen from her.

All this time, she had bottled everything up in silence. But I could finally see the stoicism beginning to waver. Something about what she had said felt eerily familiar, but before I could place it, she declared boldly, "I'm leaving. Tonight."

"You can't," I argued, "They'll kill you."

"I've seen their tortured nightmares. You have no idea what they have in store for us," she retorted angrily.

"Nori, please stop this," I pleaded, trying to convince her she wasn't thinking clearly. "They warned us about the enchantments and leaving without permission, are you willing to risk it?"

"The risk is my own, Cress," she replied confidently. "It's my life to risk, and there's no one else for them to take. If I die, there are no other children in my family. This is my decision to make."

She may have had a point. Nori being an only child meant there were no others to deliver to the Order, but I couldn't let her go through with this. It was a suicide mission, but somehow, she firmly believed staying was a fate worse than death. I pushed aside the weight of that thought for my sanity.

"Please just wait, let me try and figure something out. I don't know, maybe I can talk to Theory and see if there's another option."

I knew what I was suggesting would be ignored. They'd made it clear. It was the Order or nothing at all. I sat on the bed across from Nori, who reached out and clasped my hand in hers.

"Thank you for being my friend, even if I am useless."

I tried to fight back the stinging tears building in the wells of my eyes. "Just give me time, that's all I'm asking."

Nori did not reply or give me any indication that she was going to grant me my request. I left her room feeling utterly defeated and on edge, trying to anticipate when she might make a move. But if she did, how would I stop her? What could I do that wouldn't put my safety in jeopardy?

All afternoon I was distracted by my encounter with Nori. I debated telling Saryn and Theory, I almost let it slip to Gia. Maybe the threat of leaving and the enchantments weren't true, or maybe Nori would find a way to slip past them. Perhaps Saryn would just let her go, since she had been nothing but a "thorn in his side."

While making my way toward the terrace, I heard a loud commotion. I looked up to see Cairis running back toward me, frantically yelling that Nori was leaving. "What?" I gasped, in shock that she would already attempt this so soon.

"Where is she?" I asked exasperated.

"She told us not to follow her and then flew down to the stream in the valley. She's walking alongside it now!"

"We have to go after her!"

Cairis' expression told me everything I needed to know before he said it.

"No one will go. They're heeding the warning about the boundaries."

I took off sprinting back into the stronghold, desperately searching for Saryn or Theory. I finally found them together, strolling casually toward the flight deck for class. I worked to catch my breath and string together a coherent thought.

"Nori's trying to leave. We have to stop her!"

Saryn looked at me, zero surprise on his disinterested face. "Great, this solves the problem of what to do with her."

If I hadn't already panicked into action, I might have taken a moment to try and punch that disinterest off his face, but I didn't know how much time she had left before encountering some invisible border along the valley.

"She thinks there won't be any consequences because she's an only child, she's not thinking straight!" I hunched over, resting both my hands on my knees, heaving deep breaths.

I heard Theory let out an amused laugh. "She's very misinformed. If her life is forfeit and there are no other children, they'll come for her mother. From what I hear, she's still quite young. I hope she'll be more pliant than her daughter."

My eyes bulged with horror. To be eligible for the Offering, you had to be of age for conscription and childless. If Nori was gone, then that makes her mother eligible. If she had known this outcome, she would've never attempted this. She'd never let her mom take her place. Were they telling the truth or just trying to scare me? In any case, I had to stop this somehow.

As if Saryn had been reading my mind, "Don't waste your energy, Cress. She will drag you all down. She already is, with this whole charade. Let her be useless in the afterworld."

His harsh words set off an overwhelming chain of thoughts in me that narrowed with perfect clarity. I thought back to what Nori said this morning: *"I've seen their tortured nightmares," "run a knife across a stranger's neck," "to witness someone I care for be intimate with another."*

She had been inside my head. My dreams. There was no other possible way she'd know. The flashes of dreams flooded back into my mind. Me holding a knife to the neck of a person I'd never seen and sliding the blade across, blood splattering over my hand. Then Trace, undressing another female, causing my jealousy to boil. She'd been in our dreams, all of us, including Saryn and Theory.

I gritted my teeth, seething my words at Saryn, "She's not useless you piece of shit. She's a Dreamwalker, and I'm getting her back!"

Saryn's eyes narrowed with disbelief. Before I let him say a single word, I spun and took off running toward the tunnel to the terrace.

I saw everyone on the landing looking out over the valley.

Cowards. That's all I could think as they stood there idly.

There was no time for hesitation, and I prayed that my wings would come quickly when I called to them. With each stride, I closed in on the ledge, and yet my wings did not stir. My will was focused sharply on stopping Nori. I leapt from the ledge, knowing full well if my panic stopped my wings from unfurling, I'd be falling straight to my death.

As soon as my feet left the ledge, I looked out into the valley, seeing the sunlight blanket the trees, and felt the weight of my body dip for just a second before my wings finally splayed outward, catching me and carrying me on the wind. I began to fly lower, scanning the river, looking for signs of Nori when I finally spotted her.

I flew so fast that the crisp air cut at my cheeks. I swooped in and prepared for an abrupt landing. When she heard the thump of my arrival a few feet behind her, she looked over her shoulder, surprised.

I raised my hands trying to show her that I meant no harm and began to pace slowly toward her. "Please stop and just talk to me."

But Nori did not stop. Instead, she took off in a sprint full speed toward her destination. I gathered my resolve. I had to stop her, to at least tell her about her mother, and then she could decide; from there I'd have to respect her decision.

Nori moved fast in spite of her shorter legs, but my strides were still longer. We weaved in between boulders and tree roots as I chased her through the forest. No matter how many times I called her name, she did not relent. When I was finally nipping at her heels, I took one giant leap and tackled her to the hard ground.

She writhed below me. Screaming and crying, fighting to break through my grasp.

"Get off me! Let me go! Please just let me go…"

I held her tightly in my arms, hoping her panic and adrenaline would subside. She felt small in my arms, but she fought me with all her strength until she could fight no longer.

"Just listen to me," I begged. "I promise if you listen to me, I'll let you go and I'll respect your decision."

Nori looked at me with distrust, the first time I'd ever seen this expression directed toward me—though I had witnessed it many times toward Saryn and Theory.

I loosened my grip and released her. She shoved herself off of me, both of us sitting across from one another on the mossy dirt ground. She looked as exhausted as I felt.

"If I must meet the Gods today then let it be of their making, I welcome my creators," she practically spat at me in insolence.

"They'll come…for…your mother," I panted out the words.

Nori's attention perked up in alarm. "…What did you say?"

"Saryn and Theory assured me if you leave, you will perish and then the Order will come for your mother."

"What? That's impossible… Why? How?" Nori's worry dripped from every urgent question.

Still trying to catch my breath, I replied, "She's of age, she'd be childless, and she's young. With you dead that makes her eligible for the Offering."

More tears began to stream down Nori's face as I watched her hands curl into frustrated fists.

I began to crawl toward her slowly, trying to remain non-threatening.

"I'm so, so sorry. I couldn't let you go through with this without knowing." I paused, then added, "Please don't go."

Nori's head hung in despair for a moment longer, but when she raised her gaze, I beheld a rage unlike any I'd seen before. A glow appeared to ripple across her deep black eyes.

I held my hand out and waited, hoping for her to take it, as I said, "You're not useless. I know what you are."

Nori tilted her head, assessing me, and her eyes terrified me.

"You're a Dreamwalker, Nori. You are more than useful. You're unique."

Her voice trembled. "Ever since I arrived here, I've been accidentally slipping in and out of people's dreams while I'm sleeping. The people here are tormented and plagued with nightmares. I wish I had never bathed in the waters of Mirtith. I don't want this."

"Come back with me. I promise it will be ok. We will find a way to control your gift." She finally took my hand and I helped pull her up to a standing position.

Nori didn't face me but continued to hold my hand, staring into the distance, back to the terrace where the rest of our companions stood.

"They have no idea the monster they've got on their hands now that they've threatened my mother."

Her statement was a warning, and a promise. I could not deny her this fury. It was probably the only thing that was going to motivate her to stay. We were told to let go of our past and sever those ties, but I knew that Nori needed this to fuel her. If this was the thing that hardened her, then she needed to embrace it.

We flew back to the stronghold, and most were surprised to see Nori return with me. I knew she was angry; I could still feel her energy resonating, but there was also a hint of embarrassment.

"Look what the cat dragged back," Saryn remarked with displeasure.

"Shut your mouth!" I sneered. "You want to collect little gifted monsters, well here she is. You're lucky I brought her back because as far as I know, she's the only Dreamwalker amongst us, isn't that right, Saryn?"

The rest of the group had surprised looks plastered across their faces, but Theory began to circle Nori, assessing.

"True, but what good is she to us if she refuses to fight?" Her question addressed the group, not Nori.

I turned to face my peers, pleading with my eyes for them to trust me, to believe in Nori. No one spoke, and none of them seemed specifically inclined to welcome Nori back into the fold after she had just tried to escape.

If they understood her beliefs, they might have had some semblance of empathy. However, before I could come to her defense, Nori spoke to the entire group.

"You shall have my sword, but you shall never have my chastity. I will walk every enemy dreamscape you ask of me. I will defend you all with my last breath, whether you take me as your family or merely let me stay to protect mine. This is my offer."

Her conviction was admirable. Part of her words rang true for each of us who were here in place of our siblings, instead of someone else, for someone else. We were here to protect the ones we loved and that they loved, and so on.

"Who will accept these terms?" I asked, directing my plea to the others.

Deafening silence in the hollow valley hung over us for a long time. Nobody moved or spoke. Worry began to set in that perhaps they would reject Nori entirely, that her gift would not be enough, when suddenly Varro stepped forward. The sunlight beamed off his golden skin, his eyes sparkling like cool blue water.

"I accept."

His earnest words were music to my ears. I could have fallen to my knees and cried as I took a deep, stuttering breath. I felt like I'd been holding it since we arrived back on the landing, and Varro's alliance was the release I needed.

Gia stepped forward. "Well, I'm not going to disagree with the golden boy here."

Cairis followed next. "I'm in, but you better stay out of my dreams. I can't be held accountable for what debauchery you might encounter." He laughed and Gia rolled her eyes.

There was only one left. Trace. In typical fashion, he stood there, arms folded across his chest defensively, expression riddled with concern. I gave him the same pleading look I had given the group, but now my gaze was solely on him. Why wasn't he stepping forward for her? For me?

He finally stepped toward the group, and just when I thought he'd remain silent, he added, "If you prove to be reckless again, if you put anyone in this group at risk, I will take care of it myself."

Saryn smirked in Trace's direction, nodding in approval. Trace's words were cold and cruel. A shadow of the black cloak he had warned me I knew nothing about.

Saryn offered a slow clap. "I'm glad we could keep the family together. Let's hope your little diplomat and her Dreamwalker are worth the accommodation."

I was utterly drained from the way the day had unfolded. My muscles were sore from chasing Nori. A soak in the waters of Basdie had quickly become the solution I sought. Begrudgingly, I made my way to the bottom of the falls. It was truly ironic how far one had to travel to get to the healing pools. Each step I took put further strain on my already too-tight muscles.

When I finally reached the pool, I heard the sound of quiet singing, a song that felt oddly familiar. I walked farther down the hall toward a different door from the one where Trace and I had met. Leaning my ear against the door, I listened closely, trying to make out more of the song. The words and soft melodies danced through my memories. I closed my eyes, letting them seep into my bones.

A song of the sea; one of many my father would hum to us as a lullaby. He never sang the words, but the tune was undeniably recognizable. The sound was intoxicating, luring me toward it. I found myself reaching for the doorknob, seeking out the source.

The room was another healing pool, but much larger than the one next to it. This one was long and narrow, water snaking its way into a deep cave-like tunnel. The glowing light of the pool barely illuminated the darkness at the end of the tunnel. The song of the sea echoed along the cave walls, resonant, and caused goosebumps to form on my arms. The voice was beautiful and hypnotic, growing louder as a shadowy figure approached from the cavernous opening.

I swallowed a nervous lump in my throat as a glistening wet, shirtless, golden Varro approached, and when he saw me, his singing came to an abrupt end, snapping me out of my haze.

Feeling like I had intruded, I quickly apologized, seeking to make a swift exit. "Ugh, I'm sorry, I didn't realize this pool was taken." Why did I say that? Of course, I realized someone was in here, the noise is what drew me to it.

"You sure about that?" He smiled teasingly.

I tried to look anywhere but at him. I failed. The water droplets speckled along the lean muscles that corded every inch of his body. His short white curls were dripping and the glowing pools reflected off his bright blue eyes.

"Oh, I had just heard a familiar sound," I replied, realizing immediately I'd just contradicted myself.

"I thought you didn't realize this pool was taken?"

It was clear he was not going to let up. Before I could pivot with some other excuse he added, "This pool is larger than some of the others. You're welcome to join."

In my head I acknowledged how much larger this pool was than the other, and I tried to hide the embarrassment of why I knew that. I regretted my arrival instantly, knowing I could be elsewhere, healing in solitude.

But now I was here, with someone I didn't particularly like, and I'd look ridiculous if I entered the pools fully dressed. I began to undress, trying not to trip over my attire. I stripped down to just my undergarments and tied my hair up to avoid getting it wet.

Varro watched me the entire time, never once turning his gaze away. He may have tried to act unimpressed, but his clenched jaw and slightly raised eyebrow were a tell that I didn't entirely disgust him.

I entered the waters and made a small gasp as the heat consumed my limbs. He stood there, unmoving, with his hands resting on his hips while he assessed me.

Walking through the pool, the water level hit just above my waist, which meant on Varro—who was much taller than me—I could see the rigid angles of a striking V-shaped muscle hovering above the drawstring of his submerged white trousers. I made my way farther back into the tunnel, taking a seat on the ledge and relaxing into the warmth of the waters, letting them begin their work on my aching muscles and bruises.

Varro intended to keep me company, apparently, even if I didn't ask for it. To be fair, he was here first. He positioned himself on the ledge across from me. We sat there in silence for a few minutes. During that time, I noticed that strange hum once more. It felt like small waves of vibration against my skin. I looked to the surface of the water to see if there was evidence of the vibration rippling along the top, but there was none.

I had never felt this strange sensation before. Not until I was delivered to the king and took the Bath of the Four Mothers. I had convinced myself it was the magic awakening in me from a long-dormant slumber.

Given Varro's actions earlier, I figured I owed him some semblance of thanks. I certainly didn't want to be indebted to him, but I could show my gratitude.

"I appreciate you stepping forward earlier, for Nori." I was about as good at showing gratitude as I was apologizing; whether he realized it or not, this was a leap for me.

"I did it for you."

His words pierced through me. I tried not to let the shock of it appear on my face. I thought he disliked me, the way I disliked him. Why would he do anything for me?

"And because it was the right thing to do. We're all here instead of someone else, right?" he added.

I exhaled with relief trying to ignore his initial remark and took that as an opportunity to redirect the conversation.

"Who are you here for?" The question felt intrusive, but he'd left the door open for that by even mentioning it at all.

His once calm expression now flickered between sadness and anger.

"My sister."

He had a sister too.

"Oh, is she younger than you?"

If he was here instead of her, then that meant she, too, was of age.

"We're the same age," he answered.

Clarity eluded me for only a moment.

"Wait, are you a twin?" I asked excitedly, as I had never met another twin in my life.

"You could say that."

His reply was heavy, loaded with more than I could discern. But I was too consumed with the fact that I'd finally met another person who might know what it's like to have another half from birth.

"I'm a twin as well!" I offered, sounding much more elated about this rare encounter than him.

"I know," he said, "I've overheard your conversations."

I cocked my head at his admission. Had he been eavesdropping on me, particularly, or had he been spying on all of us?

"Too bad you got stuck with the lesser beauty of the two Corliss twins," he joked. I tried to imagine what a female Varro looked like. I bet she had long white curls and the same warm golden skin and rosy pink lips.

"I should say the same," I said, thinking of Versa and all her soft, delicate features.

"I very much doubt that."

Varro's eyes now had a hint of lust swirling in them. My cheeks blushed at the implication of his words. I felt awkward and wrong, sitting here with the son of my father's enemy. It would be easier to just ignore that, but occasionally I found it eating away at me.

"What did you mean by *you could say that*?"

A pained look flashed across his face as he turned to look away from me for the first time.

"My sister and I were triplets. Our baby brother was the smallest of the three. With my father having one strong male and female heir, he decided a sacrifice to the old Gods of the sea would bring him good favor. He tossed our brother into the Endless Tides. He broke our mother's heart that day. And he severed a tie that my sibling and I will never recover."

My heartbeat stilled and I sat frozen in horror. His father had killed his own son, an infant, at that? Lord Corliss was even more barbaric than I ever fathomed. What kind of evil existed in his heart to do what he'd done? The crisp blue of Varro's eyes that usually seemed alight with life now appeared dim and cheerless.

"With only one male heir, what are you doing here?" I asked, knowing undoubtedly that males were favored over females when it came to lineage.

"My sister was the Offering. But when my father was finally captured, I demanded they accept me instead. I'll be damned if my sister is ever taken to a place where her will isn't her own, her body isn't her own. I am here, and always will be, so she never knows this fate."

He paused before continuing, as if questioning whether he should.

"I am saddened for you and whoever didn't protect you from this," he said wincing, realizing the full meaning of his words.

Immediately he apologized. "I…I'm sorry, I didn't mean to imply…"

"Yes, you did. But that's okay. I understand. Could my father have done something more? It's pointless to question that now. I know I'm far more equipped to be here than my sister, and for that I'm grateful. She is betrothed and gets to be loved, to live the life she deserves."

It's possible I misjudged Varro. While we did not broach the subject of the rebellion—I'd save that for another time—we had found common ground. Both of us were here so our siblings weren't. More than that, we could relate to the deep unwavering connection to those siblings. It's not something he needed to say, I knew he knew. I knew he felt a similar pain in being here, detached from our other halves.

Varro made his way toward the exit of the pool. I stayed tethered in my seat watching him walk away. The muscles of his back were just as much if not more defined than the ones on his front. As he walked up the steps of the pool, his soaked britches sagged low, hanging just low enough to allow the tight arches of his buttocks to peak out from them. He was truly a masculine specimen sculpted in the image of the Gods. I was glad his back was turned to me, otherwise he might have noticed just how little I concealed my gawking.

He turned to face me and continued with an inappropriate show. The drenched pants emphasized a clear outline, indicating he was very well-endowed. I watched him dry himself and shake his curly locks. He knew exactly what he was doing, and he finally looked at me with a coy grin. I was staring and he knew it.

"Tomorrow. Same time. Same place, Moirai," he said, before strolling out the door. He did not wait for my response, or for me to realize the words he'd spoken were in the old tongue. The sound was like a sweet caress. But despite all my learning, I did not recognize the last word.

The next day, my body felt revived, with no hints of aches or pain. Part of me dreaded the day ahead. Nori was back, but today she would need to show some commitment to the cause.

When we arrived in the training room with Theory, she placed herself close by and followed along with all the stretches and warm-up exercises. But this was not unusual; she had already been willing to do those things. When we transitioned into sparring, I was nervous that once more she'd refuse the activity.

I walked toward Cairis, who I'd made my official partner—once he agreed to trade me for tutoring. His hair was tied up in a bun atop his head, and it was a unique look that highlighted his sharp jawline and high, pointed ears. I wanted to practice with the biggest and strongest among us, this way anything less than that would feel manageable.

Nori shyly followed me around and stood awkwardly to our side, looking for some sort of invitation. Cairis gave me a strange look, nodding his chin at her.

Before he could unintentionally destroy her courage, I chimed in, "Cairis, I'd like you to show Nori some of the basics today."

When he made no indication of interest in my request, I added, "Please."

"What's in it for me?" he questioned.

I rolled my eyes. "You mean besides preparing your ill-equipped team member so they can have your back?"

Many things with Cairis always felt like bartering. This had to be the sort of thing he was raised with, never being given anything for free.

"You get Nori up to speed in basic combat, and she'll tutor you on spiritual and religious studies."

He looked at me, unenthused. I didn't know what else to propose. There was little chance her gift of dreamwalking was applicable in this negotiation. I tried to play to her strengths, at least the ones I knew of.

"And after every training session, she will personally heal you. Then you don't have to make the long trek to the bottom of the falls."

His ears perked at the mention of this, and he nodded. I may have abused my knowledge of Leatherwings' notorious distaste of water. I didn't want to oust him, so I made it more about the trek than the water.

I turned to Nori, looking for signs that the deal I'd just brokered would be one she accepted, and she gave me a tiny, grateful smile.

"I can't wait to see her dancing circles around you, Cairis. Consider this a chance to work on your endurance!" I quipped, trying to give Nori the encouragement she needed.

"Fine," he acquiesced. "But who are you going to train with?"

I looked around the room, assessing my options. Gia and Trace were already engaged in a practice duel with blades. That left only one remaining partner.

I scanned the rest of the room looking for his bright curls. He leaned up against the stone podium, looking at me like he had already expected my arrival. I turned my back to him, rolling my eyes.

"I'll be back when you've got her decently up to speed. Then we will practice two-on-one."

"I'd like that…" Cairis replied with a smirk and a wink.

"I bet you would," I said snarkily while parting ways and making my way toward Varro. I didn't dare look, but I could feel Trace's eyes on me as I paced toward my new sparring partner.

"Hello, friend." He smiled nonchalantly.

I looked up at him, giving him no signs of amusement. "Guess I'm yours today," I stated, begrudgingly.

"Just today? What a shame." He looked delighted with himself.

I turned my back to him, taking a few steps away, and as I began to ask, "What would you like to pract—"

I suddenly felt a hard kick against my legs, cutting off my words and forcing me to fall forward on my face.

"What in the…" I rolled over onto my back, infuriated to see Varro now standing over me looking tickled.

He had just attacked me unprovoked. I already felt soreness on the wrist I had used trying to brace the fall.

"What are you doing?" I fumed.

"Practicing the element of surprise."

Without hesitation, I saw him lift his fist. I rolled away quickly, just in time for him to miss his mark, and stood, readying myself. So, this is how he wanted to play it.

He lunged forward into me, swinging left and then right, each fist missing me just barely as I ducked and twisted out of his path. He was fast, but I could tell he was intentionally holding back. If he wanted to provoke me, he had succeeded.

As he stalked toward me, I quickly ran around him, using the stone podium for leverage. I kicked my foot out and pushed off, jumping onto his back. My arms squeezed tightly around his neck, and my legs wrapped around his large frame.

In a swift motion, he threw his body forward, flipping me over his head and onto my back before him. Right where I had started.

I gritted my teeth, my brow furrowing in frustration. "You're going to regret that."

He looked down upon me, unconvinced. "I hope so," he retorted, and before he could straighten his stance, I kicked my foot out into his groin. A satisfying look of pain and bewilderment spread across his face.

He stepped back, hunched over and coughing. Good, I hoped that took the wind out of him. But I knew better than to let up.

In a move that had taken me a while to master, I did a kick up straight from my back and landed lightly on both feet. I swung with all my might in an attempt to land a blow, but he recovered enough to dodge. When I swung again with the other arm, he grabbed my fist in his palm, spinning me into a tight hug. I writhed, unsuccessfully trying to free myself.

He held me in place with his giant muscular arms, then leaned in close to my ear and said the words that he knew only I could understand.

The sound of the old tongue once more prickled across my skin as he taunted, "Just making sure you need that bath later."

Enraged with his audacity, I immediately kicked backward against his shin, breaking his hold just enough for me to slip away. He was stronger than me. I was going to have to beat him with speed and agility or by complete surprise.

He stood there; legs spread wide in a stance waiting for me to make my move when I took off running straight toward him. I faked a quick movement to make him think I was going high, then I immediately ducked low to slide between his legs and ended up on the other side of him with his back once more exposed to me.

But before I could take advantage of his vulnerable position, he twisted around quicker than I expected and grasped my neck tightly in his hand, holding me in place and keeping his arm locked straight so my strikes couldn't reach him.

He looked at me, expecting me to yield, but that was not going to happen. He squeezed tighter, but I did not react. He shoved me back against the stone post and squeezed harder. The pain of his iron grip around my neck began to cut off my airway, and I winced.

"Yield," he said, cocking his head at me proudly.

I said nothing.

When I remained silent, he began to tighten his grip so much that he lifted me off the ground, my back still against the podium and the tips of my toes now barely grazing the floor. I was feeling the lack of breath, my face growing red.

There was a brief exchange between our gazes, his blue eyes piercing into me as I felt my consciousness beginning to teeter. I felt wrong for enjoying the intensity of his stare—and his hand around my neck. I reasoned it was probably the lack of blood flow getting to my brain.

Once more he said, "Yield," between gritted teeth.

But for some reason, my stubbornness would not let me bend to his will. I would let him choke me out before I uttered the words. And just as I began to feel my eyes flutter and consciousness leave me, I saw Trace reach for Varro's arm, yanking it away as he growled, "Let her go!"

I dropped to the floor, hitting my head, and with that came nothing but stars and darkness.

When I awoke, I was alone in my bed. My head pounded with a pain I had never felt, and I could feel aching all over my body, quickly reminding me of how I had gotten here. I had no idea how much time had passed or who had brought me here. It wasn't Nori, or I'm certain she would have done her best to heal me and ensure that I did not awake feeling as awful as I did. I rolled over on my side, trying to find the energy to sit up.

Thoughts of Varro squeezing the life from me and Trace's rage-filled voice flashed back into my mind. I had no idea what had transpired since that moment, and Gods I hoped he had found a way to control himself. This was my fault. I was the one who was too stubborn to give in to Varro when I had already lost. Just as stubborn as Saryn when I held a blade to him.

When I peeked my head out into the hallway it was quiet and dim, indicating it was clearly past dinner time and most had likely gone to sleep. The sound of Varro's words echoed through me. His words from last night, and today in training. I began to hobble my way toward the baths at the bottom of the falls.

Unsure if I wanted to see him or not, anger wrapped around me like a warm blanket as I envisioned drowning him for this. My viciousness surprised even me. When had I become so vengeful? This place was getting to me.

This time there were no melodies drawing me back to the door, yet I knew he'd be there even before I turned the knob. I found Varro soaking in the same spot as last night. I quickly removed my clothes, uninterested in whether he was looking at me or not. I needed the comfort of the waters, badly.

I submerged my body and rolled my shoulders in relief. I relaxed, letting the warmth bring me a reprieve from the day. I inched my way slowly toward Varro, unsure of what our encounter would be like, and sat across from him.

He did not speak, but his eyes said many things. I tried to decipher their meaning. Was that guilt or anger, perhaps a little of both? While staring into his eyes, I noticed the swelling on his right cheekbone marked with a tiny cut. I did not recollect landing a blow there.

The awkward silence filled the room like the steam wafting above the pool.

"What made you think I'd need motivation to return?" I asked with a bit of venom, referencing his comment about the bath.

He winced at my words; he knew he'd gone too far.

"I didn't go too far..." he snapped, and then I realized I had dropped my mental shields in a moment of distraction.

Before I could argue that point, he added, "If you were mine— If you were my teammate, then I'd want to make sure you're prepared for the worst, for anything someone might do to hurt you."

"I am your teammate," I whispered, trying to ignore his delicately phrased words.

Although I can't say I enjoyed being choked to the point of blacking out, he did have a point. Theory would have likely approved of his methods. She wanted us to push our limits, and she would never approve of the males treating us differently. Regardless, I was caught off guard by his willingness to go there our first time sparring.

"Why didn't you just yield?" he questioned, as if he had been counting on that.

My answer came quick and uncalculated, filled with anger boiling from places within that I had kept bottled up until now.

"For my father, and for the merchants and sailors your family slaughtered. Did they yield when hundreds died, the blood soaking the bay crimson?"

I had only realized it myself as I spoke... I'd rather him see the life drain from my eyes than bend to the will of a member of House Corliss.

"You speak of things you know nothing about, just what you've been told. Don't pretend you have any reason to define me by anything other than what I show you here and now."

His voice grew louder and echoed off the walls. He wasn't yelling, more like pleading.

Against my better judgment, I continued to press him. I could not let this go.

"Tell me you had nothing to do with it. Tell me you weren't at your father's side while he led the massacre!" My voice rose louder than his.

"I wasn't involved. The instant I learned of my father's plans, I only had so much time. I acted selfishly. I protected the two most important people in my life and immediately got my mother and sister into hiding, away from that abusive piece of shit."

He paused, eyeing me intently to make sure I was hearing every word.

"Someone would have come for them, to take them as ransom or worse. Do you think my father would have bargained on their behalf? He wouldn't have raised a finger. Not someone who throws an infant into the sea or beats on his wife while biding his time to sell off his daughter in a betrothal of his choosing."

He took a deep breath and continued, sounding distraught.

"Once I had gotten them away from him and his enemies who would do them harm, I returned. But I was too late. So much death and destruction had already been done."

I watched his hands curl into tight fists below the water.

"The Erisas Bay painted in red will haunt my nightmares for the rest of my life. Don't you think I regret not doing more? Don't you think I wish I had chosen the selfless path? I couldn't watch him treat them that way anymore and saw a window of opportunity and seized it. But I never wanted the rebellion to happen in the first place. I pleaded with him to seek a diplomatic approach, but he was intent on sending a message."

My cheeks warmed with embarrassment. Suddenly I felt small, like a child being scolded when they'd done something wrong. His sharp words punished me and I searched my thoughts for a retort—but could find none.

I didn't deserve the last word. I'd judged him harshly, and yet I would've done the exact same thing. If it meant getting my family to safety, I would have chosen them.

In the complexities of war and bloodshed, we often lose sight of the small stories, and the histories only speak of the conquerors and conquered. I hung my head in regret. He must have noticed the silence of my shame.

"I can't fix what happened at the rebellion, but when the time came, I did the only thing I thought I could to right my wrong…" He paused. "I was the one who told the black cloaks where he was hiding."

"Really?" I whispered, looking up through my lashes.

"Yes. I'm the reason my father was captured. I'm the reason he'll spend a long time being tortured until they finally put him out of his misery."

"He deserved it," I said coldly.

"He did. Nevertheless, sending my own father to his death is something I have to live with, along with what happened at Erisas."

Varro looked utterly torn. I cannot imagine the choice he had had to make in doing so. He ran his hand through his wet curls.

"You're the only person I've ever told. Not even my mother or sister knew it was me."

My eyes widened at the confession. Why tell me? Why seek my approval? He could have left that out of the story and still made me feel just as terrible for all my brash words.

"By then, I knew I was going to demand they accept me as the Offering. Without me around, turning him in was the only way to ensure he'd never be able to lay eyes or hands on them again. And as you said…he deserved it."

I tried to imagine Varro's mother and sister somewhere safe, finally free of their oppression, and how that must bring him such peace. The way it brought me some semblance of peace to know that Versa would never know what happened to me, and that she got to live out her life on her terms.

Somewhere smiling, holding a babe in her arms in the gardens of her flourishing estate while her husband looked on fondly from a distance. I hadn't let myself fantasize about her happiness since I had arrived, but now I allowed myself a brief moment.

Varro cupped some of the water in his hand and poured it along his bruised and swelling cheek, drawing my attention back to the present.

"How did that happen? I never landed a punch."

Varro began to shake his head back and forth in amused disbelief.

"Unlike the rest of us, you brought your past here."

"...What?"

"Who do you think hit me, Cress? Multiple times, at that."

A small gasp left my mouth in realization.

"Trace did that?"

"Yes, he went after me like a rabid beast and Cairis had to pull him off of me. He's lucky I restrained myself, especially since I was more interested in assisting Gia to get you off the ground."

My Gods, what kind of altercation had I missed? What had Trace done? He and I were careful to maintain appearances and control our emotions. This was my fault. If I had just yielded and hadn't been stupid enough to make so many assumptions about Varro...

"It's dangerous for you both," he added.

I played innocent, making an excuse. "I don't know what you're talking about, or why he reacted like that. He probably can't stand watching females take a hit."

"He certainly doesn't mind putting Gia at risk with a blade, and he didn't come to your rescue when Saryn slapped you, though I could have had his hand for that."

Varro's words were like riddles. One minute he was chiding me, the next he was sounding protective.

"Deny it all you want, Cress. I saw it... We all saw it, what you mean to him."

I wanted to sink below the waters and drown. My chest already felt like my lungs were filled with water. I didn't know what more to say. I didn't want to sit here and keep lying to Varro, not after he'd been so honest, not after he'd made it abundantly clear that he knew I was full of it. But I also wasn't keen to divulge or admit anything about mine and Trace's past.

The only thing I could offer was this promise: "It won't happen again."

CHAPTER 24

After weeks of training and evaluations, it was abundantly clear how worthless I remained. Compared to everyone else, I didn't bring anything I found particularly special to the group's arsenal of magical abilities. Even Nori had proven to be more valuable, and she didn't even want to be here.

Yes, I spoke the old tongue, but Varro did as well, and he'd improve with help from me. But what good was that when no one else here spoke it? I put it extremely low on the list of things we'd need to survive.

Cairis knew how to track animals, but it was Trace who had helped teach him to track people by scent. To practice, Cairis constantly enlisted Nori's help, forcing her to participate in his never-ending game of hide and seek. He'd instruct her to hide somewhere in Basdie until he found her based on scent alone. I hadn't even known Trace was capable of this until we started training here. Just one more thing I didn't know about him.

Like the others, Trace was good at lots of things. He arrived here with more skills than most of us, and I hated leaning on him for anything. Ever since he ousted us with his altercation, I'd been cordial but distant with him. No one other than Varro made mention of it, but I could tell the others were suspicious, and I hated how I felt their eyes on us anytime we spoke to one another or trained together.

Trace never spoke a word of it to me, but he had to know why I was always treating our interactions like they were strictly business.

He was the most skilled with a blade. The memory of him holding one against the gambler at the tavern seemed lifetimes ago, and yet not much time had passed at all. Sometimes his demonstrations with Theory put even her skills to the test. Watching his swift and intentional movements was like witnessing someone dance in between flickers of silver reflections.

Varro was by far the best of us in any sort of hand-to-hand combat, a fact I knew all too well. At first, I had found myself jealous when I'd witness Trace tumbling and rolling on the ground to pin Gia or Nori.

But the feeling waned, and I grew numb to it. I stopped witnessing the closeness as intimacy and instead recognized it as survival. But when he was the one pinning me, I just felt angry, trapped, and worried that everyone's eyes were on us. Questioning our connection, questioning if we were still something, nothing more than liars bound to put them at risk. Varro watched us the closest. Holding me accountable to my promise.

Theory pushed us hard. Every day it was a routine of sleep, eat, sweat, fly, focus, heal, sleep. It could have felt monotonous, but it didn't. There was too much to learn, too much to master before we'd amount to anything. I liked routine and staying busy. It brought me some sense of normalcy.

Many nights ended with a visit to the healing pools. Sometimes in groups, other times alone. Cairis was the only one who never made an appearance, and my arrangement with Nori was one he'd come to take full advantage of. But Nori was more than glad to be useful, and dare I say she'd made a friend in Cairis. Warmth finally returned to her cheeks, diminishing the ashen color that befell her during our early days at Basdie.

He treated her like a little sister; they certainly argued like siblings. Each day she got better under his guidance and Theory only pushed enough to give her more encouragement. As I expected, she was quick and nimble. Extremely difficult to keep up with when Cairis tripled her size.

She took longer to gain comfort with a blade, but Trace was patient with her. Given he was the last to offer her forgiveness, I was shocked to see the level of attention he gave her. He always made sure to select weapons that were more appropriate for her size.

Not surprisingly, Trace was also the best flier of the group, with Gia being a close second. Out on the flight deck, they worked our wings to the bone. Trace insisted we all practice flying with weights in our arms, forcing our wings to grow stronger against the resistance. I hated those days, as they were guaranteed to land me in the bowels of Basdie. No attempt at self-healing would cure my back from that kind of pain.

I imagined Trace and his brothers when they were little and their cruel father forcing them to leap from the edge with heavy stones in their arms until their wings were stronger than anything required to carry their own small bodies.

I may not have improved when it came to in-flight combat, but I was quickly becoming the standout when it came to flight agility. My evasion technique was superior to all but Trace and Gia. I still considered it a small victory since I always felt like I was the one lacking.

I couldn't imagine a life before this when I never showed my wings and rarely used them. They felt like such a natural part of me now, and when I called upon them, they answered every time, without hesitation. I loved the feeling of wind on my face, the free falls and dives, staring at the sun cresting the mountains. They ached for me to fly farther, beyond the boundaries of the valley in the Elorns.

One evening, after everyone had gone inside from flight training, I found Gia sitting on the stone wall, her legs dangling over the ledge. Interested in the sunset, I made my way to the spot next to her.

"Want some company?" I inquired.

"Sure, why not?"

"The view is incredible," I said, noticing how the orange and yellow hues of the setting sun rippled across the forest below. Reds, burgundies, and browns all melted into each other as the autumn leaves turned, beckoning the frost of winter.

"He used to watch the sunset with me, even though he preferred sunrise," she said somberly, looking into the distance.

"Who…?" I asked, feigning ignorance of her former mate.

Maybe she wanted to keep forgetting him, like we were all expected to forget everyone we ever loved. But to forget the bond of a mate? Was that even possible? She remained quiet, and I feared I'd overstayed my welcome.

"My mate. He was, by all accounts, wrong for me. Wrong for me in that he was not wealthy, not a Royal, not even an Honored. He was just a commoner. He managed our family's growing collection of prized horses."

I thought about what she'd said when we first arrived and how she didn't care if anyone was Royal, half-blood, or otherwise.

"I think I knew he was the one even when we were young. Something drew me to the stables, and it wasn't a love for horses—though I pretended to be more than interested in them just to spend time with him. We practically grew up together. It wasn't till we were older that the visits to the stable, the long rides through my father's lands, and the way he'd help me off my saddle became something more. I acted first. He never presumed to be worthy of a High Lord's daughter, but I wanted him and nothing was going to stop me."

Gia recounting the story of how she'd fallen for her mate delighted and distracted me from this place as I sat there enveloped in her words, imagining young forbidden love. Her story reminded me of the books back home in my library; stacked in piles on the floor of my room. It reminded me of the times Versa and I would gossip over her escapades. Thoughts of my family had become fewer and farther between, I realized.

"I knew from the moment my lips met his, and I knew it every day after. I was the one who asked for his hand in marriage and arranged the ceremony in secret. While I may have been the one with everything to lose, he was the one I was putting at risk. Some days I regret that, but I was willing to fight for our bond. For a year, I evaded my father's attempts at securing a match for me. Unbeknownst to my parents, I had already wed my mate, and if it came down to it, I was prepared to lose it all and leave everything behind for him."

Before all of this, I'd have liked to know that kind of love. Conceivably if things had been different, then that is what Trace and I could have blossomed into. But could a flower ever bloom with only blood and darkness? We were a seed planted with false intention, and given no time to grow beneath a sunless sky.

"My mate and I were ready to escape if my father brought news of a betrothal. However, when that day came, I was delivered something far more crushing. I was the Offering. My older sibling was with child and the others, much too young, so that left only me. For days, I hid away in my room claiming to be sick, unable to face him, unable to tell him the truth of what was happening. I still wonder if what I did was right."

"What did you do?" I whispered, nervous about her answer.

"I lied and told him I was betrothed to another Royal, very wealthy, someone who lived very far away, and that I could not go against my father's wishes after all. I broke our bond and told him to find someone else to love."

I felt myself holding my breath at her confession, and I could see her teeth clenched just to get the words out, like she was hearing herself admit them for the first time.

It was wrong of me to ask, I knew it even as the words were leaving my mouth, but it was too late.

"What does breaking a bond feel like?"

Gia whipped her head to face me, thick tears filling her beautiful eyes before spilling over.

"Like death by a thousand cuts and unimaginable grief. In the first few days, it's like gasping for air when you're unable to catch your breath. Some weeks you ebb and flow between numbness and endless rage. Sometimes the sadness gets tired of being contained and it comes out like violence. Screaming, thrashing, violence."

A few more tears dripped down her soft cheeks.

"Some days it's like being asked to wander the woods blind, where you try to make your way but realize there's no point, no purpose. On the days where you think you're fine and moving on, you experience small things that trigger your memory. A scent, a place, or something someone says, and then you either lock away your feelings and push on bravely or you let yourself crumble for just a short time."

Gia's honey eyes looked glazed, and her face was soaked with tears; the dimming sunset illuminated her long blonde curls.

"Is it worth it?" I asked, anxious to understand.

"If I had to do it all over again, I don't know that I would have sealed the bond. If I had known what the pain of breaking it felt like, I don't know that I would have gone through with it. This place may have my body, my fealty, but I don't know that anyone else will ever have my heart. To be honest, I don't think I have a heart anymore. I think I cut it out myself and left it at his feet."

I sighed, wishing I could shoulder some of Gia's pain. I hoped that in some small way, this was cathartic for her. Each of us grappled with letting go of our past. Some more than others. Some had lost more than others. Some had sacrificed more than others.

I stood to give Gia some time alone as the sun made its final descent. Eventually, the valley would be lit only by the moonlight. As I began to walk away, she looked over her shoulder and I heard her whisper over the wind, "Count yourself lucky you're not bonded."

That evening we were all reading in the common room when Saryn requested that I join him in private. I placed my book on the table and gave Gia a nervous side-eye. What could he possibly want from me?

He pulled me into the mess hall and wasted no time.

"You're making plenty of progress with Theory, but you haven't shown enough improvement with your abilities. It's unacceptable."

His words were intense and oozing disapproval. The worst part being that he wasn't wrong.

Saryn pored over his notes, making mentions of my various failures, improvements, and few successes.

"I see that the library has served you well along with the arrival of the requested materials. You're the only one who has spent any time exploring poison-making and showing signs of promise. However, your toiling doesn't fool me. I know that you've only done this to make up for your lack of elemental manipulation beyond water."

He paused, looking at me accusatorily, waiting for me to acknowledge the truth. When I said nothing, he continued.

"Many find that they have an affinity for one element over others. I suggest you set aside the powders and potions and spend more time concentrating on honing abilities that require actual magic, not just stirring and a steady hand."

I rolled my eyes. Nothing was ever good enough for him. I'd quite like to try one of my latest concoctions on him. He didn't need to read my mind to know what I was thinking.

Before I could utter any excuses, he asked, "How often are you training with a Vesper?"

And with that question, he had me pinned. I hadn't visited the Vespers at all. Not since we were introduced. The others had, and it was paying off, but I was too scared. Too scared that I wouldn't have enough self-control to avoid the "drowning pools" of my past as Theory had warned. My lack of response made Saryn's judgment transition quickly to frustration.

"You're now assigned to visit a Vesper nightly, until I see improvement and say otherwise."

I didn't dare go against his instruction, but everything inside of me wanted to as I bit my lower lip against the urge to argue.

"Face your fear, Cress," was all he uttered as he exited the room, leaving me there with my guilt and hesitation.

CHAPTER

25

I had been sitting in the room staring at the glowing amber orb in the corner for a good hour. I knew it wouldn't move or do a single thing unless I willed it to, but still, it scared me. Countless times I played through the scene of Saryn knifing that poor girl in my mind. I could convince myself that the orb felt no pain, but what I couldn't convince myself of was that I wasn't going to feel it inflicted upon me. Because that was the point.

I'd often walked past these doors on the way to the healing pools. The sound of screams coming from behind the doors haunted me. I knew why my peers were outperforming me, and it's because they had thrown themselves into training with the Vespers. I was too scared to ask any of them about it, but now I wished I had. Where should I start? How should I begin?

The Vesper could only form from my imagination. But how was I to pick a face? I'm not supposed to have it embody people from my past I was attached to, so is the solution to pick a stranger? Someone I've seen walk by on a street, someone whose name I didn't even know? But would the nameless or faceless motivate me to fight or hurt someone?

I pondered the thought for some time, and the best I could come up with was the gambler from the tavern. The way he grabbed my hand and the sharp words that were about to leave his loose lips before Trace had intervened. It was the closest I had ever been to being assaulted, and the closest thing I had to this kind of motivation.

I stared at the floating Vesper and set my intention in my mind. Recalling the greasy drunk from the bar as I watched the orb twist and quake, finally taking its new form. I gasped at the eeriness of the stranger's silence, combined with once again seeing someone new in the isolation of Basdie.

His lack of movement and dead eyes frightened me. I slowly approached, keeping my guard up. His eyes followed me, and when I got close enough to his face, I could smell the alcohol on his breath and the sweat coming from his pores. I recalled his voice clearly and said the command, "Speak."

Suddenly, the haunting sounds of the drunken gambler filled the room as he slurred his hateful words. "You're a cheat and a filthy little whore!"

The words echoed through my memory and I stepped back fearfully. His words were full of spite, but he didn't move, not a single flinch.

"How about I take you upstairs and let that pretty mouth of yours earn back your coin?"

I breathed deeply, feeling my anger flare. It was working. Letting him speak to me this way riled me up, and so I set my intention further.

"Whores like you belong on their knees. I'll make those doe eyes water for me."

Now I was seething, my skin feeling hot while my fingers twitched at the blade anchored to my thigh.

"When I'm done with you, I think I'll break your sister in next…"

It was a split second before the intention was set, and the command echoed abruptly through my mind. "Fight me till you're dead."

Suddenly, the gambler lunged for me, his saliva foaming as he grabbed my shoulders and tried to tackle me to the ground. I spread my stance firmly and kneed him in the stomach. He bellowed in pain, backing away a few steps before lunging again.

He slammed into me, knocking me flat onto the cold stone ground. I could feel the weight of his body pressing me down as I writhed underneath him, trying to keep his mouth away from me.

"Stop fighting me, you know you want this, all the greedy whores do."

I tried to shake myself out of the frozen shock—this wasn't like sparring.

His words burned through me, and as I began to feel him rip and pull at my clothing, I could take no more. I reached for the blade at my thigh and began stabbing blindly, over and over, into his fat belly.

I could hear his shrill screams and wails. I felt the warmth of blood pouring over the blade in my hand, but I did not stop. I continued to scream and struggle below him, shoving the blade in till I felt him go limp and heard only my heavy breaths. I rolled his body off of me, and laid there panting, letting the panic recede.

I turned my head to the side to meet the still icy gaze of my attacker, when suddenly he began to quake and shrink, returning to its original form. The beauty of the glowing orb was a stark contrast to the ugly, terrorizing figure of the gambler. I braced myself on my elbows, still trying to catch my breath while staring at the Vesper, and when I turned to look down at my bloodied hands and clothes, I was shocked to discover them pristine.

I moved myself back up to the cot and sat there trying to calm myself, but nothing would bring me down from this heightened state. My veins coursed with adrenaline. I knew who I wanted to call upon, but I wouldn't let myself. Not yet. Not until I was strong enough to know the difference between truth and this false reality.

Instead, I called upon someone with a calming energy. I looked at the Vesper and let myself remember all my favorite of Nori's features. The dimples when she smiles. The way her hair is somehow messy but kempt.

Slowly the orb shifted, and she was standing there before me. Or at least, something that looked just like her. Needing someone just to hold me, she walked over to the bedside joining me. She placed her hand atop mine and as I began to sob, she embraced me. I let her hold me until my breathing returned to normal and I was able to grapple with how real it all had felt.

How the fear of him trying to hurt me had felt, how the knife felt piercing the flesh, and the wetness of the blood pouring out of him. I had never imagined how details could be fuzzy and clear all at once. When the intensity of the moment passed, I watched as I allowed the Vesper to return to its original form.

I found myself frustrated that I had relied on my combat skills to beat my opponent. How was this helping me channel strength and focus for my magical abilities? If anything, this room would break me before it built me up. I stared at the light of the orb in the darkness like it was some code that I had to crack.

⟜⟜⟜✦

Henceforth, I returned night after night to the hall of Vespers. Not because I was assigned to, but because I'd become plagued with nightmares. I'd rather be training in a room with a Vesper than letting the aftermath of these sessions torture me through attempts at sleep.

The bags under my eyes made it obvious, and Cairis had even made some remark about me needing to get my beauty rest, but I just brushed it off. Every night that I pushed myself to the brink in a tiny room with a Vesper was one less thing I had to fear.

I knew I'd become addicted to it and I didn't care. I didn't mind putting myself through the pain and torture because every time I walked out of that room, I felt more powerful, less of who I was and more of who I would become. I delighted in my creativity, thinking up new ways to test myself.

I had no idea if this was what we were meant to do, but it was working for me. I may have been tired, but I was mentally stronger than ever. The lack of fear had me engaging in riskier behaviors in the flight valley and in the sparring room. I was numb to pain and less focused on healing. It was like a callous slowly building over time, and with each session, I hardened.

When I showed up to Saryn's class each day sporting more cuts and bruises, he asked me why I wasn't healing myself in between sessions. I replied, "We should know when to show our scars and wounds to blend in amongst our enemies, should we not?" I quirked an eyebrow like I was teaching him something.

He smirked and gave me a nod of pride. Saryn may have been approving of the new methods to my madness, but I couldn't say the same for my peers. However, I took no stock in their opinion. This was working for me. They may have had years of experience over me and plenty of motivation, but I was finding the monster within and they had better stay out of my way.

Fighting the nameless faces of strangers was getting old. Over time, I got brave enough to explore my limitations. One of my biggest fears was being the weakest link in the group and giving up priceless information. Saryn had discussed the numerous ways in which we could end up being tortured behind enemy lines. Sadistic ways I had never fathomed, and now I couldn't get them out of my mind. They stayed with me, which is how I knew I feared them, which is how I knew I must overcome those fears.

I set my intentions very clearly with the Vesper. Most of the time, I made it embody Saryn. I don't know why, but I did. I set a safeword and instructed it not to stop. No matter how much I screamed, begged, or cried for help, it was not to stop unless I said the safeword. It was my only form of safety in these exercises. Knowing that I could push myself far enough to the edge and as soon as I needed it to stop, it would. If these experiences were ever to come to pass in reality, there would be no reprieve.

I reserved these activities for the latest hours, long after the others had gone to bed. When no one would hear my screams or find me a mess in the healing pools. These wounds would not be ones that I would wear to class. I'd let myself experience the wrath of water, fire, blade, poison, and searing mind-meddling. With each test, I grew stronger and my endurance peaked.

Each night, Vesper-Saryn would try and pry secrets from me about the Offering, the Order, and Basdie. Even about my relations with Trace, my true feelings about the others; each time I would absorb the pain and let it swell. I'd let the thick tears stream down my face in between my cries. I'd lick my dry lips till those tears tasted more like victory than pain. I didn't know what I was working toward, but I could feel it. I just couldn't explain it. Something dark inside of me was evolving.

When I finally understood the art of torture, I got brave enough to try it myself. This time I tied up the Vesper and repeated the same exercises that I had subjected myself to. I had to admit, it was far easier to be the victim than the tormentor. The first few times I tried, I found myself retching and vomiting in the corner of the room.

Inflicting repeated violence on someone who was unable to defend themselves was the hardest thing I'd tried to accomplish yet. I truly felt parts of myself dying each time I attempted it.

I'd begun to lose weight; lack of sleep and of eating had me looking quite miserable. No one—except maybe Saryn—would believe me, but I felt stronger than ever on the inside.

Trace's disapproving looks were around every corner. One day he grabbed my arm, pulling me aside.

"I don't know what you're doing in there, and I know it's none of my business, but you need to slow down."

"You're right, it is none of your business," I spat. "You don't get to decide what kind of monster I become. We all know how you feel about useless people."

My words were venomous, and the shock on his face quickly turned to sadness. His mouth agape but silent, I pulled away from his grasp and headed back to my studies.

When Nori showed up at my door, I knew the group had elected her to try and get through to me when the rest couldn't. They knew I had a soft spot for her. Nori sat on my bedside, trying to get me to open up about my training and offer some glimpse into what I had been doing with the Vespers.

I evaded the subject, explaining that I had been fulfilling my assignment as prescribed by Saryn. He didn't exactly articulate what I was to be doing with them but seeing his approval when I got better at wielding only motivated me. My shields were stronger than ever, my glamour improving with each day, and I had even dared to attempt shapeshifting under Gia's guidance.

Even if I couldn't hold it for more than a few minutes, I had tried. I was improving and that was the point. Menial magic like lighting fires and warming baths had become nothing to me, barely requiring any energy or thought.

When she tried to convince me that I should focus on training other skills, I snapped back defiantly, "I will not be the weak one amongst the lot of you. I will be feared, too!"

"Cress, *you're* the brave one! You befriended me when no one would, you fought Saryn, you came after me with no knowledge of the repercussions, and you stood up for me to the others, risking everything. You are fearless, and that is more valuable than being feared!"

she pleaded.

I tried to listen and hear her words, but I'd become used to blocking out all the noise.

"Please, let me help you," she offered earnestly.

The familiarity of it echoed our struggle in the valley, when I begged for her to return. I didn't know how to accept help anymore. I had isolated myself completely in an attempt to become like the others.

Here I was looking into the pitch black of Nori's kind eyes, seeking answers and reprieve.

"There is one thing you could do," I whispered, not letting the darkness of my dreams hear me utter a plea.

"I'm suffering from terrible nightmares, because of my training…" I paused, hoping she would understand how bad it had gotten.

"If I could just get some good sleep, then I think I'd feel differently."

A sweet smile spread across Nori's youthful face.

She nodded. "Go to sleep at a decent hour tonight, and I promise to bring you much-needed rest."

That night I didn't visit the hall of Vespers and I didn't care if that would get me in trouble with Saryn. I did as Nori had instructed and crawled into bed shortly after dinner time. I pulled the blanket up to my chin and began to fiddle with my hands. I waited for the onslaught of shadows and nightmares to take me. As my heavy eyelids fell, I thought of the stories my mother had once told me and prayed that a dream-dancer would come and keep the darkness at bay.

Nori had been an absolute Godssend. I couldn't remember the last time I had slept so well. I awoke feeling renewed in every way. Although one good night's rest wouldn't eliminate the dark circles around my eyes or put back on the weight I'd lost, it was the first step.

Breathing felt easier; the unbearable weight of anxiety from nightmares or sleeplessness had finally receded, if only momentarily. I don't know why I hadn't asked her before now. I suppose I'd felt awful asking her to use such a rare gift on something like this, or maybe I had been just too embarrassed to admit I needed help. Either way, I was indebted to her—though she would say we were even.

That morning at breakfast, I was surprised to discover Gia sporting copper-colored hair and blue eyes. Nothing compared to Varro's eyes, but they were different, nonetheless. She told me she was practicing her shapeshifting endurance.

She intended to spend the whole day with this new look—or as long as she could without exhausting herself, at least. This was proof that no matter what Gia did she was always going to look stunning. But even I knew what she was doing was a mere shade of what Saryn expected of her.

I'd seen brief glimpses of it in class. She'd fully transfigured her body and face into an entirely new form. It was slightly less scary than when the Vespers did it. At least I had the relief of knowing I trusted Gia. No matter how she shifted, there was someone I knew behind that stranger's gaze.

Gia was very convincing, but only for short periods. That was why she had practiced extending her abilities in small increments over time. She'd never be able to keep up the charade while fighting, being tortured, or "fucking," as Saryn said. Initially, it was alarming to hear Saryn talk about our bodies and intimacy like it was some weapon at our disposal, but the more he spoke like that, the more numb we became to it.

Over time, there were fewer awkward glances amongst one another each time he'd make some crass remark about these "tactics." That morning, Saryn had plans for us. Plans none of us could have prepared for.

"Today's lesson is going to take creativity, the ability to read someone, emotional intelligence, and above all else, confidence."

We all listened intently, some of us with arms crossed or hands fidgeting to hide our nerves. Unlike Theory's predictable classes, Saryn's classroom was something entirely different.

"Since most of you lack confidence and let your conscience dominate your decisions, we'll start with something easy, but that's only because I'm feeling kind today. I will not feel kind tomorrow."

I rolled my eyes, hoping he didn't notice.

"Manipulation comes in many forms. You must master this. Seduction, deception, and persuasion are delicate art forms, and if you do this well, you can control all who cross your path. Wield weakness to your benefit, tap into their deepest unspoken desires, and use it against them. An unaware enemy cannot see the knife at their back or in their beds."

Saryn had such a way with words. Making the maniacal and questionable sound noble and important. The only person better at it than him was Idris, whom we hadn't seen since our arrival.

I heard Nori let out a small gasp next to me, knowing this was extremely uncomfortable territory for her given how chaste she was. I had my own concerns, and they were brewing above me like a dark storm cloud waiting to downpour.

"For this exercise, you will be paired up with each other and let down your shields, allowing your partner to easily access your mind. You will then manipulate them by using your mind to paint a vision or an illusion. This is not the same thing as accidentally or passively letting your enemy read you. This is using someone's mind reading against them. At the end of the exercise, I will ask you to repeat aloud what your partner showed you, and we'll see who amongst you has a knack for this."

Anxious dread consumed me. Who was I going to be paired up with? Saryn proceeded to call out our pairings and instructed us to place our chairs directly in front of that person so we were facing one another but not touching.

I felt myself begin to perspire when Trace was instructed to partner with me. When he plopped his chair down in front of mine, I could barely bring myself to look at him. I shook my head in annoyance, knowing the others were likely amused at our pairing. The tension of it spread quickly across the room. To my right sat a red-headed Gia across from Varro, who wasn't looking in my direction, and next to him was Cairis seated in front of Nori.

Thoughts of my and Trace's time together began to flood back to the forefront of my mind from the depths of my memory. Memories I had tried to keep locked away once we knew we simply could not be. But I had not let my shields down; there was no possible way he was bearing witness to this bombardment.

I found myself tapping my foot, itching with defiance against this exercise, but I knew there was no escaping it. I had toyed with the idea of practicing some of this with a Vesper given my limited experience, but I settled for torture over pleasure. The regret was not lost on me as I sat stone-faced across from my former lover.

"Ladies will go first. I've always found you to be the more creative gender. Drop your shields and let's see if you've got what it takes to bring them to their knees."

Trace stared ahead, giving me a pained look. I tried to think quickly. I wanted it to be something that showed I knew Trace, but not too well. This should have been easy for us, but for that very same reason, it was all the more difficult.

Suddenly, I remembered the Nightwing feather sitting in the drawer of my dormitory, and it sparked an idea. I closed my eyes and gripped both sides of the armrests, digging my nails into the wood. I dropped my shield, letting him into my mind.

In my thoughts, I showed him a fantasy. I was standing in a barely-there sheer dress lit by nothing but moonslight. A plunging neckline exposed the curves of my breast. The backless piece of fabric draped over me, hiding only the parts of me that mattered in this illusion.

I let out a deep exhale and continued.

In my right hand, I carried one long, rigid black Nightwing feather and I lifted it to my mouth, holding it there gently against my lips like a sweet caress, awaiting a kiss that would not come. I filled the thought with heavy emotions of longing and the pain of missing someone. I began to slowly drag the feather along my neck and down the middle of my chest, tickling the edges of my breasts and causing my nipples to peak in the cool night air.

My breathing grew more ragged as I let my imagination carry me away into this illusion.

The feather continued to roam downward across my body and the thin fabric. I felt my legs clench together, tightening from the ache deep in my belly as I thought of the male with the Nightwing feathers. I pulled the dark fabric to the side, exposing my bare leg and the dip along my hip. I ran the feather along this sensitive area over and over, letting the ticklish feeling send electric surges down my core.

I licked my lips with want, feeling my palms grow sweaty as they gripped the chair. I would not allow myself to open my eyes or become distracted with thoughts of how Trace might be feeling. That was not the assignment.

I moved the feather farther inward and gently glided it across my sex, causing my legs to tremble. When I could take the teasing of the feather no more, I mouthed the word, "Trace."

I opened my eyes when I realized I hadn't mouthed the name in my thoughts but had done so out loud, a mere whisper for all to hear. No one reacted, except Saryn who had a fiendish smile on his face. My cheeks were already turning bright red with embarrassment as I looked up to see Trace, wide-eyed and jaw tight. He stretched and flexed his fingers in and out of fists, trying to release the frustrated tension my fantasy and illusions caused him.

I looked down the aisle again to see if anyone else had noticed my awkward mistake. Most of them were concentrating on their assignments, but I swore I saw a flicker of something on Varro's face before he turned to look back at Gia.

After a few more minutes passed, Saryn walked menacingly behind the males' chairs, placing himself behind Cairis first.

"What did our sweet and innocent little Nori have to show you, Cairis? Did she please you, or get under your skin?"

The thought of those two doing anything like this made my lips curl in disgust. They were as platonic as it got.

Cairis gritted out his answer with a hint of venom.

"In her illusion, I was a High Lord, head of my household, respected by all of the staff. Servants at my beck and call. She presented herself as a Madame. A collector of beautiful females…fanciful, exotic, submissive, all types. She brought them to me as a gift. They were all for me—"

Cairis was cut off by the sound of Saryn clapping and praising Nori.

"Well, well, dreamweaver, looks like you have quite the knack for reading people. Abundance, power, and respect. You read Cairis like a book. Splendid."

Nori frowned at Cairis, a pleading look seeking forgiveness for exposing him that way.

Saryn moved on, stepping behind Varro and placing his hands on both his shoulders.

"Gia, dare I say you make a stunning redhead. Golden boy, what did our shifter sweetheart have in store for you?"

Varro's glance flickered briefly in my direction before returning quickly back toward Gia.

"I was at sea, and in the distance, there was a beach. I could faintly make out the shape of a maiden. Long, dark brown hair, her skin almost pale as snow. A stark contrast to the deep blues of the sea and the warmth of the sandy beach surrounding her. I sailed furiously toward her for what seemed like forever. She called to me like a siren's song. No matter how far I sailed, I could not reach her. The distance never closed the gap. I could never truly make out her face. She had to have been a mirage, but I could not bring myself to stop sailing toward it."

"Very interesting," Saryn commented. "I like it. Longing, a sense of freedom, yet feeling trapped. Wanting something unattainable."

Gia just smiled at Varro knowingly, but he did not return any reaction.

I'd become horrified with the fact that thus far I was the only one who'd used an overtly sexual illusion. Not manipulation, deception, or persuasion.

The embarrassment warmed my cheeks as I prepared for Trace to oust me in front of everyone. Saryn stepped to the side, standing behind us and waiting for him to unveil what I'd shown him. I took a deep breath, my nostrils flaring in preparation for his words to recount the vision.

"I was shown a female." He paused before continuing, "She was very beautiful, bathed in moonslight and wearing very little clothing. In her hand, she held a single Nightwing feather. She ran it all along her body, remembering the way her lover had made her feel. When she could take no more of her longing and teasing, she aimed to please herself."

When he stopped, I took a sigh of relief thinking he'd end it there, but he didn't. For some reason, he turned to his left—towards the group, or just Varro, I was unsure—and said, "She called for her lover, by his name."

He didn't say what the female looked like, but he didn't have to. It was obvious, and I wanted to crawl into a cave and hide for the next century. I kept my eyes locked on him, unable to turn and face the looks of the others. Surely, they heard me whisper his name earlier, and he'd all but confirmed the rumors at this point.

"Cress, ever the brave one amongst your lot. I have to give you credit, I didn't think you had it in you to go straight for seduction and to use a Nightwing… The attention to detail in your creativity is impeccable. It's almost as if you knew exactly what would make Trace feel special."

The tension in the room turned palpable and I couldn't bring myself to take Saryn's words as a compliment.

"And this is why kingdoms have crumbled over queens and courtesans. Males are simple creatures, easy to read. Well done, ladies. Now, let's keep this going and make things more interesting with a partner swap. I like to keep you on your toes, after all, with fast thinking and less planning. Rely on instinct!"

All of the males stood up while the females remained seated, pushing them each down one partner while Trace made his way back to the other end where Nori sat. Face-to-face with Varro after everything that had just transpired was almost worse torture than I'd experienced with the Vesper.

I gave Varro one last look that begged, *Please, go easy on me*, before he closed his eyes and I followed suit.

He let down his shields and showed me what he'd created just for me. My lungs began to feel tight and suddenly seized. I could feel my hands still on the chair, but I felt the breathlessness consuming me, everything going cold and dark. Suddenly I gasped out loud for air, breaking myself from a vision that felt terrifyingly real.

Varro opened his eyes and stared at me while I panted in front of him, trying to calm my erratic breathing. Saryn walked toward me, looking thrilled to hear about what Varro had done.

"I'm on pins and needles to hear more about what just transpired between you two."

I began to recite the illusion Varro had created, still trying to make sense of why it felt real, too real.

"I was on a ship when suddenly I fell into the water. The waves were strong and pulled me under. No matter how hard I tried to swim toward the sunlight, I only sank farther into the darkness of the sea. With each passing second, I lost more breath and I struggled to survive. When I thought I'd almost succumb to drowning, I heard a song of the sea echoing through the water from a distance. My body felt heavy, but there was no strength to fight the sinking. Suddenly, I felt someone or something press its lips to mine, giving me air, a breath of life, and then I awoke here."

Saryn turned his head, lifting a brow at Varro.

"No one said we couldn't add a little extra to make the illusion feel real," he replied nonchalantly, disregarding Saryn's accusatory look.

My eyes widened in fury.

"How dare you make me feel like I was drowning!"

Varro raised his hands in the air as if feigning innocence. "I thought you were one for torture…"

Before I could lunge at him, Saryn had already placed his hand in front of my chest to stop me. With my mental shields down, he had easy access to read every intention before I even made a move.

"I'd say low blow, Varro, but we all know that I'm a huge proponent of 'all is fair in love and war.' And we are indeed preparing for war. That being said, not sure what you two have to work out, but I'm going to give you points for creativity and bravery, because as you pointed out, there were no rules to be broken."

The anger coursing through me was deafening as the others went down the line. I made a concerted effort to listen, but was distracted with thoughts of wanting to rip Varro limb from limb.

Gia was recounting the vision Cairis had crafted for her. A world where she was the most powerful amongst us, having mastered shape-shifting and numerous other abilities. She wreaked havoc as she pleased. She had the power to bend another's will at leisure. Males were play-things to her, she chewed them up and spit them out without hesitation. Gia smiled the whole time.

I knew Gia liked being the best at everything, but I had never realized how truly power-hungry she was. Perhaps what was most saddening about all of this was that none of them realized why she wanted so badly to exercise control over everything and everyone. No amount of power would repair her broken bond. Instead, she used that power to build a fortress around her broken heart.

Nori was the last to share the vision she had been granted. I had no idea what Trace would have done in this scenario; Trace being a violent person and Nori the opposite.

"When I flew down into the valley the day I decided to leave, no one followed me. No one tried to convince me to stay. I walked along the stream to the valley's edge, content with my decision to leave at all costs. When I went to cross what I perceived was the threshold, nothing happened. I returned home to my loved ones, only to discover that Ilithyia had blessed my mother and father with a newborn. I finally had a sibling to love. And I never saw or heard from the Order ever again."

The room was silent, mostly shocked that Trace hadn't bestowed some horribly violent vision upon her. Saryn looked irritated, and Trace looked indifferent.

"If you think I'm going to applaud you for knowing our escapee desires freedom, then you'd be mistaken," Saryn chided.

Trace retorted snidely, "You're a fool. She doesn't crave freedom. She craves the belief that her Gods don't allow good and innocent people to suffer, and she can't reconcile that they do. She desires a world that has never existed and never will. So, I guess you're both fools."

However true his words were, I was fuming at him. At least now I took comfort in the fact that Nori knew she had friends here who cared for her; she wouldn't let Trace or this exercise get to her.

He was being cruel just to be right. These were the sides of Trace that I had never seen before Basdie, that I didn't know existed. That is why I knew that I was the one who was the real fool.

Ever since Saryn's exercise, the energy amongst all of us had shifted. People were distant in the flight field, opting to train alone rather than together. After that, people sat apart in the common area, heads down in their books. Just when I had thought we were starting to come together as a team, something like this sent us spinning off center. I knew it was wrong to be grateful that others had crossed lines or hit sensitive spots, too. I welcomed anything that dimmed the spotlight on Trace and myself.

I dragged myself to dinner, knowing that we'd either be sitting in awkward silence for the entire meal or something was about to explode. My instincts told me that everyone was tired. Tired of it all. Tired of being taken, kept here against our will, told nothing but how to train. Who'd have thought a dinner roll would have been the catalyst to that explosion?

As we made our way through the supper line filling our plates, Trace placed the last dinner roll on his and began to step away when we heard Varro mutter, "Fucking black cloaks, always selfish, every one for themselves."

I knew it was coming even before I heard it. The sound of Trace's plate slamming on the table behind us as he stepped forward into Varro's space.

"Yes, I was a black cloak, and if I wanted to kill you, no one would ever know it was me. Your body would never be found, and I'd make sure you'd regret your last moments. Are you willing to die for a dinner roll, Goldie?"

Surprisingly, Varro didn't flinch at Trace's words. He seemed mildly amused. I was horrified for him. Trace was not someone to taunt or take lightly.

Varro turned to Trace, placed a spoonful of soup into his mouth, swallowed it intently and replied, "No, I'm watching my figure."

He then proceeded to step around Trace and take his place at the table disregarding the threat.

The rest of us made our way through the line and took our seats. I went to gulp my water when I found myself suddenly alarmed by the unexpected sweetness. I almost spit the drink out, which would have undoubtedly ruined my meal.

"I took the liberty of transfiguring the water to wine. Seems like a night where everyone could use it. If any of you tell Saryn, I will find you," Cairis said as the others began to inspect and smell their cups.

Gia raised her hand, lifting her cup to Cairis'. "About time. Cheers!"

Trace followed the brief silence with an encouraging remark, "If you're taking requests…ale next time. Not wine."

I wished their banter made the air in the room feel lighter, but it was a minuscule improvement, at best.

We chewed our food and sipped at our wine, lucky that neither Saryn nor Theory had been there to witness any of what had transpired. We could have just kept to ourselves, tried to enjoy the rest of our meal, and gone to the Vespers or bed—but luck was not on my side.

Varro shoved his emptied bowl to the center of the table, leaned back with folded arms, and inquired, "When are we going to get to the bottom of what's going on with you two?"

He pointed his finger back and forth between Trace and me. Cairis shook his head in disappointment and slumped into his seat with a knowing look. Trace appeared beyond perturbed.

"What, Varro, are you upset that I've seen her wings? And I don't mean on the flight deck…"

I could have strangled Trace for giving them an ounce of confirmation without aligning with me first. The past, our secret, it belonged to both of us, not just him. He didn't care how I felt. He just wanted to piss off Varro, but he'd done that and more, because now I was livid. I kicked my chair back and rose to a stand, leaning over the table and hoping they could feel the anger pulsing off me.

"You two are pathetic. Who gives a fuck if he was a black cloak? Who gives a shit about the last dinner roll? And most importantly, who cares who I've slept with? Our past is as good as dead. Move on and grow up!"

The words spilled out of me without an ounce of regret or hesitation. Nothing about my choice words sounded lady-like, and that was fine by me, because they needed to know I'd had enough of this. Enough of the staring and the whispers. Enough of the unspoken accusations.

"You put us all at risk. How can we trust you? How do we know you both aren't going to be a liability?" Varro wouldn't let it go.

I seethed. "The past is in the past. Trust that."

I stormed out of the room and headed toward my quarters, anxious to put distance between myself and the others. I heard footsteps behind me but did not turn to see who followed.

Before I could slam the door shut behind me, a hand blocked it and Trace stepped through the entryway.

"Why did you do that?" I pleaded, trying to hold back frustrated tears.

"Because even if I cannot have you, you are mine!" he snarled back angrily.

"No, I'm not," I shouted. "I'm not yours, no more than you were ever mine. We were never each other's to have."

The sad truth of that washed over me like a tide. The hurt spread across Trace's stunning features like an eclipse.

"I'm not the same person as when you met me, and neither are you. Maybe those two people could have been something, but we will never get that back. They've taken everything from us. Don't you see that?"

"'Like seeing something that's already gone'..." he trailed off in a whisper, haunting me with my own words.

His hazel eyes began to glisten, betraying his stoic facade. He reached for my hand but I pulled away from his embrace, keeping my arm tight against my side. It was then I knew... We were truly broken.

As he exited my room he turned to say, "If you don't choose fate, just know that I'd choose you."

He shut the door behind him, leaving me solitary and wordless. What could he possibly mean by that? Our fates were already chosen.

CHAPTER
27

I tried to sleep, I really did, but tossing and turning while wide awake was all I had accomplished in the last hour. I'd given up on trying to rest because I was too riled up from the events of the day. I decided I'd blow off some steam with the Vesper and made my way down the winding hallway.

Lazily I picked the first door, a different room than I normally went to. It made no difference because a Vesper was a Vesper, no need to be particular. That irritating buzz was back again. Coursing through me like a low hum, making my skin prickle and itch.

I sat on the cot and stared at the glow of the Vesper, welcoming the familiarity of the soft amber light. I let out a deep exhale, trying to rid myself of one of the heaviest days since my arrival. My mind was a mess, and deciding the best way to clear it was the issue. I couldn't reconcile if I just wanted to fight someone, inflict a little pain, or have some pain inflicted on me. Perhaps I'd just let some pretend version of Nori hug me till I cried myself to sleep.

After several minutes, I heard the noise of a faint conversation coming from the room next to mine. I couldn't make out the words, but there was a male voice. I stood up and scanned the wall with my eyes, looking for signs of where the sound might be coming from. On the far-left side of the room, there was a small crack in the stones, leaving a tiny hole. If I held my eye up to it, I could see a hint of the chamber on the other side.

I knew it was wrong, and I should have probably gone back to minding my own business, but once it was clear that Varro was on the other side, curiosity got the best of me.

From what I could see, he was on his knees shaking his head in what appeared to be desperation. Sitting on the small cot before him was a beautiful girl. She was as bright as a pearl in sunshine, with long white curls sweeping past both sides of her youthful face. She placed a comforting hand on his shoulder, trying to calm him. It seemed like he was arguing with her, but not aggressively; more like he was dismissing her advice.

He then leaned over and placed his head in her lap, giving her access to run her fingers through his hair. She then began to hum a tune, soothing him with her song. I started to feel like I'd been intruding on something very private. But who was she?

When I heard the hum of the song slow to an end, I moved my head and held my ear against the hole, trying to make out any of the conversation. "I will never be given a fair chance," he was pleading quietly. "It hurts in my ribs; my heart feels caged. I feel it in the marrow of my being."

I muffled my gasp, pulling my ear away from the cold stone wall, fearful of having spied on something too intimate to witness. Whoever it was, she had a hold on Varro. It was clear from the way he clung to her.

I occupied myself with the Vesper, doing some light sparring that allowed me to sweat off all the built-up tension. I tried my best to put it far from my mind, but I couldn't stop thinking about Varro and the other female.

When I heard the door close, I deduced he had finally made his exit.

I peeked out of my door and noticed he was heading to the baths rather than his room. I reasoned that after all the sweating I'd done, I needed a quick dip. I sent the Vesper back to its original form and waited just a bit longer so he didn't notice me following behind him.

I knew he'd be in his favorite pool, which made locating him easy. When I entered the steamy room, he paid me no attention. He didn't even turn to acknowledge me. Varro just stood there with his back turned to me, making his way farther into the cavernous pool.

I hadn't realized it till I was waist-deep, but after what he'd done to me earlier, I was feeling a bit nervous in the water. It was shallow, nearly impossible for me to drown, but the eerie memory of that feeling was now ever present.

I sat down on a stone bench under the inlet, something that was becoming a familiar routine for Varro and me anytime we were both here. He sat across from me, stretching his muscles in the milky water.

"How'd you do it?" I demanded.

"How'd I do what?" he asked, playing coy.

"You know exactly what I'm talking about. How did you make me feel like I was drowning?"

Varro slowly moved toward me, and I was unsure why he needed to approach me to answer the question. I shrank back in my seat.

From below the waters, Varro suddenly grabbed my foot and refused to let go.

"You're so tightly wound. You need to relax."

"Tell me..." I fumed, trying to tug my foot away.

"I'll tell you if you just relax," he demanded as he began to slowly knead his fist into the bottom of my aching foot.

Gods, that felt good. I eyed him suspiciously, but he was rendering me defenseless with each squeeze and tug along the arch of my foot and up my toes.

"How did you do it," I gritted out, sounding far less relaxed than I was becoming.

"It's like mesmerization. We call it 'Siren Song.' Instead of mesmerizing you to take action, it controls how you feel. I made you feel like you were drowning, even though you were perfectly safe."

He said it so matter of fact, like I shouldn't be shocked by any of it.

"How come I've never heard of that ability? Saryn has never mentioned it."

Varro lowered my foot and released his grip. It had felt so good, the second he let go I longed for it again, but then he grabbed the other foot and proceeded with the same movements on the remaining leg.

"Because it's not an ability. It's a gift."

"Like Nori and dreamwalking?" I prodded.

"No, that's an ability, albeit a rare one. Siren Song is a gift, and you have to earn it."

I was excited to understand this unique thing Varro was capable of.

"How do you earn it?" I prodded.

"When I was young, I participated in the same troublemaking that all youth get into. There is lore among my people that if you're brave enough to swim to the darkest depths of the sea and kiss a siren, then they will bestow the gift upon you for your bravery."

"But you can breathe underwater, how hard could that have been?" I exclaimed, pointing to the gills behind his ear.

"Ever the astute one." He smiled. It brought him joy to know I had noticed.

"To find a siren, you have to swim very deep, much farther than most Sea Fae ever need to go. You landlocked Fae can't even begin to understand the horrors that reside down there from what you read in your texts. Why would you? You're long dead before you could witness the world at those depths."

My eyes widened with fear—intrigue.

"But I was determined to get that kiss."

I tried to picture a young Varro arguing with his mates on the edge of a ship. Each daring the other to leap.

He rolled his thumb down the curve of my foot, and I swear I almost let out a moan.

"So, you swam to the deep blue to impress your friends, fended off a few monsters, locked lips with a siren, and now you have this gift and you used it to make me feel like I was drowning. What else can it do? Do you have to sing for it to work?"

I refused to drop the subject till he fully explained it to me.

He let out an amused laugh and when I tried to pull my foot away again, he refused to let it go.

"No, Cress, you do not have to sing for it to work. You can pretty much make someone feel anything, but once you stop, the effects wear off. They aren't long-lasting."

"If you don't have to sing, why is it called 'Siren Song'?" I pried.

"Because the sirens lure sailors to the bottom of the sea with their song, making them think they can breathe, that nothing is wrong when they're drowning them slowly, toying with them till the song turns to silence."

I knew the lore about singing sirens, their haunting songs, and the traps they set for sailors, but it hadn't made sense till now. The stories from my childhood just became that much scarier knowing they were somewhat rooted in truth. No wonder my father had tried to scare Versa and me from going in the water. I wonder if he knew the secret the Sea Fae had been keeping about those vicious creatures.

Varro continued to massage my foot, occasionally moving his strong hands along my calf, distracting me.

"With the gift, I can make you feel calm." Suddenly I felt more relaxed than I could ever remember. "Or I can make you feel sleepy." An inexplicable yawn escaped my mouth, and my eyelids felt heavy. "I could make you feel sick." And nausea overcame me.

"Stop, stop," I yelled, throwing my arms up in exasperation. "Couldn't you have picked something nice for a demonstration?"

Varro smiled, releasing my foot. "Like what? Love? Lust?"

He raised a playful eyebrow at me, and I couldn't believe I was entertaining jokes with the same person I would have strangled earlier. Varro was disarming like that. Or charming. I wasn't entirely sure yet.

"Just one more unique person with some special ability I have to contend with," I drawled.

It was the most pitiful thing to say, but it felt true. Every time someone excelled, I felt further behind.

"You don't have to contend with anything, Cress, we're a team. Everything we have in our arsenal helps all of us survive."

He wasn't wrong, but this place was less encouraging. Theory and Saryn rarely praised or complimented us. When they did, it always had a hint of disdain. You were never sure if they meant any of it, and their expectations seemed unachievable. It was a never-ending battle to not doubt myself at every turn.

It was a stark contrast to being in the academy back home. There I had been good at everything and professors weren't shy about letting me know. My family was proud of my accomplishments and humbly bragged frequently. I knew it was juvenile to expect anything like that, but there were times I just needed to hear it.

"I believe you're going to be the one to make or break this team. We need you, even if you can't see it yet."

His words struck me. I wanted to believe them, badly.

Varro grabbed my chin, tilting it up toward him intimately. I glanced to the side nervously, unsure why he'd touch me like that.

"Keep your chin up, Moirai. All that matters is who we become, not who we were."

That word again, in the old tongue—the one I didn't know. He'd only done it a few times. Passing in the hallway, occasionally on the sparring floor. He released my chin and began to walk toward the exit of the pool.

"What is that word you keep calling me?" I questioned, showing more intrigue than I cared to admit. I had tried to find the translation in the library but my search revealed nothing.

He responded to me without so much as a glance over his shoulder, his answer echoing across the stone walls and ceiling.

"Maybe I'll tell you someday. Maybe I won't. It's more fun this way."

Over the next handful of weeks, we all trained harder than ever before. Each of us put in the work with Saryn, Theory, and one another. The snide remarks had come to an end, and I had to admit I was a bit relieved that Trace and I had come clean about our history. The stares and whispers were finally gone.

I'd be lying if I said the thoughts of that Vesper girl with Varro hadn't occupied my mind more times than I cared to admit. It was an unwanted distraction, but I was too nervous to ask him about it since I'd then have to confess to spying.

Saryn finally showed hints of being impressed with us. Gia was sustaining her shifts for longer and longer periods of time. Cairis and Nori could have been a sideshow with their elemental manipulation. Trace finally got the ale he requested. As I sipped my cup at dinner, it was bitter with memories of the tavern.

Our formations and combat drills in the flight valley were much improved. It had become second nature, weaving between one another, playing to one another's strengths, shielding each other's weaknesses.

As of late, I'd gone easy on myself when it came to the Vespers. Far less torture meant my sleep cycle had returned to normal and I no longer needed nightly visits from Nori.

I always knew when Trace was with a Vesper. The shrieks and bellows of unrelenting pain echoed down the hallways, impossible to ignore. But it was never the sound of Trace screaming.

Growing up with a father like his, and as a black cloak, I'm sure it was all second nature and I prayed I'd never see the horrors of what he was truly capable of. But if he was going to be on someone's side, I was grateful it was ours. I'd never want to be on the other end of his blade when his hazel eyes went to that haunted, unfeeling place.

It was strange that the Order wanted us to completely forget who we were, but the lives we had left behind were our strongest motivations to become the darkest, most terrifying versions of ourselves. I know that's why I struggled the most—because before Basdie, I had struggled the least. It's why I had to train harder and longer because I had to dig deeper than they did to find that spark. The spark that would give me the energy, the anger, to carry forward when the exhaustion began to set in.

Stretching in the sparring room, I glanced down at my hands, inspecting the changes my efforts had wrought. They were bruised, calloused, and raw. Different from the soft, smooth hands that used to grip the reins of my horse as I explored my family's land on spring days. Autumn was nearing its end, and I worried about how much snow we might see in the Elorns.

Trace warned us all that we must be prepared for setbacks in the flight field when the elements were against us. The thought of frost glistening across my wings as we plunged through the icy valley, wind cutting at our cheeks, seemed alluring, but I knew I'd regret the fantasy I'd built up in my head. Still, there would always be the warmth of the healing pools.

But once we left Basdie, resources such as this would not be guaranteed.

CHAPTER

20

Saryn and Theory gathered us in the common area, each of us standing anxiously around the long table where it lined the largest bookshelf.

"It's time to test your skills beyond the hollow of Basdie." Theory eyed each of us intently.

My stomach tightened into anxious knots at the prospect of getting to leave this place for any amount of time.

"You're being given your first mission, which means you need to plan and prepare as a team," Saryn clarified.

"You're going with us, right?" Cairis questioned, and I knew the answer before either instructor spoke.

"No, you're going alone. It's time to put all this training to good use."

I could see Nori fidgeting, picking at her nails, something she always did when her nerves were getting the best of her. If she wasn't so damn good at healing herself, her fingertips would be a regular bloody mess.

Trace spoke up, looking confident and intrigued, "What's the mission?"

Always all business with him.

"You're going to be attending a party, a ball, in honor of a celestial event."

Cairis chimed in obnoxiously before Theory could finish her thought, "A party? Ha, what kind of challenge is that?"

"Silence!" Theory looked like she was a second away from back-handing him. From that point on, the rest of us waited patiently in silence, listening carefully to each detail.

"The party is just the means to get you all onto the premises without being detected. A very wealthy family will be hosting, but their son, who resides on the estate, has been dealing in illegal goods under their noses. Your mission is to retrieve a particular box of items that he should not possess. The retrieval of said items is essential to your future missions. It goes without saying that failure is not an option."

I inhaled deeply, letting the weight of her words settle in.

Varro's voice rang out. "What are the rules of engagement?"

Saryn smiled slyly. The same look he always gave when he was thinking something truly devious.

"There are none. Get in and get out with the box. Go undetected if possible, and don't get caught. If you happen to make that filthy thief disappear for good, you wouldn't be hurting my feelings."

We all knew this moment would come, when all the training suddenly coalesced with reality. Hearing Saryn speak so flippantly about a stranger's life, as if it were nothing more than collateral damage, was still shocking. Trace didn't seem fazed.

Hands tucked nonchalantly in his pockets; Trace began his questioning. "What intel do we have?"

Theory rolled out a scroll across the table, covered in faded drawings.

"We managed to get ahold of some of the original designs of the household from the bricklayers who built the place. There's no guarantee that they are up-to-date, but it's the best we've got."

My eyes scanned the illustrations, noting how massive the structure was. It was practically a palace, but these weren't Royals or Honored Fae.

"What else?" Trace probed.

"We have reason to believe he is hiding the stolen goods near or around the bedroom of his youngest siblings; so young they are still tended to by a nanny."

Nori gasped at the thought of children being put in harm's way.

"There will be many guests at the ball, plenty of dancing, plenty of wine, and—knowing these people—plenty of debauchery, but you're not to be distracted from the task at hand. There will be a chime when the celestial event begins, and most guests will make their way out to the terrace. This is when you should plan to make your move. If you're quick about it, you should be gone before the guests even return. The details of how you accomplish this we leave up to you."

My mind was already spinning, playing out every scenario, thinking of the roles we'd each need to play. I was a planner, a list maker with a propensity for overthinking, but now I was focused on how we didn't end up dead, or worse. And I knew what "worse" was. I'd practiced that art many nights with the Vesper.

Just when I thought Theory and Saryn had offered all they were going to give us, they added, "Tomorrow, a tailor from the king will be arriving. You'll each be fitted for the ball with custom attire of your own design or request. That same tailor will be measuring you for custom weaponry. You'll make a list of what each of you want, and it will be crafted to your exact sizing and delivered shortly thereafter."

"And who should we expect to pay for all of this?" Cairis questioned.

Saryn smirked. "The Order has direct access to the king's purse. Whatever we desire, whatever we require, shall be ours." He winked.

Before walking off to leave us to our scheming, he said, "The event is in two weeks. Get your plan together. I suggest someone teaches Cairis to waltz, otherwise he'll be a dead giveaway."

That night none of us visited the Vespers or the healing pools. We pored over the designs of the estate, planning our movements. Two weeks might have seemed like plenty of time, but not to us. I'm glad everyone was just as ready as I was.

Most of us were focused, but Cairis would not shut up about all the fancy weaponry he was going to order. I rolled my eyes at his obnoxious tangents, but it was amusing how much he was hyping up Nori about the prospect of getting an entire arsenal sized just right for her petite stature. He'd whip around her, pretending to jab at her with tiny little Nori-sized daggers.

Trace, Varro, and I were heads down in a debate about the best approach. Gia sipped at her mulled cider and instructed us to "just tell her what to do."

Late into the evening, we had devised the following concept. Gia would serve as the bait for the host's son. Fully shifted in disguise, she would lure him to a spot far from his siblings' bedroom, seducing him into distraction, while many of the guests made their way onto the balcony.

Nori would glamour the children into thinking she was their nanny. With a brief glance at the real nanny, she could pull it off, especially because young children were significantly less perceptive about the illusion than adults. Her job was to get them away from their room, freeing up Trace to find the goods while Varro used Siren Song to lull the real nanny into a slumber.

Cairis would be standing guard at the end of the hallway, ready to alert us if anything was going awry and be the first line of defense if things derailed into chaos. My job was to intercept anything and anyone that kept the plan from happening.

While it seemed like I didn't have a real role, they assured me that having me on alert and ready to improvise was going to be pivotal if the need arose. Whether that meant obstructing and distracting a guard, sending a warning signal, or coming to Cairis' aid if things got really messy. The possibilities of my position were endless.

Varro said I was the one that acted on instinct. I had proven I could adapt, and that he was certain I'd spend every day until the mission playing out every possible scenario.

I didn't know whether or not to take that as a compliment, but since no one disagreed with the plan, the first night was a small victory.

The next day the tailor showed up as expected, and we each held private appointments with him to get measured and discuss our outfits. The ball was going to consist of extremely wealthy attendees. Each of us knew that our attire needed to be just ostentatious enough to blend in.

Nori read aloud from a book that attempted to explain the celestial event they were celebrating, which was referred to as the "Canary Veil." Every twenty years, the night sky would be blanketed in yellow, with the stars twinkling in the background. Unlike a solar eclipse where day briefly turned to night, the sky would remain bright, even when it was supposed to be dark out. The book described a God who was punished for his vanity and had his vision permanently altered. He was only able to see shades of yellow henceforth. On this one night, all others would see the world through his eyes.

It is said that those who stand under the Canary Veil would be granted extra youth from the eerie light of the sky. Why a bunch of Fae needed more youth was beyond me. We already lived an extremely long lifetime, assuming we did not fall ill or get struck down.

It's no surprise I'd never heard of it. Apparently, I'd lived too far south my entire life to witness it. It was more of a regional celebration.

When I explained what I wanted for my dress, the tailor looked at me wide-eyed, unsure as to whether I was joking or not.

I had planned to be modest with my weaponry request, especially since I'd have nowhere to hide them. But then I saw Cairis' long list of items, and he had reminded me that no one said the request had to be just for the party. I followed his logic and added a handful more items to my parchment.

I demanded that everyone attend a few classes led by Gia and me on dancing. We weren't certain if we'd be pulled into the festivities, but if we were, we would need to blend in like each of us had grown up dancing at these sorts of events.

Cairis and Trace needed the most work, simply because their size worked against them. Cairis was clunky in his steps, constantly jamming Gia's poor toes.

Trace was extremely stiff. I tried to tell myself it wasn't because he was practicing with me, which forced his hands to be wrapped around my waist and our bodies closer than they'd been in a long time. I continued to critique him. He wouldn't let me get off easy in the flight field; I wasn't about to let him mess this up for us just because he didn't have a musical bone in his rigid physique.

To no one's surprise, Varro was a great dancer. He was fluid like water, his body bending and curving with each dip of mine. Maybe his sister or mother had taught him to dance. I imagined him whirling his sister around, the sea breeze tousling her hair with each turn. Nori was light and graceful on her feet, but we all knew that if she had to dance with a stranger, the intimacy of it might be more than she bargained for on our first mission.

Over the next few days, Cairis improved. He emphasized that he'd been putting in work with the Vesper. We all laughed at the thought of Cairis waltzing in that tiny room, especially given the fact that most of us practiced violence with a Vesper, not dancing. I wasn't about to criticize his commitment, though.

By the end of the week our custom weapons had arrived, as well as the final adjustments to our attire. I purposefully hid my dress from the others. I wasn't sure I was going to get up enough courage to wear it, but since I had nothing else in my closet, I knew I had no actual choice.

When I had lain in bed at night imagining what it meant to be part of the Order—an assassin, a spy, a weapon of his majesty—I hadn't imagined it would involve ball gowns and parties, but here we were.

The night before the mission, tension and anxiety could be felt amongst all of us. We'd gone through the plan many times. I'd played out every possible scenario in my head. We were feeling confident, but it also felt strange. Like a prisoner's day out. This was the first time we'd be leaving Basdie in months. Would anyone be tempted to flee? What would the consequences be if they did? Worse than that, what if someone got hurt? What if we lost someone?

Saryn constantly lectured us that this was a real mission, the risks were all legitimate, and not to underestimate anything. He said never to minimize this to a retrieval mission because things rarely go to plan. He was excellent at dampening any confidence with his incessant warnings.

I heard cracks and quakes within the walls of the stronghold, but it was not the waterfall. I wandered toward the flight deck and found Trace out there by himself. In the distance, dark gray storm clouds were lurking in, and I could see the intermittent flashes of lightning scattered all about. The sound of deep thunder rolled our way.

Trace sat there on the ledge, sketching the landscape before him. I had almost forgotten he drew at all, and was quickly reminded of how much natural talent he possessed. Despite the effortless sweeps of the charcoal across the page, his shoulders remained lifted, uptight with a tension that coated his entire frame. He never seemed at ease anymore. Always on edge, always ready for a fight. I hated seeing him like that, but I knew he was prepared for anything and that brought me a sense of security.

"My father always taught me that a clear mind the night before a mission is more decisive and purposeful," he said, continuing to sketch.

"How many missions did your father send you on?"

"Enough to know that they rarely go to plan."

"You must have learned to improvise, then."

"At a cost." He sighed. "A storm is a bad omen amongst my people."

Those were words I did not need to hear the night before our mission. I tried to sound confident when I replied, "We're your people now. I'm going to let the thunder soothe me like a lullaby and sleep like a babe. I suggest you do the same."

I turned on my heel and left his side before he could respond.

CHAPTER

29

Looking in the mirror, I was unable to reconcile myself with the refined lady looking back at me. I reasoned that I had spent too long wearing fighting leathers, and it was the fact that I was wearing a dress again. The female in the mirror was a mere shade of the girl who arrived here; scared, unsure of herself, longing for everything she'd lost. The reflection in the mirror was confident, intense, and ready to be unleashed on the world.

The dress only added to the power I felt coursing through me. If I had been trying to downplay things, I might have chalked it up to the excitement of finally leaving Basdie even if for just one evening, but that wasn't it. I was ready for this mission. My gown wasn't armor, but it was perfectly designed to disarm anyone who crossed my path.

We arranged for each of us to travel in a handful of carriages. Some of us solo, others in pairs. We staggered our arrival times to ensure we did not appear as a group, making it easier to blend in with other attendees. With the help of Saryn and Theory, we knew the fake names to use upon arrival. The others had already departed. Gia and I were last.

When I stepped into the carriage she gave me a shocked look, remarking, "Damn, Cress, and I thought I was the belle of the ball."

I blushed at her words, taking it as a compliment but also starting to worry that maybe I had gone too far.

She could see the concern on my face and cut in, "Don't worry, you're not going to ruin anything. I'm going to be exactly what he wants and more."

Gia looked beautiful, but I knew this was not her final appearance. She'd arrive looking like herself, but as soon as she could spend a few minutes getting inside our target's head, she'd shift and look like the object of his desire for the rest of the evening while we carried out our mission.

The clopping of the horse hooves and the rich scent of polished mahogany was a welcome trip down memory lane. I hadn't accounted for the longer-than-expected carriage ride when I chose this dress design, but Gia and I made small talk in between rehashing the plan—for my sake more than hers. Her job was pretty straightforward: Keep the target distracted while the rest of us acquired the goods.

When I heard the wheels of the carriage transition from the sound of the beaten dirt to that of stone, I knew we had likely reached the premises of the estate. I felt the coachman bring us to a halt, and I looked at Gia with nervous trepidation. My confidence wavered briefly. Were we ready? Were we going to pull this off as a team? Was the plan the right one? Gia reached across and grabbed my hand tightly, looked me square in the eye, and said, "No mistakes, no mercy."

Her words were electric, bringing my focus back with a jolt. I nodded at her. As we both made our way out of the carriage, I looked up at the massive stone building, firelight beaming from every window. The escorts each took our hands with their crisp white gloves and ushered us to the entry line.

The circle drive was filled with countless carriages dropping off guests, one after another. Each person attending was dressed more elaborately than the last. The ladies were draped in jewels, from diadems to necklaces—the real stars of the evening. The males were merely more accessories.

I did not see the rest of our team as we continued to step forward in line, preparing to give our false names at the door. The wait felt like both an eternity and a single moment. I tried to calm my breathing and think back on everything Saryn and Theory had taught us. Mental shields up at all times. See beyond distractions. Listen to what is not being said. Always be aware of the exits. Anything out of the ordinary is not a coincidence.

So many lessons, wise words, and instructions swirled through me that I initially hadn't even heard the greeter ask for my name. The insistence in his voice interrupted my distraction and told me that this was not the first time he had asked. I said the name I had been given, and Gia squeezed my hand as he nodded and let us pass. I let out a small sigh of relief. We were in.

The giant rectangle room was two stories, with us having entered at ground level—which was also the top floor. The clean white marble covered every inch of this place. Floors, pillars, walls, it was all stone of the highest quality, and it was clear that their wealth far exceeded that of even my own family. It was possible that someday the king would have made them Honored Fae if it weren't for their son's criminal dealings.

I had a suspicion that Gia's family had this kind of wealth, if not more. She didn't seem to balk in the way I did, which made me remember that someone who belonged here wouldn't be gaping at the scene. I composed myself and continued to assess the room, trying to remember the layout from the drawings and orient myself.

The distractions were plenty. Bright yellow flowers filled the room with a thick floral scent at every turn. They adorned every inch of the room. Wrapped around stairwells, covering long banquet tables. They paired perfectly with the white stone and the golden filigree throughout. This home was more than lavish; it was borderline gaudy.

Gia and I stood at the top of the wide stone staircase that led down one level into the open ballroom. On the opposite side was another staircase. This gave those on the main level the ability to look down and admire the dancing from above. Multiple golden crystal chandeliers hung from the ceilings overhead, canvasing the dance floor in abundant light. Since this floor was underground, there were no windows, but the walls were lined with wall-to-wall mirrors, making the space look even larger and more mazelike.

There was no hiding in here. Everything was bright. Too bright. I had hoped for dim lighting, dark corners, a way to become one with the shadows, but that would not be the case this evening. We started to make our way slowly and carefully down the staircase.

Across the dance floor, I was relieved to spot more of our team. I made sure not to stare at them and scanned my eyes across the dance floor with delicate ease and confidence. As my gaze moved back across the ballroom, I could see the expression on Trace's face as clear as day. He was staring at me with molten hot intensity.

Gia whispered to me, "Next time you can design my dress."

His eyes widened almost imperceptibly, and I had to admit I did take the smallest bit of pleasure in knowing that I could still get his attention. It was then that I realized it was likely I had gained the notice of more than just him.

Suddenly, all eyes were on me and people were clearly whispering, some even going so far as to point. As we arrived at the bottom of the stairs, I found myself face to face with a very handsome male, but there was something sinister in the way he looked at me.

His eyes quickly roamed the length of my body, drinking me in. My back was completely exposed, and the bottom of the dress was a shiny, milky white satin that hugged my hips and flared and flowed behind me. In front, my hip bones protruded from above the waistline, exposing my navel.

But the bodice of the dress was what made it truly unique. Two giant feathers, dyed canary yellow, hugged the sensuous curves of my figure, beginning at the waist of the skirt and continuing up my chest. They splayed out across my breasts, covering me but leaving little to the imagination.

They had said this party would be ostentatious and debaucherous. I was fitting right in, and now I was regretting it. This wolf of a male had a feral intensity about his appraising gaze. He grabbed my hand and lifted it to his lips, placing a soft kiss atop it.

"My name is Fenix, but you may call me Nix."

A small gasp escaped my lips. He probably thought I was just nervous about the kiss, but Gia's eyes flared at me and I could see her begin to shift nervously. This was our target. The host's son had already intercepted us, and it was all my fault. Why did I wear this stupid dress?

"And what shall I call this exotic bird before me?"

Flustered by the unplanned encounter and misdirected attention, I fumbled, trying to remember the name I was supposed to say. Suddenly, Gia interrupted and put her hand out for him, expecting a similar treatment. He turned his head in surprise and kissed her hand as well.

"My name is Lorne and this lovely specimen is my dear friend Astrid."

A sly smile spread across his face.

"Well ladies, welcome to my family's estate. Good of you to join us for this evening's celebration."

I remained speechless because I could feel his desire towards me and that was most certainly not the plan.

Gia continued, "We're delighted to be here. Your home is just as stunning as I had heard. Would you be so kind as to grab my friend and me a drink?"

Nix nodded and began to step away to fulfill Gia's request. Once he left, I let out an enormous, panicked breath.

"Cress, listen to me, we have to pivot. I've been inside his head this whole time, and there isn't a single female I can shift into that is going to lure him more than what you just presented him with. He's enamored, and we're fucked. You better be ready for this impromptu change in plans. You're the bait now!"

My palms began to sweat. I had not ever accounted for a scenario where I was the bait. That was the shifter's job. Get in his head, find out what he likes, transform and distract him.

Just as Nix arrived back with our drinks, Trace approached us, bowed, and put out his hand to offer me a dance. I grabbed it, not knowing what else to do, but welcomed the quick exit from Nix to buy myself some time to figure out how we were going to pull this off now.

Trace pulled me in close to him, and as the string quartet echoed the next waltz, he began to quickly shuffle us farther out onto the dance floor, and farther from Nix so he would not be able to hear us. I knew Gia could handle him, but I would eventually have to come back to her aid. Trace moved us through each of the steps, practically carrying me along the way as my mind raced with possibilities.

All I could utter was, "I'm…I'm so sorry. I messed up, didn't I?"

Trace squeezed my hand to reassure me.

"The dress didn't help, but even I know that your beauty goes beyond some feathers and frills. Who wouldn't want you?"

Trace continued to twirl us through the countless number of people on the dance floor. I found no relief in his compliment.

"What do we do now?" I said, worried.

He leaned into me, speaking very calmly, "Stick to the plan. Now we know exactly who he wants. Gia needs to shift to look like you, but that means you can't risk being seen near one another again. Find a way to stay far apart, and she can handle him."

I breathed a small sigh of relief and relaxed minutely in his embrace. The music seemed hollow and drowned out as a world of golds and yellows spun in swirls all around us. The dancing lessons had paid off.

"Varro and Nori are in place to handle the nanny and children. Cairis has moved to the upper level to prepare for watch duties. The plan is still good, Cress."

When the song came to an end, he held my hand out as he pulled away and acknowledged me with a bow. Then he lifted my fingers to his lips and kissed them—while staring directly back at Nix.

"What are you doing?" I chastised.

"Making sure he wants you. Males are jealous creatures, and they especially don't like others touching what is theirs." He nodded and then stepped away.

I watched him go, and that's when I noticed he was donning all black. The usual. But there wasn't a hint of his tattoos anywhere. He had glamoured them completely out of sight to keep his true identity well-hidden. Each of us were focused on mental shields and small glamours. With all the training, it didn't require too much energy or focus to keep it up for a while. Gia was the one who needed the real endurance to pull this off.

I turned on my heel and began to make my way back to her. I had to find a way to convey that the plan was still intact. When I arrived back at her side, she smiled cheerfully, sipping her champagne, and Nix handed me mine. I was grateful for a drink to calm the nerves and cool me down, but Saryn's words echoed in my mind: "Be careful of ingesting anything handed to you."

Since Gia didn't adhere to the rule and hadn't dropped dead from poison, I figured it was safe and lifted the glass to my lips. Suddenly, I felt Nix's warm hand resting on my lower back.

"You're quite the dancer, Astrid. I had hoped to be the first in line, but I guess we'll consider the fellow in black a warm-up."

I let out a small fake laugh and nodded at him sweetly, realizing I would need to play along with this seduction for the time being. I lifted two fingers to my head and pressed them against my temple just for a second before bringing my hand back down to my side. To most this looked like I was developing a headache, but Gia would recognize the signal. It meant that I was going to briefly let down my mental shields and give her access to my mind.

I conveyed through my thoughts the instruction Trace had given me and as soon as I saw her deliver the return signal my shields were back up. Nix grabbed my hand and I passed my empty glass back to Gia.

"You two enjoy yourselves. Astrid, meet me at the ladies' room afterward."

Nix was smooth and charismatic. He danced even better than Varro, but the feel of his hot breath on my neck and the way his hand wandered too low made me feel sick to my stomach. I did not envy Gia. Her role as the bait was not a pleasant one, and I would gladly give it back.

I tried to focus on the fact that he was handsome and took comfort in the blade adhered to my inner thigh. I ran my fingers along his velvety jacket, noting the rich merlot color.

His dark brown facial hair was trimmed neat and short. His deep brown eyes weren't anything special, but they matched perfectly with his slicked back hair. He smelled of foreign cologne. Not a natural scent, like Trace. I leaned into him, letting his body press against mine, knowing that this would be exactly what Gia would do.

Trying to muster more confidence, I snaked my fingers behind his head and ran my fingers through the hair at the nape of his neck. I could feel him stiffen in delight, but this was all just a game to me. A means to lower his defenses.

With him focused on dancing and the feel of our bodies now closer than ever, his mind was an open window for me to peer into. There I found lustful thoughts, but they were not sweet or kind. This host who was charming on the outside was anything but in that imagination of his. Whether it was myself or Gia, we could not let him be alone with us or in control. Shivers went down my spine at the thought. He felt the goosebumps on my skin under his hand.

"Do I make you nervous, little bird?"

The nickname sounded gross coming from him, especially after I'd seen thoughts of just how he wanted to treat this little bird. It was clear he liked his females innocent, pliable, and willing. Everything I wanted to say back to him was the opposite of that. I had to stay focused. Be what he wanted. Do what Gia would do.

I leaned into his ear and whispered back sweetly, "No, but I am a bit chilled. Will you keep me warm?"

I pressed my peaking nipples into his chest, letting him feel me. That got his attention. As the song came to an end, he twirled me one last time and ended with me in a dip. When he pulled me back up to meet him, I remembered where Gia had said to meet her.

That's when we heard the chiming of the bells. We knew this meant that guests needed to transition to the terrace if they wanted to see the Canary Veil.

"Come, Astrid, let us see if the sky truly is canary yellow."

As he said the words, he ran a finger gently along the yellow feather covering my breast. I couldn't believe the audacity of his touch; I was practically a stranger to him. He thought I was in his trap, but he didn't know the web was mine.

"Aren't you afraid I'll fly away?" I teased. "Let's get Lorne first so she can join us."

Without waiting for his agreement, I grabbed his hand, leading him up the staircase toward the back wall and in the direction of the ladies' room. When Gia was not there waiting for me, I took the opportunity to part with Nix just for a moment.

"Wait here, let me see if she's still in there."

He looked annoyed, but also knew that he probably wouldn't have much luck winning my favor if he commented.

I went inside the room to find Gia behind a curtained stall, and it was like looking into a mirror. She had shifted into me and transformed her dress to match mine. I could see there wasn't a hint of difference.

"Gia, he doesn't like strong females. Be careful," I said with a warning.

She nodded. "Trust me, I know his type. I'll be his sweet little daffodil."

"He's going to lead you toward the viewing on the terrace, but he's as warmed up as they get; keep him busy. I'll make my way to the others."

When Gia left the restroom, I could hear the bells still ringing and peeked around the corner watching guests scurry by toward the terrace exit at the other end. Gia locked her arm in Nix's and let him begin to lead her away. I heard her say, "I'm not sure where Lorne went, but you'll stay with me, won't you?" Gods she was way better at this than me.

With the guests heading in the opposite direction, I hastily performed a glamour trying to conceal myself as I walked away from the terrace towards the bedrooms.

When I arrived, Varro was standing in the doorway. Inside the room to the immediate right was a closet. When he gave me the hush sign across his lips, I knew it meant that the nanny was secured and sleeping. He needed to remain in close proximity for his Siren Song to keep her asleep. I ignored the fact that I could see him eyeing my dress, just like all the other guests had.

It's just a dress was all I could think, especially after the debacle it had caused us thus far.

Across the bedroom, I saw a young lady in a simple work dress and apron talking to two small children, a boy and a girl. She was whispering to them, and they appeared to trust her. That's when I realized it was Nori. She had glamoured me and them to think she was the nanny. If you studied closely and knew what to look for, the illusion became more apparent, but there's no way those sleepy children and their untrained eyes would notice a thing.

She grabbed each of their hands and began to lead them away from their nursery room.

As she passed me, I heard her say, "Don't you worry, just come with me, let's get a special treat. We won't tell anyone."

Once she exited the room, I peered back down the far hallway where I could see Cairis. He acted disinterested in the celestial showing and pretended to focus on his smoking pipe and the glass of liquor in his hand. People passed him one by one, ignoring his presence entirely. The guards that stood nearby treated him no differently than any other guest.

These people were so focused on guarding their wealth that no one seemed to think about the children, and it was sad—but worked in our favor. What an unbelievably wicked thing for Nix to hide these stolen goods near his innocent siblings. It was reckless, putting them in harm's way like this.

When Trace arrived, I took my place at the midpoint between Cairis and the bedroom. Trace and Varro began to dismantle the room quietly in search of the box. Saryn said we'd know it by the king's emblem etched into it.

Ever since receiving the mission, I was curious not only about the box but also what other illegal items Nix might be hiding. I had made sure not to distract myself with those thoughts, ever since we built the plan for the mission. But now that we were here, it was harder to ignore them.

Part of me wished I was in the nursery helping them search, but I remained steadfast in my position. I waited for what seemed like ages. With each passing minute, I grew more nervous. Trying to look inconspicuous, moving about the upper balcony acting like I was fixing my dress, or admiring a painting. I made my way toward the wall of windows, and from there I was able to see the Canary Veil. It was truly a sight to behold.

The whole sky was lit in a yellow haze. Unlike the auroras which looked like smears of watercolors painted across the night, this was only one color, an entirely yellow sky. I could barely make out the faded twinkling of stars behind the blanket of color. It wasn't anything like sunlight. I can only describe it as a yellow pane of stained glass held up over the pitch-black night sky.

I could hear the onlookers outside *oohing* and *ahhing*. I glanced back at the nursery and could hear Varro and Trace shuffling about. Nori and the children were still gone, off somewhere keeping them distracted with milk and cookies. Cairis, still on watch, had not sent any alerts or concerning signals.

As I continued gazing up out the window at the miraculous sky, I felt a warm hand snake around my waist.

"It's beautiful, isn't it?" the silky-smooth voice said in my ear.

I turned to meet a male that was familiar, and yet not. He looked so much like Nix, but there were slight differences. Almost imperceptible, but there.

Before I could stop myself, I said, "Didn't we just meet earlier?" Trying not to sound as confused as I was or too irritated that a stranger had touched me like I was his property.

He let out a small chuckle. "Ahh, my apologies. You must have met one of my associates. Someone with my wealth and business endeavors must employ specific practices to keep certain guests at a distance. I'm Fenix, but you can call me Nix."

My teeth clenched tightly, and I tried to keep my breathing even and calm. I could not show him the alarm that was coursing through me. If this was the real Nix, then who in Gods' names was Gia with?

"I'm Astrid, and what endeavors are those?" I whispered back nervously, before realizing a delicate flower would not pry—but it was too late.

His foxlike features twisted into a grin. "I'm in the business of procuring rare and beautiful things, hence why I find myself drawn to you."

I ignored the flattery. I could smell alcohol on his breath, and his eyes were glossy with bad intentions.

"You know, there's an absolutely stunning view from the private terrace of my room. Let me show you."

Before I could deny him, he grabbed my hand and began leading me toward a door along the same hallway as the children's room. I was panicked that he'd hear Varro and Trace tearing through the nursery in search of what we came for. I needed to somehow alert one of them and do something to get their attention.

I began to walk with him and then pretended to trip and fall on my dress. I let out a loud yelp, hoping one of them would take notice. Nix helped me up from the ground, and I acted embarrassed.

"You ladies and those high heels. I don't envy you. You can slip them off in my room, don't worry."

The implication was not lost on me, and I began to worry about my safety and Gia's. Since Nix arrived at my side, I had tried to penetrate his thoughts. But despite the intoxication, his shields were unbreakable. Unlike the male from earlier whose mental shields were nowhere to be found, thoughts oozing off him like he might as well have said them aloud, this one was a steel trap.

If I was with Nix, headed to his bedroom, where was Gia? Was she okay? As we passed through the threshold of his doorway, I saw Varro out of the corner of my eye and gave him a hand signal to let him know something was off.

When we entered Nix's bed chamber, he closed the door behind us and the echo of the lock clicking caused a pain in my chest.

"Take your shoes off, we can't have you taking another tumble, can we?"

There was a padded bench at the end of his bed and I sat down, doing as he instructed but also using it as a way to stall. I began to work on the buckle of my high heel, when suddenly Nix was on his knees before me and taking my foot into his hand.

He fumbled slightly with the latches, but insisted on helping me remove my shoes, giving him a chance to greedily run his hands along my feet and up my bare leg. I anxiously pulled away and stood, trying to make my way to the terrace he mentioned.

"We really should check out the view, how much longer will it last?" I questioned, trying to sound like we were running out of time to see the veil.

When I turned back toward him, he was hovering over me. He grabbed my chin, squeezing it a little too tightly, turning it up toward him. "What do you mean? I have my view right here."

He ran a finger down my bare chest, in between where the two yellow feathers covered my breasts. Then he placed his other hand on the white fabric of the skirt by my hip and began to drag it upward slowly as he said, "And here is my veil…"

His words were sour with drunkenness and potent lust. I needed to give the team time, but I was beginning to worry that if he ran his hand any higher, he was going to be quite surprised to find a blade on such a delicate bird.

Every fiber of my being didn't want to do this, but I knew I had to find the courage. *Be the bait*, I kept repeating to myself. Control the situation, don't let it control you. I leaned in and kissed him gently on the lips, pulling his hand from my hip up to my face and keeping him far away from finding that blade.

He showed no patience or restraint before his tongue was sweeping into my mouth. The taste of liquor on his tongue made my stomach twist. His kisses became deeper and more fervent with each passing moment. He was sloppy and stumbling, and I tried to keep us both upright as he pressed his body further into me. Then his hands began to roam once more. He pushed them against my chest and began kneading my breast.

I needed to scream, to cry, but instead, I focused my fear inward and let anger turn me hard like a stone. No matter where he touched or fondled, I would not let myself feel it, I would not let my body react the way it would as if this was welcomed or wanted. *Just buy the team time, failure is not an option.*

I let out a fake small whimper here and a moan there to make him think he was in control, that I was enjoying this. It only fueled his passion further, and that's when he turned forceful. He shoved me down onto the bed and crawled on top of me.

I could feel the sheath of the blade along my leg beginning to dig into my skin. I wanted to grab it and stick it in his side, over and over, just like I had done with the Vesper, but I knew I could only do that as a last resort.

Saryn had permitted us to do whatever we wanted with Nix, but what if that set off a whole other chain of events leading to more chaos, leading us farther from getting what we came for?

He began to fiddle with his belt buckle and I tried to reason with him, "Maybe we could slow down, I'm not ready for that. Let's go slo…"

Before I could finish my words, he put his hand over my mouth to muffle the sound of my voice. "Stop talking, little bird, and start singing."

He tried to position himself over me and shifted his grip in an attempt to lift my dress. I felt his sweaty hands groping at my legs as he tried to reach between my thighs. At the same moment I felt his hand touch the sheath, I heard the loud banging of celebratory fireworks from outside.

Suddenly the doors to his bedroom flung open and Varro was standing there, having kicked straight through the lock. His eyes were wide, brows furrowed in anger as he took in the sight of Nix pinning me to the bed. Despite my attempt at acting, he could see the fear and distress written all over my face. Varro's features were painted with frantic rage as he scanned the situation before him.

Behind him there were loud noises, yelling, and the sound of rapid footsteps. I knew we had to go quickly; with Nix distracted by Varro's interruption, I reached for the knife, jamming it into his side and hopping from the bed as fast as possible.

Nix screamed in pain yelling, "You bitch! Guards! Guards!"

He crawled across his bed, blood pouring from around the dagger sticking out of him, and pulled a corded rope. A bell sounded, clearly used to alert the staff that danger was on the premises.

I left my shoes behind, because in reality I was better off barefoot than in those things, and ran toward Varro. The scene on the other side of Nix's door was unraveling quickly into chaos we had not planned for.

Cairis wasn't too far away but would have to handle the three guards who were storming in from the terrace all on his own. Nori and Gia were nowhere to be seen.

Two guards ran up on Varro and me with swords raised, but they both suddenly grasped at their throats, knees buckling, as they began to gasp for breath. Siren Song. Varro had rendered them defenseless before he walked up, grabbed them by the scalp to expose their necks, and ran his blade across each of their throats. I shuddered at the blood spurting and pouring out of them.

"Come on!" Varro instructed me as he stormed toward the exit, both of us still wary of our surroundings.

The booming sound of fireworks continued outside, the guests completely unaware of the small battle underway inside the house. The nanny, now awake, the effects of Siren Song diminished, came running out of the children's nursery screaming. She wasn't a threat, but she was only going to alert more guards. I gave her one swift punch to the side of her face, knocking her out cold. She'd wake up with a massive headache, but she didn't need to die for this. In between unsure steps and exasperated breaths, I asked, "Did you find it?"

Varro and I continued to walk in a defensive stance ensuring no blind spots.

"Yes, Trace has it. Just focus on getting out of here alive."

He had never sounded like this. Panicked and unsure. Cairis had finally plowed his way through those three guards when Varro shouted, "Go, just go. I've got her!"

I looked up to see a clear exit near Cairis. He was covered in blood—not his own. With no other guards in his way, he could make it out under the cover of the celebratory commotion and get to the rendezvous point. All I could hope was that Gia and Nori were already there.

Down in the middle of the ballroom, we spotted Trace. Box in one hand, guard's sword in the other. He had already hacked his way through half a dozen fighters all on his own. He began to make his way up the staircase on the opposite end of us, almost to the exit, when suddenly more guards rushed in, flanking Varro and me. There were more than the two of us could handle.

Varro and I had the same thought. We both ran down the steps and across the dance floor to the place where Trace just was, but he didn't return. When I looked up, he was still at the top of the stairs, staring down at us. The echoes of guards' footsteps encircled us from every angle. Why wasn't Trace coming to help us fight?

Varro shot me a concerned look, but I couldn't entirely discern what he wanted me to do.

"We need to fly, it's our only way out."

Out of breath and with my heart racing, I unfurled my wings just as Varro did. The minute we were both airborne, I felt a sharp stab through my shoulder and I quickly plummeted back to the hard marble floor.

I writhed in agony, screaming. An arrow had pierced my wing and was embedded in the back of my shoulder. The pain seared through me and my blood began to pool across the pale floor. Shocked, I looked up at Varro and saw fear in his eyes, and then I looked back at Trace, where he stood near the doorway.

His stare was hollow. He took off through the exit door, box in hand, leaving me and Varro to fend for ourselves.

The words echoed in my mind as I began to feel lightheaded.

Failure is not an option.

That's when it became clear to me what this was all about. I knew we were a team, but the mission came first. I was the reason the mission went downhill to begin with. No one else deserved to get hurt because of me.

"Go…go now!" I choked out toward Varro, still hovering above me.

Guards were everywhere, but if he flew fast and possibly straight through the nearest window, he could make it.

"No," he fumed and landed beside me.

I looked up to see Nix standing at the top of the stairs we had just run down, holding his side and still bleeding as he yelled, directing his guards, "Kill him and bring me that wretched whore! She's mine to deal with."

Instinctively, Varro raised his wings over and around me, trying to shield me as I lay below him on the ground.

"Pull the arrow out," I begged him.

"No, you'll lose too much blood!" I'd never seen Varro look truly scared, until now.

The thought that at any minute arrows would begin showering down upon us terrified me, but then I looked up at Nix and that terror shifted into hate.

I heard the countless clicks of crossbows, and it was as if time had slowed down. Varro hovered protectively over me, and I looked into his bright blue eyes, eyes that said goodbye. My rage played through my mind like the pages of a book: the gambler at the tavern, my father delivering me to the king, Saryn slapping me, hours upon countless hours under the torturous hand of the Vesper, Nix's hands all over me, Nix forcing himself on me, the way the dagger felt sliding in his side. Suddenly, all that rage exploded out of me in an indescribable burst of energy that flared out in all directions.

Varro and I were wrapped in the warmth of safety, like a cocoon that shielded us from everything. Power flowed off of me, quaking the ground beneath us, shattering every window, and blasting every guard and Nix through the air to slam into the walls closest to them.

A sudden silence reigned, only broken by the echoes of cracking walls, falling glass, and the guards' pained moans. Outside, the fireworks ceased, and the sounds of screaming guests took their place.

The ruckus grew fainter with each passing second. I felt incredibly tired and drained. What had just happened? I wondered if the blood loss from the arrow had become too much. I felt myself slipping into a fog, and in the distance, I heard the faint echo of Aster's words, *"How strong is faith, when arrows nocked?"*

Varro tucked me into his bloodied, golden arms, and I was overcome with an unexpected sense of comfort before the sensation of whooshing air skimmed past us as he flew us out of the destroyed ballroom. My eyes fluttered, and the last thing I remembered was how warm Varro's hands had felt on my too-cold skin.

CHAPTER 60

When I came to, bright lantern lights were all around me, and I could feel a sharp sting along my shoulder blade. But it was nothing compared to the pain I had felt the moment the arrow pierced me. I was lying flat on my stomach and the hard wooden table below me was doing nothing for my comfort.

I looked up, barely lifting my head to the side, and saw Nori there tending to my wound. Thank Gods she was alright. I let out a sigh of relief as she continued to work on me.

"Thank you," I whispered, licking my dry lips.

I was parched and my body felt extremely hot, like I'd been battling a fever.

Nori looked down at me calmly. "It's going to be okay; I promise. Just relax."

When I tilted my head to face the opposite direction, I realized I was laid out in the middle of the common room. That's when I looked toward the bookshelves lining the wall across from me and saw him.

Standing there in the same black attire from the ball, looking back at me—no, through me.

That's when the memory of him abandoning Varro and I to fight alone, to die, came searing back with a fiery intensity. Uncontrollable anger engulfed me, immediately I was numb to the pain in my back.

I leapt from the table, pushing a surprised Nori back and charged towards him yelling, "You left us to die! You fucking left me, you left us *both*!"

I caught myself from tripping as the dizziness from blood loss overcame me, but it did nothing to deter me as I continued to march across the room toward Trace.

He stood there, motionless, with arms folded across his chest. That's when I noticed his tattoos were back, but this time, they were red, red like blood. Not black like they had always been. Had he been glamouring me…again?

"Tell them!" I continued accusingly. "Tell them how we needed you, and how you left us!"

Angry tears were beginning to well in my eyes now that I was practically nose to nose with Trace.

"How could you?"

The words he whispered were only for me to hear. "Now you see me."

And I did, crystal clear. The monster he had warned me about. The black cloak, always bound by duty. Morals be damned.

Balling my fists, appraising the now red tattoos sprawling over him, I gritted out a reply, "Guess it's a good thing my blood isn't on your hands…yet."

Fuming, I turned my back to him and began to return to the table, wobbling with each step. Cairis came to my aid, holding me up as I made my way to a chair, and Nori quickly arrived with a cup of water as if reading my mind.

My mental shields were down, and I didn't care. I hoped he was reading every single damn thought running through my head. His deceit spread like a plague through my mind, infecting every pleasant memory I'd ever had of us. I felt all those emotions wither and die. Our trust, our friendship, and countless nights of lovemaking, once sweet, turned sour by one simple decision—by one unforgivable action.

Saryn arrived, and I was less than thrilled to hear anything he had to say about this mess of a mission. The calm from the others indicated we hadn't failed entirely, but that didn't mean we'd done well, either.

"You successfully completed your mission. And despite Cress's accusations towards Trace, you managed to return with your lives intact. Before anyone else gets the idea to critique Trace's decision, you all should remember the number one rule. The mission above all."

Theory took over, saying, "The mission requires sacrifice. Your lives are few, but the work you will do is for the lives of many and the protection of your kingdom. If you want to keep your lives, then train harder and plan better. Work as a team, or perish as individuals. Failure is not an option, and Trace took that seriously enough to make the necessary sacrifices."

Before she could say another word, I was yelling again.

"Sacrifices? Are you *kidding* me? Tell me, Trace, what sacrifice did you make on that mission? Were a stranger's hands roaming your body against your will? Did they try to take you by force? Did you take an arrow to your wing?"

I could feel the anger building, my hands shaking, balled into fists at my sides, when suddenly Varro was there gently grasping my arm. "Cress, look at me. Breathe. Calm down. You have to control your anger, or it might happen again."

I was relieved to see Varro. His face was no longer stricken with horror, but his words made no sense.

"What might happen again? What are you talking about?"

Varro glanced quickly at Saryn and Theory, then back to me.

"Don't you remember the blast?"

My head was pounding again as I palmed my forehead, trying to stave off the headache.

I tried to think back to when we were surrounded on the floor of the ballroom with blood pooled all around me, but all I could remember is blacking out in his arms and the vague feeling of wind rushing past me, then waking up here. Everything else was hazy and unclear.

"What blast?" I asked Varro, unable to remember what he was referring to.

Saryn was suddenly at my other side. "Cress, let's have Varro take you to the healing pools. Get some rest, and tomorrow you and I can discuss your abilities."

What abilities? That's when I looked around the room at the rest of my team, noticing the hints of hesitation and fear in their expressions. Theory looked at me with accusing curiosity.

The healing waters sounded lovely. I turned to look up at Varro, giving him my arm as I didn't trust myself to walk the entire way down on my own. I didn't bother to look back at Trace as I left the room. Saryn and Theory can praise him all they want for securing the mission, but this went deeper—this was personal. This was betrayal.

Varro escorted me the entire way in silence, which I was content with because, honestly, I didn't know what to say. My head and body ached. I was trying diligently to remember more about everything that had transpired, but my mind was blank. I remembered stabbing Nix; I remembered Varro and I being surrounded and that traitor abandoning us. I remembered the piercing feeling of the arrow…but then nothing much after that.

When we got into the room, I tried to lift my arm and immediately winced at the pain. Nori had stopped the bleeding and mended the wound, but it still felt incredibly sore.

Fear lingered heavy in my heart. What if I wouldn't be able to fly again? I gasped at the thought, but then Varro grabbed my chin and lifted it toward him. "You will fly again. I promise."

I pulled my chin away. "Stay out of my head," I retorted in annoyance. I was too tired to maintain my mental shields.

Nori or Gia must have removed the dress that ruined it all and put me in looser clothing while Nori worked on repairing me. I tried again to lift my shirt, but felt the sharp pang again.

"Let me help you," Varro commanded.

I was too sore to argue when he stepped behind me and gently began to tear away at the fabric, ever so slowly as to not jar my shoulder.

Well, that was one way to undress without lifting my arm. I saw the bloody fabric fall to the floor, and Varro remained close behind me. I could feel the heat radiating off his body, unsure if I wanted it to be from him or just the steam room.

But then he gently ran a finger down the fresh scar along my shoulder blade. "The waters should take care of this, though battle wounds look good on you."

My mouth was dry, unable to come up with some quippy reply. I swallowed the awkward lump in my throat, surprised by both his compliment and the fact that he'd left me exposed in barely-there undergarments.

He gently grabbed my shoulders, turning me to face him, and bent down to his knees. He placed his hands on my hips at the top of my pants. Gently, he began to slide them down my legs. Slower than necessary, and with fingertips grazing my skin.

His head hung low, avoiding my gaze but allowing him to drink in the length of my legs. They were still covered in dried blood from my injury; it must have seeped through the dress. I wanted to ask him what he was doing, should have stepped away, but I just stood there still and nervous, unsure of what was happening. I would have apologized for the blood, but silence enveloped us and there was no need to speak.

He stood before me, casually removing his shirt and tossing it to the floor beside my bloodied garments. He grabbed my hand and carefully led me down the steps into the pool. Once the warmth of the water hit me, I felt like I could breathe again for the first time since I awoke on that table. I inhaled the steam, letting its warmth fill my lungs.

I went to pull my hand away from Varro's grasp. "I'm fine now."

But he did not release me and just kept walking me farther into the cavernous pool. Once I was sitting on the ledge across from him, he finally dropped my hand and took his usual spot, perched on the other side.

He sank into the waters, rolling and relaxing his shoulders, but still keeping his gaze fixated on me.

"Why did you stay with me?" I asked, itching to know the answer.

Why was it so easy for him to stay, when Trace had left me behind, seemingly with no issue? He could have died.

"You saved Nori. Do you not deserve the same?"

That was different. Varro put himself in the path of imminent danger.

"I suppose I owe you a blood debt," I said discouraged, knowing that maybe I wouldn't be as brave if the situation was reversed.

Now that my headache had subsided a bit, I could feel that nuisance of a hum itching at my skin again. I hadn't mentioned it to anyone until now.

"Do you ever experience a weird sensation, sort of like the feeling of humming against your skin? Sometimes it itches and prickles, occasionally it's more like a tickle."

Varro raised an eyebrow with intrigue.

I started to say, "I know it sounds stra—"

"When did you start feeling it?" he cut me off, sounding more serious than I'd expected.

"The first time was when we all bathed in the waters of Mirtith at the palace. I thought it was our powers awakening, but no one else has mentioned it to me," I hypothesized.

"I felt it too, it started at the same time as yours. I don't know if it's what you think it is…" Varro confirmed.

I was too ecstatic to hear someone else had experienced this and that it began at the same time as mine. I ignored his doubts about what had caused it. I was almost certain it had something to do with our magic, or these waters, and I was going to make sure to ask the others about it.

"You really don't remember anything, do you?" Varro inquired.

"Remember what?" I replied, confused and not wanting to leave the topic of the strange sensation now that I had found someone who could relate to it.

Varro stood, slowly making his way toward me.

"There was an explosion. It was big enough that it shattered everything in the vicinity. It was so loud that my ears still haven't stopped ringing. That's what stopped Nix and all his guards."

By now Varro practically hovered above me.

"Who set off an explosion?" I asked, curious to understand how we were saved when we needed it most.

He reached out, cupping both sides of my face in his rough hands. I leaned into the warmth of the gesture before he uttered the words, "You did, Cress."

I yanked back from his touch, wide-eyed, unable to make sense of what he had just proclaimed.

"What did you just say?"

"Cress…you caused the explosion. I can't explain it. We were seconds away from being impaled by a mass of arrows. I was covering you to protect you, but there's no way either of us would have survived. Suddenly, everything went still. It was as if the entire room shattered with one large burst of energy."

His words were rushed, and with each detail he recollected, the memory of it became clearer in my mind.

My hands started to tremble under the water, and my skin began to crawl as the images returned. The memory of Trace's blank stare. All of the bloodied guards strewn about. Some injured, others dead. Shards of glass, everywhere. The sound of distant screams.

"Oh Gods, what did I do?"

He could tell I was beginning to panic, the reality of having hurt so many people, even killed some—real people, not Vespers… The tears sat at the edge of my lashes, begging for release as a deep uncontrollable sob climbed up from my chest and erupted.

Varro reached out instinctively and pulled me into a tight hug, holding my limp body while I wept. Confused and scared, no longer familiar with myself after what I'd done. I didn't know how I did it, or what it meant.

Pulling me into his firm golden chest, he held me, letting me fall apart. He began to gently caress the back of my head and whispered, "You're okay. I got you. You did good, Moirai."

I awoke in the morning to the sound of banging on my door. Groggily, I pulled myself away from the covers and cracked the door to be greeted by none other than Saryn himself. This wasn't the person I wanted to be face-to-face with.

"Get dressed and come with me," he ordered.

I shut the door and quickly threw on clothing, uninterested in following Saryn anywhere but knowing it really wasn't a choice. I had built up quite an appetite and would rather be making my way to the dining hall.

I was surprised to discover my pain had dissipated. Now and then I felt a phantom jolt, but I knew it was all in my head and hoped with a few more days I'd forget the feeling entirely. Wouldn't it be nice if I could also forget how Trace had left me for dead?

When I stepped out the door, Saryn shoved an apple in my hand. This was as close as he got to being considerate. I began to devour the apple while following closely behind him as he led us in the far opposite direction of the dormitories. The only thing I knew about this hall was that it had to be where Saryn and Theory stayed, since we'd watched them head off in the same direction each night.

We arrived at a solid-black metal door, its cold severity contrasting the wooden ones throughout the rest of the fortress.

"Hold out your hand," Saryn requested dryly.

Unwilling to argue with him this early in the morning, I did as he asked. Holding my raised hand in his, my palm facing up, he said, "Get ready to bite into that apple."

I had learned by now not to question him, and the second I bit into it, Saryn pulled out a blade and ran it across my hand. I yanked my hand back in anger, clutching it to my chest.

"What was that for?" I exclaimed.

"Place your hand on that door handle, the bloody one."

He did not explain further. I lifted my hand to the doorknob, feeling my blood coat it as I gave it a good twist. The door swung open soundlessly.

Saryn shook his head in disbelief. "Figures."

He stepped into the small chamber, ushering me to follow him.

"What is this?" I questioned, looking around at the dark, tiny room consisting of a small study desk, a chair, and shelves of books and tomes that looked like they hadn't ever seen the light of day. They were covered in cobwebs and dust; I wasn't entirely sure of the last time anyone had stepped foot in here, given the state of the room.

"This is a room with a door that only you can open, thanks to the blood bond you just made with it. Even though you can grant me entry, that does not make the items within accessible to me."

He demonstrated by reaching out to grab a book from the shelf only to wince and quickly release it, as if the book had burned him.

After seeing that, I was not the least bit inclined to try it myself.

"Grab one of them," Saryn directed me impatiently.

I reached my hand out tentatively, ready to pull my hand away the instant I encountered any pain, but as my fingers grazed the dusty books, I felt nothing. I slid one from the shelf and set it down on the small writing desk.

"Cress, only you can open that door, and only you can open these books. Think of it as a double layer of security. However, if you tried to leave the room with them, I'm almost certain you would not be able to."

Confused and missing his implication, I questioned, "Why would I be the only one that can access these?"

Saryn sighed.

"There was one of you in our Order before. She's gone now. But I would see her coming and going from this room nightly, a room none of us could access but her. Likely an enchantment created by someone long ago. Perhaps during the earliest days of Basdie. We hope that in every Offering there will be at least one of you, but that in itself comes with its own risks and dangers. It often skips a few generations, and for many bloodlines, it has died out completely. If I'm being honest, I would not have pegged you as one of them."

Enough of this monologue. "As one of *what*?" I asked with annoyance.

"As a Dark Wielder."

Saryn's response was monotone and matter-of-fact. The words sent shivers down my spine.

"What is a Dark Wielder?" I questioned, nerves clinging to the words.

"They are Fae who can control dark abilities. It goes beyond simple magic like illusions and manipulations. Dark Wielders don't even need weapons—they are one."

"No, no…I'm not anything like that," I argued.

"Varro told the team what happened. You did that, albeit unknowingly, but it was you who produced enough energy and power to create a blast radius that took out numerous enemies all at once."

My mind raced, thinking about how Varro had described it last night, and the vivid memories that had rushed back. But I didn't want this. I didn't want to be a Dark Wielder. It sounded scary and awful, and I just wanted to be as good as my team.

"What if I don't want this? I'll find a way to control it and won't let it ever happen again," I said, begging Saryn to give me a reprieve from any obligation to explore this further.

We could just pretend he never showed me the room, never told me anything at all.

"You don't have a choice, Cress. You just became our strongest asset. Which means you're our biggest advantage. Well, I should say 'will become,' because right now you don't even know what you're capable of. But you *will* find out."

"I don't want to be different. I want to train with the group."

The sound of my pleas shocked me. All of this time, I'd only ever wanted to be special and excel, find a way to keep up with my peers. And here I was, finally being told I was unique, rare, one in a few generations, and I wanted to avoid it at all costs.

"I am not a Dark Wielder, but I will do my best to help guide you and train you. But only you can put in the work here in this room, where generations of Dark Wielders from the Order documented everything they could about their abilities."

Saryn could feel the tension between us and the silence that hung in the stale air of the tiny room.

"Can I have the day to process this? Please, don't make me stay here today."

All I wanted was to be in the dining hall with my team eating breakfast, or getting the sweat kicked out of us by Theory in the training room. I was scared, struggling to wrap my mind around all of this, but I didn't want to be isolated in some closet far from the group. Saryn had never gone easy on me; I half expected him to lock me in this room.

"Yes. You need to take care of yourself from now on. Dark abilities take more than just a lot of energy and focus. The wielder I knew seemed like she wasn't always there, like she was…absent," he warned me.

"Will the others be scared of me?" I questioned, remembering the looks on their faces last night.

"They should be," was all he said as he led us away from the room, directing me to be the one to close the door behind us.

CHAPTER 31

I was relieved that Saryn hadn't locked me in, but the weight on my shoulders from what I'd learned made me feel like my chest had caved in on itself. I fought back the uneasy feeling and tears from the moment we left and began heading toward the common room. I glanced to my side, noting the rushing falls behind the glass, a visual representation of how I felt on the inside, a constant bombardment of one thought to the next, the fear of the unknown, a never-ending list of questions with no answers.

I'd never heard of Dark Wielders or their abilities. Saryn said it could skip generations, but who in my family line had this within them? Did they know it and conceal it? Was this from my mother or father's bloodline? Would this ever have come about if I hadn't been delivered to the king and forced to bathe in the Bath of the Four Mothers?

I looked down at the gash on my hand and used what little energy I could spare to heal myself. I now feared myself, but I was even more fearful of how the others would feel about this, or how they'd treat me.

It was an odd thing, to want special treatment until all of the attention was actually on you—but for all the wrong reasons. Had they heard of Dark Wielders? What if their powers just hadn't been unlocked yet, and I didn't have to carry this burden alone? I shouldn't pity myself, but it sure felt that way. I didn't feel special, I felt like a freak.

When I entered the room behind Saryn, they each looked at me with a different emotion. Nori's expression seemed the most optimistic of all of them. Varro's, something more akin to pride or admiration. Gia's eyes flared with a hint of jealousy, and Cairis bore an amused smile. I only let my gaze flicker to Trace for a second.

His expression was hollow and empty. My skin warmed as I tried to keep the anger from boiling over, which might lead to another outburst. This wasn't the time or place.

"Gather around, I want to show you all what you managed to retrieve and why it's valuable." Saryn motioned for us to join him at the table where the box etched with the king's emblem sat.

As we gathered, I took special note of how Trace intentionally positioned himself the farthest possible distance from me. Varro towered over me to my right, and Nori was to my left.

Saryn carefully lifted the lid to the box revealing a satin cushion, upon which sat a handful of smooth, polished stones. There were ten of them, all oval in shape. Each of them was milky white with a bluish, sometimes purple hue.

They were beautiful and mesmerizing, unlike any stone I'd ever seen. Growing up alongside Gris, I had encountered rare and precious gemstones of all varieties. That and the ridiculous collection of jewelry in our estate.

"Does anyone know what they are?" Theory asked expectantly.

"I'd wager to say they're moonstones," Gia chimed in confidently as she leaned in to get a better look. "I read about them in one of the books you have here. I'm guessing that's why they were worth risking our lives, given what they can do," she continued, eyeing Saryn.

"Beauty, brawn, and brains?" Cairis teased her. She gave him a typical roll of the eyes and turned back to Saryn and Theory, expecting them to give her credit.

"What can they do?" I asked, desperate to know what Varro and I had almost died for, what was worth Trace's betrayal.

Saryn picked one up between his thumb and forefinger, angling it toward the light, "I'd rather show you…"

Next thing we knew, a swirling cloudlike hole appeared mid-air behind Saryn, and without hesitation he stepped into it and disappeared. We each let out an audible gasp of surprise.

Seconds later, the same swirling cloud appeared on the other end of the room, and Saryn stepped out with a knowing grin, looking unfazed.

"That's impossible," I whispered to myself.

I felt Nori reach out and squeeze my hand, glad that someone else was feeling the same shock and concern. Were my eyes playing tricks on me? What sorcery was this?

"Your eyes aren't playing tricks on you, Cress. Get your mental shields back up before I make you pay for those missteps in the training room."

I was fuming that Saryn had called me out like that, but he was right. I was full of distractions. Distractions and thoughts that drained me and took my focus off simple things like mental shields.

The cloud-like mirage dissipated behind him and he walked back towards us, holding out the small stone in his palm.

"These are moonstones, also known as portal stones. They're illegal for anyone but the king to possess. They're extremely dangerous when in the wrong hands. They have the unique ability to open gateways between time and space."

Gia, tickled that she'd guessed correctly, questioned with excitement, "How does it work?"

Theory replied, tossing one of the stones back and forth between her hands. "The stone must be on you physically. You can only travel to and from somewhere you've already been or can actively see. You have to be able to picture that place with clarity, for the moonstone's precision relies on it. The longer you concentrate, the portal will begin to materialize. Keep it clear in your mind's eye; failure to do so can result in ending up somewhere else entirely, or worse…lost. The farther the distance you travel, the more energy it's going to take out of you.

"The short distance across the room was nothing at all, but if you were to try and portal from here back to your home, you might as well be crawling out of the gateway and preparing for a rather large meal and a long slumber."

When she paused, I glanced all around the room, observing the reactions of my peers as they learned what could be done with the power of these tiny iridescent stones.

"Moonwalking requires massive amounts of energy and focus; doing it well means remaining undetected."

Cairis snorted. "Moonwalkers?" he questioned with amusement.

Saryn looked especially irritated with his remark. "Laugh all you want, you're lucky you haven't encountered a Moonwalker. One minute you're sleeping alone in your bed, and the next there's a blade pressed firmly against your throat. Does that seem amusing to you?" He paused, waiting for Cairis to risk making another misguided statement.

"Everything is about energy and focus. All of your abilities require these two things to fuel them, and using the moonstones is no different. You may have earned these, but now you have to prove to us you deserve them."

We all sat there, processing the severity of Saryn's words. He was right. We had retrieved the stones, but they belonged to the king. If he was willing to let members of the Order have them, that had to mean it was a gift that came with a certain level of trust…and expectations.

Lost in thought of what it would be like to travel from one space to another from memory alone, I was snapped out of my daydream when I heard a familiar low voice question from across the table.

"How much energy and focus did it take her?" He jutted his chin in my direction, and we all knew what he was asking.

Saryn shook his head in disappointment. "You couldn't just let us concentrate on the moonstones, could you, Trace?"

He growled back in defiance, "I want answers, we all do. Did you train her to do that?"

"No, I did not. Had we known she possessed such abilities, that would have been part of the plan…or at least the backup plan."

I was convinced the two of them were going to lunge at one another any minute. I interrupted, not for him, but for the rest of my team.

"He didn't know; I didn't even know."

Trace looked at me like it pained him. "Then how do we know if you can control it? What if you end up hurting one of us, or yourself?"

I just loved how he decided to pretend he was minutely worried about me at the end of his question.

"What? Are you afraid you might end up dead because of another team member?" I spat back venomously.

Before I could argue further, Varro stepped forward. "I was there, and she didn't hurt me." He glared at Trace.

"What was it?" Trace demanded while ignoring the Sea Fae, forcing an answer from Saryn.

"She's a Dark Wielder."

You could hear a pin drop from the silence.

"Be lucky there is one amongst you. With proper training, she will bring to the table an arsenal of abilities most of you can't even fathom. She needs your support, not your criticism."

I had never heard Saryn stand up for anyone or anything. Belief in duty and honor towards the Order was the only thing he cared about. There was an overwhelming sense of gratitude in my chest, but I knew better than to thank him.

Theory snapped the lid closed on the full box of moonstones. "You don't deserve to work with these yet. Not when you can't act like a team. I'll return these when you all show some semblance of maturity."

Seeing her clutch our prize in her hands, refusing to let us have them, strongly irritated me. We had risked our lives for them, not her.

My fury must have been written all over my face because Theory chided, "Good, Cress, let that be motivation to make sure the team gets their act together, and you'll have these back soon enough."

In truth, she was probably right. The team was volatile, at best. Between the palpable tension, curiosity about the stones, and my new untapped ability, we probably didn't need anything else in the mix while we sorted through this mess.

Saryn exited at Theory's side with the box, likely to hide it.

Varro walked up to Trace and leaned into his face. He spoke quietly, but loudly enough that I could still hear his words as I watched Trace's jaw twitch.

"Don't give her a reason to lose control again, or you might find yourself a victim of her wrath."

CHAPTER 32

I wasn't entirely sure how I felt about my ability—or curse. The only person who treated me no differently was Varro. The others showed varying degrees of hesitancy, nervousness, and outright curiosity. But for every single question they had, I had two more of my own. I was torn between desperately wanting to understand this side of myself and fearing what came with that knowledge. The unspoken expectations from the team and Saryn weighed heavily on me. Even if I could learn to channel it properly, how could I practice it safely? Was this something I could even practice with a Vesper?

Since the mission, the group had been spending most of their time training, trying to demonstrate to Saryn and Theory that they were taking their duties seriously and could be trusted with the moonstones. Each of us was now equipped with quite the arsenal of weapons, custom made. Nothing was more satisfying than when a blade fits like a glove, with perfect hilt, length, and weight. Each swing felt like a second skin.

While the others got to enjoy their new weapons, I, on the other hand, had been locked in that dusty room for the past few days trying to keep my eyes open and sleep at bay while I scoured page after page. Many of these texts were written as journals, not instructions. With each passing word, I felt more empathy for these individuals from the past. They had been scared, felt like outsiders, and felt afraid of themselves and what they could do. If I had been journaling myself, I would have expressed similar sentiments. Instead, I was consumed with learning all I could.

At times, I felt guilty and unworthy of my stewardship of this great knowledge, but I didn't feel compelled to put my thoughts on paper. I just let them fester. Perhaps writing them down would provide some sort of release or reprieve, but instead, I just kept absorbing their stories, trying to find my own path woven in between their testimonies.

The common thread was that most of them had had no idea about their power until some inciting event. I guess mine was the stress and fear caused by almost dying and taking Varro with me.

Some of their powers manifested as something they were already skilled at, but evolved to cataclysmic levels. One such example was a Dark Wielder who was gifted in elemental manipulation, but when he sought to control fire, it practically decimated everything in the vicinity.

Another similarity was the constant mention of how drained they felt. It wasn't just about the amount of energy required to expel the power, but honing their control of it. Without exerting enough energy and focus, chaos would ensue. Precision, aim, balance, and restraint were all of the utmost importance when this kind of power was in one's possession.

If someone wanted to just lay waste to everyone and everything around them, they could, but that was not what the Order was for. Not unless it was absolutely necessary. Every journal entry usually began with the tracking of one's daily regimen: how much they slept, how much they ate, what they ate, and when. Wielding the abilities, even in practice, was so taxing that it was difficult to recover in time to prevent a reprisal. It was very apparent that I would need to take my routine much more seriously than I had before, ensuring that all the essentials to remain strong and alert were present before I practiced channeling these abilities.

As I pored through the books and journals, I was looking for one very distinct answer. I needed to know what I had done during the Canary Veil. I barely remembered it, and Varro was the only one in the Order who saw it with his own eyes. I'd asked him to describe it to me a handful of times so I could continue to look for clues. Eventually, I found some information that felt as close to an accurate correlation as I could get.

This wielder explained in their notes that the physical manifestation of a shield can encompass the individual upholding the shield along with anyone or anything they can manage to encapsulate. The larger the protection area, the greater the amount of energy needed to maintain coverage of that space. This explained how Varro was also kept safe. This tiny dome of energy had protected us from the onslaught of arrows pouring down from overhead.

My curiosity began to feel satiated as I continued through the notes, knowing I had finally found what I was seeking. A more advanced version of the shield included projection, which converted the defensive ability into an offensive one. The shield could move outward in a display of explosive energy, overwhelming anything in its path. For some, this could be a tremor causing the ground to quake. For others, it could be something more akin to a powerful gust of wind.

These descriptions most accurately reflected what Varro had described. I remembered shattered glass and stone rubble strewn all about. Guards writhing in pain with shards of the destroyed ballroom embedded in their flesh, while others had been unable to survive the impact itself.

Reading onward conveyed the countless possibilities of the shielding when used in such a manner; more gruesome and crueler than I could have ever imagined. Some had the ability to suffocate anything within range; another described the victim's bones breaking one by one. It made me think of Varro's Siren Song and how he could make people feel awful, terrible things. But this was beyond that—it wasn't an illusion. Their enemies suffered through the real thing.

Hours would pass by in the study no bigger than a closet. As time went on, the solitary flame by which I read generated enough heat to stifle the air. After I told Varro about the need for me to focus on a well-rounded regimen, he took it upon himself to ensure I stuck to it. He was the only one who made sure to drop by, regularly bringing me meals or something to drink. His visits, however brief, were welcomed.

He was the only one I felt comfortable sharing my learnings with besides Saryn. Perhaps it was because he had been there and put himself in harm's way for me, or because he was the only one who wasn't the slightest bit scared of me and what I could do…or would learn to do.

The more I learned, the more I knew that reproducing this ability was not going to be anything I could just conjure at will. That's where I needed to get, eventually, but the one and only time I had done it was under immense duress.

I was not surprised when Saryn implied that we may need to recreate a similar scenario to force it out of me. This time I'd be able to remain conscious and aware of the feeling and my surroundings, and then learn how to tame it. But recreating the feeling of being that threatened was not something I was looking forward to.

When I mentioned Saryn's proposal to Varro, he was not overly keen on the idea either. Though he expressed concern and displeasure, he also understood that he knew nothing about what it would take to master my ability. He knew that, despite all my fears, I craved understanding and control of it. He gave me unwavering support and believed that I could do whatever I set my mind to.

He was the only one who had verbally offered up the notion that he didn't care if I was ever able to use this power again. He said it made no difference to him, and that even without it I was still essential to the team with everything I'd already brought to the table.

The others' silence spoke volumes. They could fear it or be jealous, but they knew after that first mission that we could not hide behind the belief that training, sparring, and planning would always be enough. Whatever we were headed into would have real consequences, ones where our lives were at risk.

Beyond my initial outburst at Trace, no one had spoken about how we'd almost lost two of us. We had made too many assumptions and did not have enough backup plans prepared.

Yes, we told Cairis to go when we saw the window of opportunity, but that was assuming we'd be fine with the three of us. We had assumed Trace would come to our aid, even with the goods in hand. We had assumed our enemy would not be smart enough to have decoys in place. We assumed we could get in and out mostly undetected.

We would have to mend as a team to survive. We needed better planning, better communication, and quite frankly, the callousness to assume everything out there was far worse than we'd imagined. It was us against everyone.

I was deep into my reading when I heard a knock on the door. I opened it to find Varro there, informing me that I needed to come with him immediately.

Idris had returned.

All of us gathered in the common room, surprised to see Idris for the first time since he drugged us and delivered us to the doors of Basdie. From my limited encounters, he was normally the picture of calm and collected. This time, though, close observation revealed a twinge of nerves. Something wasn't right. I feared this visit of his would not bode well for us.

"I come with urgent news. King Baelin of Artume has been assassinated by his brother Silas. He has overthrown his rule and is installing his new regime as we speak." Idris eyed Saryn and Theory intensely before continuing.

"Silas is a traitor. It is no secret there is a following of dissenters that have grown in numbers over the past few years. He does not wish to honor the peace treaty between Cambria and Artume that his brother has adhered to since the great war."

I glanced around the room, watching the others take in the news with concerned looks flitting from one face to the next. Saryn shifted uncomfortably from side to side. He appeared the most bothered, which was unusual.

"He has made no further acts at this time, but King Aeon has preemptively deployed an increased number of Kingsguards along the Ledor River. We cannot be certain if they will strike, but are unwilling to take any risks."

I felt my palms sweat in wary anticipation of more details. I had known this moment would always come for us. The day they'd need us to leave Basdie. When we'd find out the real mission and true purpose. When the king finally came calling. From the corner of my eye, I could see the blood-red tattoos along Trace's arm as he ran a hand nervously through his tousled hair.

Idris continued, "There will be a change of power, meaning Baelin's court will be overhauled to root out anyone who will not support the new regime and Silas as their king. Now is the time to embed our assets. Chaos is our doorway."

Theory stepped forward. "They're not ready, Idris."

In a rare display of impatience, Idris spat back, "War does not wait! It was your job to make sure they were ready."

Theory glared at him through silver eyes. "They don't always operate like a team, and they haven't even learned to use the portal stones yet."

Idris stepped forward, practically nose to nose with her. "You have four days to teach them, and then I'm taking at least two south of the river to Nasallus. I will be back for the rest shortly thereafter."

Saryn grunted in agreement with Theory, but Idris cocked his head and spoke before Saryn could add more, "I'm swearing them in tonight. I speak for the king."

I knew I wasn't the only one holding my breath, trying to accept the fact that we were running out of time.

We all sat in near-complete silence during dinner. Saryn, Theory, and Idris did not join us. My guess is they were discussing who was most prepared and would leave with Idris first. I'd never been to Artume, I doubted any of us had. Though, I'd heard the road south could be treacherous. I had studied it briefly on maps, but those who resided in Cambria under the rule of King Aeon did not travel across the border along the Riverlands. Travel to the other side was reserved for diplomatic and trade envoys.

The peace treaty was delicately maintained. Each had agreed to the established border and which lands were granted to which kingdoms. Rules of engagement were adhered to and, for the most part, peace was manageable. Both sides wanted to focus on restoring their lands and livelihoods, and so it was for many, many years. Until now.

I felt the weight of the moment shifting the flow of history back toward a time when tensions ran high, fighting was rampant, and years were marred by senseless bloodshed. Generations erased.

I was lucky to have not been born then, but I had read the texts and been taught everything there was to know at the academy. A chivalrous line on a map represented nothing more than the words of two kings and signatures on parchment. It could easily be washed away like sand under the tide.

The three of them arrived at the dinner hall dressed in full black regalia, their silver talismans hanging from their necks and reminding me of our invisible brands. They led us out to the terrace where the sun had almost finished setting, instructing us to stand shoulder to shoulder with one another in a straight line. To my left was Varro, and to my right, Trace shifted uncomfortably. Next to him was Gia, followed by Cairis and then Nori.

"Your families delivered you to the Offering. Your king delivered you to the Order. But only your peers can deliver you to the Imperi. Tonight, this ceremony represents embracing the blood of your true brethren beside you. They are your family; they will be with you until your last breath. Trust them with your life, for your people are trusting you with theirs."

I inhaled deeply, attempting to steel my emotions against the gravity of Idris' words.

Theory approached Varro with a small blade in hand as Idris continued. "The latest member sworn to the Imperi carries the burden of swearing in the next. A tradition that has been in place since our inception. One by one you will recite your oath... Theory, place your blade on Varro's throat and repeat after me."

Eyes wide, my nostrils flared in fear at his instructions. No one moved, not a single flinch, but the energy radiating between the entire group was palpable as I watched Theory lift the small blade to Varro's throat and hold it against his golden skin.

"I am offered but give myself freely.

I am ordered but follow freely.

I am the Imperi.

This is the beginning to no end.

My loyalty is bound to you and our cause.

In words and in blood."

Each phrase, Theory repeated the words aloud, staring into Varro's eyes and keeping the blade pressed firmly against his neck. When the last word left her lips, she quickly swiped the blade across Varro's neck.

I watched his body react in panic, and though I could not see his eyes, I knew there was terror in them. Before I could reach for him to offer aid, Theory quickly grabbed his bleeding throat with her other hand and held it firmly for only a second before pulling it away, revealing she had quickly healed his wound. Her ebony hand was still covered in his blood, but she showed no hint of concern or regret. I watched Varro's hands tremble at his sides before he grabbed for his neck, checking to make sure the wound was not there.

Theory then handed the blade to Varro, nudging him to face me next. This was pure insanity. My pulse raced, my chest rising and falling with immense fear as I gazed up into those crystal blue eyes, knowing what was coming next. He didn't have to say anything. I could see it in the way his jaw was clenched tightly; he could have cracked a tooth.

I gave him an almost imperceptible nod, knowing we would not escape this. With my small gesture of permission, he raised the blade to my throat, still wet with his blood. His hand was unsteady and I could feel it quivering against my skin. Idris repeated the words, but I could only hear Varro's voice as he spoke the oath emptily.

Our gazes locked and I could see small tears forming in his eyes. All of a sudden, I felt a warmth spread over me like a blanket or a tight hug, immediately calming my nerves and diluting my fear completely. Then Varro grabbed the back of my head at my nape, tilting my face back ever so slightly before swiping the blade across my throat as gently as he could while still drawing blood.

He immediately dropped the blade, and before I could even react to the pain, his other hand was there over my throat, soothingly hot. There was no pain, only the warmth of his fingertips woven into my hair and pressed against my throat.

He held them there, and only when he removed both hands did the dreamlike state I had been in recede and everyone else came back into view. He turned his attention to the bloodied blade on the ground. He picked it up and placed it carefully in my hands, letting his fingers linger.

I gulped down my nerves as I turned to face Trace. Had I known we'd ever be doing something like this, I'd probably have practiced healing others much more diligently. Would I be able to pull this off quickly? How much pain would he feel if I wasn't quick enough?

There I was staring into his hazel eyes, realizing how we'd come full circle. The first time my eyes had met his, he'd held a blade to a stranger's neck. Since then, much had changed between us and about us. Part of me felt like he was a stranger now.

I held the blade against his throat and began to repeat each line of the oath, following Idris' words. Time seemed to stand still as my thoughts waged war on my heart. There were so many feelings of betrayal between us; I'd never felt more distant from him than in this moment.

Two distinct feelings battled deep inside my heart. One being indescribable sadness, and the other being uncontrollable anger. Trace's expression screamed *Forgive me* but there was no forgiveness in my heart. Not as I took an oath to protect him with my life, knowing he had already failed to protect mine.

I slid the knife across his throat, and he didn't even flinch. It was as if he was accepting of this fate, of the pain that would ensue. His ambivalence welcomed it like an old friend. I let myself witness one drop of blood before I held my hand firmly against his throat and used all my focus and energy to heal him quickly and thoroughly.

When I removed my hand to reveal that the wound was no more, his expression was numb. My breath hitched as he grabbed the blade from my hand and turned his back on me to face Gia.

Each of us took the oath, culminating with Cairis swearing in Nori. We all turned to face Idris, our throats and hands smeared in each other's blood forcing us to realize the fragility of our existence.

"Welcome to the Imperi, brothers and sisters. May the enemies of our king never see us coming." Idris smiled wickedly.

The next morning, they began our crash course in utilizing the moonstones. Most of their focus was on ensuring Trace and Gia knew what they were doing, since it had been determined they'd be the first to leave with Idris. This meant the rest of us would have only slightly more time to hone our skills. I was not shocked that I was chosen to stay behind, since Saryn and I had barely made a dent in my training.

I had to admit, I did not like the idea of two of our members being sent off on their own. It seemed better for us to go together, but no one had asked for my opinion. The plan had been determined by Saryn, Theory, and Idris without room for argument.

Gia was going to be planted as a member of the new queen of Artume's court; one of her ladies-in-waiting. Everyone knew the risks that came with this, and I was almost certain that was Idris' intention. Ladies often ended up as some sort of concubine or consort for the king or his inner circle. Once again, she was being set up as bait. This was what she got for being the most beautiful and gifted in shapeshifting.

Trace, not shockingly, would be inserted as a member of the military, which would allow him to demonstrate loyalty, work his way up the ranks, and eventually be in charge of protecting the Royal family themselves. This would also keep him close enough to Gia to allow them to coordinate and exchange information.

Additionally, by embedding himself in the enemy's military he'd have more exposure to any plans to march on or attack the border. Most importantly, he could gauge how many of them were truly loyal to the new king versus just trying to keep their heads attached to their shoulders.

Most of the time, we watched and listened as Trace and Gia practiced using the moonstones to portal from one space to the next within the confines of Basdie. The rest of us were anxious to give them a try but remained patient, knowing that their time with us was dwindling, and it was far more important that they felt comfortable and capable with the stones.

They needed to understand how to use them, how to hide them, and the associated risks on top of what little briefing they could receive from

Idris about where they were headed and the plans to install them in the inner circle.

About a day ago, Trace started wearing a glamour full time. His tattoos were completely hidden now, and the scar on his brow missing. While the black cloaks did not operate in Artume, the kingdom had likely heard the rumors. He could not run the risk of being identified; he'd need to keep up a constant front not only of his physical appearance, but also his mental shields. Gia would be doing the same, keeping her mind locked down while determining when and how it made sense to shift in order to gain information and access.

We'd been so focused on their exit and ensuring they were prepared that I spent little to no time focused on dark wielding. But I knew as soon as they left, my training with Saryn would intensify ten-fold.

Idris would be back soon and likely expecting that the remainder of us were ready to go. We weren't, but now was the time.

When I had been sent to serve the king, I had never thought we'd be crossing the border to infiltrate Artume. But I had also never thought the southern king's brother would assassinate him.

CHAPTER

64

The day had arrived where Idris would escort Trace and Gia south to their next destination. I was nervous for them, but I needed to appear confident for their sake. If I were being sent behind enemy lines, I'd want to know those closest to me actually believed I'd be okay.

Nori helped Gia pack what little she'd brought, even though most of her belongings did not matter. Instead, the king's tailor had already prepared an assortment of gowns and fineries packed into ornate trunks. Vastly different from the attire of a Northern noble, these thin, delicate pieces concealed little, bordering on indecent. If Gia was going to success-fully convince them she came from wealth, then she'd need to appear so. Solid gold accessories ranging from chains, charms, and intricate head-pieces to compliment her beauty were packed neatly in a velvet lined chest.

Similarly, Trace had received several Kingsguard uniforms. They looked very different from the uniforms worn by the Cambria military. To his dismay, they were not black.

I had no idea what role myself and the others would play once we too were implanted, but seeing all of these items felt like props, essential to the façade.

It was then that I realized being a member of the Imperi was just as much about acting, deception, and lies as it was about abilities and strength. I didn't think I had fully understood that till now. We were not a show of the king's brute force, we were what came before. We were the silent warning. A warning that, if executed properly, would ensure there'd never need to be anything more.

We joined the two outside the doors of Basdie as their belongings were loaded onto carriages. Idris would escort the unmarked caravan, which meant this was goodbye until we could join them.

The lump in my throat ached at the thought. Things between Trace and I were unresolved, but he was one of us. I worried about him just like I worried about Gia.

Cairis wrapped his giant arms around Trace, an embrace to which he reacted with a frozen uncertainty. Nori went up and did the same, and I was pleased to see him slacken a bit and relax into her arms with the faintest hint of a smile.

Varro walked up to Trace, giving him a nod of respect. That was more than I had expected from the two of them. Now it was my turn. My mouth watered trying to find words, any words at all.

I approached him slowly, silence filling the space between us.

"Take this for later," he said quietly, as he handed me a folded piece of parchment.

Ignoring his words, I began to unfold it, but he quickly placed his hand atop mine. "Later," he repeated.

I nodded in acknowledgement, tucking the piece of paper into my pocket. I glanced over to my side, catching a glimpse of Gia, and turned back toward him.

"Protect her. Please."

"I will."

"And yourself, too. Be careful." I swallowed the lump in my throat.

He looked at me, guilt and confusion in his eyes, as this was the first time I'd shown any semblance of concern for him since he'd left me for dead.

"Goodbye," I added somberly, hoping he would do better for Gia than he had for me or Varro.

He leaned down and said softly into my ear, "I will right my wrongs, this I promise."

Realizing I had momentarily lapsed my mental shields, his response was no surprise, and yet the weight of it felt heavy on my heart. I stepped away from him and made my way toward Gia's carriage. Cairis lifted her feet off the ground in an embrace, squeezing her tightly, and she squealed for him to put her down.

I was much more worried for Gia than I was Trace. Having experienced firsthand what can happen when you play the bait, I had nothing but trepidation regarding what may be in store for her.

She can say she has no heart; she can try and convince me there's not a single chink in her armor, but I know now the kind of monsters she will face. I know what it feels like when the hot breath of vile intention is upon your neck, groping your body, and it makes my stomach churn so much that I have to fight back the bile.

I grabbed both her hands, clasping them in mine. "No mercy," I said, echoing the same words she had offered me.

A knowing smile spread across her gorgeous face. "They have no idea what's coming for them," she said, voice steady and controlled.

The monster that flickered beneath the surface of her gaze looked like it was truly ready to be unleashed. I wouldn't be shocked if, given the chance, she'd bring Silas and his entire damn court to their knees before we even arrived.

Idris indicated it was time to leave and Gia began to make her way into the carriage. Suddenly, that odd humming sensation began to buzz under my skin again, reminding me that I had forgotten to ask either of them about it.

"Wait!" I exclaimed as I leaned into the carriage door. "I meant to ask you, have you felt any sort of new sensation since the Offering? It's like a humming feeling, a low vibration; I'm not sure how else to describe it. Sorta makes your skin tickle or itch. I've felt it since—"

Wide-eyed, Gia cut me off before I could continue my hurried explanation, "You've felt a bond calling?"

"…What?" I looked at her incredulously.

"What you're describing is the call of the mating bond. I knew it the moment you said it," she exclaimed. "What do you mean you've felt it since the Offering?"

It was then I heard Idris whistle and the sound of the carriages starting to shift forward, indicating they were leaving. I stared into Gia's confused expression with horror. "Wait, what? No! Hold on!" I called out to her as I stepped down from the moving carriage, left with a swirl of overwhelming confusion.

Unable to control the onslaught of emotions and questions rampantly overtaking every fiber of my being, I took off running inside, farther down, all the way down to the bottom of Basdie where I entered a door I knew about but had never opened.

The noise was deafening. The sound of the waterfall running straight through the center of Basdie with nothing to muffle or contain its power.

I walked across the slick stone, feeling the mist coating my skin. I stood there behind the waterfall as it crashed down in a constant show of unrestrained power; nature at its peak.

I fell to my knees, unable to quell my outburst any other way. I began to scream; I screamed over and over, my voice completely lost to the sound of the falls. I screamed until I was hoarse, fighting back the stinging tears trying to escape.

It wasn't possible. It couldn't be. Please, Gods, do not do this to me.

From the corner of my eye, I saw Varro peer into the chamber. By now I was soaked from head to toe. I didn't understand how he had found me. He beckoned me toward him, looking nervous.

I was not ready for this. I was never going to be ready. I wanted to jump into the falls and let it drown me, but something began to distract me. There it was again. The incessant humming that made my wet skin prickle and my hair stand on end.

Still trying to fight back tears, I walked carefully toward the exit making sure I didn't slip and fall. When Varro shut the door behind me, I could finally hear my own thoughts again.

"Are you okay?" Varro asked exasperated.

I stood there silent, staring at him and unsure how to answer.

"Cress, you were shaking the entire damned mountain. What's wrong? What happened?"

Oh no, I thought to myself. I had done it again. I had lost control. But now, something else consumed my focus completely.

"Moirai," I said through gritted teeth, "What does it mean?"

Varro's shoulders sagged and the expression on his face changed immediately. "It's just a nickname, Cress."

"What does it *mean?*" I demanded.

He took in a deep breath, looking like he'd had it knocked out of him.

Licking his lips, he met my accusing gaze and answered, "It means fated one."

"No, it doesn't!" I lashed out. "I know the literal translation for those words, and it's not Moirai."

"That's because it's the word *my* people use for fated one."

We stood there staring, locked into one another, silent tension the only thing keeping me from falling to my knees in shock.

"You... All this time. You're my mate?"

The tales of Forgotten Fae and the Imperi will continue in Book Two,

Fate awaits.

BONUS CONTENT

Varro's POV

I felt my mate's presence before I ever saw her. The moment I beheld her with my own eyes, hers were transfixed elsewhere. Her thoughts were flooded with every range of emotion, all of which indicated her heart lay with another. Shock, surprise, relief, lust, desire, confusion—I watched it all consume her as she locked gazes with the dark-haired male beside me. A stranger whose appearance distinctly contrasted my own. All of my fear and concern about what the Offering entailed had come to a halt when I saw her.

When each of us stood, the thin, soaked garments clung to our bare skin and outlined the form of our bodies, and there was nowhere to hide. She stared at him, and I stared at her. Momentarily, I struggled with the notion that I should show a modicum of respect for this female whose name I did not yet even know. I should not gaze upon her shapely beauty without her permission. Shamefully, though, unable to turn away, I continued, noting how the dim glow of the pool surrounding us highlighted the angles of her soft features. Her thoughts were singularly focused on the sight and presence of his body across from hers. Who was she? Who were they? Was I misreading this strange feeling?

Those who have found their fated ones have always described it as a unique sensation akin to humming or thrumming that sits just beneath the skin. It was the bond calling to the other once in close proximity.

The relentless sensation of which would only cease when the bond was sealed through the act of lovemaking, binding themselves to one another for eternity.

In the stories passed down by our elders, the God of the Sea became heartbroken when he was separated from the Goddess of the Moons, for they were mates. The sea, once calm and predictable became fierce and tempestuous, reaching for the light of the moons with each crashing wave. And so, the Sea Fae of old embarked on great voyages in hopes that their travels would lead to that sacred pairing. They made sacrifices to the Gods they worshipped, praying their pursuit was just. Some people, like my father, sacrificed too much. As if any offered soul could quench the sorrow of the mighty sea.

Is it possible these strange waters we were forced to submerge in were playing tricks on me? Was this something else entirely? But I could not ignore the undeniable truth that I felt tethered to this female.

As we exited the pool, I tried to make my side glances appear inconspicuous. My mouth watered, my skin warmed, my gills flared and my ears perked at just the sound of her footsteps. Everything felt oddly attuned, like she was the only one there—but we were most definitely not alone.

Once we were outside, standing before the carriages, we were instructed to drink an unidentified liquid. My instincts wanted me to knock the vial from her hand. This near-instantaneous sentiment of protection was new and hard to comprehend. I needed to do my best to have my wits about myself. The Offering was very much underway. I found myself surrounded by other Highborn and should have been making note of them and any other details that might unveil more about our destiny. It was impossible, though, when every fiber in my body felt like it was straining to know her, to touch her—to hear the voice of my fated one.

Ever since arriving at Basdie, Trace's mind had been unreadable. He was guarded and aloof, even with her. Cress's mind, on the other hand, was the exact opposite. She foolishly—and regularly—left her mental shields unattended; her naivety and innocence made her overly trusting. But her weakness was an open door for me. It was intrusive, but I couldn't have stopped myself if I tried. Once she realized the need to guard her thoughts, the advantage of this doorway would close, and who knows how tightly?

The sound of her name played through my head on a loop, like an unforgettable song. When we introduced ourselves and she finally looked at me, I could have stayed locked in that moment forever. I felt a blush overcome my golden skin, knowing that she actually found me handsome. One tilt of my head, though, and that was all it took for any semblance of attraction to dissipate.

Once she saw my gills and quickly deduced who I was, who my father was, I could feel her fury lunge across the table like a rabid wolf aiming for my throat. I was used to this hatred by now. Numb to it. But, *Gods, please, not her.*

The irony of her affections being intertwined with a black cloak... It was absurd. By all accounts, she seemed soft, kind, and unaffected by the hideous truths of our world. Nothing like him. The Gods were cruel. A member of the Orni here with me, with her, consuming her every thought. I didn't recognize him, but it was possible he had been with the ones that came for my father and had concealed his true face. You never can tell with the black cloaks. He didn't deserve to look at her, let alone speak to her. I clenched my teeth as thoughts of him touching her clouded my mind like a storm rolling in. I noted the indisputable signs like the inky tattoos along his arms. The same ones the entire brotherhood displayed like badges of honor. It was nothing more than proof of their vicious, murderous hearts.

Before I could stop myself, I was making remarks about his past.

Unsure if it was really about him, or just the fact that each second she looked at him with admiration made my stomach roil. Her first impressions of me were already marred by her own bias, adding a physical altercation with him wasn't going to win me any favors.

I kept my distance from her—by sheer force of will—but still attempted to listen in on her conversations and thoughts. I admired how she attempted to socialize and fit in with the others, while I remained guarded. All my focus on Cress served as a near-constant distraction from everything else going on.

She was the only Honored Fae among us, and you'd think that she'd understand what it felt like to be judged for things beyond your control, but that wasn't the case. Not after everything that had transpired at Erisas Bay. No, she was intent on making plenty of assumptions about me. Maybe the increasing desire to speak to her had me acting a bit outlandish. Even if that meant arguing, I was willing to entertain it.

I had figured if she was going to hate me, she might as well know the real truth about her lover, or whatever he was to her... I hadn't expected to be so direct, to aim my words like sharp arrows, but they soared out of me with little composure. The more we bickered, the more the tensions caused the bond to ripple and nearly sear my skin.

Attempting to make my exit and avoid any further banter, I could not deny the pull reeling me in as I intruded on her space. Curiously, I reached out and pushed aside her hair, revealing that her ear no longer bore the feather. I could still smell him on her skin where it had touched her flesh, but even then, I was pleased to find it absent. Patience was my ally, I told myself, for circumstances would arise to sever their ties.

The longer we remained in Basdie, the more certain I was that if I could do anything to get Cress out of here, I would. If I was granted only one wish, it would be that, to help her be free of this place. I wouldn't care if she never knew it was me. I barely knew her, but I desperately wanted to. Despite feeling locked out, I still felt a deep responsibility to protect her.

I had grown up around people like Saryn, Theory, and Trace. My father and many of his inner circle were manipulative and evil. Dark-hearted and wanting to mold us into the same. Each passing hour it broke me a little more to think of her stuck here and waiting to be subjected to their teachings. When Theory stated that she expected us to treat each other as equals in the sparring room, I could feel the bile rise in my throat. I couldn't stand the thought of any of them, male or female, laying a hand on her. My fears were answered all too quickly.

The sound of Saryn's hand across her face almost sent me into a frenzy. I gritted my teeth, my hands clenching as I prepared to pounce, when suddenly our unsuspecting Cress unleashed a side of herself we'd never seen. I watched in awe as she took on Saryn with full measure; violent swings, one after the other. I could feel her anger emanate from across the room as sweat pooled at her brow. Her precise movements were like a dance, and it was clear she had been trained. Trained well. Temporary relief washed over me, knowing she wasn't entirely helpless.

I remained on guard but had relaxed my arms a bit when, to my surprise, she called for a blade. I smiled, watching as she bested Saryn and held the sword to his belly. When she yelled "yield," it dawned on me…her exposure to this type of confrontation came from courtyard sparring and classroom instruction. No warrior would cry "yield" to an opponent on the battlefield.

It pained me to see her not understand his silence. Members of the Order did not yield. *Oh, Cress, these are not the kind of people you're used to.* When she finally pulled back, realizing she did not have the courage to draw blood, she did something even more surprising. She returned Saryn's brazen slap. The bond tingled as she put him in his place.

Today was hard. Much harder than I had expected it to be. I had never put much thought or sentiment into showing my wings—until her. Suddenly, the foreign customs seemed like they mattered. Watching her look up at Trace's wings was just as painful as being forced to share ours with each other for the first time in the presence of others.

I knew I hadn't made much progress in the way of gaining her affections, but everything at Basdie moved quickly. This place had stripped us of our autonomy before we had even realized it. Its momentum was unstoppable, inevitable. We complied as commanded or our lives were forfeit. A fact we were constantly reminded of.

Seeing his black Nightwings, I was reminded of her earring. It stung to think of their intimacy; I was glad she had not worn it since that first day. One less thing to torture me.

I stepped up to the ledge with the others and stared out into the expanse of the valley, surrounded by the gray mountains of the Elorns. I didn't know if I wanted to see her reaction. Looking at her might give away my true feelings, and that seemed unsafe in a place like this. I let them unfurl and felt the dry, harsh air, so different from the warmth of the sea breeze.

I longed for home. I longed to be submerged in the salty waters, or sprawled out on the shore letting the tide rush over me with the sun warming my skin. I wished to be anywhere but stuck here in this rocky prison far from the places familiar to me. I took solace in knowing that all this distance had brought me to her. Did she enjoy the mountains? From the handful of times I'd slipped in and out of her thoughts, I was almost certain she preferred the refreshing moisture of the sea, like me.

Though she was not yet mine, I had a potential mate, and I let the hopeful shiver of the bond overpower me until I could no longer control myself. I turned to meet her gaze—I had to see her emerald eyes. To see if she had accepted me, or if she still looked at me with misdirected disgust.

When I turned, her eyes locked with mine and I felt seen by her, well and truly seen for the first time. There were no hints of judgment or displeasure, instead she exuded admiration and awe. Surrounded by the others, we lacked any privacy, but in the brief moments that passed, it felt completely exclusive, just us two.

When she moved to take the spot next to me, my hands began to tremble with nerves, and yet I was the one who gave her a reassuring nod. When her wings splayed, I worried that she heard the audible hitch in my breathing.

The beauty of the greens with iridescent hints of yellow and gold had me awestruck. I looked at her often, probably more than she ever noticed. Someone with more subtlety might have passed them off as stolen glances, but mine were unashamed and intentional. Occasionally, she'd meet them, glaring back in defiance. It was amusing and adorable. But out on the ledge, standing next to one another with our wings on display, there was only desire. She had destroyed me, and she had no idea.

⊷

Fideli Cœur. In the old tongue, this referred to the way two bonded mates' connection was more than physical; it was also mental. It was like an invisible cord between two souls, allowing one another to speak with their hearts and minds, without the need for words.

Saryn considered whether it would be a tactical advantage, but decided two people with loyalties that deep would cause more problems than they solved. His reaction to the ability only mates can achieve and how quickly he breezed past the discussion of it told me everything I needed to know and confirmed all my fears. It was obvious this wasn't the kind of place two people get to know one another, let alone fall in love. Since being conscripted to the Order, it was abundantly clear that our loyalty was to the king first and each other second.

It didn't matter if Cress knew or if we ever tied our bonds. It was impossible to ignore my feelings for her. I would always put her first. In a room of one hundred Fae, I would always seek her out before any others. I would fulfill my duty to Aeon and the Order, but she would remain firmly at the forefront of my mind.

This was another reason why I wished I could get her out of here and free of these obligations. It was dangerous for both of us to be here, but it was even more dangerous for me, knowing that this bond compelled me to protect her at all costs. I feared the day this would be put to the test.

⫘⫘⫘✦

I kept an eye on Cress, whether she knew it or not. That night, I heard the creaking sound of doors and footsteps in the hallway, far past any hour one should be awake. I peeked my head out of my door, trying to look inconspicuously into the hallway at whoever was roaming about Basdie. When I saw Trace trailing quietly behind Cress, I felt my breath leave my chest in a rush.

I found myself gripping the wooden door frame so tightly that it was beginning to crack against my grasp. My skin warmed with anger and… jealousy. I wanted to follow them and spoil their meeting with an unexpected interruption, but I knew my actions would be foolish.

Maybe they weren't meeting to rekindle anything? Could they simply be trying to find some way out of the Order? It's not like any of us actually wanted to be here. If that was the case, I'd murder Trace for putting her in harm's way. Basdie was magically warded, of that I was certain. If he encouraged her to participate in some scheme to escape and she ended up injured, or worse, I'd have his head.

Though I could tell Basdie was beginning to harden her, she was still so impressionable. She'd probably do whatever he asked of her. I resolved to step back into my quarters and read a book to distract myself. It was nearly impossible. My chest was heavy with anxiety, and thoughts of them together, alone, doing anything, weighed on me. Patience, I reminded myself.

⸎

When I saw Cress run full speed for the ledge of the flight deck and take the plunge to chase after Nori, I felt compelled to follow her. Saryn commanded the rest of us to stay put. As the sensation of the bond dwindled with the reduced proximity to her, I became overrun with nerves and concern for her well-being.

This was the first time we had been far enough apart that I couldn't feel her since having arrived at Basdie. If we were bonded, it would be different, but since she barely acknowledged my existence, we were far from it.

It seemed like forever until, thank the Gods, she arrived back on the flight deck looking disheveled and exasperated. Surprisingly, Nori had returned safely with her, but she looked like a Fae possessed. I listened as Cress stood her ground to Saryn and Theory, spewing defiant words and pleading Nori's case. A plea for us all to accept her trespass and the terms of her involvement in the Order. No one else had been granted any accommodations, and it seemed unlikely they'd be honored either.

I admired her courage and conviction. When no one else would step forward, I chose to be the first. It wasn't for Nori. It was an olive branch to Cress. She had built up such a wall between us, I had to try anything to soften it. Witnessing her relief when I offered my alliance brought me contentment. She had no idea how much I wanted to take her side, be by her side, if only she'd let me.

⸎

Spending time in the healing waters at the deepest parts of Basdie was probably the only thing allowing me to cope with being separated from the sea. Each time I visited, it brought me back from the edge of insanity.

I missed my sister, my mother, and my ship. My skin was dry and scaly, and my gills were irritated from the altitude, leagues from the nearest shoreline. In the solitude of the water, I'd often find myself humming or singing the songs of my people, the shanties that stirred the Seafarers to work in unison or the dirges that lamented shipmates and soulmates passed on into the next life. It had become a nervous habit to help the anxiety recede, but it worked.

To say I was surprised and serendipitously pleased when Cress happened upon me one evening would be an understatement. She tried to pass off her intrusion as an accident, and before she could make a swift exit, I welcomed her to join me.

The last time I'd seen the stunning curves of her body was beneath soaked garments in the Bath of the Four Mothers. I tried to hide how pleased I was at the sight of her stripping down, but it was hopeless. Gods, was she stunning.

As she placed herself across from me to soak, I felt the ripple of the bond strengthen. Something about the water, her proximity, and possibly the lack of others around to interfere made the sensation undeniable. I wondered if her body responded the same way, if her fingertips burned with anticipation and her senses sharpened. I dared not ask, for fear she would discover the meaning behind my question. If something was indeed stirring beneath her porcelain skin, she was either unaware or intent on ignoring it.

She swallowed her pride and thanked me for stepping forward on Nori's behalf. Before I could calculate my words, I stupidly replied that it was for her then quickly recovered my remark by adding that it was the right thing to do. When she opened the door for me to share more about myself, I took the opportunity, as I may not get many others. If this was the encounter where she was finally going to talk to me openly, then I'd embrace it.

I had hoped to find a connection, and found an unexpected one given our rare commonality that we were both twins. In my case, trip-lets, reduced to twins by a hostile act. I couldn't hide from the truth of my situation. Not when she knew what it was like to have that kind of heightened bond with a sibling. There was no defending my father. He was terrible, by all accounts. Murdering my infant brother was just the start of his brutality. Telling her was only risking she'd further correlate his vile behavior to me, but she had to know I was not my father, not even close.

Taking my sister's place as the Offering wasn't something I had even needed to think about. She and my mother had suffered long enough at the hands of my father. I did think about how strange it was, the order of events. Had I not stepped in for her, I would have never met Cress. I'd have gone my entire existence without laying eyes on my mate. Occasionally, I had let myself wonder if this was exactly how it was all meant to be.

I could have stayed and talked to her all night in the comforts of the warm water, but I reminded myself to be patient. Tonight was one small step. She let me in and I, her. There would be more of this; I would forge my own path into her heart and let her see the real me. She would know my truth one way or another. Then she'd have to be the one to reconcile the undeniable predicament of our intertwined fate.

As I made my exit, I turned to say in the old tongue, "Tomorrow. Same time. Same place, Moirai." I knew very well she had no idea I was calling her the very thing I'd longed to since the moment we met.

Cress was clearly the diplomat of our group. I watched as she single-hand-edly persuaded Cairis to train Nori. Their size difference was amusing. This left Cress without a sparring partner. When she eyed me from across the room, she had already accepted the inevitability of training with me as she made her way to my position on the floor.

By now, I knew Cress was a worthy sparring partner. She had nearly eviscerated Saryn in their exhibition, and it brought a smile to my face each time I recalled the surprise and fear on the instructor's face, her sword poised at his belly. I also knew Theory would realize if I was pulling my punches when it came time to face Cress. Still, I had convinced myself I could act overly aggressive at the onset, initiating conflict before Cress had a minute to get her bearings, then ease into a pattern of parrying her attacks afterward.

When I swiped her feet out from underneath her, she fumed on the ground beneath me. She was actually quite cute when she was angry, I just hated being the one it was directed at. It was more fun to watch her take it out on Cairis or the others. I took a few swings in her direction. Some I allowed her to dodge, but others she danced around and under with an impressive display of skill. She was trying, so I tried harder.

The feeling of her legs wrapped around me and her chest pressed hard against my back was an unwanted distraction. This was not how I wanted to feel her body against mine for the first time. I flipped her over abruptly, and again she spit her venomous retort at me just before she shoved her heel directly into my groin. This cheap move had me bent over and heaving for air in between coughs. This was not how I had wanted the first time she touched me there to feel, either. Not even close.

She continued her assault on me, and when I twisted her tightly into my arms, I held her there while she writhed for freedom. I whispered a taunt in the old tongue, knowing it would only incite her further. Someone not as attuned to her as I was would have fallen for her next move. But I caught her with my hand and grasped it tightly around her neck.

She was trapped. There was no way she could beat me, not without magic, but Theory's class was about physical skill not abilities. I squeezed a little tighter, indicating she should yield. I was trying to offer her the same out she had given Saryn, but she did not flinch. I watched as her eyes began to water and blood rushed to her face. From the corner of my vision, I saw Theory give me a nod of approval, indicating I was not to give in until Cress forfeited.

I hated every minute of this. *My strong, resilient girl, please just give in, don't make me do this.* I squeezed tighter and shoved her back against the podium, hoping she would take it as a warning and yield. I watched as she doubled her resolve, even as her lungs spasmed, and I could feel her pulse struggle beneath my grip. I commanded her to yield, begging her to swallow her pride and do as I asked, but she wouldn't waver. I could see her lashes begin to flutter with loss of consciousness when suddenly I heard the sound of Trace yelling, "Let her go!" as his knuckle struck my cheek and caused me to drop Cress to the ground.

I returned to the baths that night, unsure if Cress would ever feel comfortable being alone with me again. I felt terrible about how things had transpired during training. I should have known better. Trace's brutality all but confirmed his will to possess her. It wasn't chivalry. He'd taken Gia to the mat many times and never so much as blinked at the bruises he left on either her or Theory. He could not stand to watch me touch her. At least the outburst was in front of everyone. They saw it with their own eyes, their silent concern corroborating our suspicions. Some made it more obvious than others.

When I asked her why she hadn't just yielded, her angry words flowed out of her mouth like they had longed to be free for days. We were finally going to have it out. I had vowed to myself to never tell the truth about what had really happened to my father and how he was captured, but that was before these circumstances. My past, her past…none of it mattered anymore. Who was I protecting by keeping it a secret? I was so tired of bearing the brunt of her prejudices.

For the rest of my life, I would grapple with the decisions I made, how I put my mother and sister first before the lives of strangers. We argued back and forth, and I only hesitated for a few seconds before I told her my biggest secret.

The truth was, I had handed over my own father to the black cloaks. I had to make sure he could never lay hands on either of them again, and so I sealed his fate with my decision to turn him in and let him answer to the Gods for his crimes. But first, he would answer to the hands of the Fae. Fae whose viciousness was the only thing to match his own. Cloaked males whose arms were covered in the exact same markings as Trace.

The sting of Trace's blows was ever present as I cupped the water to my sore cheek, letting the healing do its work. Did she really not remember him attacking me before she hit the ground? I wondered, if she had been conscious, would she have found his actions admirable or out of line? Her mental shields were getting stronger with each day, which meant opportunities to know her true feelings were less frequent.

The accusations I'd been considering and that I'd already been hinting at in so many ways were sitting on the tip of my tongue. I don't know whether it was the exhaustion of being stuck in Basdie with my mate seemingly unaware of my affections, or the frustration from us all playing along like we didn't know something was going on with her and Trace. But I let my self-control recede—if only for a moment—and accused her of lying. All she could offer me in return was a cold, knowing remark.

"It won't happen again."

It became obvious when Cress began to take things too far with the Vespers. If her mental state was anything like her physical state, then I feared what kind of irreparable damage she was doing to herself. Part of me wanted her to be strong, prepared for whatever horrible things might lay ahead for us. But the other part of me longed to hold her, to shield her from the madness those sessions could inflict.

Luckily, the others were also aware of her withering in front of us. Her cheeks, once rose-kissed and full, were now withdrawn and white as chalk. Dark circles encompassed her eyes and her gaze was unfocused, exhausted. I knew we needed an intervention, but choosing the right person was key to its success. Cress was stubborn and, despite her weary state, her emotional walls were strong. We decided Nori was our best chance of bypassing those defenses and reaching her with our message.

Expecting her to stop would have been against Saryn's wishes. We just wanted her to pace herself, to get some rest, and for Gods' sakes, protect her mind from crumbling due to whatever relentless torture she'd been putting herself through in those rooms. I understood the Vespers and the purpose they served, but in the wrong hands they were a trap, one that could pull any soul into its darkest depths and never let go. Saryn and Theory had warned us. But their warning was one of caution, that hanging onto your past was not recommended; a warning I did not heed.

I had only done it a few times. The Vesper looked identical to my sister in every way. Pulling from my memories and imagination, it brought me some small happiness to know I hadn't forgotten her. I missed her dearly. She was my best friend, and watching my father's horrific treatment of her and my mother had been enough to make me wish death's cold hand would take me on more than one occasion. All those times I couldn't protect them, all the regret that I'd never overcome. At least now they were free of him...and of me and my guilt-stricken face.

I did it because I needed someone to talk to, or else I was going to come apart at the seams. It was impossible to trust anyone here with the information that I was almost certain Cress was my mate. Even with Gia, who could possibly find some way to relate, in spite of her broken heart, I wouldn't risk it. I knew the conversations weren't real, and every response was just one I had imagined, allowing myself to hear what I wanted. But I granted myself those small comforts, otherwise my heart or head was going to explode. Which would happen first, I did not know.

⟨⟨⟨✴

There were times when I wasn't sure if Saryn actually wanted us to be a team or if he just enjoyed pitting us against one another for his own amusement. When he asked us to practice manipulating one another through mind reading and illusion exercises, I already knew we were in trouble. I watched with jealousy as Trace and Cress were paired up first. That jealousy quickly boiled over into rage when I heard her whisper his name. I chewed on my bottom lip while I focused on calming my breathing.

Even as I meddled through the thoughts Gia was projecting, I felt myself distracted by the intrusive nature of those two. Each person's manipulation was unique and personal, but hearing Trace recount Cress's vision might as well have been a confession. My stomach churned.

When we finally shifted partners, I could see the embarrassment plastered across every one of Cress's features. Her eyes begged me for reprieve, but I could offer none. I needed her to know how I felt. How I'd felt since I first saw her and discovered she belonged to another, that she longed for him all the while I pined for her.

She had no idea the number of times I had held my breath in her presence, every time she passed me in the hallway. How I had longed to reach out and grab her hand, to pull her to me. She had to know she had been suffocating me since the moment I felt our bond calling, and for this brief, selfish illusion I would take her into the undertow with me. All the way to the bottom.

It was a mere heartbeat to transition from illusion to the reality of her gasping for breath and gripping her chair, all while believing the dark, cold terror of the water engulfed her. I let my Siren Song weave its way down her beautiful mouth and steal all the air from her lungs. Lungs

426

next to a heart that I feared would never beat in rhythm with mine. I relinquished her once the smell of her fear pierced my nostrils.

I should have expected her to lash out. I'd have done the same if someone used Siren Song on me with no warning. I wasn't proud of my words, but I couldn't let the real reason be known for why I was at my breaking point with her.

I was spiraling out of control. Between what had happened in the sparring room, and then in the exercises with Saryn, I wasn't doing myself any favors to win hers. Trace tried to provoke me during dinner, but his threats didn't faze me. I had to hold back a small laugh of amusement. I quite enjoyed getting under his skin like this. Tensions were at an all-time high, and not even Cairis' water-to-wine was enough to cool me down. I was tired of the charade we were all playing on their behalf. Family, right? It was time to get the secret out on the table.

Pointing my finger between the two of them, I asked accusatively what was going on. I wanted the answer, and at the same time, I didn't. Unsure if I was prepared to hear if there was still something between them or if this was just the past unwilling to relinquish its claws. Trace confirmed everything and did so in a way that showed her no honor, but I'd expect nothing less. Before I could react, Cress had jumped in with a rage-filled diatribe, chiding us both. She wasn't wrong, but I pressed my luck anyway.

I had secrets—we probably all did—but they felt like liars and I wasn't entirely sure who had dragged who into the lie. If they had just been honest when we got here instead of forcing us all to dance around the truth, then I wouldn't have been so bothered. I hated my own words. I was just so frustrated. When she angrily replied, "The past is in the past. Trust that," and stormed out of the room, I breathed a sigh of relief—even after I watched him chase after her.

I was exhausted and embarrassed by my words and actions. I could have fallen into a deep sleep, but I needed to see my sister. Or, at least, pretend to. I told her about everything I'd done and said. How badly I'd messed up, but that I'd gotten the confirmation I needed. I wanted to believe that Trace and Cress were over and nothing more than a fading part of our pasts, washed away like everything else that had once mattered. I knew I was being unfair, even to both of them, but I was being eaten alive by this thing inside of me.

Why had the Gods done this to me? Was this punishment for how I had handled the rebellion at Erisas? Was it for all my mother and sister had endured while I stood by idle, reasoning to myself that there was nothing I could have done, just to make it through the day?

Why would the Gods bring her into my life now? Why would they bring with her a past lover who I was supposed to embrace as a brother? There is a reason that most plays of the Gods are comedies. Tragic comedies…

I dropped to my knees and placed my head in my sister's lap, letting her run her fingers through the curls of my hair while she hummed one of our favorite childhood songs. I embraced this selfish comfort, because I felt so utterly lost. I was burying my chances of Cress ever feeling any semblance of affection for me, and I'd sealed that with how I'd acted earlier. I didn't know exactly what I'd do if Cress did return my feelings. What could we even become in these circumstances? "I will never be given a fair chance. It hurts in my ribs; my heart feels caged. I feel it in the marrow of my being… My Moirai," I whispered to my sister. I took in the silence of the Vesper, and the chill, stale air of the stone room.

Cress had every right to be furious with me about using Siren Song.

Nothing I was doing was working. I had to find a way to render her defenseless so she'd calm down. It was a risky move, one that could have resulted in her kicking me in the groin again—and maybe I deserved that. I reached for her foot under the water, grabbing it tightly.

Slowly, I began kneading my fist into it, massaging firmly, and she quickly relented her protests—though continued her interrogation. I became excited with the thought that this was the first time I'd been allowed to touch her with any sort of affection. I answered all of her questions truthfully, recollecting how I'd won my gift of song.

When I released her foot, I could see a hint of disappointment in her expression. She wanted more and it pleased me. I quickly resumed my efforts on her other foot and watched as her shoulders slackened once more. Although I couldn't say I enjoyed telling her I had kissed a siren, I think it was pretty obvious that it was all on a dare.

She pointed at my gills, questioning why obtaining such a gift was considered a feat when I could already breathe underwater. I hoped she did not find them displeasing. I mentally noted the three crescent moons of Demir tattooed behind her ear. Whether she realized it or not, they resembled my gills, and the thought warmed my cheeks.

When I rolled my thumb down the arch of her foot, I watched as her eyes fluttered, and I could tell she was fighting back a whimper or a moan. I had to focus on controlling myself from finding too much excitement in that.

Our conversation carried on as I shared more about the lore of my people and the vast misunderstandings of our lifestyle. I enjoyed that she was intrigued. This was the first time I had noticed just how many questions Cress asked. Was this a sign she was finally opening up to me? I'd entertain her curiosity if it kept her talking.

She tried to pull her foot away during another barrage of questions, but I wouldn't allow it. I continued to hold it tightly, acknowledging internally how tiny her foot felt between my large hands. Occasionally, I'd get bolder and move my hands up and down her lower calves, rubbing them with dedication. It felt a bit like I had been performing parlor tricks for her, showing the various ways Siren Song worked, but she walked right into my quip requesting that I try something nicer.

Even just mentioning love and lust in front of her made my bond tingle, but she quickly diverted the conversation to more self-deprecation about her abilities, or lack thereof. I'd gathered enough information to deduce that before the Order, Cress had rarely used magic, and the fact that she was playing catch up with the rest of us ate away at her confidence.

I couldn't explain why I knew it, but I felt so strongly that Cress was going to mean more to this team than she realized. I argued with myself that my judgment might be biased, but this wasn't the bond; I just had faith in her, even if she didn't have it in herself.

By now I was riding high on our time together and feeling a bit too confident, but I reasoned that if I had this window of vulnerability, I was going to take it. I gently grabbed her chin and tilted her face up toward mine, forcing her to look at me with those eyes.

"Keep your chin up, Moirai. All that matters is who we become, not who we were."

It's everything I'd wanted to say to her since we'd arrived. As I made my way out of the room, secretly wishing the night hadn't ended there, I smiled to myself knowingly as she continued to pry about the nickname.

⟨⟨⟨✦

Thank the Gods I was left to ride alone in a carriage on the way to the party where we'd carry out our mission. The thought of riding in a pair with Trace or with Cress was an intimidating prospect. Alone with Trace, I don't think I would have been able to bite my tongue the entire ride. And with Cress…well, I had ideas and none of them were in service of the mission.

We had planned well, and I had confidence in us if we worked as a team. Gia being the bait instead of Cress brought me much needed relief, as I knew I'd already be distracted with thoughts of her whereabouts and safety.

The mission had been going according to plan by my account. My Siren Song was successfully keeping the real nanny subdued in a slumber while Nori glamoured the children to lure them away from the room. When Cress arrived, I almost didn't recognize her. My breathing came to a halt and I checked to ensure my mouth wasn't agape. What in the three moons of Demir was she wearing? Was she trying to seduce every male and female here? I tried to keep my focus on the sleeping nanny while Trace and I began to search the room for the box, but I was more than distracted with thoughts of the yellow feathers outlining the curves of her breasts. If I took notice, there was no way Trace hadn't.

Cress left the room to continue her duties of patrolling the hallways and keeping watch, along with Cairis. Only a few moments passed before I heard her yelp in the hallway. I poked my head out of the room to ensure everything was okay, when I discovered she was being escorted into a private room by someone. Her eyes were a warning long before I saw the hand signal at her side as she entered the threshold of the nearby bedroom. Something was awry.

I turned to Trace and told him we needed to hurry, and that I thought Cress was in trouble. He continued to tear apart the nursery, searching and becoming more flustered. I warned him again, thinking we should split up so I could keep an eye on her.

"I know!" he growled back at me. "You heard Saryn, failure is not an option. We have to find this thing, whatever it is, or we might as well not come back alive."

I'd never seen Trace so intense, and though his reminder of Saryn's words made sense, I just couldn't find myself able to take them more seriously than protecting Cress, or any of the others for that matter—even him. We continued to search frantically, but I had a terrible gut feeling something bad was happening to Cress. The thrum of the bond was faint but erratic, unlike anything I'd felt thus far.

I grew impatient. "Keep searching; I'm going to check on her!"

I stood by the locked door trying to listen in for any sounds of distress, but over the noisy crowds outside it was difficult to hear anything with clarity. The bond now beat under my skin with a pounding force, a sensation which made me dread its meaning. That's when I smelled it; her fear. It wafted out from under the doorway and up through my nostrils causing my eyes to widen in panic. If the fear I'd felt when I used Siren Song on her was any indication of how bad things were in there, this was ten-fold worse. I wasted no time kicking down the door.

When I saw her there, pinned on the bed under some stranger, his hands aggressively pressed against her, my vision turned red. I scanned the scene intensely, then witnessed Cress jam a knife into the side of her assaulter. Angry and wounded, he pulled the bells, alerting his guards. We were now in an unplanned chain of events where we'd need to improvise.

As we exited, Cress at my side, two guards came running up on us with swords raised. I did not hesitate before I sent them to their knees gasping and clutching at their throats for air. I stood behind them, yanking their necks back and focused all my rage from witnessing her in peril mere moments ago. I ran my dagger across their throats and felt the warmth of their blood coat my hands as I ushered her to follow me.

The ballroom was quickly descending into chaos. The nanny, now awake, ran screaming from the bedroom. I was about to put her down too, but Cress interjected, knocking her out with one swift strike to the face. All I could think about was getting her to safety, and yet she had the mind to ask me if we had found what we came for. I confirmed for her that Trace had it in hand and walked in the same defensive stance we'd practiced many times in the sparring room. I saw a small window of opportunity for Cairis to make an exit and yelled at him to go ahead.

Unsure of where Gia or Nori were, I remained solely focused on getting Cress out of here. More guards ran in to flank Cress and I on both sides, and I assessed the situation nervously, knowing they outnumbered us. Almost as if our minds were in sync, we both ran down the steps to the center of the room where Trace had just been, thinking he'd join us and we'd stand a better chance together.

When I glanced up at Trace, holding the box tightly in one arm and a sword in the other, his expression was unreadable. I shot Cress a concerned look, acknowledging that we were both wrong in assuming he'd aid us. However, there was no more time for thinking, only action.

"We need to fly, it's our only way out," I whispered to her, and she unfurled her wings ready to take flight.

We had barely been airborne, just a few feet off the ground, when I heard Cress's shrill cry and saw the arrow embedded in her shoulder, blood already streaming down the green iridescence of her wing. I winced at the sight of it and her slamming back into the marble ground as she began to writhe in pain.

I saw her glance over to the top of the staircase, and together we witnessed Trace leaving to make his own escape with the box. The sound of more guards' footsteps grew louder as they encircled us and leaned over the balcony surrounding the ballroom.

"Go…go now!" She croaked in pain, looking up at me as I hovered above her, flapping my wings in desperation.

Absolutely not; I wasn't going to leave her. I landed by her and wrapped my wings around us, trying to shield her from any more incoming arrows. She screeched for me to remove the one from her shoulder, but I knew she'd lose too much blood. I was terrified, watching her already bleeding profusely from the wound. There was silence, and then I heard the most awful sound.

Click after click of crossbows echoed all around us. Instinctively, I leaned in closer, trying to shield both our bodies with my wings splayed as wide as they'd go, preparing mentally for the onslaught of pain. Then, suddenly, everything went quiet and still, as if time had frozen. I felt the ground quake, then the sound returned with the loud crashes of mirrors and windows shattering throughout the room. Next came the screams of injured and dying guards, followed by the sound of guests scattering about and yelling in terror.

I had no idea how it had happened, but I looked down at Cress who was quickly losing consciousness and I tucked her into my arms. I used what remained of my strength to fly us both out of there to the rendezvous point to get her help as quickly as possible.

Every minute of that flight was horrific, as I focused intently on the hum of our bond to assess if she was still alive. I wanted to take her far away from the Order, Basdie, all of it—but I knew it was outside of our control. Those hidden and mysterious brands on our wrists would surely serve as a beacon to find us, no matter where we went. I tucked her tighter to my chest, inhaling her scent and trying to ignore the frustration of being unable to protect her from this life.

☾☾☾✦

If I hadn't been so focused on Cress's well-being and practically hovering over Nori while she worked to heal the gash on her shoulder, then I might have found time to be angry with Trace. Ever since arriving back at Basdie he had kept his distance from both of us, but stayed close enough to still keep a watchful eye on Cress. At the rendezvous point, the others were shocked to see the state of us both; but not Trace. He knew better than the rest what had transpired. But he had not seen what had truly scared me, whatever had saved us. And I was fairly certain Cress had something to do with it.

When Cress's eyes finally opened, I had hoped to be the one to comfort her, but she didn't wait a single minute before she let rage take over at the sight of Trace. I worried she'd cause the wound to re-open, but there was no stopping her fury as she berated him. I felt the betrayal just as much as she had, my brother-in-arms, or so I'd thought, but I knew exactly why this betrayal ran deeper for her. All of us did. His features were unflinching with every angry word, and I could not make out what he whispered to her in response. It must have done nothing to quell her anger, and Cairis immediately went to aid her steps as she wobbled away dizzily.

Up until now Cress had kept up a strong mental shield, but then they ceased completely. Maybe she was intentionally letting him, letting all of us know exactly how broken their trust was. Weeks ago, I might have delighted in knowing that anything residual between them was severed, but I knew the value of working as a team far outweighed my personal desires.

Saryn did nothing to ease the tension, implying that Trace was the only one who ensured we completed the mission successfully. This sent Cress into another fit, spewing rhetorical questions in Trace's direction and I watched as the anger began to grow out of control. I had every reason to be concerned with what might come of that if I didn't find some way to distract her, so I gently grabbed her arm, trying to make it clear I was not a threat.

"Cress, look at me. Breathe. Calm down. You have to control your anger, or it might happen again."

When she did not understand my warning, I glanced quickly at Saryn and Theory whom I'd briefed somewhat while Cress was still unconscious, concerned that it might impact how we needed to treat or heal her. Part of me worried I should keep what happened a secret, but the situation was beyond my knowledge.

It was not a conversation I wanted to have in front of the others. Grateful that Saryn suggested I escort her to the healing pools, I walked silently beside her the entire way, carefully observing whether she was steady on her feet or not.

She began to undress, and I shuddered as she winced at the pain from lifting her arms. With her mental shields still down, I tried to reassure her that she would heal and fly again. Cress stubbornly attempted to undress on her own, again, when I demanded she let me help her. I stepped behind her and began to gently tear at the fabric till it could be removed easily and slide down her arms without her having to raise her shoulder.

I bit my lip, acknowledging the long scar across her shoulder blade, the memory of that arrow striking her playing on repeat in the back of my mind. *My strong Moirai,* I thought to myself. I would take her wounds, scars and all. She was still perfect in my eyes.

I turned her to face me and lowered myself to my knees. I could not bring myself to look up at her, for fear of her gaze laying me bare. I placed my hands on her hips and began to slowly slide her pants to the ground, hoping with each passing second that she'd let me care for her rather than retreat. Shamefully, I let my fingertips run down her legs across her soft skin and clenched my jaw at the sight of all the dried blood that had seeped its way through her clothing.

When I stood, I grabbed her hand and led her into the waters, unwilling to let go of it even when I was certain she had balanced herself. I continued to lead her farther into the waters, to the ledge she normally sat on every time we'd meet here. Once relaxed into the warm healing waters, she questioned why I'd put myself at risk to save her. I couldn't bring myself to tell her the whole truth, though everything in me wanted to.

I reasoned with her that she was worth saving, just as she had done for Nori, but now she was convinced she owed me a blood debt. She had no idea how badly I wanted to bind my blood to her for eternity, and that losing her might have killed me too. How could she not recognize the call of our bond?

As if she read my mind, she mentioned for the first time ever the sensation, and that's when it became clear she really had no idea what it meant. I breathed a sigh of relief knowing, now, that she had felt it too, but had reasoned with herself it was related to our abilities. I didn't have the courage to tell her she was wrong for fear of how she might react. I wanted to talk about the feeling further, but there was something more pressing.

She really couldn't recollect what happened during the mission, so I shared with her the explosion from my point of view. When it still did not stir her memory and she asked me who had caused it, I embraced her face in both my hands and told her that she had been the one to do it. There was no other plausible explanation. Saryn and Theory had a hypothesis, but they did not share it with me.

The black center of her eyes widened as the memories began to return. Her confusion now turned to panic. She'd never killed anyone, let alone many. No amount of training with Vespers would prepare someone for their first time. A sob wrenched from her chest and I pulled her in tightly to mine, hugging her as she went limp in my arms. I let her cry until she was so exhausted she did not protest when I lifted her to carry her back to her bed. She had already fallen into a slumber by the time I laid her down.

⫷⫷⫷✦

I struggled to sleep. The images of Cress, the arrow in her wing, the blood on the floor, it all became too much to bear. I didn't know what Saryn and Theory thought had occurred, but I had a far-fetched idea.

It was clear that some of the others had been made aware of what had happened. It irritated me to hear them whisper about her, but I didn't have much clarification to offer. When they finally showed us what we had risked our lives for, I was too distracted by Cress to give much attention to the portal stones. Though Saryn proclaimed them powerful and unique, to me Cress was those things and more. Knowing we had risked our lives for stones, however rare, tainted them a bit in my mind.

When Trace shot an accusatory remark at Cress, I mustered all the self-control I had remaining to avoid choking him with my Siren Song. He was lucky she was alive, no thanks to him, and he wanted to imply *she* was a problem? Of course, Saryn hadn't trained her to do that, and knowing Cress she certainly would have told us if she had something like that in her arsenal of abilities. After all, she had been the one to struggle most with embracing magic since our arrival.

With Trace's pointed questions, I got the funny feeling he had an inclination as to what her powers were; otherwise, why would he continue to press the matter? I tried to defend her, but he pushed for more answers. When the words "Dark Wielder" left Saryn's mouth, I could feel the hairs on my arms stand on end. I knew it was a possibility, but an unlikely one. Dark Wielders were as uncommon as Seers. Most had heard the legends, been told the stories, but no one actually had ever seen or met one. Now I was to grapple with the fact that my fated one is supposedly a keeper of this dark magic?

Before any more questions could be asked, Theory chided us and took the moonstones away. I did not like the way Trace had looked at Cress ever since getting the confirmation he so clearly expected. I walked up to him, putting my body squarely in between his and hers.

"Don't give her a reason to lose control again, or you might find yourself a victim of her wrath."

I'd pay a good handful of Lorcs to watch Cress put him on his ass for having the audacity to question her after he left us for dead. He can keep his little box of rocks, if that was more important to him.

It was apparent that Cress was intent on carrying the burden of her news alone. If I was being honest with myself, I was wrestling with it, too, but doing my best to have confidence for her. She was prone to self-doubt even before finding out she was a Dark Wielder. None of us had any real knowledge of what it meant, and if Trace did, he certainly wasn't sharing it with the rest of us.

When Saryn isolated her in what could only be described as a small closet to study, I made it my mission to make regular visits to her, finding excuses like bringing her food or water. She kept emphasizing the need to stay focused and keep her energy levels up with sustenance and good sleep. I was equally curious about her secret studies and missed her presence during training and in the flight field. Nori also checked in with me frequently to ask how Cress was doing, and I appreciated her genuine concern despite her obvious nervousness. The others still seemed mostly fearful of Cress.

I tried to make sure she understood that I personally didn't care if she ever found a way to use her power again. Sure, it would be an advantage, and I loved the idea that she'd probably be able to defend herself better than any of us if she did learn to wield it properly—but at what cost? You'd have to be a fool to think there wasn't a price with that kind of magic.

Idris returned, and I knew in my gut it did not bode well for any of us. I went to notify Cress that we were being summoned to the common room for his arrival. The news of King Baelin's assassination was cause for concern. I hadn't thought of us going south into Artume when we joined the Order because they were no longer our enemies. The peace treaty had been diligently upheld.

His brother, Silas, apparently had little regard for those treaties, and when he assumed power the peace our two kingdoms had once forged now hung in the balance. Hearing Saryn tell Idris that we were not ready to infiltrate our enemy was an understatement. Idris only said we were all expected to prepare for the evening's ceremony that entailed only Gods-knew-what.

Idris, Saryn, and Theory donned all black with the silver talismans matching our brands hanging from their necks. We hesitantly followed them out onto the terrace. The air was much cooler now, as dry winter winds blustered through the valley below.

The Imperi.

The words echoed through my mind and sat at the tip of my tongue, begging to be said aloud. We had been the Offerings, then became the Order. What other oath was there to give? We had already bound ourselves to King Aeon, was that not enough?

Theory approached me with a blade in hand and lifted it to my neck. I tried not to swallow the lump in my throat for fear of it chafing against her sharp dagger. I listened nervously as she repeated each word of the oath, following Idris' instruction. The second she said the word blood, I felt the abrupt sting of the blade slide across my throat. Not deep enough to maim or kill, instead it was done artfully and intentionally.

It scared me, nonetheless, and I could already feel the warmth of blood beginning to surface. Suddenly, Theory's hand was tight against my throat compressing the open wound and when she lifted her hand away any residual pain or bleeding ceased. I checked the wound myself, feeling for anything at all, but there wasn't even a scar. The oath was a test of trust and commitment.

When Theory handed me the blade and nodded for me to turn to Cress, I thought I was going to be sick in front of everyone. What if I pressed the blade too hard? What if I could not heal her fast enough? *Please, Gods, anyone but her.* I turned to face her, looking down and assessing her features. Did she trust me? Didn't she understand how impossible this was for me? I felt the blade trembling in my hand as I sought to find courage to do what was expected of me. Expected of each of us.

Cress stared into my eyes and gave me a knowing nod. Without it, I don't know that I'd have found the strength to do it. I lifted the blade to her delicate throat and began to repeat Idris' words. With each passing phrase, I grew more nervous and felt tears welling in my eyes.

"This is the beginning to no end."

As I stated my oath to the Imperi, I hoped she felt my intent as I bound myself to her. To always protect her. My fated one. To No End.

I felt the fear begin to emanate from her skin and let my silent Siren Song weave its notes around her, across every inch of her body, wrapping her in a warm embrace. I gently grabbed the back of her head and intertwined my fingers in her hair, then swiped the blade across her throat. I used every ounce of my magic to ensure that Siren Song exceeded any possible pain.

Hurriedly, I moved both my hands to her throat and funneled all of my magic to healing the wound as quickly as possible. I hadn't even realized I'd dropped the blade. I retrieved it, placing it in the palm of Cress's hand and let myself feel the warmth of it for a moment just to reassure myself she was okay before she turned to Trace to repeat the same act.

I was relieved to find out that at least if they were going to split us up, however briefly, I wasn't going to be forced to part ways with Cress. Saryn was going to intensify her training, and I wanted to be nearby to ensure he didn't take anything too far. I'd be lying if I said I wasn't pleased to know that this would also result in me finally having time with Cress apart from Trace. I shouldn't have cared because it's not like she knew who she was to me or my true feelings, but the prospect of not seeing him around every corner with skeptical eyes was a welcome one.

All of this commotion did mean things were getting more serious. Thoughts of infiltrating Artume, a kingdom none of us knew well, was one that had struck fear into all of us. Trace transitioned into a glamour and I had to admit, it was strange to see him without tattoos or that noteworthy scar through his eyebrow. I was glad they were sending Gia. Her stone heart and stubborn attitude was far more prepared than Nori's, and Cress had barely scratched the surface of her new ability.

When Idris arrived at Basdie with the carriages, we all joined together to say our goodbyes. As I approached, I overheard Gia muttering to herself about the state of the carriage and questioning how she was expected to get any beauty rest hunched in that small space. I pulled her into an embrace and hugged her tightly, so she knew I'd miss her—complaining included.

She pulled away from me and said quietly, "Make sure she's ready when you join us; that she can rain down the power of the Gods on our enemies."

Gia's request only affirmed my own belief that my place was by Cress's side while she learned to embrace the power of being a Dark Wielder. I gave Gia a nod and moved aside for Cairis.

I walked past Trace and gave him a nod of respect. We hadn't really spoken much since the fiasco at the Canary Veil, but I needed him to understand he was still my brother by oath. I was bound to him just as much as I was to the others. I could forgive him for leaving me behind, but I would not forgive or forget that he left her.

I tried to watch Cress and Trace's interaction from a distance without seeming conspicuous. The tension was palpable even from across the stone pathway. I witnessed him hand her something that she quickly pocketed, piquing my curiosity. My jaw tightened when I witnessed him lean in and whisper something in her ear. *Gods, grant me the patience to not put my hands on another member of the Imperi.* I took a deep breath in and exhaled the dry mountain air through my nostrils. What I wouldn't give for just an ounce of sea breeze.

Cress gave Gia a much warmer farewell before walking away. Suddenly, I saw her turn back to Gia's carriage and climb along the side door, leaning her upper body into the window while trying to convey something she must have forgotten to tell Gia. At the sound of Idris' whistle, the wheels began to turn as the horse's hooves clacked against the stone. Gia's carriage started to roll away, and Cress stepped down while mouthing frantic words.

Cress took off running back into the entrance of Basdie like something was very wrong. I paced quickly behind, trying not to look like I was chasing her or give a reason for the others to be alarmed. She sprinted towards the bottom of the falls. With each winding turn, my anxiety grew.

When I reached the bottom, I noticed she had entered the door to the atrium leading to the falls. No one ever went in there, and it was assuredly dangerous and slick. Then the most unexpected thing occurred: the whole of Basdie began to shake. The ground quaked underneath my feet and I braced myself against the wall. I remembered this feeling at the Canary Veil just as Cress unleashed her power. Was it happening again?

When the brief quaking stopped, I peeked my head into the doorway, worried about her. The deafening sound of the waterfall crashing downward made it difficult for her to hear me, so I gestured her back toward me. She was on her knees and appeared quite distressed. I watched as she stood carefully, soaking wet, and made her way back to the doorway.

Once the door was shut, I could finally hear again. In nervous exasperation, I asked if she was okay and if she knew the entire mountain had been quaking. Was she even aware of when her gift activated?

"Moirai," she said through gritted teeth. "What does it mean?"

Oh no. "It's just a nickname, Cress." I tried to play it off casually, the feeling of dread and worry washing over me.

"What does it mean?" she demanded angrily.

I licked my lips, preparing to tell her the truth, my mind wanting to keep the secret but my heart unwilling to comply. Not when she was looking at me this way.

"It means fated one," I said.

"No, it doesn't!" she shouted. "I know the literal translation for those words, and it's not Moirai."

Oh, my sweet Cress… "That's because it's the word *my* people use for fated one."

Our gazes were locked and the silent tension between us was drowning me. Finally, the truth that I'd been hiding, something she never saw coming. She was the vibration to my soul, and with every passing second, I was filled with doubt that she would ever have me.

Her words were a cracked whisper, "You… All this time. You're my mate?"

I tucked a wet strand of hair behind her ear. "The Gods are cruel, aren't they?"

PRONUNCIATION GUIDE

Aeon: A-on

Alcar: Al-car

Artume: Are-tomb

Aster: Ass-tur

Asterius: Ass-tear-e-us

Astrid: Ah-strid

Baelin: Bay-lynn

Basdie: Baz-dye

Blackthorn: Blac-thorne

Brynmawr: Bryn-marr

Cairis: Care-iss

Cambria: Came-bree-uh

Ciaran: See-air-an

Corliss: Core-liss

Cress: Kress

Cressida: Kress-ah-duh

Doorlae: Dor-lay

D'eliar: Dee-el-e-ar

Demir: Duh-meer

Elorn: A-lorne

Ennae: Een-yay

Erisas: Air-ugh-sus

Evenus: Ev-ugh-nuss

Fenix: Phen-icks

Fideli Cœur: Fih-day-li Cur

Gaia: Guy-ugh

Gia: G-ugh

Gianna: G-on-ugh

Gris: Gree

Huxley: Hucks-lee

Idris: Eye-driss

Ilithyia: Ih-lith-e-uh

Imperi: Im-peer-ee

Kasparov: Cass-par-aaf

Ledor: Lee-door

Lorc: Lork

Lorne: Lorn

Magnus: Mag-nuss

Miran: Mere-un

Mirtith: Mur-teeth

Moirai: Moye-rye

Nasallus: Nuh-saul-lus

Niall: Nigh-ull
Nix: Nicks
Nori: Nor-ee
Nyla: Nye-luh
Orni: Or-nye
Saryn: Sair-in
Sav: Saav
Seraphine: Ser-ugh-feen
Silas: Sy-luss
Taran: Tear-un
Tinsilor: Tin-sill-or
Theory: Theer-ee
Tiernan: Tier-naan
Trace: Tray-se
Varro: Var-o
Versa: Verse-a
Vesper: Ves-purr
Wendell: Wen-dull
Wick: Wic

ACKNOWLEDGMENTS

To the readers, thank you for taking a chance on me. Always take a chance on yourself. I hope you'll continue with me on this journey.

For my father, for instilling in me the belief that something can be made from nothing. I carry on your legacy of believing in yourself, of forging your own path against all odds. Getting lost in the pages of writing this story is the only thing that allowed me to survive the grief of your loss. I can only hope to live up to your larger-than-life storytelling.

To my mother and all the strong, independent, amazing women who I call family and friends... Your own trials and tribulations handled with resilience and a few cuss words will always inspire me and the characters I write.

To my brother, the definition of perseverance. We've got grit and I leaned into that while learning to do something new and challenging.

To my husband, there is no one else I would rather "ever after" with than you. I'm so glad I found someone to stay forever young with. You, me, the pups, and the horizon will always be my greatest adventure. Thank you for being my partner in brainstorming, critique and my brave alpha reader.

To my beta readers, Dani and Kelsey, your feedback and enthusiasm gave me the empowerment to keep pushing myself. Thank you for believing in this story.

To my faithful supporters, Dani and KP, I couldn't have done this without your endless cheerleading and encouragement.

To the Kansas City bookish community, I am forever grateful for the doorway you opened that inspired the next chapter of my life.

To my legal counsel, Reece, your guidance has been invaluable in helping me become an entrepreneur and woman-owned small business.

To Jade, you breathed life into my brand. I'm so grateful for your rare and endless creativity.

To my editor, Noah, you have proven that writing a book is a team sport and I'm immensely grateful for your talent and polish that helped me elevate this story.

To my map illustrator and interior designer, Travis, you quite literally put the place on the map. Thank you for helping readers see the world I created and reminding us why every book can be a piece of art.

To my proofer, Rachel, the journey to the finish line can be tiring but your hilarious and sincere commentary and true passion for the book was the spark I needed to move me forward. Thank you for making your mark on this story.

To my cover artists at Krafigs Design, perhaps the most nerve-racking part of putting a book into the world is giving it a face. Thank you for encapsulating the magic so perfectly.

451

ABOUT THE AUTHOR

Lexy Night has always looked to the stars. Growing up, feeling like maybe this planet wasn't where she was supposed to be, it became practically impossible to ignore the indescribable pull of the cosmos. The next closest thing to that are the stories and adventures we can envelop ourselves in, making us feel like we lived a thousand lives in a single lifetime. Whether you find your peace between the pages or the notes of a song, she hopes you find the feeling of home.

Born and raised in Kansas (there's no place like home) she loves Midwest hospitality and is a big Chiefs football fan. When not writing, Lexy can be found snuggling her dogs, cosplaying, attending fantasy balls, binging movies/series, and playing board games. What she enjoys most are giggles with her bookish friends and exploring national parks (and the world) with her husband. Her favorite content genres are Sci-Fi and Fantasy, and she has always appreciated the villains more than the heroes.

You can find more updates, social links, and what's coming next from author Lexy Night at LexyNight.com.